# The Villains

*After Ann had let Hansen out of the door, seeing the tail lights of his car vanish around a bend in the road, she sat for a long time thinking about him. Then, to kill the time until he might return, she undressed and took a leisurely bath.*

*She was seated at her dressing-table making up her face when she heard the chimes of the doorbell. There was no conscious coquetry, no intent to provoke a response in Hansen, in her answering the door in the towelling bathrobe that was all that covered her perfumed nudity.*

*Her mouth opened in terrified shock when she saw Toffler, an insolent triumphant grin on his mouth, his foot already jammed against the door she tried desperately to close against him.*

*' 'Ello, doll,' he said. 'We 'ad a date. Remember?'*

## Other titles in the Walker British Mystery Series

JOHN
ROSSITER
# The
# Villains

WALKER AND COMPANY · NEW YORK

First published in the United States of America in 1976 by the
Walker Publishing Company, Inc.

This paperback edition first published in 1985.

ISBN: 0-8027-3115-5

Library of Congress Catalog Card Number: 75-36550

Printed in the United States of America

10   9   8   7   6   5   4   3   2   1

# Foreword

The events and their consequences I have described might, with the growing flabbiness of the law and the venality of some of its so-called servants, easily become fact.

Although fictitious, neither Weizsack nor Sinter is an overblown caricature. Unscrupulous lawyers like them exist. They use the law for their own ends, twisting it and perverting it for personal profit and aggrandizement, with a flagrant disregard for justice and the safety of the community.

People who feel that they have been denied justice by fraud and trickery are apt to seek redress outside a law that has failed to protect them. A bad thing, but understandable. There have been recent instances of it, fortunately none so serious as I have depicted.

Anyone caring to spend a few hours listening to the trial of a criminal such as Toffler (and he, too, is no caricature) may hear something of what I have written in the early chapters of the legal skirmishing and the twisting of facts to the advantage of the accused by counter-accusations against witnesses doing no more than their duty as citizens. A witness in such a trial is indeed fortunate if he leaves the stand without being labelled a fool, a liar or a knave. Sometimes, all three together.

A defence counsel's duties are fivefold: he has a duty to his client, to himself and to his opponent, the prosecutor; a duty to the court and to the State. It is difficult to accept that the lawyers to whom I refer have any intention of venturing beyond the first two.

If I have taken minor liberties with the rules of evidence, using the license happily extended to writers of fiction to ensure brevity and clarity, I have taken none with the form of advocacy I have so often seen used to concoct defences and to attack, without justification, police officers who, in the vast majority, endeavour to present their evidence as honestly and in as unbiased a manner as possible.

J.R.

# Chapter 1

In the beginning was pain and darkness, the limitless black cave of his skull overshot with threads of forking red. And floating, like a vivid moon in the inkiness, he saw the vicious mocking face of Toffler. Then the numbing nothingness of a void, his body nerveless and melting into the floor. Later, his shoe heels dragging on a smooth surface, tightness constricting his collar so that he heard his choking breath whistling in his throat, a tactile awareness of its happening to another's body. The sensation of lifting, of softness beneath his back and a fumbling and coolness on his loins; of hearing deep laughter booming from the outer edge of the spinning universe; of perfume and the gentle pressure of a moist mouth, a warm living pointed insertion ... somewhere a flash of bright fire through his eyelids and into the eyes that ran hot liquid down his cheeks and into his ears. And still the grinding pain in the epicentre of his brain, a confused mumble of voices drifting through his mind. He thought he heard a name floating towards him in the darkness ... not *hers*, but S ... S ... S ... S ... He shaped his mouth in a nightmare's soundless scream of iron lips and rigid tongue, his eyelids dragging open to shadowed faces that receded and loomed and the bigger sweeping shadow that brought engulfing oblivion again ... down into the consuming darkness where savage unseen teeth brought an unspeakable crunching agony to his testicles, and on to a deeper darkness and vomit in his mouth ...

Detective Sergeant William Gault, standing in the witness box, held with one hand the gilt-painted iron rail separating him from the formidable presence of the Honourable Sir William Timbrell, OBE, TD, four yards away in his carved,

7

high-backed chair. With the other hand he held the purple-stamped court bible, repeating the oath dictated to him by the Clerk of the Court below him.

*I swear by Almighty God that the evidence I shall give to the court and jury sworn between our sovereign lady the Queen and the prisoner at the bar shall be the truth, the whole truth and nothing but the truth.*

He said it with difficulty, for his fractured lower jaw had been clamped together with surgical wire, his tongue struggling to manipulate the words in the mouth cavity. That wasn't his only disablement. He saw only with a monocular vision, a cottonwool-padded black patch covering the empty socket where his right eye had been. He stood with his legs apart, allowing space for the more comfortable accommodation of the bandaging supporting the tubes and stitching inserted in his genitals.

He was a tall, slim man with dark good looks and a moustache, normally neat, that he had allowed to straggle during his two months in hospital. The one eye left to him was a deep brown, dull now from suffering and dejection. He wore a quiet grey suit, the jacket pockets bulging with small pads of gauze.

The jurors faced him, seated on oak benches with only a thin covering of foam rubber to give their buttocks comfort during the long hours of sitting. They were men and women unknown to Gault; chosen, not for their intelligence or their understanding of the law's complexities, but from a Voters' List, their names suffixed J on the assumption of some anonymous employee of the Local Authority that they were representative of the common average citizen. Which meant they could be an unpredictable amalgam of selfishness, compassion, obtuseness, commonsense, crass stupidity, decency and bigotry. They were here to decide the issue between two special pleaders; one saying 'He did it', the other arguing that he hadn't. To isolate them as far as possible from the truths of life, nobody was allowed to mention the undeniably pertinent fact that Toffler, the man on trial, was a brutal bastard with a criminal record which included convictions for kicking men he hadn't liked very much into bloody pulp; a man who called himself a company director because there wasn't a socially 'acceptable name for the parasitic villain he was.

Rain beat against the narrow mullioned windows set high

up in the lofty, mouse-grey, stone walls of the court. The lower half was panelled in a pale snuff-coloured wood. A massive Royal Arms in gleaming gilt and blue and white was spiked to the wall above the judge's head. The lights were yellow in the leaden grey of the wet morning leaking in through the windows.

Seated with the Judge was the morning-suited High Sheriff with his ivory wand of office, a Lord Lieutenant in his blue gold-braided uniform and the Judge's Chaplain. None took any part in the proceedings, being only the law's window dressing.

The legal functionaries' primary interest in Sergeant Gault's injuries was not a sympathetic one, although sympathy might have been implicit in the Judge's allowing a male nurse to stand in attendance on him. Their main concern was to decide whether or not his injuries fell within the ambit of Section 18 of *The Offences Against the Person Act 1861* under which the accused, Edward Harry Toffler, a company director of 27 Cleveland Road, had been committed for trial: to prove that Gault had been maimed, disfigured or disabled exactly as defined in the statute and, if that were proved to the letter, that the acts had been done unlawfully and maliciously by the accused Toffler. For Gault, however, the issue was the intolerable misery and torment of a crippled life, with tubes fitted surgically and painfully into the scrotum to drain out the stinking fluids, a wired-together jaw allowing only mashed or liquid food, and a crater-like hole beneath the eye patch letting in nothing but utter blackness.

It was neither necessary nor desirable that Gault should himself detail his physical sufferings to the judge and jurors assembled, to the black-robed, wigged barristers seated around the huge green-baize covered table beneath the judge's bench, to their attendant solicitors or to the crowded public gallery. That might inject unsettling passion and pity, blood and sorrow and anguish, into the arid emotionless atmosphere.

Doctor Nicholas Llewellyn had entered the witness box while Gault waited outside the courtroom to be called. It had probably been as well that the sergeant had not heard the brutally clinical detailing of his injuries.

Llewellyn, having taken the oath, was led into his evidence by Michael Quibbell of Counsel, instructed to prosecute by the Director of Public Prosecutions. He was a plump, pale-faced man whose amiable features were made studious by the addition of heavy-framed spectacles his eyes didn't wholly need. He was too gentle with witnesses to ever be briefed for the defence by a villain's solicitor, too honest to join in the money-grabbing tactics of his less principled brethren. He was an unemotional and objective prosecutor.

He opened. 'You are a Registered Medical Practitioner and an appointed Police Surgeon for this city?'

'I am.' Llewellyn, a cadaverous and swarthy man, was familiar with the giving of evidence. What he had to say would be said bluntly with little regard for over-tender suscep-tibilities.

'As a Police Surgeon you have a general medical overseeing of Sergeant Gault?'

'Yes.' He opened a file of papers on the ledge before him.

'Will you tell his Lordship and members of the jury of his medical condition on the date of his admission to hospital.'

'I first saw Sergeant Gault on Sunday morning the seventh of October in an intensive care ward at St Edmund's Infirmary, he having been admitted five hours previously and already under treatment for his injuries. The more obvious of these was the rupturing of the right eyeball by a kick or a blow from a fist, more probably the former. There was a gross tear-ing of the sclera and cornea, the fibrous protective envelopes of the eyeball and a discharge of the vitreous humour from inside.' Llewellyn knew his judges, knew that Timbrell dis-liked the latinization of any but legal terms and these he explained to juries in the tone of voice usually reserved by teachers for children.

'This,' Llewellyn said, 'is a jelly-like material which, once gone, cannot be renewed. It had been considered necessary to remove surgically what was left of the eyeball...' He waited, watching both the judge and Kaufman Sinter, Toffler's defend-ing counsel, making notes of what he had said.

'There had been,' he continued at a slight nod from Quib-bell, standing and following his evidence from a deposition, 'gross injuries to Sergeant Gault's private parts. Several violent impacts to the penis and scrotum had resulted in major crush-ing injuries to the testicles, lacerations of the epididymis ... the spermatic tube, my lord,' he clarified before the judge could object.

His Lordship spoke nevertheless. 'Does this have any effect

other than that common to mechanical injuries, doctor?'

'Yes, my Lord. It is improbable that Sergeant Gault will ever be able to father a child.' What he didn't add was that a gangrenous condition was supervening and that surgery might be necessary to remove the testes.

'He has children?'

'I understand not.'

'Please go on.'

'He suffered also a fracture of the lower jaw necessitating its immobilization by wiring. There was severe bruising in the parietal region of the back of the skull caused either by his falling or by a blow. The flesh was not broken, indicating the probability of a blow. There was evidence of a similar blow on the frontal bone above the left eye. On admission to hospital he was in a concussed state with shock supervening. There is subsequent evidence of an amnesia associated with the concussion.'

Quibbell asked, 'Does this leave Sergeant Gault with a memory of the circumstances causing his injuries?'

'This, of course, is something only he can answer,' Llewellyn said cautiously. 'Amnesia can leave a patient with no recollection whatever of events following the blows causing it. Or it may leave him with only a partial recollection.'

'Are you able to speak of Sergeant Gault's mental condition from your own observations?'

'He has spoken to me, of course; discussed the circumstances of his being injured. He has a partial recall; confused in some respects, apparently clear in others.'

'Is this likely to be a temporary amnesia, doctor?'

'I would hope so, but neither science nor medical knowledge has a definite answer to that.'

'How in your opinion were these injuries caused?'

Llewellyn had not hesitated. 'As I indicated when detailing them, there are alternative possibilities. But my opinion is that the injuries to the eye, jaw and genitals are consistent with their being repeatedly kicked. Those to the head...' He shrugged. 'Almost certainly blows with a padded instrument of some kind.'

'Such as a cosh?'

'Leather or cloth-covered, yes.'

'Would the blows to the head render him unconscious?'

'Undoubtedly. I understand he was so when found. He

could, of course, suffer loss of consciousness from shock, but either way he was unconscious. This man was beaten to a degree I have rarely in my professional experience encountered and shock would be inevitable and severe.'

'Thank you, doctor.' Quibbell sat and Sinter rose to cross-examine. He was a fat man; a grossly-fleshed man. From his small pink mouth could float beautifully enunciated words, persuasive honeyed pleadings. But from it also could rasp caustic biting phrases when the need arose. He was a dangerous opponent of argued fact and logic and never more so than when he was being polite.

Behind him sat his shadow, Alfred Weizsack, a struck-off solicitor; a cunning old man with an organic mitral incompetence, surviving sixty-four years against all medical opinion. Unable to practise openly as a solicitor, he did so nonetheless in the paper-thin guise of chief clerk to a figurehead partner who drank too much whisky to care what Weizsack did in his name.

Sinter tugged at the lapels of his gown and flattened the starched collar fillets with the palm of his fat hand. He looked as if he was smelling himself and loving every fragrant second of it. He kept Llewellyn waiting, acting apocalyptic disclosures about to be unleashed, making significant what he was about to extract for his gallery of twelve jurors.

'What exactly *is* amnesia, doctor?' he asked, smiling encouragingly at an unresponsive Llewellyn. That smile too was for the jury, warming them to Sinter's sweet reasonableness.

'Briefly, a functional disturbance of the memory.'

'And that is how you would describe Sergeant, ah, Gault's condition?' He smacked his lips at the conclusion of the sentence as if tasting his words too and finding them good.

'I would.'

'His Lordship and members of the jury have heard from you the symptoms of amnesia, doctor. May we take them a little further? Are you familiar with retrograde amnesia?'

'Not familiar. I am aware of it.'

'I see.' Sinter raised his eyebrows. He lifted an open book lying on the table in front of him. 'May I quote to you a revelant opinion on amnesia?' He read from the book. '*In cases of retrograde amnesia from concussion, events which occurred immediately antecedent to the injury are occasionally remembered indistinctly or not at all. There can be a complete amnesia of events even after recovery.* I am quoting the authority of Kuhn and Geller's *Traumata of the Brain,* doctor. You are familiar with it?'

'I know the book and I agree in general with what the authors are saying.'

'And to make certain that members of the jury understand what retrograde means in this context, may I clarify it means a loss of memory of events occurring before the injury causing the amnesia?'

'It does.'

'Thank you, doctor. May I, ah, quote further? *This retrograde amnesia may result in the patient making false accusations against persons he mistakenly believes connected with the causation of his injury.* Will you agree with me again?'

'No. That is something outside my knowledge.'

'It is within the knowledge of two very eminent brain specialists, Doctor Llewyllyn,' Sinter said sharply. 'Are you disagreeing with their expressed opinion?'

'I said I don't agree with *you*; that I have no knowledge of the effect you are quoting. But I will accept the findings of Kuhn and Geller as authoritative without necessarily agreeing with them.'

'Thank you, doctor. That is all anyone can ask.' He closed the book, dropping it carelessly on the table. The noise it made drew the jurors' attention to it as a solid, demonstrable fact. Which was why he had dropped it. 'Is this the picture we now have of the mental condition of Sergeant Gault? Firstly, that he is suffering a form of amnesia?'

'He is.'

'Secondly, that it might be retrograde amnesia?'

'There is no evidence of that.'

'Is there evidence to the contrary?'

'No,' Llewellyn conceded. Sinter was fishing, the most difficult of cross-examinations to counter.

'Is it a possibility?'

'No more than that. Anything from a brain injury is a possibility.'

'But there?'

'Yes.'

'Thank you.' He smacked his lips. 'So, should Sergeant Gault be unfortunately suffering from retrograde amnesia, his recollection of events immediately prior to the blow causing it could be wholly or partially obliterated?'

'Assuming he is, yes.'

'And, assuming again a retrograde amnesia, it could result in his making false accusations against another person?' He tapped his forefinger on the book, reminding Llewellyn of its authority.

'I will accept the validity of Kuhn and Geller's conclusions,' Llewellyn said carefully, 'in respect of similar cases they have investigated.' He was clearly unhappy at being forced to support a hypothesis of which he knew little.

'I am indeed grateful,' Sinter said. He flipped his gown open at the back and sat, regarding the jury with the air of one having made an incontrovertible, unarguable point.


Knowing none of this, Sergeant Gault waited in the witness box while Quibbell referred to the depositions in his hand.

'You are William Austin Gault, a Detective Sergeant of the Regional Crime Squad, attached for special duty to the Headquarters Branch of the Criminal Investigation Department of this city?'

'Yes, sir.' The words came misshapen through the rigid jaws and saliva immediately ran down the corner of his mouth. He dabbed at it with the gauze pad he took from his pocket.

Quibbell spoke to the judge. 'If it please your Lordship, may the witness sit? I am instructed he finds standing for periods longer than a few minutes a great discomfort.'

The judge regarded Gault with his heavily-pouched eyes. His was a stern, bloodless face with deeply-incised lines cutting into the flesh that sagged away from the bone structure. His robe showed a solid and brilliant scarlet in the light from above his chair.

'He may be seated.' Although the seat was an uncushioned wooden ledge, he was doing him a favour, putting the dignity of the court at risk, and it showed.

'Thank you, my Lord,' Quibbell said. He spoke to Gault. 'Is it fair to say, sergeant, that your memory of the incidents leading to the infliction of your injuries is, to some extent, impaired?'

'I recall some things clearly; other things not so.'

'You remember Saturday the seventh of October last?'

'I do. I reported on duty at six o'clock.'

'And were you—without naming him—instructed to keep observation on a particular man and were you doing so in Bernard Street in this city?'

Sinter rose to his feet. 'My Lord! My learned friend cannot admit to an impairment of memory in this witness on the one hand and, on the other, supply him with information in the form of leading questions.'

'I am entitled to lead on introductory matters,' Quibbell protested, 'as my learned friend well knows. There can be no dispute...'

Sinter interrupted him. 'There can be, my Lord, and there is. My friend is choosing to feed the witness's faulty memory.'

The judge leaned forward. 'I think in this case, Mr Quibbell, it were better you did not lead, even in introductory.'

'As your Lordship pleases.' Quibbell spoke to Gault. 'You recall where you were on duty, sergeant?'

'Yes, sir. I followed the man concerned from an address in Conduit Street to Bernard Street.' The man concerned, Gault thought bitterly: Toffler himself, and protected now from identification because to say he was being watched by a Crime Squad detective was tantamount to identifying him a suspect, a known criminal.

The two counsel and their solicitors knew; the judge knew and the police knew. Detective Chief Inspector Hansen, waiting in the court to be called himself, knew more than anybody. It had been at his request that the Crime Squad were keeping detailed observation on Toffler. If the jury used its collective imagination, it too would know from Sinter's failure to disassociate Toffler from that part of the evidence.

'Do you recall the time?'

Gault creased his forehead. 'About nine, sir. I can't be certain.'

'Will you tell his Lordship and members of the jury what you can remember of that night.'

Gault remained silent for a few moments. From outside he could hear the muffled sound of moving traffic. He felt fibreless in the dead air of the court, the dull ache in his belly depressing him. His single eye sought for and found Ann's face in the public gallery. He hadn't wanted her to be there. It was no place for a man's wife. Not when, as he suspected, Sinter would be attacking him over his identification of Toffler. Nor was he certain what her reaction would be. His mind worked on two levels. One level was the now, when mental perception and vision were clear enough for him to follow the legal arguments, arrange his own thoughts; for him to see the sheen of talc on the judge's jowls, see each knotted horsehair in his wig; feel minutely the roughness of the painted rail between his fingers. The other level, his recall of things past, was fogged by confusion. His mind shied away from the emotive words he was on the verge of identifying and which escaped him. He imagined, floating in his skull, small black discs that blocked off segments of his recall. Occasionally his remaining eye would feel expanded and engorged with a pulsing hot fluid, giving him a blurred superimposed vision, distorting his thinking. Then, it seemed, he lost contact with the world around him.

He spoke directly at Quibbell, slowly and deliberately, forcing each word past the unmoving gate of his locked jaw.

'The man I followed parked his car in Bernard Street. He was accompanied by another man. They left the car and I lost them in the darkness while searching a place in which to park my own car. I remember waiting in a doorway, expecting them to reappear, to return to their car which I had located. There was a woman...'

Below him, Sinter made a note on his pad and stared significantly at the jurors.

'I remember a woman...' He creased his brow in concentration for it was at this point that the black discs of non-recall clouded the pictures of his memory. 'She was in front of me ... telling me about a man. He had done something ... I think it might have been her husband.' He dabbed fluid from beneath the black eyepatch with gauze. 'I think she was asking me to help her ... she sounded frightened. Then I must have gone somewhere...' He trailed off. The silence in the court was total.

'Go on, sergeant.' Quibbell was gentle with him.

'I must have gone into a building. I have this feeling of being enclosed ... of a place with no light, but yet I could still see ... glass, perhaps a window or door. I felt this blow...' He touched the back of his head with his fingers. 'I remember my legs giving way ... not being able to stand. It was then I saw the accused.' He looked directly at Toffler sitting in the dock with a prison guard at his side and more than a hundred eyes moved with his single one.

They saw a man utterly composed, indifferent to the multiple stare. A man with a powerful muscular body and the bottle-neck shoulders of a fighter; cold butcher's eyes in a narrow face with tight-stretched, sunlamp-tanned skin and a knifeblade nose. His mouth was a gash of insolence, always open enough to show his strong white teeth. His hair, coarse and cut square at the neck, was the cream colour of sheep's-wool. He wore a sharply cut tan suit with a yellow-flowered tie. The overall impression he gave was that of a bird of prey and there was menace implicit even in the relaxed confidence of his sitting.

Gault's sick loathing of Toffler was crystallized in his steady regard of him, feeding on the face of the man who had mutilated him, emasculating him as surely as if he'd done it with a razor. *As God's my judge,* he told himself, *I saw the bastard. I know I did.* He hung with his fingertips to that small extrusion of fact on the steep wall of his non-memory, the only thing holding him from falling into purposeless confusion.

'Sergeant!' Quibbell's voice brought him back from his contemplation of Toffler and he broke contact. 'You are clear about your identification of the accused?'

'Quite clear,' he said firmly.

'You know the accused by sight?'

'I know him.' He had to. He had been following him, an invisible shadow, for over a week.

'Was he doing something when you saw him?'

'I don't know. I saw only his face and then only for the moment before I fell.' He could see it again, even in the confused recall of that night. As he had seen it in the nightmares that followed. The cruelty in it—masked now from the jury—the mocking insolent mouth, fading as darkness had swept into his mind. 'He was standing near me and to one side. No more than reaching distance from me.'

'Do you allege he was the man hitting you?'

'No. I don't know.'

'Where was the woman at this time?'

'I don't know.'

'The other man?'

'I didn't see him either.' He shrugged helplessly, wiping saliva from his mouth with fresh gauze. 'I must have lost consciousness straight away.'

'Do you recall anything following that?'

'I believe I was carried ... being handled. I have a recollection of a woman being present at one time and I heard voices...'

'Can you recall what was said?'

'No. I don't believe I heard the words at the time.' His fingers touched the eyepatch. 'Shortly afterwards ... I believe it was afterwards ... I felt a blow to this eye. Yes, it was before that I heard the voices ... I think I saw vague outlines of people. I believe I vomited then...' He remembered clearly the bitter taste of the vomit; its choking his nostrils. But preceding that, before the pain in his eye, the perfume and smell of a woman. Both had had a nightmarish intensity. He remembered being kissed and it wasn't anything he could explain or wish to. And the name: just the faint echo of an echo on the far distant periphery of his fading consciousness. S ... S ... S ... S ... something beginning with an S, but it wouldn't come. He clung to the reality of his stroboscopic-like flash of the vision of Toffler's face that had printed itself unmistakably on his memory circuit; the one coherence in the phantasmagoria of moving shapes haunting his mind.

'Do you recall the blows to your jaw and genitals, sergeant?'

'No.'

'And the next thing you remember?'

'Very vaguely being in an ambulance. Then speaking to Mr Hansen at the hospital.'

'Have you since been taken to Bernard Street?'

'Yes.'

'Is it fair to say you were unable to identify the house in which the assault took place?'

'Yes.'

'Is it within your knowledge that you will almost certainly be discharged from the police service on medical grounds?'

'It is.' It would, he told himself miserably, have been kinder to have put him down with a humane killer like a racehorse with a broken fetlock or a run-over dog. He couldn't think of any pressing reason for keeping him alive.

Quibbell turned and whispered to the Director's representative sitting behind him, said 'Thank you, sergeant,' to Gault and sat.

Sinter lifted his fat bulk with a studied deliberation, his eyes

18

on Gault, his expression one of stern denunciation. He waited, posed with his fist holding a lapel of his gown, his other hand spread like a pink starfish on the green baize of the table. When the chamber was completely silent, he spoke.

'You don't really remember very much do you, sergeant?' The tone of his voice was already contemptuous of Gault's value as a witness.

'No. Not too much,' Gault admitted.

'And what you do remember is confused, is it not?'

'Parts of it are clear enough.'

'Oh?' Sinter's fat face expressed enormous astonishment. He referred to his notes. 'Allow me to, ah, remind you of what you said directly and indirectly about your ability to recall. *I can't be certain. A woman ... telling me something about a man. I think it might have been her husband. I think she was asking me. Then I must have gone somewhere. I have this feeling. I don't know.* Three times you said *I don't know*, sergeant. *I think I saw vague outlines of people.* These are all words you used.' He smacked his lips. 'I put it to you they, ah, indicate anything but a clear memory of past events.'

'I said, parts of it are clear.'

Sinter hardened his voice. 'Such, for instance, as identifying the accused, Mr Toffler?'

'Yes.'

'But not the woman?'

'No.'

'Nor anyone else you allege or imagine was there?'

'No.'

'You don't think that your identification is providential? Providential, I mean, for bolstering the charge preferred against the accused?' The sneer was there, barely concealed beneath the fleshy features.

'My identification is a fact,' Gault said as curtly as his malformed jaw allowed. 'It led to the charge and not the other way around.'

'So you say. So you say.' Sinter was patently disbelieving. 'Is your memory of any other part of this alleged incident so vivid? I cannot recollect your saying so in your evidence-in-chief.'

'I didn't say. Nor did I say my identification of the accused was vivid. I said I saw him clearly. No doubt had I known

19

the woman as I know him, I would have identified her as well.'

'Ah, yes, sergeant. The woman. You really do not know her?'

'I don't.'

'You are sure?'

Gault felt a tiny glow of anger. Since his injuries, he could lose control of his temper easily. 'I am quite sure. I had never seen her before in my life.'

'Could you identify her from a photograph?' That barely concealed sneer again.

It surprised Gault. 'A photograph?' He passed a look of mute enquiry at Hansen to see if he knew anything of it. The Chief Inspector replied with a just-perceptible shrug of incomprehension.

'Yes. A photograph.' He was playing cat-and-mouse with Gault and the sergeant knew it.

'I wouldn't know until I have seen it.'

'You will be given the opportunity, sergeant.' He produced a coloured photograph and a square of green notepaper, handing them to the Clerk of the Court for passing to the judge. 'My Lord, I would like to put these documents to the witness.'

The judge scrutinized the photograph and looked at Gault, frowning distaste in his face. He read the note. 'I see, Mr Sinter,' he said noncommittally. 'Under what circumstances have these come into your possession?'

'They were delivered by post to the offices of my instructing solicitors this morning, my Lord.'

'Is the witness supposed to recognize the woman from this?' He sat back stiffly.

'It may prompt his memory of events, my Lord.'

'It may indeed.' He handed the photograph and paper back to the Clerk. 'You have taken the necessary steps to trace the writer?'

'We have, my Lord. The most assiduous, unremitting enquiries are being made.'

'And you wish to use them to cross-examine the witness on his credibility?'

Gault waited dully, his mind frozen like a wounded animal's. *The bastard's cooked something up for me*, he told himself. It would be unlike Sinter not to.

Sinter replied to the judge. 'I do, my Lord.'

'You are unable to prove either the photograph or letter?'

'No, my Lord. Should there be any suggestion that the photograph represents anything other than what the camera saw, I do have the original negative which was enclosed with it. It is what is known as a Polaroid-Land colour film, my Lord, self-developed in one minute inside the camera and, I am instructed, impossible to tamper with.'

'I am aware of the process, Mr Sinter,' he replied tartly. While he seldom objected to witnesses being treated as though ignorant of the obvious, he did so in his own case. 'You may put the photograph and letter to the witness.'

When Quibbell was given his courtesy viewing of the exhibits he pursed his lips, not looking at Gault. The sergeant felt again the glow of resentful anger. The bastards were setting him up for a monkey. It wasn't Toffler on trial now. It was himself. He swallowed spittle and grimaced. Not being able to clean his teeth made them as rough as plaster to his tongue, tasting of unremoved tartar. He came out from under the black cloud of his anger as Sinter spoke to him.

'Please read the letter, sergeant.'

He took the piece of paper handed to him by the court usher. He dabbed gauze to his eye and read the ill-printed message.

MR WIEZACK, LAWYER.

DEAR SIR RE MR TOFFLER. HE IS INNICENT FOR ASUALTING DECTECTIVE GAULT. I DID IT. HE HAS RUNED MY MARRAGE. HE TOOK MY WIFE AND MADE HER INTO A COW. THAT NIHGT SAT OCTOBER 7 I FOLLOWED THEM WITH A FREIND (PRIVATE DECT) AND TOOK THE PHOTO. THEN I WENT MAD AT WHAT I SEEN WITH MY OWN EYES AND KICKED HIM BAD. MY FREIND STOPED ME KILLING HIM. PLEASE TELL THE JUDJE. DONT LOOK FOR ME I AM LEAVING WITH MY WIFE TO START A NEW LIFE. IM NOT SORRY FOR WHAT I DONE ONLY SORRY MR TOFFLER GOT BLAIMED. YOURS RESPECTFULLY. A WRONGED HUSBAND.

Gault kept his face expressionless, knowing every eye in court was on him. Despair ate holes in his confidence. 'This is absolute nonsense,' he said shakily. 'The man's insane, whoever he is.'

'That might be a matter for the jury to decide, sergeant,'

Sinter said coldly. 'Not for you.' He held out the photograph. 'Please look at this and tell his Lordship and members of the jury what it, ah, depicts.'

Gault took the photograph and examined it, the blood draining from the veins in his face. He felt sick.

The glossy coloured print was explicit in detail. The naked woman, her large breasts pendulous over him, straddled a man lying supine on a bed. Her face overhung the man's, her pink tongue out, its tip just penetrating his open mouth. His trousers' front was unfastened and, although one of her thighs shielded the man's loins from the camera, he was manifestly exposed to her attentions. The woman's face was turned three-quarters away, showing only the curve of her cheek, a fringe of sooted-up artificial eyelash and dark hair. Despite the hard shadow of a flashlight falling across the man's features, he was unmistakably Gault himself; his eyes closed in apparent concentrated ecstasy, one hand clamped between the woman's thighs. It was a picture of a man with not too much time to waste in getting unclothed for a casual fornication and apparently happy to be a passive partner to the woman.

Gault's first wild thought had been of *her*, then knowing it couldn't be, remembering the feel of a woman's mouth on his and the flash of bright light through his closed eyelids. And, even knowing, it knocked the little composure he had remaining to him off balance, unhinging him from his professional competence as a witness. He was unsure now because the black holes in the spaces of his mind had become a threat to his memory. Conceivably, just conceivably, he could have.

'Sergeant Gault!' Sinter's voice cut through his stupefaction. 'Are you looking at a photograph of a man and woman engaged in an act of apparent sexual intercourse?'

'Yes,' Gault whispered. He wondered despairingly where his backbone had gone. He felt limp and incapable of resistance, wanting only a deep dark hole into which to crawl.

'Do you recognize the woman?' The inexorable voice pursued him.

'No.'

'I see,' he said meaningly. 'Do you recognize the man?'

Gault twisted his head, casting an agonized look at his wife, then turning back to Sinter. 'Yes.'

'Is the man, ah, yourself, sergeant?'

'Yes,' he ground out, 'but it's not true...'

'You mean that it isn't you?' The barrister raised his eyebrows in exaggerated bewilderment.

'No ... it's me ... I must have been unconscious. I didn't know it was being taken. That needs emphasizing...'

'I see.' The mobile lips curled in disbelief. 'Is that all you can say? Could it not be that you have forgotten?'

'No ... no it couldn't.' He was regathering his courage, his determination not to allow this fat conniving bastard to walk roughshod on his face, to malign and denigrate him under the guise of instructions from his client.

'That, sergeant, is something of which you may not be the best judge. Would you agree the photograph was taken on the night of the assault on you? Not on some other, ah, occasion?'

'There has been no other occasion.' The detective was more aggressive now, his voice stronger.

'If you say so. Please refer to the photograph again, sergeant. Can you see any signs of injuries?'

He ignored the photograph. 'I don't need to. The blow on the head wouldn't show anyway.'

'Or the absence of one?'

Gault remained silent.

'Are you going to answer me, sergeant?'

'You know the answer. As the back of my head is away from the camera, it's obvious it wouldn't.' He was brusque with Sinter now, rallying his depressed mind and flagging body to meet the challenge of Sinter's intent to dissect and destroy him. The disciplines of his profession, the conventions and rules of a criminal trial, pressed less weightily under the nagging pain and raw nerve-ends of his unhealed wounds. Nor, basically, was he a man to be crucified meekly without fighting back at his executioners.

'Thank you, sergeant,' Sinter said, coldly ironical, 'but you obviously need reminding you were struck on the forehead as well.' He twitched his gown straight on his shoulders. 'But no matter. Do you know what amnesia is?'

'Loss of memory.' He moved restlessly on the wooden ledge.

'That and more. Have you heard of retrograde amnesia?'

'No.'

'Please allow me to, ah, explain.' He was bland now. 'It can result from a blow on the head. It can result in a loss of memory of events not only following the blow, but prior to it. You understand me?'

'I understand its definition. I don't understand I suffer from it.' But the fear was there and the knowledge of those black discs of non-recall floating in his brain

'Doctor Llewellyn in his evidence agrees there is proof only that you suffer a form of amnesia,' he conceded as if anxious to be scrupulously fair. 'Retrograde amnesia, however, is provable by example...'

The judge intervened. 'Non-medically, Mr Sinter?'

'I believe so, my Lord.' His irritation at the judge's intervention was thinly concealed. 'Given the opportunity of testing the witness's recollection of events. However, should your Lordship consider it necessary to recall Doctor Llewellyn...?'

The judge thought that one out, tapping the end of his ball-pen on the Archbold *Criminal Pleading* open before him. 'No, I do not. But please confine your questions to the non-medical aspect of amnesia.'

'As your Lordship directs.' Sinter turned back to Gault. 'Would you not agree, sergeant, that forgetting about an event that actually happened is a symptom of amnesia?'

'Yes.'

'Would you accept Doctor Llewellyn's agreement that retrograde amnesia specifically involves the forgetting of something that happened prior to the causation of the amnesia?'

'Obviously I can't dispute it.' His empty eye socket leaked fluid, feeling as if the heel of a boot was grinding into it. The fuse of his self-control was shortening.

'Thank you.' He made it appear as if he were deeply grateful. Then his voice hardened. 'Now, sergeant, having regard to the photograph and letter, is it not the truth that you were, in fact, engaged in sexual intercourse with this woman? That you were, in fact, surprised *in flagrante delicto* by the husband and a private enquiry agent? That you are suffering as a result of the blows you received from the husband, a form of amnesia blotting the events completely from your mind?'

'*No!*' The word came harshly from between the clamped jaws. 'That's a lie and you know it is!'

The judge lifted his head and stared disbelievingly at Gault. 'That was a most abusive and outrageous reply to learned counsel.'

Gault held the judge's angry gaze, not answering but with obstinate defiance in his one eye.

'You will control yourself, sergeant, and behave under cross-examination as a disciplined police officer is required.' He spoke to the fat barrister. 'Please proceed, Mr Sinter.'

'May it please your Lordship.' He bobbed his wigged head, returning his attention to Gault.

Gault's wife had watched despairingly from the public gallery, seeing the spectacle of his normal decisiveness and confidence being stripped from him, his struggling to defend himself with mangled words and a faltering memory; his transition from confused irresolution to undisciplined aggression, his uncertainty about what had happened to him; his fighting back hopelessly, but not fighting hard enough or with his usual precision. She had strained her eyes to see the photograph, but from her position it was postage-stamp size, a meaningless square of colours. She wanted to stand and scream at them all; at the cold inhuman fat man butchering Bill with his monstrous accusations about a woman; at the autocratic old judge for not stopping him, for his harsh words to a sick man. She suddenly hated the stupid-looking jurors for even listening to the remorseless chopping away of her husband's integrity, at the people around her for having nothing better to do than to sit and watch his crucifixion. But most of all there was a cold sick loathing and hatred for the man in the dock. It was something she wanted never to lose or to have diminished.

Sinter was stern and accusing with Gault. 'We have a somewhat different picture now, have we not? Not a Detective Sergeant engaged in his lawful duties as it would at first appear; helping a woman in distress...' He was to Gault a whole fat sneer of a man; belittling him, treating him with contumely, denigrating him both as a man and a police officer. 'You were none of those admirable things, sergeant, but a man photographed in squalid *coitus* with a woman he alleges he does not know. Being assaulted, not by the accused, but by a no doubt righteously outraged husband...'

Gault wasn't hearing the rest of his words. He had now the desperation of a cornered animal, not wanting to crawl behind the protection of his bandages, just wanting to die with his teeth in the flesh and tissue of his tormentor's throat. He wasn't wholly sane at that moment. He rolled his eye at the judge, reading his stern features without comfort, then back to the moving moist pink mouth of Sinter. 'As you wish, sergeant,' he was saying. 'No doubt the members of the jury will choose to put their own construction on your refusal to answer.'

Gault hadn't even heard Sinter's question and he stared at Quibbell, wordlessly demanding to know why he wasn't objecting to the tearing-apart, the goading, of his witness, but the barrister avoided his regard. His attitude was saying he had lost faith in Gault, was not prepared to battle for somebody in whom he no longer believed.

Sinter was talking to him. 'Allow me to come to my second point, Sergeant Gault.' He held an open book in one hand. 'This is a well-known medical text book; Kuhn and Geller's *Traumata of the Brain* to which I have already referred Doctor Llewellyn. Not a book, sergeant, with which you would be familiar but one, I assure you, held as authoritative by the medical profession. It refers, among other things, to amnesia. I will quote. *This retrograde amnesia may result in the patient making false accusations against persons he mistakenly believes connected with the causation of his injury.*' He closed and flung the book down on the green baize. 'Isn't that precisely what you have done? Falsely accused Mr Toffler of being the author of your injuries...'

Gault had again lost the words behind the noisy throbbing of his eye socket, and his disfigured face, pale with anger, glared at Sinter. Furious resentment welled up from his stomach, seeking release in savagely articulated words.

'Suppose you and Toffler both get stuffed!' He swivelled his head to get the judge in his vision. 'Have you finished?' It was as near a shout as he could get. 'Because I've had a gutful of what you call a trial!'

He heard an agonized 'Bill! Bill!' from the gallery, but kept his angry regard on the judge who was working his mouth, his face shocked and beginning to redden over the cheekbones with his own anger.

Gault felt raw and humiliated; no longer caring for the justice so assiduous in proving him a perjured liar and a cock-happy fornicator. He didn't care any more for the so-called majesty of the law and the Crown Court, the God-like sacrosanctity of High Court Judges, the supposedly liberty-preserving role of defending counsel: nothing even for the neutral role of Quibbell.

He grasped the railing of the stand and pulled himself upright, even as the judge found his own words.

'How dare you, sergeant! That was the most unprecedented impertinence and contempt for a court of law I have...'

Gault interrupted him. 'All right!' he forced out with a terrible intensity, his voice straining to get past his teeth. His eye was glaring at the judge as he had never been glared at before. 'I'm guilty of whatever it is you're all trying so bloody hard to prove against me! I arranged to have my balls kicked to a pulp, my eye ruptured, my jaw broken, just so I could frame that filthy grinning bastard in the dock! So I didn't see him if that's what you all want me to say! I dreamed it up! Said I did because I'm a lying, bloody-minded, fornicating copper who wouldn't be interested in finding out who actually did this to me! So now find out your bloody selves!'

He swept the bible from its shelf with a vicious sideways swipe of his hand and stumbled from the stand, white-faced and furious, almost incoherent with the sickening rage that had engulfed him, making blindly for the door.

The judge broke the shocked silence in the court. 'Bring that man back to me,' he rapped out.

Gault stopped and turned slowly to face the equally furious judge. A trickle of clear fluid leaked unchecked from beneath his eyepatch, saliva ran from the corner of his trembling mouth. His eye was red-capillaried, injected with his physical suffering. He stood with his legs apart, the wreckage of a man, demolished with violence and torn apart by calumny, with nothing to fear except more grinding pain and discomfort and needles being pushed into his body. The judge was no longer awesome, but an old man with only the power to commit him to prison for contempt. He wasn't God, able to strike him dead for blasphemy and, even had he been, that wouldn't have stopped Gault either. He staggered, his legs suddenly boneless, putting out a hand to support himself and not quite making it. Chief Inspector Hansen caught him, holding him upright with the help of the male nurse.

Gault's fury had evaporated, but not his resentment. 'I feel ill,' he said faintly, his voice only a little above a whisper. He wanted to get away and die like a sick cat. 'I've nothing further to say to you or anyone else.'

'Be quiet!' The judge put shaking fingers to his forehead, looking down at his notes. He had conquered his need to shout back at this impertinent, disgraceful sergeant and he considered matters with his dry lawyer's mind while Sinter and Quibbell waited, both standing.

'Have him taken outside, Mr Quibbell,' he said at last, 'and ensure that he is seen by a doctor immediately. Except for reasons of his well-being, he is not to leave the precincts of the court without my express permission. I will adjourn for fifteen minutes.'

The Honourable Sir William Timbrell badly needed time in which to recover his lost equanimity. He needed almost as much the narcotizing smoke of one of the cigarettes waiting for him in his retiring room.

In the dock, Toffler made no effort to hide his sneering, mocking grin.

# Chapter 2

Detective Chief Inspector Robert Hansen needed to see Gault. The production of the photograph and letter had been as much a surprise to the Prosecution as it had been to the unfortunate Gault. But, compounding Quibbell's surprise, had been his reluctance to argue against their genuineness, the question of their doubtful admissibility in evidence. Everything about the exhibits stank of a concoction; the alleged anonymity of their sender, their late receipt by Weizsack, the too-carefully posed picture of the woman lowering herself on to Gault.

Although Gault was not in his department, Hansen possessed a strong loyalty to him as a fellow-policeman. To have seen such a palpable fix worked against him, accepted as a weapon to destroy his credibility without serious opposition or doubt from either judge or prosecuting counsel, made him want to spit at what was masquerading as a justice that was not only meant to be done, but seen to be done. The justice he had once respected as holding an equally-poised balance all too often seemed to stand with one pan tilted, loaded with solicitors and barristers who fixed the evidence, manufactured it, distorting and destroying with lying persuasion and argument what couldn't be fixed.

Hansen was a big man in his early thirties. Although he wore his black hair a little closer trimmed than current fashion deemed necessary, he was no buttoned-up, short-back-and-sides man. His face had the used look of a man who had dealt with too much of the rubbish and filth of criminality, of human depravity. He had a cat's bold eyes on the orange side of brown. His cheeks were flat, his jaw hard-planed. He looked more Calvinistic than he actually was; a man who, attacked or insulted, would predictably respond with something other than sweet reason or forgiving gentleness.

In deference to the formality of a Crown Court, he had dressed himself in a charcoal-grey suit and a white shirt. His wristwatch and cufflinks were of stainless steel and these matched the man.

He found Gault in an anteroom off the main corridor. It had *Interview Room No 4* painted on the varnished door, its indicator panel saying *Engaged*.

Gault was slumped in a green pvc-covered armchair, his face candle-coloured, his single eye closed.

A dark-haired woman sat near the window at the far end of the room. She wore a fawn belted coat with a blue scarf at her neck. She was slim and elegant and attractive enough to draw Hansen's immediate attention. Her unhappy expression made her, he thought, Gault's wife. He gave her a small smile.

Doctor Llewellyn was adjusting the shoulder of Gault's jacket. He held an empty hypodermic syringe in his hand. The male nurse, a podgy man with a florid complacent face and wearing a tight-fitting grey jacket with his name and *The Royal College Hospital* stitched in red on the patch pocket, dabbed cottonwool beneath Gault's eyepatch.

Hansen spoke to Llewellyn. 'Can I have a few words with Sergeant Gault when you've finished, doctor?'

'If you're not too long.' He touched his finger on the syringe and mouthed silently, 'Sedative.'

'The judge'll be pleased,' Hansen said ironically.

'Bugger the judge.' Llewellyn spoke softly to Hansen alone. 'I'm a doctor, not a bloody lawyer.' He unscrewed the needle from the glass barrel of the syringe and shook it free of fluid, then casing it in a small silver box. He put fingers in Gault's hair and ruffled it. 'You feel all right now, Spartacus?'

Gault's eye opened and he nodded.

'Five minutes and no more,' Llewellyn warned Hansen.

When he had gone with the nurse, Hansen walked over to the woman. He smiled at her again. Close to, she was lovely. Something in him reached out and made an immediate connection. Her skin was without blemish and creamy; her wide eyes a clear deep green. The nose was small, the mouth generous and smooth, opening to show teeth of peeled-almond whiteness. Her black hair, cropped short, exposed small gold rings in the lobes of her ears. She looked obsessively neat and clean. Even the slim wedding ring on her finger shone as if polished daily with jeweller's paste.

'Mrs Gault?'

She nodded, her smile a formal one.

'My name's Hansen. Do you mind my having a talk with your husband?' He meant, on his own.

'You want me to go?' She was surprised, her widened eyes looking up at him.

He hesitated, but there were awkward questions to be asked. 'Do you mind? For a few minutes.'

She rose, taking her handbag and gloves and leaving him, not glancing at her husband.

Hansen sat on a table opposite to Gault who watched him without expression. There was compassion in the detective for the disabled sergeant, but also a thin edge of disapproval for his emotional collapse. Hansen expected a CID sergeant to be able to stopper down the extreme emotions of hysteria and furious abuse, even under the grossest of provocations. But he conceded he had been provoked.

'You won't get the Queen's Police Medal for what you said to old Timbrell,' Hansen started with a slight grin. 'But speaking as a bystander, it was educational.'

Gault didn't respond to his senior's reassuring humour. 'Don't expect me to say I'm sorry.' The words were even more slurred than they had been in the court. 'That bloody bastard Sinter ... I'll say it again if they make me go back in.' He was smouldering still.

'I don't think they will, sergeant. I don't think they need to.'

The eye looked away from him. 'You mean, I ballsed it up?'

'I imagine so. You more or less retracted your evidence in the heat of the moment and Sinter will seize on that.' He tried to keep his rank out of his voice, using something between his senior authority and friendliness and finding it difficult. 'I haven't much time and I want to know about the photograph. Can you remember more than you gave in your evidence?'

'You heard what they said.' Gault was abrupt, at war with authority and expecting trouble. 'It showed me screwing a bloody woman. What I say doesn't apparently go for much.'

Hansen turned down the corners of his mouth. 'Don't dish out any of your self-pity on me, sergeant,' he said sharply. 'We

31

both know it was faked. But it's fresh evidence and it'll have to be enquired into.'

'Don't rely on me.' His fingers were picking jerkily at a pad of gauze. 'I'm told I have retrograde amnesia.'

'For Christ's sake, sergeant,' Hansen snapped. 'We're supposed to be on the same side. Stop fighting me. Is there anything more you can tell me? *Think*.'

'Ann was there,' Gault said woodenly. 'She heard it.'

'You mean your wife?'

'Yes.'

'She won't believe it any more than I do.'

'No?' The eye watching Hansen didn't look convinced.

'Not when I've told her.'

'I hope you're right.' He wiped saliva from his mouth and shifted his position, wincing. 'There is one thing ... a name. I couldn't remember it before except it began with S. I've got it now ... at least, I think I have. Sheila. Somebody said it when ...' He trailed into silence.

Hansen waited, then said, 'Go on.'

Gault turned his head, leaving Hansen only the blankness of the black eyepatch. 'That's something else I've remembered. A woman ... kissing me ... putting her tongue in my mouth ... laying on top of me. I must have been coming round.' He was awkward with his embarrassment, feeling like a raped schoolgirl.

'A good time to remember it, sergeant,' Hansen said ironically.

'It wouldn't have helped. Only made me look a bigger prick than I am already. And don't forget,' he said bitterly, 'I could have dreamed it up like the rest of it.'

Hansen stared at him, not altogether blaming his intractability. 'But you're sure you heard the name Sheila?' It wasn't much to go on, but a lot better than nothing.

Gault nodded.

'You can't remember what she looked like? That she was the same woman who got you into the building?'

'No. That's gone. Only what I saw on the photograph.'

That wasn't much either. Quibbell had showed it to Hansen before he left the courtroom for a cigarette during the adjournment. Dark hair that could have been black or brown, artificial lashes over closed eyes, big hanging milk-coloured breasts and a foreground of a lot of non-identifiable buttock;

her nose concealed behind the curve of Gault's face, her mouth open and distorted by the extruded tongue. She wasn't recognizable as anyone he knew.

'It's enough,' Hansen assured him optimistically, putting a comforting confidence in his voice. 'I'll find her.'

'Yes.' Gault's attention was drifting away from him, his eyelid drooping. 'But I've still ballsed things up.'

Hansen shrugged his big shoulders. 'Don't fret about it. Worry about me. I don't know yet what Sinter's got up his dirty sleeve marked with my name. Only that it'll be something nasty.' He smiled. 'I'll try and not be too bloody-minded with the judge. He's...'

The door opened and Detective Chief Superintendent McGluskie entered. He was as huge in his fat as his antithesis Sinter, but without the soft overhanging belly. His was hard. He was shiny bald, his teeth big and square like ivory dice and yellow from smoking. The intense blue eyes rarely joined in the joviality of his features. Like most fat men he was often physically underrated but, in action, he was as indestructible as an iron door. He showed surprise at seeing Hansen and frowned.

'You shouldn't be here, Robert,' he said reprovingly. He had a fat man's voice that rumbled in his chest and belly. 'It could be misconstrued. You know that.' A defending counsel could make heavy bricks of the straw of even a few casual words between witnesses.

Hansen slid off the table and stood. 'I heard his evidence, sir,' he replied. 'We can hardly be collaborating...'

'He hasn't finished it yet,' McGluskie interrupted him sharply. 'Sinter could make sausage-meat out of you and we're in trouble enough already.'

He followed Hansen outside and lowered his voice. Mrs Gault was seated near the door, waiting to rejoin her husband. 'Watch out for a sly kick in the goolies,' he warned. 'I've heard word that Weizsack and Sinter are hatching out something nasty for you. Apart from having a couple of witnesses prepared to swear on their mothers' graves that Toffler was somewhere else altogether.'

# Chapter 3

The atmosphere of the court had settled back into its accustomed *gravitas* and heavy decorum following the fifteen minutes of reorganization and redeployment caused by Sergeant Gault's unprecedented outburst.

The judge had returned with his retinue, expecting Quibbell and Sinter to have reached some acceptable form of agreement on questions they could anticipate his putting to them. Externally, he appeared to be in a more appeasable state of mind.

When there was a proper silence and cessation of movement, only the rattling of rain on the windows heedless of any judicial admonition, he spoke, informing at large the array of barristers below him that he understood the officer causing the unseemly and indecorous scene was deemed medically and emotionally unfit to continue his evidence. He looked enquiringly at Sinter. 'Mr Sinter?' The fat barrister had already risen. 'Had you further cross-examination in mind?'

'I had indeed, my Lord,' Sinter said. 'But neither the accused nor I wish to prolong the witness's ordeal nor add to his sufferings.' He looked as if he really cared. 'If it pleases your Lordship to direct the witness to be held available within the precincts of the court, the defence will defer further cross-examination.'

'Mr Quibbell?' The judge's tone of voice made Quibbell very definitely the second-string advocate.

Quibbell stood. He was about to surrender tamely any chance Gault would have in that court of refuting Sinter's scurrility. 'I, too, my Lord, had intended to re-examine Sergeant Gault on matters arising from his cross-examination by my learned friend. However, I understand from Detective Chief Superintendent McGluskie, who has spoken to the officer since, that he refuses quite firmly and categorically to give further evidence. In view of that and his medical condition, my Lord, I do not feel I can properly ask for an adjournment.'

'Thank you, Mr Quibbell.' The two barristers had been agreeably co-operative in helping him avoid the unwelcome hysteria of further evidence from Sergeant Gault. He thought of the sergeant with extreme displeasure. He frowned judicially, showing the cutting edge of his lower dentures. 'I will, of course, require that Chief Superintendent McGluskie makes a full report of this occurrence, the officer's behaviour and remarks, to his Chief Constable.' He wasn't as all-forgiving as his opening remarks might have indicated.

Alfred Skeffington, Bachelor of Science, Associate of the Royal Institute of Chemistry, a Principal Scientific Officer employed at the South Eastern Forensic Science Laboratory, took the oath. He told the judge and jurors of his examination of a pair of tan-coloured suède shoes (Exhibit No 2, marked Toffler), which he produced suitably protected from further contamination in a clear polythene bag. On one of them—the right, he said—he had found eleven grey-coloured fibres of interwoven worsted wool and Acrylan, all within the range of ten to fifteen millimetres long. On the side of the welt of the shoe, he had found a spot of blood. From the fibres of a pair of brown woollen trousers (Exhibit No 4, also marked Toffler), he had removed a human head hair. The condition of its root indicated that it had been forcibly removed from the scalp.

He had compared the hair microscopically and chemically with head hairs taken from Sergeant Gault. They were identical in pigmentation, in breadth, in the character of the cuticle and cortex and in the presence of a medulla. He was, in plain English, prepared to say that the hairs had a common origin; that is, the hair found on the trouser leg of the accused, Edward Toffler, was identical with the head hairs of Gault.

He could further state that the eleven fibres found on Toffler's right shoe were microscopically identical with those he had taken from an overcoat worn by Gault on the evening of the attack on him. The blood found on the shoe had been subjected to an agglutination test, resulting in its being identified as Group O. A specimen of Sergeant Gault's blood had been similarly examined and it too had been identified as Group O.

The jurors began to regard the nonchalance of Toffler with a little less credulity.

Sinter cross-examined Skeffington and elicited, as if wringing from him an admission of guilt, that it was possible—Skeffington qualified it as remotely possible—for another man to possess head hair with the identical cuticular scaling, with an exact medulla diameter of six-hundredths of a millimetre, with a medullary index in Gault's case of 0.26. He also obtained from the chemist the information that Blood Group O occurred in about forty-five per cent of the white population. Which, as Sinter pointed out and with which Skeffington had to agree, would amount to about two hundred and sixty thousand people in the city alone. What Sinter was not required to elicit in quoting these figures was that two-thirds of them would be women and children; that of them all, few, if any, would also possess the characteristics of Gault's hair, wear an overcoat such as he had, or be identified (as Toffler was) as being at the scene. Nor was it incumbent on him to point out (which was never commented on) Toffler's utter refusal to provide a specimen of his own blood for comparison, and the law's flabby inability to require him to.

Hansen followed Skeffington into the witness box. Having witnessed the destruction of Gault as a witness and remembering McGluskie's warning, he didn't suppose he was going to be an exception to Sinter's special kind of legal malignancy. But he couldn't be sure from which direction the attack on his credibility would come. Only that it would come. That he had conducted his investigation scrupulously and strictly by the rules would mean less than nothing to Sinter in his efforts to get Toffler off the hook.

Hansen gave his evidence straightforwardly and without any prompting from Quibbell, without any reference to his pocket book.

'On Sunday morning the eighth of October last at one o'clock,' he said, 'as the result of an earlier interview with Detective Sergeant Gault in the Casualty Department of St Edmund's Infirmary, I went to twenty-seven Cleveland Road with Detective Sergeant Connach. I there saw the accused at the door of his flat. He had apparently been in bed and was dressed in pyjamas and a bath robe. I identified myself and told him I was arresting him on a charge of unlawfully wounding Detective Sergeant Gault of the Regional Crime Squad earlier that evening in Bernard Street. I cautioned him and he replied, "I don't wish to say anything until I have seen my solicitor." '

That was a euphemism, Hansen thought. An acceptable, necessary lie. What Toffler had actually said, apart from furious obscenities, was *The stinkin' law again. I'm sayin' nothin' to you bastards without my brief tellin' me what, an' that'll be bugger-all.*

'I accompanied the accused to his bedroom and in his presence took possession of a suit, a shirt and tie, underclothing and a pair of shoes and socks; all being on a chair at the side of the bed and having the appearance of being placed there on the accused's undressing. I asked him if these articles of clothing were his and had he worn them that evening, but he made no answer.'

Not really an answer. Toffler had said, *Push off! You mus' think I'm bloody soft!* Nor did Hansen say that the bed had been occupied by a naked girl who would have looked more at home in a school uniform and pigtails, but who had sworn at him with even more fluency and virulence than Toffler on no worse basis than that he was the law and to be despised and hated as such. At all costs, Toffler must be presented to the jurors as a moral and honest citizen.

'I returned with the accused to Headquarters where, at one-fifty, he was formally charged with the offence with which he stands indicted and to which he made no reply. Mr Weizsack, his solicitor's representative, having been informed, arrived at two-five. In the presence of Mr Weizsack, the accused was cautioned a second time and asked if he wished to make a statement in answer to the charge. He replied, "I do not wish to make a statement at this stage." '

The right of the accused to remain mute, to deny an answer in the face of accusation. Sticking two derisive fingers up at justice. The biggest ever bar to arriving at the truth. Which, Hansen believed, was what justice should be all about, but wasn't.

'On Monday the ninth of October I handed the clothing of the accused, together with the other exhibits in this case, to a receiving officer at the Home Office Forensic Science Laboratory at Bankish.'

Quibbell put down his deposition and sat. A prosecuting counsel, representing injured or wronged society, deals only with undecorated and unvarnished facts in an unemotional manner, his aim that justice shall fairly be done to both society and the accused. Not for him the special pleadings, designed not to test the evidence of witnesses, but to confuse the issues, to throw doubt on prosecution facts, to turn them upside down to his own advantage or to bleach them of significance. But criminal lawyers such as Sinter did just that, using their knowledge ruthlessly, not to ensure a just and equitable verdict, but to fight or coax for the acquittal of the clients they appeared for. Misrepresentation, accusation and smear were Sinter's primary weapons.

As he rose to cross-examine Hansen their eyes met, each measuring the enmity of the other. They had met before. There could never be a cause in which they met without a mutual loathing. It lay between them like a bitter black river.

'Isn't it true to say, Chief Inspector,' Sinter commenced, 'that you visited Mr Toffler that night determined already of his supposed guilt?'

'I was in possession of sufficient information to justify my believing him to have committed the wounding; sufficient to justify his arrest and subsequent charging.'

He recalled seeing the terrible hulk of Gault lying on the leather-topped examination table in Casualty; the punctured depressed eyeball leaking thin blood and fluid down his cheek; the monstrously swollen shape of his genitals straining against the cloth of his trousers; the crooked lower jaw and bloody tooth sockets. Hansen, inured to blood and smashed bodies as he was, felt sick in his stomach at the inhuman savagery of the beating. Semi-conscious, fighting against the pain-killing drug injected into him, Gault had managed to articulate 'Toffler ... did ... it. House ... Bernard Street ... *Toffler ...*' from his misshapen jaws before letting go and dropping back into merciful unconsciousness.

That and the witness they had found almost immediately in Bernard Street who, arriving back at his lodgings there, had seen Toffler—who he knew by sight and reputation—lifting a man he had assumed at the time to be a drunk into a car, had formed the basis for his arresting Toffler. That the witness had since abandoned his lodgings without leaving a forwarding address was, to Hansen, one of a piece with the concocting of Toffler's defence.

'Isn't it true to say also,' Sinter continued as if Hansen hadn't answered him, 'that you forced your way into the accused's home in the middle of the night without a search warrant?'

'No, it isn't.' Hansen kept his voice even, unemotional. 'I arrested him in the doorway of his flat. He was in pyjamas and I returned with him to the bedroom in order that he could get dressed.'

'So you say,' Sinter said meaningfully. 'And while you were in the bedroom you chose to seize some of his clothing, bundling it up for examination?'

'I seized the clothing, yes. That is essential, justified procedure. I bundled it up, no. I packed and sealed each item separately in polythene bags supplied for that purpose.'

'Oh? You came prepared to seize his clothing?' He put a sinister interpretation on that.

'Only in general terms. I carry the bags in my car with other equipment. When I saw I needed them the sergeant with me collected them on my instructions. I packed the clothing in the presence of the accused. He was invited to sign the sealing tapes and he refused.'

'Only, Chief Inspector,' Sinter said, again ignoring what Hansen had said, 'it seems a very fortunate thing in terms of evidence against Mr Toffler for you to have done, was it not?'

'Fortunate?' The contempt was in Hansen's eyes, not showing on his features. Sinter was plastering it on thick, even for this jury. He knew as well as any police officer when and why it was done. 'It is routine investigative procedure in the majority of crimes of violence.'

'Really? I'm glad to hear it, Chief Inspector. Is it also routine procedure for you to say to your prisoner when he asks to see his solicitor...' He lifted his note pad and read out, *You'll see him when I think you will. And then only if you co-operate?*'

'I said nothing of the kind.' Hansen's voice was clipped and brusque. 'Mr Weizsack was contacted by telephone immediately on our arrival at Police Headquarters.'

'But you continued to charge Mr Toffler although he wasn't legally represented?'

'Of course I did. Not to have done so would have been wrong; inviting criticism.' Whatever you did or did not do; how you did it or why, was going to be criticized. It made for a very strict adherence to procedures; allowing no room for the humanities when a cigarette or an extra cup of tea could be twisted by

39

astute counsel into evidence of an inducement to confess.

'Did you not at one time, Chief Inspector, attempt to intimidate Mr Toffler into confessing to a crime of which he is completely innocent?'

'That is completely and utterly wrong. Sergeant Connach was with me,' he pointed out, 'and will support my version of the accused's arrest and charging.'

'No doubt he will,' Sinter sneered. 'He is your subordinate, is he not?'

'He will be a police officer sworn to tell the truth,' Hansen said coldly.

'Yes.' He dismissed that as not being worth very much. 'Did you make a remark to Mr Toffler as you entered his flat? On the way into his bedroom?' He put a fat hand on the top of his wig and straightened it.

'If I did, it was in terms of my telling him to precede me or that I wanted him to dress.'

'I am instructed you said *"I'm going to get you, you bastard, if it's the last thing I do"* and . . .' He referred again to his note pad. ' *"You did Sergeant Gault and I'll see you get ten years".*'

Hansen was conscious of the judge's eyes on him, so obviously wondering whether Hansen had actually said the words that he could have been thinking aloud. This was it, the detective told himself. It would be boring in its hackneyed sameness, in its paucity of inventiveness, were it not so eminently believable by jurors. Alleged in a high court of law by a barrister, the words gathered to themselves a legal truth and authority. He could hear them saying: it stands to reason, Toffler's bloke wouldn't have said it if it wasn't true. Not in front of a judge.

'You've been misinstructed,' Hansen said precisely. 'No such thing was said. Nor anything that could remotely be imagined as it.'

Sinter flushed. 'Please don't tell me I was misinstructed, Chief Inspector. Mr Toffler . . .'

'I *am* saying it.' Hansen had no intention of allowing Sinter to bulldoze over him. 'If those are your instructions, then the accused has misinformed you.'

The judge frowned at Hansen over his half-moon spectacles. 'Don't continue on those lines, officer. Confine yourself to a denial or an agreement.'

Hansen acknowledged him with a curt nod. He was being

told to fight back one-handed. *Yes* or *No*. These words, un-qualified, were feeble, inadequate and misleading replies under an attack that chose its own words for their effect.

Sinter said, 'Thank you, my Lord,' and swivelled himself to face Hansen again. 'You don't admit saying those words to the accused?'

'No.'

'So be it, Chief Inspector. We shall, ah, see. Now, I don't want to trap you...'

Hansen interrupted him again. The word 'trap' was deliberately emotive, planting the thought of underhandedness, something to hide, in the jurors' minds. 'There is nothing to trap me over and it is improper you should imply there might be.' Sinter's baiting was beginning to irritate him.

'Oh, no? I'm glad to hear it.' He showed his own raw edge of irritability. 'And please do not interrupt me, Chief Inspector. Just listen to my question. Who collected Sergeant Gault's clothing? The specimens of his head hairs?'

'A scenes-of-crime sergeant who will follow me to give evidence of it.'

'And they all came into your possession?'

'They did. I handed them to a laboratory officer with the exhibits taken from the accused.'

'They were sealed in proper containers?'

'They were.'

'Is there a possibility that the clothing and shoes you took from Mr Toffler's bedroom have been subject to accidental contamination by the other exhibits?' His expression was of an eminently reasonable man seeking a fair explanation. 'That they have been, ah, exposed to the contact of hairs and fibres and the blood about which we have heard Mr Skeffington give evidence?'

'The possibility is too remote to consider. They were all in separate sealed exhibit bags and the two groups kept apart, even on delivery to the laboratory.'

Sinter bared his teeth and said, 'Thank you. I will gladly accept your assurance that no accidental contamination could have taken place.' He concentrated his regard on Hansen, holding him with his chilling grey eyes. 'So we come to the only acceptable explanation, Chief Inspector. Mr Toffler, knowing that he has had no contact with Sergeant Gault on the evening in question; or, indeed, on any previous occasion, has instructed me of the only possible alternative. One that makes significant the remarks he alleges you made to him. "I'm going to get you, you bastard, if it's the last thing I do" and "You did Sergeant Gault and I'll see you get ten years".'

'I have already categorically denied saying that.' He felt the concentrated attention of the jurors and the spectators on him.

'So you have, Chief Inspector, but I suggest that you did.' His words came hard and accusing. 'I suggest further that in your efforts to carry into effect what you had threatened, you deliberately tampered with Mr Toffler's clothing and shoes.'

Even in the shock effect of Sinter's monstrous allegation, Hansen wondered what was expected of his reaction to being called in legal language a dishonest, unscrupulous bastard. A pallid 'No' in accordance with the directions of the judge? He subdued his undisciplined impulse to raise his voice at Sinter. 'That,' he said evenly, trying hard to control the shaking of his anger, 'is an outrageous allegation without an atom of substance in it.' He was conscious of the jurors' eyes on him. Christ! he thought. Why shouldn't they consider it? No doubt they'd been conditioned to such denigrating rubbish by books, by television. How would they know that no detective officer, his moral honesty apart, would be brainless or reckless enough to invite such trouble. And advocates like Sinter knew how to make the most of their credulity.

Quibbell came to his feet, late but willing. 'My Lord,' he protested, 'I must object to this line of cross-examination by my learned friend which clearly tends to degrade the witness's character.'

Sinter remained standing. 'I make the charges seriously, my Lord, and only after very painful consideration of the consequences entailed. So far as my instructions are concerned, the complete innocence of my client and this witness's specific denial that accidental contamination could have occurred, leave no alternative acceptable explanation for the otherwise inexplicable appearance of these hairs and fibres on the accused's clothing and shoes.' He lifted his Archbold *Criminal Pleading*. 'If it pleases your Lordship, I quote the authority of Yewin's Case, paragraph 1350, on the integrity of witnesses. *If the question is relevant to the point at issue and the witness denies the thing imputed, he may be contradicted.* I intend, my Lord, that the accused shall give evidence to contradict parts of this officer's evidence strongly and convincingly.'

'I am aware of the case, Mr Sinter,' the Judge said. 'Mr Quibbell?' He was so obviously for Sinter that Hansen wondered by how much Gault had affected his thinking. It was so much easier for a judge to concede extreme liberties by the defence than to risk being rapped publicly on his legal knuckles by the Appeal Judges. If he leaned backwards for the accused nobody could complain, and he was leaning. For all the protected majesty of his position he was careful not to antagonize Sinter, a counsel notoriously quick on appeal and fearless of judges. Nor, Hansen knew, was Timbrell partial to the police. In Hansen's opinion he was a domineering, autocratic old bastard.

The attack on him was making Hansen sweat gently, his underclothing sticking to his body. Toffler was going to get away with it and all Hansen's fighting wasn't going to resuscitate a lost cause.

While Quibbell stumbled his way around Sinter's unassailable submission, Hansen reflected on Sinter's performing the self-contradictory feat of arguing that the fibres, hair and blood never came from Gault, but that if they did they were planted on Toffler. It was the equivalent of saying, I was never there, but if you prove I was, I didn't do there what you say I did. This tongue-in-cheek, alternative defence was a commonplace in law.

The judge gave his expected decision against Quibbell's arguments and Sinter picked up his note pad, returning his attention to Hansen.

'Now, Chief Inspector,' he began again. 'Can this allegation —charge, if you wish—be any more outrageous than the accusation appears to Mr Toffler who has steadfastly maintained his complete innocence throughout these proceedings? You have yourself,' he pointed out, 'eliminated any possibility of accidental contamination.'

Hansen's voice was thick and shaking. 'You are accusing me of planting this evidence?' He knew the colour had drained from his face and he felt the chill of the anger he had hoped to conceal. There never was an acceptable excuse for a police witness losing his temper under cross-examination.

The judge threw down his pen. 'Officer! You will answer learned counsel's questions and not initiate questions of your own.' He was irritated and it showed patchily on his parchment skin. Two police officers stepping out of line in one

43

trial was colouring his judgement.

'I find being falsely accused of dishonest practices most objectionable, my Lord.'

'Learned counsel is, as you must well know, entitled to test your credibility as a witness,' the judge said shortly. 'Please answer his questions. Proceed, Mr Sinter.'

'I am grateful, my Lord.' Sinter returned to Hansen. 'Please answer my question, Chief Inspector.' His eyes were mocking the detective, confident of success.

'Yes. It *is* more outrageous,' Hansen said sharply. 'I consider it highly improper that I should be accused of a criminal offence on no more than the say-so of somebody like Toffler.'

The judge thinned his lips at that, looking over the top of his spectacles at Hansen, but saying nothing. He made a note on his pad and leaned back waiting for Sinter.

'That,' Sinter said waspishly, 'might be something over which members of the jury may very well take issue with you when they have heard the rest of the evidence.' He knew Timbrell was now with him and he didn't push it.

He sat with a flourish of his gown, leaving Quibbell to stand and attempt to do what he could to repair the damage to Hansen's credibility. It wasn't much and when Hansen stepped down he was coldly furious, leaving the court at once, needing to get away from the pettifogging dirty atmosphere that was choking justice.

# Chapter 4

In the bar of The City Arms, Hansen was a figure isolated by his own silence, his visibly repressed anger repelling any casual approach. Not normally a midday drinker, he needed one now to anaesthetize the smart of the intolerable affront put on him by Toffler's acquittal. The appearance of him in the foyer of the court, a mocking grin on his arrogant face, had been indication enough to Hansen that the case against him had folded, needing no telling that the court had accepted the implications of Sinter's defence. Unusually for him, he felt ill-used, dirtied and frustrated. While he could guess the acquittal had been wrapped up in unanswerable judicial phrases like 'not safe to convict' and 'the benefit of any doubt that might exist in your minds', the hard and ugly facts would be left uncontested to muddy his honesty.

He had ordered a double whisky, adding only a face-saving dribble of water from a carafe and retreating to an unoccupied table in the far corner of the bar. He stuffed tobacco in the bowl of his pipe with an impatient finger, relapsing into a deep withdrawal from his surroundings, waiting for his anger to cool. He thought he could have faced up to such malicious denigration and surfaced again, sustained and able to shrug it off by the inner knowledge of his own probity. Other policemen had done so, accepting it as an inevitable part of the job to be insulted and subjected to accusations of corruption. Hansen was discovering he no longer possessed the temperament to do so; that he needed to fight back with an unpolice-manlike urge to push the lying words down their throats. Toffler, waiting in the foyer for Weizsack and Sinter to join him, surrounded by his jubilant supporters, had been more than his frail self-control could stand, and he left before his need drove him to unthinkable violence against the sneering gangster.

He looked up irritably when the woman stood at his side, then rose hastily when he recognized Mrs Gault.

'Mr Hansen,' she said. 'May I talk to you?'

There were rain spots on the shoulders of her fawn coat and on her hair. Her face was pale and unsmiling. She was near enough for him to smell the perfume on her. He felt the same tug of attraction he had experienced in the Interview Room.

'Of course,' he said. 'Can I get you a drink?'

She sat with him, stiff and unrelaxed in her chair, placing her handbag and gloves precisely to one side.

Hansen flicked his finger and thumb at the waiter and ordered a Campari with soda-water. 'I'm sorry about your husband,' he said formally. 'We lost out.'

'I know. I was there,' she reminded him.

'Then you saw the majestic impartiality of justice in action,' he said expressionlessly.

'I've seen it before. I was a policewoman before I married Bill.'

'Oh?' That had surprised him, not having seen or heard of her before that day.

'The City of London. I was CID at Old Jewry.'

'A rough patch,' he smiled. 'Teeming with savage stock-brokers and Stock Exchange clerks.'

She smiled briefly back, forcing it as much as he had his humour. 'They aren't always as civilized as you'd think. And I transferred from West End Central, which *is* as uncivilized as you might imagine.'

He measured her with a frank stare. It was difficult to visualize her as a policewoman. 'Detective Sergeant?'

'Detective Inspector.' She wanted to lose the subject of herself. 'This horrible beast Toffler,' she said. 'He's not getting away with what he did to Bill?'

He raised his eyebrows. 'He *has* got away with it. You were there. He can stick his fingers up at us now. Even admit he did it and know we can't do a thing about it. *Autrefois acquit*, they call it.'

She possessed a woman's undeviating logic. 'Only on that charge. There are others.'

'There are. If we could prove them. And, doing it, survive

46

the screams of police persecution. Nor is this case over yet.'

'I thought it was.'

'Only the public part. There'll be repercussions.' He didn't want to particularize. He and Gault had been accused by Sinter of perjury, of suppressing and corrupting their evidence to gain a conviction. None of it had been withdrawn or disproved and somebody was going to need an accounting of it. 'Disciplinary enquiries,' he said. 'Routine stuff,' he lied, not wanting her to fret about her husband more than she was already. 'And primarily aimed at me.'

'Nothing worse can happen than has already. I've lived with it for two months.' Her face showed the strain of the nightmare of her husband's mutilation.

'He's going to be all right,' he assured her, knowing he wasn't. There wasn't anything he could say; nothing to make the tragedy smell sweeter.

A man approached their table with a glass and a plate of sandwiches in his hand, met Hansen's unwelcoming stare and changed course for another.

'He isn't,' she calmly contradicted him. 'And it isn't only *his* life that's ruined.'

That he realized. What young woman could suffer for ever a husband no better than a eunuch.

'I want to know about the photograph, Mr Hansen.' She was holding the tall glass of red Campari, not drinking from it, her fingers restless.

And that, he guessed, was why she had followed him into the bar. He thought Gault a lucky man to have a wife like her. Or had been. Looking at her through Gault's remaining eye, he wasn't so sure now. She was too sexually attractive for a man to contemplate with smashed-up balls. She could be a torment to him. Hansen's own wife would have accepted the evidence of the photograph without caring much about it either way. He put the thought of her out of his mind. She was his own failure and he had yet to rationalize her parting from him to an indifference.

'It showed your husband and a woman. You heard that. He was clearly unconscious.'

'The judge didn't think so.'

'Timbrell's an old fool. I'm sure he was.'

'That's what Bill said.' Two spots of colour showed over her cheekbones. 'The evidence still suggests he was sleeping

47

with a whore.' Not sleeping with just a woman but, by her standards, she had to be a whore. 'We've got to prove he wasn't, Mr Hansen.'

'I know already he wasn't,' he said. His was a simple loyalty and he knew Toffler. 'It was all too obviously contrived.'

'I suppose it was,' she said sharply. 'But we might be the only two to know it. And that's not enough. You *are* going to do something about it? Bill's not going through the rest of his life with that against him.'

He smiled at her because the alternative was to show his annoyance. He was being pushed. 'Hold on,' he said easily. 'I'm not the Chief Superintendent in charge of the Department. He'll have different ideas about who should do it.' He paused. 'There's another little snag about my doing it anyway. I'm handing in my warrant card.'

She looked blank. 'You are?'

'Yes.' He didn't want to explain further. Nor to justify it.

'I'm sorry. Not because of the case?'

'It's been in my mind for some time.' He sensed a slight withdrawing from him in her manner and didn't want that.

He sucked glumly at his cooling pipe. She was forcing an explanation by her attitude. 'I've had a bellyful of the service,' he said. 'There seems to me there are better things to do. Not to go into details, there's not much more left in it for me but the pay.'

He recalled the dedication and enthusiasm of his earlier service. He had really believed that he was working for a society that cared; that the detection of criminality was an end of which he could be proud; that justice was a commodity without a price-ticket and available to all. His were ideals that had soon withered in the light of harsh reality, leaving cynicism in their place. That he had now seen criminality buying its way out of conviction and punishment with the use of conscienceless lawyers and faked evidence did not surprise him. He had known of the suborning of jurors, the blatant buying off or intimidation of witnesses, an erosion in even the moral standards of the courts more than often to the point where only lip service was paid to the support of law and order. The soft bleeding-heart touch for vicious criminals when punishment was thought an obscene word that nobody really liked to mention. He thought that one day it might even be shamefully printed p——, as other obscenities had once been.

He had seen the sort of flabby, misguided justice that put the brutal killer of a child on probation, that sentenced a man to a ludicrous and profitable three years imprisonment for a ten-million pound company fraud, while sending a helpless old woman to gaol for refusing to apologize to a judge. Apart from Weizsack and Sinter, he knew lawyers who were venal and corrupt; solicitors who faked fraudulent, baseless defences for use by barristers prepared to stoop to any legal trickery to earn the fat fees marked on their briefs; prepared to present the dangerous criminals who were their clients to a court painted as blameless men maliciously charged by corrupt policemen who, when they were not grossly incompetent, had lied, fabricated evidence and forced confessions from men they knew to be innocent.

She had said something he had not heard. 'I'm sorry,' he apologized. 'I was brooding in my whisky.'

'Perhaps you'll help me before you leave,' she repeated.

'Help you?' he echoed. 'Help you what?'

'Help me to prove Bill was framed.'

'I'm sorry, Mrs Gault,' he said stiffly. 'I've already told you it isn't in my hands to do anything.'

'All right.' Her face was set with determination. 'I'll do it on my own.'

He frowned. 'Do just what?'

'See that Toffler is punished for what he's done to Bill for a start.'

Hansen stared his disbelief. 'Toffler! I'm sorry to be blunt, but that's ridiculous. Your having been a policewoman should tell you that.'

'Oh? You don't believe I could do it?' Beneath the scrubbed-clean loveliness there was clearly no lack of resolution, of hard-minded competency.

'Partly. Damn it, I've never heard such nonsense.'

She coloured again and looked annoyed in her turn. 'It isn't nonsense, Mr Hansen. I mean it and I'm quite capable.'

'You'll get yourself into serious trouble. From the police as well as Toffler.' He tried hard to keep the irritation from his voice. 'Let me spell it out for you if you don't already know. He's not one of your pin-striped fraudsmen. It wouldn't be anything for Toffler to do to you what he's done to your husband. And to get anything from him, you'd have to get near him. He'd know you, Mrs Gault.'

She shook her head. 'He's never seen me. How would he?'

'It's a man's job,' he persisted.

'It was with you and Bill. It didn't help either of you.'

'Look,' he said earnestly, ignoring the implication of his own failure, 'Toffler's nobody's fool. And he knows only one kind of woman.' He was blunt about what he wanted to emphasize. 'The kind that don't have too many objections about spending most of their time flat on their backs.'

'I'm not a fool either.' She stared at him levelly with her green eyes as if daring him to say otherwise. 'I wasn't attending a finishing school for young ladies at Old Jewry or at West End Central.'

He made a small sound of exasperation. 'Please, Mrs Gault.' He leaned forward, tapping the stem of his pipe on the table top. 'You'll only buy trouble. Leave what has to be done to us.'

'There's nothing to stop an ordinary citizen from making enquiries, investigating a crime.' She was telling him, not asking.

'No,' he admitted. 'There isn't. But I could so easily queer your pitch.'

'You wouldn't. I've confided in you, Mr Hansen.'

'Unasked.' He held her stubborn gaze, then grinned, suddenly boyish. 'No, of course not. But don't push me. I might if I thought it would stop your being dangerously silly.'

She didn't react to his grin. 'It's not silly,' she said coldly, 'to want to clear my husband's reputation.'

'No. But there are other ways. I can't stomach the idea of your doing it through Toffler.' He hoped the male arrogance wasn't showing too much. 'Something will be done.'

'Not by you. You're resigning. And what will anyone else do?'

'Check it out. Try and trace the woman; the man who took the photograph.'

'You've already said any further action by the police will be called persecution.' She was politely disbelieving. 'And they'll have copies of *Police Regulations* in their pockets . . .'

'If you mean by that they'll operate by the book, I would expect them to.'

'That would be useful.' She didn't disguise the sarcasm in her words. 'I know enough about whores to know that even if the one with Bill is identified, she won't admit a thing. It'll all be inconclusive, Mr Hansen; as it is now. She looked down at her fingernails and Hansen followed her gaze. 'Bill told me that if anybody could find her, tie her to Toffler, it would be you.'

'He's flattering me,' he said dryly. The way, he knew, to get a reluctant somebody to do what you want. A woman's way.

'I was relying on you, Mr Hansen.'

Feminine blackmail. Designed to make him feel he was failing her, and that was just how he felt. There were several reasons why it shouldn't worry him, but it did. He had his own share of troubles already without adding hers to them.

'I'm sorry,' he said.

'So am I.' She stood, retrieving her handbag and gloves. There was nothing soft about her even in her apparent defeat. 'You were the only one I could speak to.'

'Please sit down,' he said. He hadn't risen himself. 'Let me think about it.'

She sat and the movement of her clothing released perfume from her body. He felt again the strong pull of her personality, of her sexual attraction; degrees more powerful than he had experienced with his own wife. She had been instant sex, palling in the end like a surfeit of sugar because there had been nothing behind her loving but shallowness and her use of him as a resident phallus.

'You don't know me, Mrs Gault. Why do you assume I'm likely to help you? And don't say I've a kind face because I know I haven't.'

She said simply, 'I'm a woman, Mr Hansen. When I saw you giving evidence, I thought you would ... knew that you'd understand.'

It began to bother him that she had witnessed Sinter's allegations against him. 'I haven't exactly come up to your expectations, have I?'

'Bill wasn't the only one, Mr Hansen.'

'He wasn't?' He didn't get her meaning.

'You too,' she said deliberately. 'I would have thought you'd want to prove you weren't a liar ... that you weren't corrupt.'

He flushed and shifted uncomfortably in his chair. 'They tell me it's all part of the job.'

'And you accept that?'

He remained silent for a few seconds, his eyes narrowed at her. 'No,' he said harshly, stung to defending himself. 'I don't. Any job that requires me to stand up and be blackguarded

51

without allowing me to defend myself; called a liar, accused of planting evidence, by a pettifogging bast ... sorry, a mountebank like Sinter, isn't worth having.'

'You could do something to prove he's the liar,' she pointed out gently.

'That appeals to me more than clobbering Toffler. He's basically rubbish and wouldn't last a month without Weiszack and Sinter to wipe his nose for him.'

'You don't have to do anything dishonest.' The tip of her pink tongue touched delicately on her lips as she regarded him. 'Only help me.'

'That could be misinterpreted.' He had the uncomfortable feeling he was more interested in her as a woman than as the wife of Sergeant Gault. And that she knew it. She was somebody he didn't need, having already as much of a woman in Norah as he could cope with. And Norah, like his wife, was someone he didn't want to think about now.

She said lightly, 'I don't see why it should. We wouldn't be doing anything morally wrong either.'

He started to refill the bowl of his pipe, suspecting he was being talked into compliance. 'At the moment I don't want to know.' He hadn't before met a woman so persistently purposeful. He looked at his watch. 'I have to go.'

She reached across and touched the back of his hand, an unexpectedly intimate gesture for the occasion. She was using her femininity, sensing his indecision, and it was potent stuff.

'Will you speak to me again? When you've thought about it?'

'Yes,' he agreed. Men he could handle; he wasn't so sure about women. Certainly not an attractive woman who could do things to his breathing, set his heart pounding, merely by touching his hand with her fingers and moistening her lips as she did it.

'I suspect you don't like Toffler,' he observed wryly.

'Mr Hansen, I loathe him so utterly that even to think about him makes me want to be sick.'

# Chapter 5

Hansen had discreetly allowed Mrs Gault to precede him in leaving the bar and she was not in sight when he emerged into the street.

The rain had stopped and bars of cold sunlight, slanting down between the grey spongy clouds, struck a bright glare from puddles and wet tarmac. The leafless branches of the lime trees edging the square still dripped water. Early afternoon traffic left a smell of burned petrol in the damp air.

Hansen, normally an equable man with an easy-going temperament, was rarely provoked enough to unleash the inner toughness that showed itself in his features. Despite his preoccupation with the violence and dishonesty of criminality, there was room for gentleness and compassion in him, differing from many in that he expended it on the victims of it and not on those committing it.

His concern for Sergeant Gault was greater than he allowed for himself. Nothing would give Gault back his eye, probably not his essential masculinity; but what had been done to him was, for Hansen, an affront also to ordered society, needing justice and punishment.

Mrs Gault had disturbed and unsettled him with her undeviating determination to act the detective. He had thought it impossible when she put it forward but, on reflection, could admit to himself that it might be his masculine arrogance objecting. In fact, it need be no more impossible for him to accept than that she had done similar work as a Woman Detective Inspector. Women detectives had been used in bringing the Kray gang to justice, leaving him with no argument against her sex as investigators. But he had not reached the point either of agreeing it desirable, or where he could consider stepping outside department procedures and regulations to help her; worrying although he was that he could be lacking the same determination to clear her husband of the smear where, without hesitation, another man might. Particularly as the opportunity was there. In resigning, he could do one of two things: walk out of the job as he had intended, to start a fresh life elsewhere, although that would mean parting from warm, comfortable, loving Norah; or to use his freedom from Police Regulations to fulfil the obligation he felt he had to Gault and, in the process, undertaking the task of exposing Weizsack and Sinter. He saw nothing dishonest or wrong in that, although his fourteen years of disciplined obedience fought it. But first, he had to get the inevitable backlash of the case settled with McGluskie, and that wasn't anything he looked forward to.

He halted suddenly on the footpath, his passage blocked by Toffler and the three men with him. He recognized one of them, an albino; a white-haired lumpy-shouldered man with a smooth pallid face from which, behind dark glasses, his pink eyes smouldered an inner hate. He had never been known to smile. Simon Ash, risen in his profession as strong-arm thug and club bouncer, from wearing brass-studded leather jerkins to aping his employer's taste for expensive racecourse storm-coats. He was an aggressive homosexual.

Toffler, apparently about to enter the bar, was grinning with the amiability he could now afford. Mockery was heavy behind the grin.

'No 'ard feelin's, Mr 'Ansen,' he said. His narrow face creased and he showed his teeth. It was a face unmarked by kindliness or pity. He was a tall man and wiry, his eyes on a level with Hansen's own. His hands were in the pockets of his stormcoat and he kept them there. He had been dragged up in the back streets of the city by the sort of parents who had once squirted fly-killer spray into his ears to cure an infection. His early education had been primarily Borstal and, as a young offender, he had been insolently indifferent to the homilies and urgings of Children's Officers and Probation Officers alike. He had learned to live well without getting too much dirt beneath his fingernails or sweat in his armpits. If he possessed any saving graces he kept them concealed behind an aggressive hatred of authority in any form.

By his familiars, he was referred to as 'Donkey', although never to his face. He had undergone the curriculum of

Remand Home, Approved School, Borstal and prison necessary to mould him into a criminal respected and admired in his own dishonest world; contemptuous of earlier efforts to rehabilitate him.

His cunning had been, and still was, unintelligent and brutish. It had taken Weizsack, whom he had met in prison years later, to round him off as a professional criminal, able to operate without too great a fear of the consequences. And Weizsack was a good, if costly, mentor.

Hansen was familiar with Toffler's background, had been prepared to give it to the court in squalid detail in the event of his conviction. Until five years previously his had been run-of-the-mill dishonesty with convictions for larceny, assault occasioning actual bodily harm, demanding with menaces from prostitutes; shop, house and office-breaking. His villainy's profit had later permitted him to afford the advisory services of Weizsack and, through him, those of Sinter; enabling him to pillage the public and avoid conviction. He now had money and connections and was arrogant in his success.

Hansen felt the onset of the anger he thought he had damped down with the double whisky, but his features remained impassive, only his eyes needing to be watched.

'You'll come again, Toffler,' he said quietly. He stepped sideways to continue his interrupted passage.

Toffler blocked his path with insolent *bonhomie*. 'You ain't takin' this personal?' He exaggerated astonishment. 'I mean, somebody's got to lose, ain't they? Tha's justice.'

'You're in my way.'

'I'm only talkin'. You can't put the collar on me for that.' He showed his teeth again. 'You should 'ave got a good brief, mate. You 'ad a good case that was buggered up.'

Hansen's face was chilled with the impotent anger that had returned, but he said nothing. Despite the passing traffic and the thickening stream of pedestrians around them, he was very much on his own.

''Ow's the poor sergeant?' Toffler asked. One of the men behind him snickered.

The detective was being baited and the book covered that too. *No police officer will permit himself to respond in kind to incivility, insolence or insult from a member of the public.*

'I've nothing to say to you, Toffler,' he said. 'Get out of my way.'

'Chris', Mr 'Ansen!' The exaggerated astonishment again that didn't reach his calculating grey eyes. 'I'm tryin' to be matey. I want to buy you a drink. To let bygones be bygones. One day you'll probably 'ave me stone cold for somethin' I've done or 'aven't done an' I won't bitch about it.' He didn't make it sound believable. ''Ere,' he said. 'You don't 'old it against me because I was found innocent, do you? Because you picked on the wrong bloke?' The two unknown men with him sniggered. Ash, his eyes unwavering and hostile on Hansen, didn't.

Hansen knew Toffler was trying to goad him into indiscreet words or violence, taking the mickey like a dangerous, overgrown street lout. He realized that whatever he said or did would, witnessed by Toffler's attendant jackals, be used by Weizsack for his own unscrupulous purposes when it suited him. Even the unthinkable acceptance of a drink from Toffler, a contemptuous reference to the result of the trial, would be enough. From none of it would he emerge with an acceptable excuse. He swore to himself that when he was free of the restraints of his profession there would be a reckoning with the evil Toffler.

From the corner of his eye he could see the greystone façade of the Law Courts and the steps rising to its entrance. There was no uniformed constable visible although he doubted he could bring himself to signal for assistance had there been. But he would have welcomed what would otherwise have been an interference.

'Get out of my way.' He wanted to add, *Or I'll knock you out of it.* That would have suited Toffler's purpose had he.

Toffler withdrew a hand from his pocket and for one welcome moment Hansen thought he was going to start the trouble himself. Instead, he held out a five-pound note. ''Ere,' he said, a sneer loosening his mouth. 'No 'ard feelin's on my side. I want to give somethin' to the Police Widows and Orphans box. Mr Weizsack said it'd be a nice gesture...'

The detective tightened his lips. He had to get away before his temper spilled over and he hit Toffler in his insolent face. He wondered how far any advocate of sweet reason would get in this situation.

'...I don't 'old no grudge, matey, for you tryin' to clobber me. You 'ave your job to do.' His mouth split again in its infuriating grin.

'Have you finished?' Despite his efforts, his voice shook with anger. He suddenly moved sideways, pushing his shoulder against Toffler and sending him staggering back on his heels. As he strode rapidly away he heard Toffler say sharply, *'No!'* to one of his men, Ash no doubt, and then the sound of mocking hyena's laughter following him across the street.

If Toffler had done nothing else, he had that day earned himself a disproportionate share of the detective's future thinking.

McGluskie's office was an Home Office approved structure, a basic standard for Chief Superintendents. Exactly square with cream-painted walls, it possessed two curtained windows overseeing a receding, never-ending view of rooftops and television aerials. Boxed-in radiators beneath the windows gave off a Sahara-intensity heat that dehydrated sinuses. A constabulary blue carpet, big and deep-piled but not so big and deep-piled as the Chief Constable's, covered the major part of the polished tile floor. A black plastic swivelling chair groaned and creaked beneath McGluskie's enormous weight of flesh. Hansen occupied one of the three wooden-armed chairs supplied for visitors. The grey-enamelled metal desk at which the Chief Superintendent sat was equipped with an anglepoise lamp, three wire trays stuffed with files and documents, a blotting pad stamped with the force's identifying badge and two telephone handsets; one black, one green. His officially issued law and reference books were supported at each end by two mounted incendiary bombs which had dropped unexploded through the roof of his lodgings during World War II. These, and an old-fashioned squad photograph of his recruits' class, were the only individual decorations he permitted himself.

The contents of the office were listed on an inventory form; denying, McGluskie often said, the current occupant any opportunity of selling or hiring them out for personal profit. He also exercised his ponderous humour by explaining that the office wasn't quite so comfortably furnished as an Home Office approved prison cell but he was permitted to leave it occasionally without giving his parole.

Behind the fat man's humour was a single-minded functionalism; the hunting down of criminals. And he was good at it.

As good as he was at picking flies out of the air when they jigged within reach of either of his pudgy hands.

He was halfway through his twentieth cigarette of the day, having just returned from a stomach-bloating four-course lunch in the Senior Officers' canteen. Provided he hadn't to move from his desk for an hour, it inclined him to a genial expansiveness.

Hansen knew him as a man who, apart from eating and smoking excessively, had few discernible weaknesses. But one was sex. He disapproved of it with all the zealotry of a man who didn't get it himself. Hansen suspected that the mountain of his belly and the hippopotamus proportions of his wife proved insurmountable obstacles to his enjoyment of it.

They had discussed Toffler's acquittal, McGluskie predictably assuring Hansen that Sinter's attack on him and Gault was part of the job and to be suffered. 'Obviously, Robert,' he said, 'nobody who matters believes any part of it.'

'Nobody but a dozen jurors.' Hansen wasn't to be satisfied so easily. 'And half the city by the time the *Evening Observer* gets to work on assassinating my character.' Bragger, the editor, was notorious for his anti-police attitude. He had once been convicted of drunken driving, since when he had nailed imagined police corruption and ineptitude as high on the paper's masthead as he could. Somebody had only to say it, to write a letter about it, and it was printed. And retraction was a dirty word to him.

'Your shoulders are broad,' McGluskie said comfortably. 'It won't be the first time.'

'Not that broad. And it's the last for me. I'm packing it in.'

McGluskie lifted his eyebrows. 'Come off it, Robert. You're not serious?'

Hansen withdrew from his pocket a folded report he had typed and signed on arrival at his own office. 'Serious enough, sir.' He passed it over the desk and McGluskie put on his spectacles and read it. Then he laid it on his blotting pad, pulled a face and screwed out his cigarette in a littered ashtray. He looked undressed without one smoking between his fingers.

'You'd be a fool,' he said bluntly. 'Chucking away a career.'

'I don't have a career. Sinter saw to that this morning.'

McGluskie sighed. 'Never argue facts with a fool who's already made up his mind. All right. So you think you're ruined. But you're running away from it, Robert.' Cigarette smoke hung motionless in the still air over his bald head with nowhere to go.

'I knew you'd say that.'

'Well? Aren't you?'

'Not running away,' Hansen said evenly. He had no intention of quarrelling with a man he liked. Nor did he intend discussing the other reasons of his folded marriage or Norah with his puritanical senior. 'I've decided there's more to life than cleaning out stinking sewers and getting nowhere doing it.'

'Come off it.' McGluskie's face developed an additional two chins as he peered at Hansen over the top of his spectacles. 'Toffler's only one that's got away. You've had enough villains convicted to prove you can do it.'

'I'm not the only copper who's felt like this.'

'No, you're not. But you should know better.'

Hansen shook his head stubbornly. 'I'm told there are other people in the world. Nice people who aren't liars; people who don't get fun out of kicking your face to pulp; people who are decent human beings. If I don't get to meet them, I'll doubt they exist.'

'Resigning won't get rid of the villains.' McGluskie removed his spectacles, sliding them back in his pocket. 'It's bad news, Robert. I don't think it'll be accepted.'

Hansen frowned. 'I've made my mind up, sir,' he said curtly.

'Ah, so you might. But the Chief Constable hasn't.' McGluskie beamed genially, wanting to soften the blow. 'Don't take it hard, Robert. You know the form. There's to be an Investigating Officer appointed.'

To anticipate trouble and then have it confirmed does nothing to soften its impact. Hansen had suspected he wouldn't be allowed to resign under the shadow of a disciplinary enquiry. He could, but there was punitive legislation against doing so without permission.

'Because of Sinter?' he asked.

McGluskie nodded. 'He made the allegations in open court and the judge insisted on a report to the Chief.' He slid a cigarette from a packet and lit it from a lighter that was miniaturized in his big fist. 'You and Sergeant Gault.'

'I thought you said nobody believed it?' he said sardonically.

'That doesn't affect the issue of an enquiry and you know it.'

'They might have spared Gault. The poor sod's going to be discharged medically unfit anyway.' He was getting quietly furious at the thought of the unfortunate sergeant and himself being rubber-heeled at the instigation of a conniving barrister with only his client in mind. 'Why pile this on him?'

He knew and was only airing his anger. Every complaint against a police officer, however ill-founded or motivated by malice, was required to be investigated. There were forms to be served, statements to be taken and, finally, where a criminal offence was alleged, a comprehensive report submitted to the Director of Public Prosecutions for a decision. Even when exonerated, a residue of dirt stuck to the police officer concerned. Complaints by criminals under investigation had become a recognized ploy, an often successful counter-measure used to erode and discredit the evidence against themselves; allegations of corruption by the corrupt; charges of perjury by liars.

'Gault's still a serving police officer,' McGluskie said patiently. It was fortunate for Hansen that the Chief Superintendent had a comfortably full belly and a narcotizing cigarette going. He would have been justified in being terse with his Chief Inspector.

'But not for long. And unless he's cleared, he's likely to lose any disability pension he's entitled to.'

'Clearing him—if he can be cleared—is part of the exercise, Robert.'

'He can be. But I'm not so sure an outsider is going to be able to dig deep enough.' He had raised his voice without realizing it. 'It'll be an enquiry to decide whether he was screwing that bloody woman on duty or off duty when it's obvious he wasn't screwing her at all ...'

'Careful, Robert,' McGluskie said. 'I'm not deaf. Get off Gault's back. And off mine too. It's the truth we'll be looking for.'

'I can find the woman. If I can't resign, I can at least do that much.' He thought of Mrs Gault. What she had said was now making more sense to him.

McGluskie lowered his eyebrows. 'You know that's nonsense. You can't touch anything connected with your own disciplinary enquiry. In fact, Robert, I'm going to anticipate the service of a Disciplinary Notice and give you a direct order not to.'

There was a few moments' silence, then Hansen said quietly,

'I see. And what about Weizsack and Sinter? Will their conduct be enquired into?'

McGluskie stared at him. 'What the hell are you on about now?'

'Christ! Let's not kid ourselves, sir. Toffler couldn't dream up that defence in a million years. Weizsack and Sinter fixed it for him, and if that's not conspiracy to pervert justice, plus subornation of perjury, then nothing is.'

'And you think you could prove it? Do something about it?' McGluskie was scornful and short with him. 'That either of them is going to tell you it wasn't all suggested in Toffler's instructions? In fact, tell you anything at all except to shut the door on your way out? No. You can forget that. Get your feet back on the ground, Robert. You're making this a personal issue.' The thought of investigating a solicitor and barrister on matters concerning their defence of a client clearly appalled him.

Hansen pushed out his chin. 'Bloody sure I am.' His features darkened. 'Is that so surprising when I've been accused of perjury and corruption? Now being threatened with a rubber-heel enquiry?'

'I don't like what you're saying, Robert, and I'm not having it.' McGluskie selected a file from a pile in one of the trays and tossed it over to Hansen. There was no amiability left in his expression. 'The robbery with violence job at the Morgan Street Co-operative. Tie up with Sergeant Ballinger about it. He needs help.' He held out Hansen's report. 'You want this back?'

'No, sir,' Hansen said formally. 'Being under investigation isn't likely to change my mind.' And nor would it while he was simmering under the injustice of it.

# Chapter 6

In his own office, Hansen used an hour with Sergeant Ballinger and his file, giving him sufficient lines of enquiry to keep him busy and out of his hair and his office for the next two days, telling him to call in when he'd collected something worth discussing.

It mightn't be what McGluskie had intended, but Hansen wasn't now disposed to be sidetracked into impotence. He had made up his mind.

His office was similar to, but differing in detail by the gap of two ranks from McGluskie's. The carpet was smaller and thinner and the windows were screened by white venetian blinds instead of curtains. Accommodation for his visitors was limited to two chairs. His desk was three drawers smaller and without a tooled leather top. Nor did his chair swivel. But, because he was attractive to women and, probably, because it was known his wife had left him, the typists' pool kept his office bright with flowers and pot plants.

He sent for the Record Cards of Toffler and his known associates, and for details from the Policewomen's Department of all convicted and cautioned prostitutes.

While he waited, he studied the copy photograph of Gault and the woman who might be called Sheila. Being self-developed in the camera, the print could not be traced to a commercial processor. That cut its usefulness in half.

Behind the two figures, eternally frozen by the flashlight in apparent concupiscence, he identified the edge of a yellow and brown curtain with a sunflower motif and the corner of a wooden bedhead. The sheets on which they performed were white, the bed cover a pale-blue linen material with a raised Paisley design.

Examining the woman's body under a lens, he saw she wore

a gold-coloured watch secured to her left wrist by a thin red strap. It was all she was wearing. Her skin was the same milk-white all over, indicating she was no lover of the sun. From the firmness of the flesh he guessed her to be somewhere in her twenties. Without clothing to type her, she didn't look particularly whorish. And not, Hansen thought with a twinge, too unlike his own wife. Just a naked woman making preliminary loveplay with Gault. The sergeant, closely examined, told Hansen nothing more than it was unlikely he would lie there, no more excited than a complaisant not-very-interested girl about to be used by a masterful partner. Gault's supine passivity jarred with Hansen, as it should have with the court.

He put the print back in its envelope and into an inner pocket. Somebody, somewhere, might recognize her. But he had his doubts.

None of the yellow Record Cards turned up any associate of either Toffler or his friend called Sheila. The smaller, mauve *Prostitution and Brothels* cards revealed only one Sheila. And she, still active as a whore, had been born in Liverpool fifty-nine years previously. She would, Hansen guessed, have withered boobs and a drooping belly with nothing of the trim, smooth figure of Gault's Sheila. He scowled at the unhelpful card and returned it to the others.

And they only represented those who had surfaced above the dirty water. There were hundreds of whores operating in the city; professional and amateur and all the grades in between; including the housewives who rented themselves out while their husbands were working; some for the money, some just for a change of scenery.

Next, he checked his desk diary for Gault's home telephone number and dialled it, bypassing the switchboard and call-recording equipment. The palm of his hand was damp on the receiver.

When she answered, he said, 'It's Hansen here, Mrs Gault.'

After a short pause, she said quietly, 'I'm glad you called, Mr Hansen.'

'I've been thinking about what you said.' The words came awkwardly. 'Can I see you?'

'Yes, of course. Soon?'

'This evening?' He was reacting like a youth making his first date.

'Will you come here?'

'Is that all right?'

'Shouldn't it be?' His caution seemed to surprise her.

'If you think so. About eight?' He felt they were conspirators already, linked by the mundane preliminaries.

'You know where I live?'

'I have your address.'

'I shall be waiting, Mr Hansen ... thank you.'

When he replaced the receiver he wiped his palms with a handkerchief. Toffler and McGluskie had, each in his own way, pushed him into a decision he would rather not have had to make.

To a degree, his wife had pushed as well. When she left him almost six months earlier, her leaving uncomplicated by any residue of love or affection, he was free but for the tying up of matters such as Income Tax adjustments, his status on the force personnel records and explanations to his friends and enemies. Now, there was nothing to keep him tethered to a conformity of sexual conduct. Or to a particular fear for the future.

*You won't be surprised that I've gone. God how you've bored me with your dull little life. Don't bother looking. I shan't be coming back. I hate you, you arrogant bastard. Get yourself a bloody servant because that's all you ever wanted. I don't want anything to do with any more coppers in my whole life.*

She had neither prefixed it, nor signed it. The writing had been spiky with malice and every spitting, bitchy word had scratched him like fingernails.

He had been unfortunate enough to have fallen in love with her and it had left scars. She was a thin, dark girl with an elfin face and almost non-existent breasts, mirroring nothing of her limitless hunger for carnality. Another man might have considered himself favoured by God above all other men. For Hansen, her nymphomania had been no sexual heaven, but a corrosive illness that generated frustration and bitterness between them.

She had drained his nervous system, burned him up in too short a time, drawing on his physical reserves in bed and out of it, leaving him little for his work. It was unbelievable to him that so schoolgirlish a body could contain such a fierce unquenchable lust. In the early days of their marriage, she had

64

eaten him alive with her greedy teeth, goading him into ever increasing ruttishness. Rarely had there been any humour or affection in her loving: never had she said, 'I love you.' Gluttonish, fleshly and, eventually, tartish; she had been all these. And Hansen, driven to his physical limits by the fire in her, burned out his need for her, her body losing its magic for him.

In the process, and painfully, suspicion had soured him. He discovered without surprise that she preferred loud, physical men with coarse appetites for lusty, crude living; crowded bars and noise; meaningless brainless banter and witticisms that never moved above the loins. Sex to her was a driving daily need and she made it clear that have it she would; if not from him, then from another. A viciousness came into her, a derision of his stamina. On the few occasions that she was less demanding of him, he suspected her friends with whom she was spending more of her evenings. She was a bitch in permanent season, needing the retinue of panting dogs that followed behind.

His pride suffered more than his body. In the final stages of their apartness she had neglected the home, becoming sluttish in the kitchen if not at her dressing-table mirrors. And, contemptuously, she eventually turned her back on him in bed. Not to be wanted by a woman with her compulsive needs was withering.

He had collected every photograph of her, every item of clothing and cosmetics she had left behind; calmly and finally disposing of them, a man intent on destroying the dirt he needed to scrub from his mind. What he couldn't destroy was the devastating hurt she had done him. He swore he would never allow himself to fall in love again.

Prior to selling the furniture, he reported briefly to the Chief Constable that, due to domestic differences (he put it no more explicitly), his wife had left him, that he was reverting to bachelor status and moving into furnished accommodation.

She had left with him Trudchen, their dachshund bitch, and the discomfort of realizing that she hated him. He had failed her, he knew that. Any single, normal man always would. It might deserve her contempt, but he couldn't believe it deserved her hatred. The thought of her in another man's arms still had the power to put a shadow in his face. But he could not return her hatred.

And now Norah. Big, blonde, pinkly beautiful and amoral

65

Norah with the flame-orange Opel *Commodore* and the accommodating husband; leaving the car outside Hansen's flat entrance one night a week as casually as she left her husband for what she called her 'Bobbie-loving'. The magic of her body wasn't volcanic, but pleasantly therapeutic and he slept at nights. Neither needed to pretend to more than a happy affection, nor could there be any misunderstandings about the future. She had no apparent intention of leaving her husband.

He had telephoned Hansen's flat late one night when Norah was there.

'Geoffrey Barsett here, old boy,' he had said cheerfully. 'Would you mind frightfully asking Norah where she's hidden the bloody door key?'

That hadn't been difficult because Norah was beneath him, her arms around his shoulders only just sufficiently relaxed to allow his outstretched hand to reach the bedside telephone.

His *amour-propre* had been seriously dented. Somehow, adultery by kind permission of the husband seemed indecent, endowing it with a patronage he resented. Norah had explained. Geoffrey was the most wonderful man there could ever be. His only discernible failing, it seemed, was his inability to say 'no' to the women wanting to share him. Norah, needing an antiserum against his infidelities, had chosen Hansen (whom she had met hugging his solitariness in the bar of the Bear and Pelican) as the needle.

'And, Bobbie darling,' she told him, pecking small kisses over his scowling face. 'He *approves* of you. He thinks a policeman should keep me out of all kinds of trouble.'

'That's bloody noble of him,' Hansen had growled, not nearly mollified. 'Why didn't you give him my office number as well? We could have cosy chats about all sorts of interesting things like *flagrante delicto* and The Divorce Reform Act.'

But he went on loving—in his guarded, bruised way—the big, silky, sweet-smelling plumpness who helped to neutralize the acid his wife had left in his stomach.

# Chapter 7

Bernard Street, terraced Portland-stone houses of architectural elegance, had fallen on hard times. One side of it had been demolished in preparation for a planned ring road, leaving a rubble-strewn emptiness quickly filled with paper debris, homeless cats and parked vehicles. From those houses left, respectability had fled, leaving behind homes that had become shoddily converted flats, linoleum hotels and continental shops. Repainting their shabby exteriors or the heavy iron railings guarding the deep basement areas would have needed an unwarranted optimism about their future. A betting shop at one end and a transport café at the other set the tone of the fallen street.

Hansen parked his car on the waste ground, inconspicuous among the others. He had changed from his grey suit to an olive-green worsted, a green and white check shirt. He wore a loose smooth-tweed coat against the cold.

Without attempting concealment, he used the binoculars he had brought with him, starting from the betting shop and examining each magnified window along the length of the terrace. When he picked out curtains with a yellow and brown sunflower motif in the third floor windows of the Queensbury Commercial Hotel, he remained with them for a short pause, then continued his scrutiny until he reached the café at the far end.

The hotel's bell-push didn't work and Hansen hammered on the door before getting an answer. The man opening the door wasn't any welcoming hotelier, but a thickset character more like a strip club's bouncer who had had a hard night of it. He was unshaven, his shirt open and tie-less, his suit creased as if he had been sleeping in a chair.

He was morose even before Hansen spoke. 'No rooms,' he growled, and pushed at the door.

The detective already had a foot jammed against it, his warrant card displayed. 'I wouldn't want one,' he said equably. 'Just a talk.'

The man showed no pleasure as he glanced at the card briefly. His manner showed him to be no stranger to them.

'Inside,' Hansen added. He stepped past the reluctantly opened door into a hall. It smelled of a recently cooked meal, strong on fried fat.

The man said, 'What's the trouble?'

'I'm making enquiries about one of your guests. The register, please.'

He hesitated, then left Hansen, disappearing through a door in the hall, closing it behind him. When he reappeared, he handed a thin dog-eared book to the detective. He said nothing, but breathed heavily, the smell of stale liquor reaching Hansen's nose. He had a beer-drinker's belly and couldn't have been in the top echelon of bouncers.

The name inside the cover was *H. Wikker*. Hansen put his finger on it. 'This is you?'

Wikker nodded, patently holding in check a natural truculence.

'How many rooms, Mr Wikker?'

'Six.'

Hansen turned the pages. The large majority of the names were prefixed 'Mr and Mrs'. None appeared repeated. The Queensbury Commercial Hotel apparently did very well; most days showing all rooms occupied.

He kept the register open at one page. 'A Mr Gault was here on the seventh of October.' He was watching Wikker's pouched eyes, seeing a glint of unease in them. 'You don't appear to have him booked in.'

'I don't know the name,' he grunted. 'If he isn't in the book, he never stayed here. You've got the wrong hotel.' He held out a broken-knuckled hand for the book.

Hansen shook his head. 'I haven't finished yet. There's a room on the third floor I'd like to look at.'

'You'll need a search warrant.' His truculence was now unconcealed.

'As you like.' Hansen kept his amiability. 'I'll get one. And take the register with me. It'll support a complaint that you're running a brothel.'

Wikker goggled, then growled, 'I ought to smack you in the kisser for saying that.'

Hansen moved a step nearer. 'So you ought,' he agreed, 'only you won't.' He smiled. 'Not carrying all the belly you do,'

Wikker's face screwed up with anger, his jaws bulging. 'Now, just a bloody minute, mate. You come barging in here making accusations ... this is a respectable hotel ...' His mouth sprayed spittle. 'What's the bloody idea?'

Hansen could have laughed at him, trying to bluff with turned-on aggression, but unable to conceal the fear in his eyes.

'You've just said there are no rooms, Wikker, yet you've nobody booked in for tonight.' He hardened his voice. 'How much investigation do you think these names and addresses will stand up to? To me, they are all toms bringing in their customers for a use of your beds. Well?' he said while Wikker struggled to say something. 'Do I get a search warrant, or don't I? If I do,' he warned him, his eyes glittering, 'I'll search every room, your living quarters and your office, if you've got one.'

Wikker swallowed. He had lost some of his colour thinking about it. 'What do you want?'

'To see one room. The room in which Detective Sergeant Gault was beaten up by some of your friends.' He stared at the man, his expression cold and giving no comfort. Wikker didn't need telling more. If he knew nothing else, he would know about Toffler's trial. 'Perhaps you helped beat him up,' Hansen added. 'So don't worry if the beds aren't made.'

Wikker's expression showed he hadn't been prepared for this and there was obvious thinking going on behind the sweating forehead.

'I don't know Sergeant Gault and he's never been here.'

'And if he had, you wouldn't know.'

'He couldn't have been.'

'I can prove he was,' Hansen said flatly, 'so save your breath. Why do you think I'm here?' When he didn't get an answer, he asked, 'Do you know everything that goes on in this place?'

Wikker said 'No' reluctantly, because he could see where saying 'Yes' could lead him. 'Things do happen ... I can't be in every bloody room. But I swear he wasn't here.'

'Show me the room. The front room on the third floor.'

Wikker turned, thin-lipped and anxious, needing a moral support that wasn't there, that rarely is when there's trouble. Hansen followed at his heels up the four flights of stairs.

The door to Room 5 was open. Inside, it was unarguably third-rate commercial and not too clean. It was furnished with a double bed, a tatty grey and blue carpet, a warped plywood wardrobe, a chair and a metal stand on which to lay a suitcase. A small table beside the bed held a plastic-shaded lamp, an aluminium ashtray and a Gideon-issue Bible for any unsaved commercial travellers who might use the room. A grimy hand basin and a wall mirror occupied one corner. If a woman's hand had touched the room, it didn't show.

Hansen produced the photograph. The curtains were identical, as were the bedhead and the blue bed cover. It had been that easy and he knew that once an Investigating Officer started his enquiries, there wouldn't be much time for him.

He covered the two bodies in the photograph with his thumb, leaving the faces visible and showing it to Wikker. 'Now start telling me I've got the wrong hotel,' he said scratchily.

Wikker had composed his features and they were expressionless. He had many fears, but his fear of Hansen was the more immediate and it showed in his eyes.

'I don't know anything about it,' he said.

Hansen ignored his denial. 'Of course, you could have taken the photograph yourself. That would involve you in something more serious than brothel-keeping, wouldn't it? Left holding the baby for what happened to Sergeant Gault...'

'Christ, no!' He was shocked, sweating profusely and chewing at his thumb, his impassivity suddenly vanished.

'Look at the woman's face,' Hansen ordered, holding the print nearer to him. 'Who is she?'

'I don't know.' Resistance was draining from him.

'Who is she?' When he received no reply, Hansen put the photograph away. 'Listen to me, Wikker,' he said, his expression stern. 'I've got your number on this. You're a knocking-shop keeper whatever else you might choose to call yourself and you're not going to go dumb on me.'

When Wikker started to speak, he silenced him. 'I said, *listen*. If I don't get your co-operation as a witness, I'm going to see you have a vice detail sitting on your doorstep twenty-four hours a day. They'll check and double-check every man and woman coming in and going out. You'll be finished, Wikker.' He looked around disparagingly. 'You wouldn't get much of a living running this place as a straight hotel.'

Wikker believed him. 'You bastard! You can't prove a thing...'

'Get your coat.' Hansen was harsh with him. He moved past him, past the amalgam of beer fumes and sweat, out of the room.

Wikker stepped after him. 'Now, just a minute. Where're we going?'

Hansen stared at him. 'To the station while I get that warrant.'

'*Harry!*' A shrill voice came from somewhere in the basement. 'Who've you got up there?' She sounded shrewish; a woman who wouldn't be satisfied with the first answer a man could think up.

'Jesus!' Wikker swore softly. 'The nosey bitch.' He shouted down the stairs, 'Wrap it up! I'm busy!'

Angry words floated up; unintelligible, but their meaning clear.

'Bloody women,' he said to Hansen. 'I don't know her name.'

'Who? Her?'

'For Christ's sake. The one in the photo.'

'Ah! But you know her?'

'She's been here. With her husband,' he added as insurance. 'Does the name Sheila ring a bell?'

The eyes flickered, saying yes. But his mouth said, 'No.'

'She'll be in the register.'

'I still wouldn't know which one's her.'

'Who does she work for?' Hansen pulled out his pipe, filling it with tobacco from a red rubber pouch; a man prepared to ask questions for ever.

'How would I know?'

'*Who*, I asked.'

Wikker looked at him with worried speculation. 'How far is this going?'

'If you're not tied in with the fixing of Sergeant Gault, no further than between you and me.'

Wikker licked his lips and lowered his voice, glancing furtively down the stairs. 'You'd swear on the Bible?'

'Not for you. You wouldn't know one if you saw it. Be satisfied with my word.'

Wikker jerked his thumb in the direction of the basement
'Not her down there either.'

Hansen couldn't imagine it. 'No,' he said. 'Not her either.
Now tell me who this woman works for.'

'She could be on CG's book.' It was out, and he wasn't happy
that it was. 'Jesus,' he whispered, pleading. 'You'll swear?'

'You're my informant now,' Hansen said. 'Don't start crying
about it. You mean Charlie Glass?'

Wikker nodded dumbly.

Charles Willson Glass. The man who started his working life
pimping for his sisters; the huckster in female flesh, now at the
top of his profession with a stable of 'Swedish masseuses' and
'photographers' models'. His grandmother was dead, but Hansen suspected that had she not been, Glass would have trafficked
in her too. He was a man who had early recognized an essential male need and did his best to satisfy it. Too cunning to
expose himself to a charge of keeping a brothel, he would
naturally use fronts like the unintelligent Wikker and his fake
hotel. And Glass was, Hansen knew, one of Toffler's associates.

'You know Toffler too, of course?'

The answer was again a quick shift of Wikker's eyes. He
wasn't very bright or he would have asked the woman downstairs for some dark spectacles. And he would have known the
detective wasn't going to be satisfied with only Glass's name.

'Toffler,' Hansen explained patiently, 'was here the same
night as Sergeant Gault and the woman.'

'No,' Wikker said hoarsely. 'I don't know Mr Toffler.' The
'Mr' made Toffler a man Wikker feared. 'He's never been here.'
Sweat poured from him and he blinked it from his eyes.

'Or Simon Ash?'

He shook his head stubbornly.

'So how did this woman get the use of the room?' He opened
the register, resting it on the banister rail. 'I see a Mr and
Mrs J. Cannon of 23 High Street, Sidcup, are shown as using
Room 5. Who booked it for them, Wikker?'

There was a heavy-breathing silence while Wikker thought
that out and sweated more. 'I don't remember that far back.
They probably just arrived here and I booked them in.'

'But the woman was one of Glass's lot?'

'I said so.'

'Sheila?'

He gnawed at his thumb again. 'I don't know any of them by name.'

That could be possible, Hansen thought, with the shrewish woman downstairs to keep him in order. Only it wasn't so with Sheila. His attitude said he knew, and that was enough.

'The man?'

'I told you. As far as I know, her husband.' He was getting impatient, wanting the detective off his back.

'I asked you if you knew him.' Hansen suspected that Wikker would be too frightened to name Toffler or Ash. He was surprised that he had gone as far as he had.

'Honest to Christ, I don't. I never saw him before. I haven't seen him since.' Had he known how to, he would have crossed himself and called on the Pope and the Sacred College of Cardinals to support him.

Hansen descended the stairs, Wikker trailing behind him. When he reached the door he returned the register, then took a wallet from his pocket. He withdrew a five-pound note, rubbed it between finger and thumb to check there was only one and held it out to Wikker.

Wikker was surprised. 'What's that for?'

'For you. Take it.'

He took it, uncomprehending.

'Now you're my informant, Wikker. My snout, grass, or whatever you choose to call yourself.'

Wikker's face flushed, but he made no effort to return the note.

'It means that you are more-or-less protected from what you've told me. Only from me, Wikker,' he warned him sternly. 'Not from any other police officer. So don't think you've got any immunity.' He opened the door. 'I expect you'll be having a Detective Superintendent calling on you in a day or so. He'll probably be more polite than I've been, but don't take advantage of him on that account and lie. You understand?'

'Christ!' Wikker protested. 'Haven't I been honest...'

'No. You've told me nothing I didn't know. Answer his questions. The only thing you *don't* tell him is that I've been here. You understand that, too? Because,' he said grimly, 'if you do tell him, I'm going to forget you're my informant and feed you to Charlie Glass and Toffler.'

# Chapter 8

There was a note on Hansen's desk. *See me, please. A. McG.*

He walked the short distance between their offices without optimism.

McGluskie, a genial version of Buddha, pulled a sympathetic face. 'I'm sorry, Robert,' he said, waving him to a chair. 'The Deputy Chief's ordered a criminal and disciplinary enquiry against you and Gault. Don't take it personally, there wasn't any choice.'

Hansen kept his features rigid, repressing his deep resentment. 'And my resignation?'

'It's been refused. You'll have to soldier on until the DPP gives his decision.'

'It's been one of my better days,' Hansen said ironically. He passed over an early edition of the *Evening Observer*. 'You've seen this?'

Bragger, the editor, hadn't missed the opportunity. The report of the trial was front page, the headlines in the paper's largest type.

JUDGE DIRECTS ENQUIRY INTO ALLEGATIONS OF POLICE PERJURY.
'PLANTING' OF EVIDENCE CHARGE AGAINST CHIEF INSPECTOR.
ACCUSED MAN ACQUITTED

Two sub-paragraph headings read *Detective Sergeant retracts identification* and *Unprecedented impertinence and contempt remark*. The text included nothing of Hansen's denials, but gave Sinter's allegations against both detectives in detail. It would make comforting reading for Hansen's enemies and good source material in future cases.

McGluskie read it, then shrugged, passing the paper back. 'Slanted, Robert, but it happens. We'll have to grin and bear it.'

'You mean Gault and I will.'

'Yes,' McGluskie agreed. 'But it rubs off on all of us.'

'And Sinter will get away with it because he's a lawyer. Because lawyers seem to have a licence to throw unjustified mud at witnesses, just to get their clients off the hook.'

'You've got a thing about that man, Robert.' He swallowed cigarette smoke, then blew it ceilingwards. 'All right. So he got Toffler acquitted by questionable tactics...'

'Questionable?' Hansen made a noise in his throat, expressive of his deep disgust. 'Dirty, unethical, smear tactics. He doesn't even have to justify them.'

'Sinter's an exception. Crooked lawyers are in the minority.' He paused, then added, 'Like bent policemen.'

'Yes, but we do something about them. We investigate and prosecute them. And Christ! Don't the bloody lawyers and judges make a song and dance about it when we do. But they don't do anything about their own crooked friends. Not unless they embezzle from a client's account and they are forced to. I can't remember an occasion when either the Bar Council or the Law Society brought a crooked lawyer to book. They pretend they don't exist.'

McGluskie shrugged. 'They exist.'

'They shouldn't exist at all.' Hansen was savage. 'And the press makes heroes out of them. Defenders of the oppressed. A blow for the rights of the individual. You'd think to read the *Observer* that Sinter's done justice a favour, struck a blow for freedom against police persecution and corruption...'

'Like I said, Robert,' McGluskie interrupted calmly. 'You've got a thing about lawyers.'

Hansen's swarthy face flushed. 'I'm talking about Sinter and Weizsack. Not other lawyers.'

'Leave it,' McGluskie said tersely. 'We've been over it before. All you need worry about is getting yourself cleared. If either Sinter or Weizsack has gone beyond his brief, it'll come out in the wash.'

He looked at his watch pointedly. 'I'm due at a conference with the Chief. Detective Superintendent Sloan from H Division is the Investigating Officer. He'll be here tomorrow. He's a first-class man to dig out the facts.' He lifted his bulk from the chair.

'He'll need to be.' Hansen wanted more convincing than McGluskie's say-so, thinking of the intractable Wikker. He stood.

'I'm sorry, Robert. I can't discuss your case further. It's all in Sloan's hands now.' He stubbed his cigarette out, preparing to go.

'Leaving me smelling like a dead dog until I'm proved innocent,' Hansen said bitterly. 'If I ever am.'

Wikker possessed a primitive intelligence, its primary function one of self-preservation. With Hansen gone, he applied its sluggish working to that purpose. It reached the self-evident conclusion that the threat of the law was watered milk compared with the terrifying probability of being suspected a police informer. The one threatened his wallet, remotely his freedom for a month or two; the other menaced his health, his ability to stand without crutches. He groaned aloud when he thought of what could happen to him. If Hansen followed up his nosy digging-out, Glass wouldn't need more than a minute's thinking to know Wikker had talked. And the thought of Glass's reaction turned his stomach. Although Glass had never personally skinned a knuckle, put the boot in, on an informer, that didn't signify. He was close enough to Toffler to get it done for him. And with Toffler being tied up in the going-over of that bastard of a sergeant ... Christ! Wikker sweated out his problem and smoked cigarettes furiously.

He waited until the woman with whom he lived had left the building, then went to a kiosk at the end of the street and dialled a number. When a man answered, he put a coin in with shaking fingers and asked if he could please speak to Mr Glass.

Gault was in a small room at the end of the ward; a square windowed box overlooking the lines of beds outside. It was furnished with a white-enamelled bed, a wooden locker with a vase of yellow flowers on it, a washstand and an uncomfortable-looking wooden chair. Radio earphones were hooked on the wall at the head of the bed, a *Daily Telegraph* lay open-paged on a small carpet at its side. The room smelled of floor polish and antiseptic and hot radiators.

Gault sat in a wheelchair, a red blanket shrouding his legs, looking with his single eye at the wall. He turned his head fractionally when Hansen entered, nodding expressionlessly and returning his attention to the wall.

Hansen unbuttoned his coat against the heat and sat on the bed. He placed his gloves and pipe next to an untouched glass of orange juice on the locker. He felt the circumstances called for a little less formality between their two ranks.

He smiled and said, 'Feel any better, Bill?'

Gault's face twitched as he struggled to articulate. 'Not much. They're taking the wire ... from my jaw.' What he couldn't say to Hansen, what his mind shied away from putting into words, was that he was going on the operating table that evening; that his scrotum was being opened and the pulpy suppurating testicles taken away. The ward doctor had told him this on his return from court, warning him that further delay might be dangerous. He had once witnessed the gelding of a horse and the ugly fearful memory of it now moved below the surface of his thoughts like a foul worm.

'That's something,' Hansen said encouragingly. Hospital visiting made him awkward, conscious that one saw only the scrubbed and drugged patient; only guessing at the pain of needles, the discomfort of changing bandages and the long dreary hours of waiting for nothing.

'Yes.' Gault was making it clear that talking was an effort.

'Is there anything I can do for you?'

'I'm being looked after, thanks.' The sergeant was withdrawn and Hansen recognized that conversation was going to be uphill.

'This is an unofficial visit, Bill. I wanted to warn you that we are being rubber-heeled over our evidence this morning.'

Gault's hands clenched into fists. 'I know. Mr McGluskie's been. When that's settled,' he said savagely, 'a Medical Board.' He managed a hard laugh between his locked jaws. 'Being pensioned off.'

'They'll find you a job at Headquarters, Bill, if you want it.'

'Yes. Civilian switchboard operator ... bloody tea boy. They can stuff it.'

Hansen changed course. 'Bill,' he said. 'Before Sloan starts, is there anything more you can tell me about this Sheila woman?'

Gault was silent for a few moments, plucking with his fingers at the red blanket. 'No,' he said finally. 'I told you everything.'

'This is between the two of us,' Hansen assured him, deciding to take a chance on Gault's discretion. 'I've checked and found the room where it happened. And there is a Sheila mixed up in it somewhere. I'm doing this against orders so I won't give you details. What you don't know, you won't get involved in.'

'And you'll nail Toffler?' He wasn't asking, he was doubting.

'If I don't, nobody will.'

It was difficult to read Gault's features, but Hansen suspected he wasn't convinced. His injuries, the shock to his system, had made him a difficult man to deal with.

In Hansen's view, Toffler's reaction to Gault's following him had been too violent, even for the brutal sadist he was. The photographing of Gault and the woman had needed previous thought and preparation, needed a more compelling reason than the circumstances revealed. Hansen was far from convinced that Gault had told him everything. He believed that every man had something to hide and he wasn't prepared to make Gault an exception.

'Bill,' he said earnestly. 'This is important. You and I are going to be thoroughly investigated. All sorts of side issues are likely to be gone into.' He paused. 'Is there anything you haven't told me about this case that Sloan is likely to dig out?'

Gault's eye twitched away from Hansen's stare and he hesitated before answering. 'Why should there be? I said ... I told you everything.'

Hansen's face was wooden, recognizing evasion when he saw it. 'You can trust me, Bill. I'm in the shit, too.'

'You mean you'd cover for me?' Gault said, bitterness in his voice.

'No, I wouldn't. But if anybody's going to find out anything, it had better be me.'

'There isn't anything,' Gault said flatly. 'You've got it all.' He turned his gaze from Hansen, withdrawing his brief attention.

'All right, Bill.' Hansen shrugged. 'You're man enough to ...'

'*I'm what!*' His head jerked and he made an ugly noise between his teeth, something despairing. 'A *man*?' His features were distorted, his eye glaring at Hansen, anger pushing the words out. 'Don't you know ... going to lose my balls! A bloody eunuch ... useless one-eyed bastard!' He dabbed a gauze pad at his mouth with trembling fingers. 'What can you do for me? I don't want anything ... leave me alone.' He was shaking,

78

looking at the wall, waiting for Hansen to go.

'Bill, I'm...'

'*Christ's sake!*' Hysteria thrashed his body convulsively in the chair, his fists banging its arms. Liquid trickled from beneath the eyepatch and he breathed heavily. '*Leave me alone!*'

Hansen closed the door quietly on the distraught man, motioning the nurse sitting at a table to go in. He wasn't sure that Gault hadn't seized on his tactless words to end an unwanted interview. And that went some way in easing his guilt at causing the outburst.

On his way out through the corridors, he realized he hadn't told Gault that he was seeing his wife that evening.

# Chapter 9

Hansen parked his car in the road adjacent to Bromham Crescent and walked the remaining distance, keeping to the shadows. The moon was rising from behind the horizon of dark rooftops like a thin bright fingernail. A wind blowing up flapped his coat skirts on his thighs, scratching dead leaves along the footpath. When he saw a gate with 18 on it, he opened it and entered the short gravelled drive. The bell push rang a subdued two-note chime.

She answered the ring promptly and he stepped inside. She wore a blue, gold-embroidered tunic over white trousers. Her black hair was loose and glossy as if just washed, her mouth unpainted. In her ears were long lapis lazuli pendants.

He followed in the wake of her perfume, approving the room into which he was led. Two huge moss-green velvet-covered chairs sat in off-white carpeting. There were gold curtains with tasselled cords and reproduction Utrillos on the walls. The lighting was concentrated over the chairs from green silk-shaded lamps. A low case of books occupied one wall. There was no television set, but a stereogram deck with a rack of records. A telephone handset in two shades of green stood on a glass-topped table. At its side was an olive-coloured percolator, the smell of coffee strong in the room. Pot plants added to the total effect of greenness. An open Alec Waugh paperback rested face downwards on the arm of one of the chairs.

She took his coat and put him in a chair where he could feel the warmth of the open coal fire. He took his coffee as she did, black and sugarless.

After the drying up of the social pleasantries, he found difficulty in phrasing what he had come to say. She affected him powerfully, making him choose his words carefully. Her personality was direct and she looked at him steadily with her green eyes, poised and calm in the chair opposite.

'As I said on the telephone, Mrs Gault,' he commenced, 'I've been rethinking. If you'll accept some advice, some limitations in what you propose doing, I'm with you.'

'Thank you.' Her eyes were warm. 'I was sure you would be.'

'I'm agreeing only because you were a policewoman.' He needed to avoid being patronizing. 'Were you otherwise ... just Bill's wife, it wouldn't be on.'

'No,' she agreed. 'But then, I don't imagine *I* would have considered it.'

'What specifically had you in mind?'

'Whatever it needs to clear Bill.'

'And how far doing that are you prepared to go?'

She lifted her eyebrows. 'How far would you expect a woman to go to prove her husband didn't prefer a whore?'

Whatever else was there, Hansen recognized bruised feminine pride when he met it. 'It depends on the woman,' he said. 'As it's you, probably farther than I'd hoped.'

'You've heard the latest about Bill?'

He nodded. 'I saw him this evening. I'm sorry.' Banality, he thought. But what else could he say to a woman whose husband was being emasculated by a surgeon's scalpel. And she still had him, for what he would be worth.

'It couldn't affect you as it does me, Mr Hansen, but you would understand ... there isn't much left of our marriage.' She was outwardly unperturbed, not allowing her feelings to show. Not asking for his sympathy either. Perhaps, Hansen thought, that side of marriage wasn't so important to her. With some women, it wasn't.

'No,' he agreed with candour, 'I don't imagine there is.'

She said calmly, 'Will you show me that photograph?'

He frowned and replaced his cup and saucer on the table. 'You're not serious?'

'I am.'

'It's a confidential document. The Official Secrets Act applies to it. To me, too.'

'Nonsense,' she said crisply. 'There's nothing very confidential about it now. I must be about the only person concerned who hasn't drooled over it. And I assume you or somebody else will be showing it to witnesses during enquiries.'

'It's obscene, Mrs Gault,' he said offputtingly, 'and seeing it won't make you any happier.'

'*Please*, Mr Hansen. I've seen dirty photographs before.'

But not one with your husband on it, he said to himself.

She took it from him with steady fingers and examined it, her features blank and unrevealing.

'I'll know her,' she said, returning it to him. She made no other comment.

'That's all I want from you ... just to identify her. When you've done that, the rest is for me and you pull out.'

She nodded, her earrings swinging.

'So what do you propose to do about it?' he asked.

'Get next to Toffler. There has to be something I can find out from him about that woman.'

'So you said before. And I told you that you were asking for trouble.'

'Not if you help me.'

'You want God, not me.'

She was eager. 'I've thought it out, I really have. All I need is a background ... something you can give me.'

'Oh? I can?'

'Will you wait? Just for a few minutes? I want to show you ...' She rose from her chair and left through the door, closing it behind her. He heard her footsteps, muffled in carpet, ascending the stairs.

He reached across and picked up the paperback. *A Spy in the Family. An Erotic Comedy*. Inside was her name, Ann Gault. He said 'H'm' to nobody in particular and poured a cup of coffee, drinking it reflectively. He knew that if he had any sense, he'd follow her through the door, turn left and quietly let himself out into the uncomplicated night. He needed a drink and a night's sleep. He had smoked two pipes of tobacco on his way to her as an insurance against nicotine deprivation, leaving the pipe in his car. Now he wanted another. He looked around for signs of Gault's occupancy and found none. He didn't know what that could mean. It was as if she had put his things away, not wishing to be reminded...

The door opened and a woman stood there. Her hair was blonde and hung loose over her shoulders, her mouth shiny pink with paste. Blue paint made her eyes glitter. She wore an orange wool polo-neck sweater that outlined her breasts

**and** nipples, a too-brief red skirt showing a lot of very attractive thigh over black calf-length boots.

Hansen half-rose from his chair in astonishment, the cup tipping in its saucer. He righted the cup and stood, then walked across to her.

The dark, decorous and elegant Mrs Gault had been transformed into a tart by a yellow wig, some heavily-applied make-up and the absence of a brassiere, looking provocative enough to bring out the randy goat in any man. Hansen was no exception and it showed in his eyes.

She was grave. 'You think I'd be recognized?' She was close enough for him to feel the heat of her body.

He leaned forward and sniffed her perfume. She had added to it and the amalgam of scents made him blink. 'You'll want something a lot less aphrodisiacal,' he said. 'You'll be savaged.'

She raised her eyebrows. 'But not as Ann Gault?'

He swallowed, wanting to smile and say, 'By me, anyway' but not sure it mightn't be too pointed, making his liking for her obvious. Talking to her was like talking to a widow, cut off from casual humour by bereavement.

'Yes,' he answered her. He was being committed to an attitude, whatever he said. 'As Ann Gault as well. Who are you supposed to be now?'

'Ann Pardoe. That was my maiden name.'

'All right, Ann Pardoe. You're a foolish headstrong woman.'

She moved away from him, sitting and waiting, her long legs drawn up beneath her. 'So you approve?'

'I didn't say that.' He returned to his chair. 'If you mean using it on Toffler, you frighten me.' The thought of Toffler mauling her did.

'It needn't,' she said. 'I've survived a few Saturday nights around Soho. Toffler presents nothing very original in men.'

'I wish I could believe you.'

'But you don't think I'll be recognized?'

'No. You'd have to dig deep for Ann Gault.'

She stroked the long yellow hair with her fingers as if she approved it. 'I haven't changed beneath it.' But she *was* different; in some subtle way the cool elegance had been flawed; she looked, Hanson considered, so bloody *available*.

'I don't really know you underneath,' he said.

'No you don't, do you.' She smiled. 'You'll help?'

He had difficulty in keeping his eyes from her breasts, from the protruding nipples, in not thinking of her as the tart she appeared to be; not yet rationalizing the change from Siamese to alley cat.

'If the alternative is your going it alone, yes.'

'It is,' she said coolly.

'You didn't lose any time in getting organized.'

'I bought it this afternoon. I didn't want it to die on me.'

'What do you want from my end?'

'A background for Ann Pardoe. She has to be somebody's girl-friend or wife. Somebody she isn't likely to bump into while she's with Toffler.'

'A prisoner,' he said. 'Inside and known to Toffler. But not too well known.' He thought about it. 'There's Dennis Garvey in Pentonville for office-breaking. Denny to all his girl-friends who're waiting or not waiting until he gets out. Which won't be for a couple of years at least. No known relatives, no fixed address ... a loner if there ever was one. He isn't one of Toffler's mob but he'd be known.'

'Can I have a sight of his record card? A photograph?'

'Having breached the Official Secrets Act once already, I don't suppose being hanged a second time is any more painful.' He could only hope he wasn't to be a Samson to her Delilah. She was still unsettling him with her surface sensuality. While she might be Ann Gault behind the raw sexual image, her blonde and tartish *alter ego* had triggered off his imagination, linking it with his liking for its original.

He said, uncomfortably, 'I'd rather you took that stuff off. I can't convince myself I'm talking to you ... talking to Ann Gault.'

She stared at him, then laughed lightly. 'I know your weakness now.' She put her thumbs under the wig at the forehead and slid it backwards, shaking her own hair free. Then she took tissues from her handbag and wiped the paste from her mouth, the blue from her eyelids. He was glad she proposed doing nothing about her breasts. They were more provocative on Ann Gault because of the contrast with her unpainted face.

'I still feel that you're taking a hell of a risk with Toffler.'

'Whoever got anywhere who didn't?' It was unanswerable feminine logic.

'Does Bill know?'

'No. Only you and I.' She made her husband's exclusion a small intimacy between them.

'You know Toffler's hang-out?'

'Bill told me. The Double Decker.'

'He's there most evenings.'

The Double Decker was a drinking club with a top-storey bar and a table-sized brass disc set in the floor for dancing and strip shows. Its clientele was drawn largely from the more affluent core of local criminality still at large; its bouncers necessarily ferocious. No policeman entered it singly and without a search warrant. Toffler had bought his way into its management by fear, his only investment being his assurance of freedom from rival parasites. In return, he took more than a carrion-eater's share of the profits.

Hansen said, 'You can't operate from here. You'll need to have another address.'

She wrinkled her forehead. 'I will?'

'Toffler's no idiot. Not just because he drops his aitches. He'll check on you; may even have you followed. He'll certainly ask questions.'

'I see.' She recognized his concern for her and she responded with warmth, amenable to his leading her. 'I'll go into lodgings.'

While they discussed the details of her metamorphosis into Ann Pardoe, each was conscious of the other's regard, conscious of the attraction between them.

Finally, he said, 'I still don't like it, Ann.' And he didn't. She might be no novice at dealing with criminals, but Toffler...

'I can look after myself ... really I can.' She looked as if she could, the vestigial policewoman in her evident.

'Don't be left alone with him. If he takes a shine to you—and I'm sure he must—he's a dirty fighter.' He meant 'lover', but couldn't bring himself to say it.

'I'll be careful, Robert.'

When it was time for him to leave, he stood with her in the tiny hall, not wanting to go. As a Woman Detective Inspector, she must have been a disturbing colleague to work with.

She stared at him curiously, sensing, he thought, his sexual interest in her. He was not certain that she approved it. Then she licked her lips with the tip of her tongue and he was sure

85

she did. Whatever it was that drew men and women together was there, strong like an electric current. If he knew women—and he thought he did—she was telling him she was attracted to him and it moved his loins. He hesitated to label what he felt for her. It was too tangled with his sexual needs for easy identification, but knowing he didn't want the sentiment of love. For a moment, he went close to taking hold of her.

What stopped him was not diffidence or a lack of male confidence. Nor that he was a married man, she a married woman. What did stop him was her being the wife of a fellow-policeman. That the fellow-policeman was in hospital and in no position or condition to object made it even more impossible for Hansen. There was a moral taboo here somewhere that Hansen needed—wanted—to rationalize. It didn't make sense that because Gault couldn't enjoy his wife's body, nobody else should. It didn't make sense, but it was there just the same. It seemed not to inhibit Ann and Hansen thought he understood this, accepting that after two months without a sexual release she would be susceptible to being physically moved by his maleness; perhaps by any available maleness that was acceptable to her fastidiousness.

He moved towards the door.

'I'm grateful, Robert,' she said softly. There was a shadow of disappointment in his eyes. 'Probably more than you realize.'

'Don't be.' He felt his heart thumping, certain it was audible. 'I shall lean on you hard if I think you're going too far.' He showed his teeth. 'Even throw my rank at you.'

Outside in the darkness, he felt that he had been pusillanimous.


He groaned under his breath when he saw the *Commodore* waiting at the entrance to his apartment, glaring its tell-tale orange and black immediately beneath a street light. He might have anticipated Norah that evening, although she would never make firm arrangements. She said it made her feel like a call-girl. He usually bought her flowers, occasionally perfume. Once he had given her a big Havana cigar for Geoffrey, but never knowing whether she had passed it on to him or not. She was as likely to smoke it herself. Tonight, he had nothing.

He felt physically tired and mentally exhausted; in no condition, he thought, to make five-star love to Norah. Curiously,

Ann had blunted the edge of the happy anticipation he would normally have generated between the street and his rooms.

Norah was, as he should have guessed, in the bathroom from which she would eventually emerge like a shiny pink Venus in a cloud of steam, her strong white teeth ready to eat a meal or to bite him. It wasn't important to her which she did first, just so long as she did both. There would be no *tristis post coitum* with her either. She might sigh dreamily at the end, but would then either happily light a cigarette or poke around in his refrigerator on the off-chance of finding enough eggs for an omelette.

She had already brought Trudchen up from the caretaker's basement and Hansen rubbed her whiskered biscuit-smelling mouth with his nose before tapping the bathroom door and telling Norah he had arrived.

After he had poured two whiskies, handing one to Norah through the bathroom door, he sat with a leg over the arm of a cretonne-covered easy chair, waiting his turn for a use of the shower. The room had been furnished with pieces from some uncertain period in the nineteen-thirties and wallpapered in crimson Chinese Restaurant flock. Everything possible had been padded and cushioned, ruched and flounced, for female comfort. It suited Hansen and, despite Trudchen's black hairs on the seat covers as evidence to the contrary, it was cleaned daily.

The kitchen was spacious enough to allow a man holding a frying pan to turn around without knocking too many articles from the draining-board. Hansen rarely used it for anything more adventurous than boiling eggs or shaking cornflakes from a packet. Norah, however, and despite her Junoesque proportions, would manage a cooked breakfast for two easily enough before her noisy, unconcealed departure at eight the following morning.

When he had come from the shower, Norah had detected some difference of nuance in the yellow of his eyes or in the set of his mouth. Wearing his best midnight-blue and gold pyjamas, she sprawled inelegantly across his lap, pressing him into the chair, already on her second whisky.

'You have worries, Bobbie,' she told him, warm whisky-smelling breath moist in his ear.

'It's been a day of sorts,' he admitted with understatement. 'Have you read the *Evening Observer*?'

'No,' she said comfortably. 'I never bother. Why? Are you in it?'

'More or less. It could tell you that you are associating with a scoundrelly perjurer, a corrupt copper,' he told her solemnly. 'I'm tired, too.' He made light of the allegations, not wanting her to even think there was any substance in them.

'I never believe newspapers, Bobbie.' She licked her lips and put her mouth over his, her tongue darting in. It was what she had come for and she didn't want to know anything else.

Before joining him in the big double bed, she pulled off the pyjama jacket, then unfastened the trousers and stepped out of them, folding and tucking them in the foot of the bed to be kept warm by the electric blanket. She straddled the supine Hansen, a knee on either side of him, hovering above him like a golden, big-breasted moth in the darkened room.

'Relax, Bobbie darling,' she whispered. 'You're a tired little boy and Mummy's going to love you.' Her hands were busy on him, gently and encouraging, while he lay, his eyes closed, letting her love him.

His thoughts drifted as he relaxed and a small coloured picture came into his mind, clear and brilliant. 'Where have you hidden the photographer, Norah my love?' he murmured into her mouth. He would have laughed, except that the possibility of his having been wrong about Gault's unconsciousness when photographed wasn't very funny.

She was lowering herself on to him, pressing him into the mattress. 'Don't be a bloody twit, Bobbie. What on earth do you mean?'

'You should have read the *Observer* ... dear God, darling, I can't breathe ...'

'That's good.'

'I'm staying with you, my love.'

'That's good too. Were you going somewhere?' Her full weight was on him now, her huge breasts cushioned on his chest.

'I nearly did,' he said, thinking of Ann and the taboos fencing him from her. 'So very nearly ...'

Gault, floating in the dark sea of his post-operative stupor, comatose under the numbing effects of the drugs injected and fed into his body, was haunted by violent dreams of sex and death, his mind squirreling around Toffler, his mocking face enlarged to a gigantic grimacing mask; seeing *her*, nearly always with Toffler, writhing in the fleshy nakedness he had tasted himself, whispering frantically with her arms around his enemy's shoulders, crying out her inexhaustible lust into the darkness, waking him with a jolting heart to lie awake in utter dejection.

Then the anguish of realization would bite him. Christ! Never to press his body into a woman's breasts again, never to feel the smooth skin of her thighs; never any relief for the simple, aching need in him to be loved. A need that castration had not obliterated. Even before the operation, he had tried to recreate his past lusts, but the memories of the women he had loved threw only colourless, juiceless, one-dimensional shadows on the screen of his imagination; the recall of times past promoting only a numbing nothingness, a bitter regret for things lost.

He could recall her with his other emotions; black-haired and vivid with sherry-brown eyes that turned up at the corners, giving her a feline expression; a tiny slim body that excited a man's imagination because it made him feel big and powerful. She was a nocturnal creature frequenting dimly-lit bars, her natural habitat a bar stool; waiting, he had thought at the time, like a beautiful cat for its prey to come within reach of its talons. He had deliberately put himself within reach, his masculinity challenged, and he had never sought release.

He could recall the bright images of their encounter, the fire she had lit in him, but never again to evoke its heat. It was as though another man had bought her that first drink and the many that followed, returning with her to her room and being possessed by her dark-furred body.

The man he was had been obsessed with her, as she had been with him, burning their lusts into a fusing heat. When he discovered she had been Toffler's mistress, and only God and she knew of how many other men, he hadn't cared. Her talons had gone deep and he would have turned in the job rather than lose her.

But that had been then. He now knew that a man's lust existed only in the present and future. And he had no present or future. He had only what was now a mockery to his manhood, a taunt to him with its impotence.

Then would come the frenzied need to tear the bandages from him and shout his bitter frustration and empty despair through the sleeping hospital.

# Chapter 10

It had been a bad morning for Hansen, frustrated by Sloan's early arrival from being able to leave his office.

Sloan, a badger-grey man with sucked-in cheeks and a permanent sniff, was nearing the end of his service, already knowing the exact day and hour of his departure, the amount of his pension and the tax deductible from it to four decimal places. He was known to Hansen as a conscientious, ultra-cautious and shrewd detective who never moved a millimetre outside the limits laid down by Force General Orders. Pointed in the right direction, he would move as ponderously and inexorably as the Judgement of God, and the debris of his passing would be ground exceedingly small.

Sloan had immediately covered himself against procedural counter-attack by serving on Hansen a Disciplinary Notice. This form outlined the allegations made by Sinter against him, then went on to remind Hansen that he was not obliged to say anything concerning the matter but he might, if he so desired, make a written or oral statement to Sloan or to the Chief Constable. It warned him that the statement might be used in any subsequent criminal or disciplinary proceedings. As Hansen agreed with Jeremy Bentham (who had expressed it first) that while guilt might seek the privilege of silence, innocence should demand the right to speak, he told Sloan he would make a statement.

He now had to move fast. Sloan, slow moving and cautious though he might be, would be no slouch in identifying the Queensbury Hotel and screwing down Wikker with the weight of his thirty years experience. And Wikker, Hansen knew, had all the frailties of self-interest. He would, under pressure, tell Sloan anything to get himself out of serious trouble. Hansen could only hope it wouldn't include disclosing his own visit.

It would all depend on the metal of the superintendent's will against Wikker's fears.

Alone in his office after Sloan's departure, Hansen made telephone calls, using the line bypassing the switchboard.

He first dialled the number of the Caulfield Arms Hotel in an adjacent Division. He knew it by repute as a one-night-bed-and-breakfaster, not a lot better than the Queensbury. Its proprietor was suspected of encouraging its use by freelance whores and homosexuals needing an hour or so of cut-rate privacy. Occasionally, the hotel accepted bona fide guests. It was not on Glass's books and the proprietor wouldn't know Hansen.

He booked a room from twelve noon that day in the name of William Jackson, giving a non-existent address in Birmingham, saying he would need to dump his case of samples in the room during the afternoon.

Next, he dialled the Olympian Massage Clinic. It was unlikely that Glass would demean his status by answering calls, but if he did Hansen was prepared to close down on him for his voice would be recognized.

A woman answered, her words low-pitched and vibrant, telling him that the clinic was at his service and calling him 'sir'.

Hansen put hesitancy and what he believed to be a touch of Bagot Street Birmingham in his speech, acting a man sweating out his embarrassment.

'A friend,' he said. 'He recommended me to your establishment. I thought, being here on a visit, I'd give it a try. You know? By a lady...'

'I understand, sir. What kind of massage had you in mind?'

'Oh? I don't really know ... what kind have you?'

Her voice became persuasive, the saleswomanship of a whore who had made the inner office at last and was selling another woman's services. 'We provide a medically-approved manipulative massage with body oil at five pounds, sir; a sponge massage and assisted shower for seven-fifty and our special full-relief massage for ten. The full-relief,' she said languorously, 'includes lower-abdominal manipulation ... *full* manipulation.' She gave the last an undercurrent of promised sensuality although there was, Hansen knew, nothing more sensual in a full-relief massage than masturbation.

He breathed heavily into the mouthpiece. 'Yes, well, I'd want that, of course. You see, I've been working hard ... feeling a bit, er, stiff...' He gave an embarrassed laugh. 'You understand? My friend said to go to you; you'd provide the right treatment.'

He felt dirty, haggling with this huckster in female flesh.

She said, 'We understand completely, sir.' She lowered her voice. 'You receive your treatment in a private room, of course.'

'Ah, yes, well, that's the difficulty. I'm booked in at the Caulfield Arms Hotel and I'd prefer my treatment there, this afternoon. You see,' he said in an apparent burst of confidence, 'I wouldn't want anyone I know to see me. I'm a sales representative and one of my customers has a shop in your street ... that's why I'm telephoning.'

'I assure you we shall be absolutely discreet...'

'No,' he said definitely. 'If I was seen, you know? People might misunderstand. You know ... you've got pictures on the front.' They had indeed. Large coloured photographs of bare-breasted women smoothing their nimble anenome-active fingers over happily-smiling prone men with towels around their loins.

'So we have.' She sounded amused at his timidity. 'Perhaps this evening, sir. We do have a rear entrance.'

'I'm taking a train from Kings Cross this evening.'

He was banking on Glass not wanting to pass up money because some out-of-town salesman with an itch wanted the service only he could provide in his own hotel room.

'Just a moment, sir.' There was silence for a few moments and the scrape of a palm over the mouthpiece, the remote rumble of a man's words. She returned to him. 'Could I have your name and address for our records, please.'

He hesitated, deliberately. 'William Jackson,' he said. 'I'm down from Birmingham on business. My address wouldn't mean anything.'

There were more seconds of muffled consultation until she said to him, 'That will be quite in order, Mr Jackson, but I'm afraid our fee for outpatient treatment is twelve pounds fifty; plus our operative's taxi fare.'

'That's all right,' Hansen said. 'I'll expect her at three o'clock. I'm in room seventeen. Er,' he said anxiously, 'This operative ... she'll be a young lady?'

'Yes, Mr Jackson. Young and pretty. I'm sure you'll be given a satisfactory service.'

Hansen replaced the receiver and grimaced. She or Glass would certainly check at the hotel on some specious pretext and the proprietor would as certainly disclose the type of booking and the Birmingham address; all of which would only confirm the picture he had given of a goatishly-inclined salesman needing a last fling before returning home.

He dialled unanswered calls to Ann and, in between, studied again the photograph of Gault and the woman Sheila. After last night's demonstration by Norah, he couldn't be so positive that Gault had not consciously adopted the passive role in which he had been photographed. He didn't believe he had, but the hard edge of his previous certainty was now blurred.

He had, too, given more thought to the question of Toffler's personal involvement. A beating-up was a job normally left to a hatchetman like Ash. It was unusual, tactically bad, that one should be planned and executed against a detective obviously known to be following him. Anybody not cretinous would know that clobbering a policeman promoted more trouble than the satisfaction it gave. Being watched, being shadowed, would be nothing new or unexpected in Toffler's experience; usually occasioning no more than a deferring of whatever villainy he was pursuing or its abandonment. In Gault's case it had resulted in Toffler's being charged and tried, something he would never normally have risked for a profitless act of violence. Gault had been detailed to check on Toffler's movements primarily because information had been received that he was an associate of a man wanted for an armed bank robbery in Kensington. Toffler would not have been at risk, even had the man been found in his company. Hansen was all the more certain there was unexpected dirt to be stirred up in the investigation; that he had to get to the woman Sheila before Sloan.

When his repeated call to Ann was answered, he gave her an address in Commercial Road at which she would be able to rent a room without having to produce her Birth Certificate and a character reference from the local vicar. It catered to the vaguely theatrical and would not be so respectable as to arouse Toffler's suspicions.

'Go there,' he said, 'in your Pardoe outfit. Carry a travelling case with you and change always in a ladies loo. A different one each time. Never go to Commercial Road as Ann Gault, or to your home as Pardoe. There's a coin-box telephone in the entrance hall. Let me know as soon as you're installed.'

Then he briefed her on Dennis Garvey's background; his date of birth, his physical description including body scars and tattoos, what he drank, where he ate and the brand of cigarettes he smoked; his date of arrest, the charge and the trial court and the counsel defending him. He read out the list of his associates; the make, colour and index number of his car and where it was currently garaged; his last address and the pubs and clubs he frequented. He described to her the lay-out of the Reception and Visiting Wing of the prison and the route to it from Paddington Station. He gave her the Governor's name and that of his Chief Officer and the days on which visiting was permitted. He finally told her that a photograph of Garvey would be delivered to her that afternoon.

The extent of his briefing was the measure of his concern for her safety. Even their remote connection by electrical impulses stirred his masculinity, made his pulse race. The rapport was there, clear and strong, and he knew it was going to be the most difficult thing in the world not to do something about it.


Because he had no wish to eat in the canteen with McGluskie and Sloan a constraint on his appetite, he walked along the street to the Trattoria Napoli, ordering an *omelet con funghi* and a glass of white Chianti.

He sat on his own, a folded newspaper conspicuously propped in front of him, advertising his disinclination for company.

When Toffler entered, followed by Ash, he knew the meeting was by intent and not by accident. He placed his knife and fork on the plate and waited, his expression harsh and forbidding, the lines of his dislike cut deep around his mouth.

Toffler waved a hand to Hansen, then spoke to Ash who went to the bar counter and stood there, near enough for the detective to see the light-sensitive pink eyes glimmering behind the dark glasses. The gangster approached Hansen's table, his teeth showing in an insolent grin. 'Mind if I join you, Mr 'Ansen?'

The detective swallowed his anger like pieces of sharp tin. 'I'm eating,' he said curtly.

Toffler pulled out a chair and sat. 'You go on. Don' let me stop you.'

'What do you want?' Hansen looked pointedly at the white-haired, boyish-faced Ash at the counter. His shielded eyes were fixed on him. He wondered, without caring overmuch, what had triggered Ash's unconcealed dislike of him. His malevolence showed as plain as a piranha's teeth. 'You think he's enough support for you to be nasty?'

Toffler put a thin cocoa-coloured cheroot between his bacon-rind lips, not lighting it. The stretched skin of his narrow features had been freshly-shaved and polished and he evaporated a strong smell of deodorant. His shrimp-pink shirt and embroidered crimson tie were new, his coat cut in an aggressive military style.

'Mr 'Ansen,' he said, 'there ain't no sense in us sparrin' at each other now the trial's done with. I want to talk.'

Hansen stared at him. He was doing something about Toffler now and talk might prove useful. And people like him usually talked only when they were worried, feeling insecure. It was a time for listening and picking the bones from whatever was said. He picked up his fork, detaching a segment of omelette. 'All right, talk.'

Toffler settled in his chair. 'Tha's the 'ammer. Now,' he said, 'anythin' you say about me ain't goin' to mean much, is it?' He looked at Hansen with a weasel cunning. 'I mean, you're already in the crap, mate, over your tryin' to fix me. Sayin' more's goin' to settle your 'ash with your bosses. Right?'

'Go on. You're telling it to me.' Somebody was keeping Toffler in the picture. Probably Sloan had already approached Weizsack.

'Right.' The cold butcher's eyes were narrowed, intended to convey a warning. 'I ain't goin' to let you be a nuisance, Mr 'Ansen. I can't. You're 'eading for dead trouble if you are. So,' he added casually, 'is your mate Gault.'

'Threatened men live long lives, Toffler.' He nodded at the still-staring albino who now held a glass of tomato juice in his hand. 'Are you going to set your pansy friend on to us?'

Ash knew he was being referred to disparagingly and bright pink coloured his face, making his glowering expression even more venomous. It was obvious to Hansen that only Toffler stopped the albino from venting his malevolence on him.

Toffler was calmly confident. 'I'm too big to be pushed around by you, mate. There's...'

Hansen interrupted him contemptuously. 'Don't you ever believe it. I've heard it before. You crooked bastards get delusions of grandeur as soon as you believe you've got away with murder; put away enough loot to buy a Queen's Counsel. You're not big at all, Toffler. Never too big not to finish up in a special security prison.' He jerked his head in the direction of the door and smiled nastily. 'Now suppose you shove off. You're putting me off my food.' If all Toffler wanted was to threaten him, he had been threatened before and there was no profit in listening.

Toffler stroked the cheroot against the side of his vulture's nose, studying the detective with calculating eyes, then baring his strong teeth. 'You ain't goin' to upset me, mate. No more'n you did Wikker.'

Hansen showed no recognition of the name, but thoughtfully speared more omelette with his fork. Wikker hadn't failed him. Whatever Toffler had been told had stung him into action.

'You're beginning to get scared?' he asked mildly.

Toffler lit the cheroot with a book-match and swallowed the smoke, shaking his head slowly. 'No, mate, I ain't. But you should be. Very, very scared.'

'So you said before. All right.' He sipped at his wine. 'So I'm scared. Does that make you any happier?' Beneath his impassivity, he was growing angry. More than anything else, he wanted to jerk the table into Toffler's belly, then smash the mocking insolence back behind the cruel face. The thought warmed that part of his brain still retaining the cells of his ancestral savagery.

'You ain't takin' me seriously, Mr 'Ansen,' Toffler said reproachfully. 'I don' aim to sit back on my fanny and let you fix me again.'

'Say what you came to say and get out.'

'I've said it, mate. I'm givin' you some friendly advice. Jus' lay off me.'

'Or?'

'I don' 'ave to say. You'll know.' He blew smoke over Hansen's head.

'You've been watching television, Toffler. All your toughness is on the outside. Inside, you're third-rate twisted sewage and you talk too much.'

Toffler's eyes were the cold grey of emulsified oil. 'You can't insult me, mate. It don' pay to be too sensitive. Let me tell you...'

'*No*. Let me tell you something. I'm putting in my ticket. Not because of you, but because it suits me to. After that, I'm my own man; not a police officer who can't hit you in your stupid face.' There were patches of colour over his cheekbones. 'Come to me then and threaten me. And when you do...' He raised his voice so that Ash could hear him. '...You'll need that pansy bodyguard of yours. Tell him to put that in his handbag and think about it.'

He saw the baby-pink flush into Ash's pallid face again, the fingers of the fist holding the tumbler of tomato juice tighten until he expected the glass to crumple like tissue paper.

'At the moment, Toffler,' Hansen continued, lowering his voice, 'I'm a police officer doing his job. And that's sorting you out for the law.'

'I 'eard you was jackin' it in,' Toffler said unruffled. 'Seems a pity you 'ave to be so bleedin' stupid now when it don' matter. Lissen.' He leaned forward, the smell of tobacco strong on his breath. 'You could say I was in business and 'ave to protec' my interests. I'd be a bloody fool to let you muck me about without doin' anythin' about it. I've got to fight you, mate. An' you'll 'ave your bleedin' 'ands full.' His teeth showed in a grin. 'But I'd rather we was mates.' He tapped ash on to the tablecloth and smeared it into a pound sign with the ball of his thumb.

'You mean you'd like to buy me off?'

'If that's what it takes, Mr 'Ansen. There's only two ways I know about people: you buy the bastards or you break them.'

'Like you broke Sergeant Gault?'

Toffler drew on his cheroot, his cheeks sucked in. 'If you will 'ave it so, mate.'

'Tell me why?'

A nerve twitched in Toffler's jaw and a brief glow of anger showed in his eyes. He stared at Hansen for a long moment, then he stood. 'Jus' remember,' he said tautly. 'There's more'n one way of skinnin' a cat.'

His manner changed abruptly and he leaned across the table, grasping Hansen's hand in his fist. It was a public gesture, designed for everyone to see. 'Nice to 'ave met you again,

Bob,' he said loudly, as Hansen snatched his hand away. 'Drop in any time.'

Ash followed him out, but at the door turned his colourless face to Hansen, glaring at him from behind the dark windows of his sunglasses, his livid mouth twisted in a soundless sneer.

Hansen knew he would have to watch for the albino. Fag strongarm men included an unforgiving bitchy viciousness in their armouries. For a year or two, until his discharge from the army with ignominy, Ash had been a guardsman, prostituted to the perverted appetites of the older men he allowed to pick him up in Piccadilly Circus. The convictions leading to his discharge had resulted from his importuning in a public urinal a young man he failed to recognize as a policeman and, when he did, attempting to fight his way out of the arrest.

He was recorded in his Crime Intelligence File as having an uncontrollable temper with a readiness for violence. With nothing feminine about him, he was as unlike the popular image of a homosexual as a man could be. He was a dangerous and unpredictable male and Hansen didn't underestimate him.

But Toffler interested the detective more. For him to follow Hansen into the restaurant meant a lot more than bloody-mindedness. His reaction to Hansen's last question had shown an unexpected sensitivity that went some way to confirming his suspicions about Sergeant Gault.

# Chapter 11

Looking down from the window of his hotel room, Hansen searched the street for indications that he had been followed.

He had driven his car to the hotel by a circuitous, leisurely route, crawling along side streets in low gear, allowing traffic to overtake him and checking constantly in his rearview mirror. Finally, he had left the car in a cul-de-sac, walking the remaining four hundred yards through a grey drizzle of rain. That Toffler had been so prompt in following him into the Trattoria Napoli was clear enough evidence he was being watched.

Hansen had told Dobkin, the hotel's proprietor, that he was expecting an agency secretary to help with some paper-work. Both men had adopted unrevealing expressions appropriate to its improbability.

When the taxi pulled into the kerb outside at three o'clock, Hansen studied the foreshortened view of the woman paying the driver off. If he had expected somebody tartish, he was disappointed. Her appearance suggested she was a modest young housewife out for an afternoon's visit to a cinema, with a pot of tea and plate of cream buns in a cafeteria to round it off before returning to prepare her husband's evening meal. Her fair hair was strained back from her pleasant features in a pony tail. Her body was heavy-breasted, her legs thick and muscular. She wore a short tweed coat over a skirt that just missed covering her knees and she carried a handbag and a plaid holdall. She wasn't a woman whose buttocks were in any danger of being pinched by a stranger.

He opened the door to Dobkin's knock. She was standing behind him and, that near, Hansen could see she wore no make-up. Tealeaf freckles blotched a tiny nose and her wide blue eyes assured Hansen they had never seen anything more nakedly erotic than a baby. She looked clean and well-scrubbed and, if she wore perfume, it wasn't reaching him. The only measure of her presumed whorishness was that Glass had sent her.

Hansen smiled. 'Come on in, Miss Smith.' He closed the door on the cynical Dobkin and led her inside, turning the key in the lock and pocketing it.

She looked around her at the shabby furniture and the two single beds, then at him, stripping off her gloves. Her fingers were ringless. In spite of her prim *hausfrau* appearance, she exuded a definite aura of eroticism. But that, Hansen admitted to himself, may have been only because of his knowledge of what she was prepared to do to him.

'You're Mr Jackson?' Her voice was commonplace and pleasant, supporting his feeling that he must be mistaken, that she was there for no more than a cup of tea and a cosy chat about the weather.

'Yes,' he said. 'And you?'

'I'm Janet.' She took off her coat. Beneath it she wore a woollen cardigan and a gold metal belt. Her waist was small.

'You don't look like a masseuse.' What small-talk, Hansen asked himself, could you have with a strange woman preparing to relieve your sexual hang-up.

'I don't?' She arched her eyebrows ingenuously. 'Well, I am.' She said matter-of-factly, 'I understand you want the full-relief massage?'

'Yes.'

'I have to be paid in advance.'

He felt inside his jacket for his wallet. 'Twelve-fifty?'

'And the taxi, seventy pee.'

He counted out notes and added coins to the exact amount and she put them in her handbag.

She became brisk and zipped open the holdall, taking from it a blue tube of hand-cream, a rabbit's-fur glove and a white bath towel. 'Which would you like, Mr Jackson? Some clients prefer the cream, others like the glove.' She smiled and brushed the glove's fur against her cheek.

'I was hoping,' he said, regarding her preparations with disappointment, 'for the full treatment. You know? Er, intercourse.'

She looked slightly offended. 'That isn't what you've paid for, Mr Jackson. I can't do anything else but give you an abdominal massage.'

'I see.'

She walked to one of the beds and laid the towel across it, smoothing the creases out. 'Would you like to get ready? I'm sure I can satisfy you.' She started unbuttoning her cardigan, as impersonal as a nurse about to give a patient an enema.

He sat at the foot of the bed, slowly removing his jacket, knowing it could never be in him to prepare coldly and deliberately for a sex act. 'Am I going to be allowed to kiss you?' he asked ironically.

'No. Not that either.' She seemed well-prepared for the client who wanted more than he had paid for.

'What am I going to get for my money, Janet?' he asked, fumbling with his cuff-links.

'A body massage ... of all parts.' A woman smell came from her as she removed her cardigan, displaying her pulpy breasts overflowing from an inadequate pink brassiere.

It was intended, he guessed, that they should hang free over him while he was being massaged, probably to excite him into a private financial arrangement for full intercourse. Some extra money that Charlie Glass wouldn't know about or get.

She untied the ribbon at the nape of her neck, her hair dropping over her naked shoulders. They were smooth and freckled too. She unscrewed the cap from the tube, squeezing a clear jelly into the palms of her small plump hands, rubbing it in with her fingertips. It was all very mechanical and impersonal, yet possessing its own sensuousness.

'Do you mean you are going to masturbate me?' he asked.

'If that's what you want for relief,' she said calmly. 'It's part of your abdomen, isn't it?'

The woman was moving him pruriently with her deceptive domestic ordinariness. He could have been her husband, being given something to think about before returning to his factory production line. Had she been an obvious tart, she would have repelled him.

He stood and retrieved his jacket, taking out his warrant card and holding it under her nose. 'I'm sorry, Janet,' he said, 'but I won't be needing your massage.'

She put a hand to her opened mouth and covered her breasts with an arm, her terrified eyes looking from him to the door, then back to her coat and cardigan on the chair.

'Don't,' he said. 'It's locked, and the key's in my pocket.'

'You're ... you're a policeman?' She groped her way blindly

into the chair and sat, numbed with shock.

'Yes. I have to point out to you that you've been soliciting me for an immoral purpose.' She wouldn't know that in the unlikely event of a prosecution, the evidence of it would be nullified by his acting as an *agent provocateur*, that she could only solicit in a public place. His lever was to be more forthright than an empty threat of prosecution.

Her mouth shaped the words 'No' and 'Only a massage', her throat jerking.

'Get dressed,' he ordered her. He pulled out the handbag wedged between her buttocks and the chair arm and opened it, taking out the money he had given her, stuffing it in his trousers' pocket while she struggled back into her cardigan, her body shaking. 'You won't want this,' he said pleasantly. 'Not having earned it.' The money was better in his pocket than in Glass's bank account.

There were two letters in the handbag and he read their envelopes. Both were handwritten to Mrs J. Liggett at a local address. He replaced them and gave her back the bag. Despite knowing what she was, he felt sorry for her.

'I think the best thing we can do, Mrs Liggett,' he said, his expression stern, 'is for us to go to Headquarters and send for your husband. See what he has to say ...'

She froze, white circles appearing around the blue of her eyes. '*No!*' she whispered hoarsely. 'Oh, my God! You *mustn't*. He'll murder me ... please! Do anything, but don't let him know.'

'What does your husband do?' His voice gave no promise of agreement.

'He's ... he's an insurance clerk.'

'And this is to help you buy the groceries?'

'Things are difficult ...'

'Not that difficult,' he said coldly, 'that a married woman has to dirty herself by rubbing off any rubbish that's willing to pay for it.' Things his own wife had done put him on her husband's side.

'Oh, God.' She flushed, her freckles standing out clear. 'You make it sound so filthy.'

'It is filthy,' he snapped. 'And it had to come out one day, didn't it? I take it your husband doesn't know?'

Her fingers attempting to fasten the cardigan were fumbling with the buttons, slippery from the jelly. 'Are you mad!' she wailed, tears starting between her eyelids. 'Of course he doesn't.'

He pulled a chair forward and sat near her. 'This would ruin your marriage.' He made it a statement of fact.

She nodded dumbly.

'Have you any children?'

'One ... a little boy.' The tears ran unchecked down her cheeks.

'And he's at school?'

'No, in the council nursery.'

'While you go out on this caper?' He was softening her up, reminding her of what she stood to lose, kneading her into malleability.

'Yes.'

He sighed. 'There *is* a way out, Mrs Liggett. It means I shall be taking a risk I don't know that you'd justify. It would mean your being completely honest with me.' He looked doubtfully at her.

'But I will,' she cried eagerly. 'Please ... *please*. Anything...'

'You can walk out of that door with no comeback if you can give me some information.'

'*Anything.*' She straightened in her chair, trying to control her trembling mouth, her eyes pleading on his. She meant it at that moment; anything.

'You work for Charlie Glass?'

She nodded, swallowing. She had abandoned the abortive buttoning of her cardigan, wiping her greasy palms on a tiny handkerchief.

'You know the other girls working for him?'

'Some of them.'

'You know Sheila?'

There was a pause and then she said, 'I'm frightened.' She was, and it showed in her face.

'Of me, or Glass?'

'B-both.'

'Be more frightened of me, Mrs Liggett,' he said grimly. 'And of your husband finding out.' He toughened his voice. 'I want her name.'

Her tongue moistened her lips. 'Sheila ... Sheila Coughlin.'

'Describe her.'

'She's slim ... black hair. It's tinted.' She waved her hand vaguely.

104

'Age?'

'Twenty-six.'

He produced the photograph, covering Gault's features with his thumb and holding it out to her. 'Is that Sheila?'

She stared at it, her eyes widening, and nodded. 'It looks like her.'

'Where does she live?'

'I don't know,' she said helplessly. 'I've only seen her at the clinic. And not since about a month ago.'

'Has she any particular friends? Men, I mean.'

'I don't know.' Her reluctance was stiffening into resistance.

'Is one of them Donkey Toffler?'

She wasn't quick enough to hide the glint of recognition in her eyes although she immediately shuttered them with her lids. 'Donkey Toffler?' she repeated.

Hansen scowled at her. 'I said complete honesty, Mrs Liggett, not covering up. Don't you damn well hold out on me now. Was Toffler one of her boyfriends?'

'She knows him ... she's mentioned him to me.'

'In what connection?'

'She used to be his girl.'

'Used?'

'That's what she said.'

'Were you?'

She wrinkled her forehead, the *hausfrau* being asked if she could remember what time the butcher's shop closed, acting out her domestic wholesomeness. 'Was I what?'

'Were you Toffler's girl?' Hansen thought her a tangle of self deceit.

'No.' She wasn't offended by the question, but cautious, and Hansen didn't know whether to believe her or not.

'But he visits the clinic?'

'Yes. In the evenings when I'm not there.'

'Because your husband's home then?'

This deliberate reminder of her vulnerability quickened her breathing. 'Please don't tell him ... please.'

'I won't if you've told me the truth.'

'I swear on my son's life ... please promise me.'

His yellow eyes searched her face, stern and uncompromising. 'I promise. But if I find you've lied...' He left the threat unuttered. Dealing with women like her inhibited him, made him careful that their lies and evasions didn't fool him, yet

105

forcing a consideration for them they didn't always deserve. 'How are you going to explain to Glass about your having no money?'

She twisted the handkerchief in her fingers. 'I don't know.'

'I do. Tell him that Mr Jackson wanted the full treatment; that he wouldn't accept anything less.'

She managed a wry smile. 'You don't know Charlie Glass.'

'Yes, I do. He'd expect you to have given it?'

'Rather than lose a client who'd paid, yes.'

'So you'd go the distance when it's necessary?'

She hesitated, enough to show it wouldn't be a fate worse than death. 'You weren't paying me enough.' She bit at her bottom lip. 'Charlie isn't going to believe I wouldn't.' She had recovered much of her composure now she had Hansen's promise.

'Tell him the truth. He'll have to believe that.'

She was startled, her mouth opening.

'I mean it,' he said. 'If you have to, tell him.' She might not think she would, but Glass would screw it out of her anyway, needing only to impose the same threat as Hansen. But meaning it. He stood and began putting on his coat. 'It's your problem,' he added indifferently.

'I don't think that'll help.' She rose from her chair and moved nearer to him, her expression coaxing. 'I don't suppose you'd give me back the money?'

He frowned. 'No, I wouldn't.'

She avoided his stare. 'I'd do anything ... make love to you properly, anything you wanted. You *did* ask me.' She looked at the bed and then down at his loins. The stuff of whorishness she had in her was showing. Hansen knew her husband was going to have problems. She wouldn't stay long in the massage and rub-down business when she realized she could just as easily earn the big money on her back. 'All afternoon,' she breathed when he didn't answer. Her cardigan opened as she thrust her breasts forward, her big thighs straining her skirt. 'I could say I was made to stay ...'

'Even if you gave me a signed receipt for my expense sheet,' he said sardonically, 'I doubt if I could persuade my Chief Constable I was doing it for the job.' She was, he saw, a shallow-minded little bitch, a sordid trollop for use by any man forced to buy his love.

When she thinned her lips and coloured at his refusal, he

snapped, 'Get dressed and go on home. Save it for that poor bastard of a husband of yours.'

He left her in the room he had used for exactly twenty-five minutes. When he paid Dobkin on his way out, he couldn't reasonably object to the sly, cynical grin he was given.


Under normal circumstances, Hansen would have put out an *Information Wanted* notice to all Divisions, asking for suggestions as to the identity of the woman known as Sheila Coughlin. Instead, he was forced to telephone to those of his colleagues he could trust not to make an official issue of his request. He also contacted his informants and put them to their scavenging. None of those to whom he spoke knew Coughlin.

He checked the Main Index which listed every name ever coming to the notice of the police, also checking the Missing Persons Register. None of the Coughlins filed in either was female. Then he asked for a name check on the nominal index held at New Scotland Yard's Criminal Record Office. Without a date of birth, he didn't expect an identification and the names he was given didn't raise any hopes that hers would be among them. Women such as Coughlin appeared to be, used aliases as often as they changed their ponces.

He wondered whether Sloan had yet identified the Queensbury Hotel and spoken to Wikker. The feeling that his position was being burrowed into from behind was unsettling.

He telephoned Ann. She had obtained a room in Commercial Road and was moving in that evening, after which she proposed visiting the Double Decker.

'You don't need to,' he told her. 'I know her name. Sheila Coughlin. I shouldn't be long in tracing where she is.'

'But you haven't yet?'

'No,' he admitted. 'But I shall.'

'There's nothing at CRO?'

'Not under that name.'

'You've a description?'

'It'll fit every other woman using your West End.' He gave it to her, suspecting she wasn't too happy with what he had discovered.

He was right. 'I know whores probably better than you, Robert,' she said. Her purpose was still firm. 'Using another

107

name, she can lose herself in the city for months.'

'All right.' Resignation or agreement are the only alternatives acceptable to a determined woman.

He promised he would check her out of the club between ten and twelve, telling her that she wouldn't see him and that she was not to look for him.

She had said softly, 'When are we going to meet again, Robert?', not sounding like an ex-Woman Detective Inspector, or a married woman either, and his hair prickled at the back of his neck. She could turn him on like an electric light-bulb by a change of inflexion in her voice.

'Perhaps when you get back to Commercial Road,' he said. Neither considered their purpose needed discussion. Nor, by an apparent unspoken mutual consent, did either mention her husband.

He had found time to telephone the hospital to ask after Gault. Gault, he was told, had had the operation which, despite its psychological aftermath, was a relatively minor one in terms of the loss of tissue necessary for the body's vital functioning. Gault was said to be comfortable, which meant to Hansen that he was probably heavily drugged and not actually screaming with pain.

# Chapter 12

When he returned to his office after eating a plate of ham sandwiches in the bar of the Bear and Pelican, Hansen found an urgent message for him, timed at seven-thirty. McGluskie wished to see him in his office.

Sloan was seated at the Chief Superintendent's side, the wire trays pushed away to give room to the green file of papers in front of him. Both men were stern-faced and Hansen was not invited to sit. That alone spelled unpleasantness. Neither superintendent was smoking, indicating an official, judicial interview. The atmosphere was loaded with formality; one in which he would be called 'Chief Inspector' or 'Mr Hansen' with a clear requirement that he'd better be formal in return.

The signs were bad for him and he had only the brief time it took for him to walk from the door to the front of McGluskie's desk in which to make a guess at what had gone wrong.

McGluskie pressed down a switch at his side. This lit a red-painted bulb outside his door; a warning that he was not to be disturbed. He opened his file of papers with pudgy nicotined fingers, coming straight to the point of the inquisition.

'Mr Hansen. Did you speak to a man named Wikker at the Queensbury Commercial Hotel yesterday?'

Sloan was watching the detective's reactions closely with his deep-set grey eyes. The quietness of the office was almost complete. Most of the staff had cleared their desks and gone out into the darkness of the streets, only the sounds of remote movement reaching the ears of the three men.

Hansen was a prisoner-at-the-bar again, this time being examined and judged by his colleagues. He said, 'Yes, sir,' keeping his voice expressionless.

'In connection with what?'

'In connection with the identity of the woman photographed with Sergeant Gault.'

McGluskie's lips tightened, the fat fleshy pads around his eyes narrowing them. 'Against my specific instructions that you weren't to make enquiries?'

'Yes, sir.'

'Did you give him five pounds?'

Christ, he thought. Wikker's been bleeding his guts all over Sloan's shoes. He said, 'Yes, I did. I gave it to him in payment for information.'

'What information?'

'About the woman.'

McGluskie made a pencilled note. 'Where is Wikker?'

Hansen looked at him in surprise. 'I don't know. Should I?'

'I thought you might.' The unblinking blue eyes held his.

'Isn't he at the hotel?'

'No, he isn't.'

McGluskie selected a sheet of paper, dropping his eyes to it before speaking. Hansen recognized it as a handwritten statement. 'Mrs Wikker has complained that you called on her husband yesterday afternoon; that after an argument in which you are alleged to have browbeaten Wikker, you forced the money on him for the renting of a room he didn't want you to have; which, he told his wife, you wished to use for an immoral purpose...'

'That's complete bloody nonsense, sir. I...'

McGluskie frowned and held his hand up, palm towards Hansen. 'Please don't interrupt me, Chief Inspector.' He returned to the statement. 'Mrs Wikker also complains that her husband was intimidated by you to such an extent that he left the hotel within the matter of a few hours, completely frightened. She states that she does not know where he is and is extremely worried. Which is why she reported the facts to the police.'

'I say again; complete and utter nonsense, sir.' His features were tightly controlled against his need to shout. 'She's lying. And if she isn't, then Wikker certainly is.' All the frustration and bitterness of being lied about was bile in his throat. Toffler's trial had disproved the naïve sentiment that truth will out. A man could be destroyed as effectively by lies and innuendo as by a knife thrust into his liver. And Wikker's were cunning, well-thought out lies.

'All right, Mr Hansen. We shall know when we find Wikker. You knew him before, of course?'

'Only by reputation. I know that apart from a couple of assaults he's got a clean sheet.'

'Do you know he's on record as a suspected brothel-keeper?'

'It would be difficult to prove he was.'

'Have you tried?'

'No.'

'Why did you want the room, Chief Inspector?'

Hansen's face darkened with anger. 'I've already said that's lying nonsense.'

'Peculiarly enough, this is the same hotel in which Sergeant Gault is alleged to have used a room for immoral purposes.' McGluskie's fleshy features were completely blank, showing nothing.

'There isn't anything peculiar about it. I went there *because* Sergeant Gault had been photographed there. For no other reason.'

'I won't ask you how you knew.'

'Why shouldn't you?' Antagonism was growing between them and Hansen regretted it, for he liked the usually amiable McGluskie. 'I knew because I did some elementary leg-work on it.'

'Yet you paid Wikker five pounds for information you could have got for nothing more than the exercise of this leg-work?'

'I paid him money as an informant.'

'You've put in a claim on the Informants' Fund?'

'No, sir.'

'You paid it from your own pocket?'

'Claiming it would have been asking for trouble.'

McGluskie hardened his voice. 'Did you also pay for the room at the Caulfield Arms from your own pocket?'

Hansen blinked, knowing Sloan would be noting his least involuntary facial twitch, analysing the reasons behind each. Toffler was fighting back as he had promised, having all the advantages of not being encumbered with a conscience about who or what was used in doing it. Nor had he lost any time. Hansen looked at McGluskie's wall clock. Seven forty-five. He had left the Caulfield Arms at about three-thirty. Mrs Liggett had done her stuff with Glass and Glass had done his with Toffler. The only surprising thing about it was Toffler's

111

unexpectedly swift reaction. And its cleverness. It had to be conceived by a more subtle brain than Toffler could boast. Weizsack would be both capable and ruthless enough.

'I did, sir,' Hansen finally said. He wasn't being given any time to do much fighting himself.

McGluskie referred to his notes again. 'You rented Room Seventeen, used it for half an hour with a woman—claiming to be your secretary—and paid four pounds fifty to the owner, Mr Dobkin. You also used the name Jackson and an address in Birmingham. Is that correct?'

Despite McGluskie's impassivity, Hansen could almost read the questions behind his features. From his point of view, half an hour would be just about the time needed for Hansen to get his trousers and shoes off, to indulge himself in what would be called discreditable conduct with the supposed secretary, pay off Dobkin and be back in his office where McGluskie knew he had been working until leaving for the Bear and Pelican. It wasn't an improbable or unfair surmise.

'Yes,' Hansen said. 'The facts are correct. The conclusions you've obviously arrived at couldn't be more wrong.'

'Have you any alternative conclusion?'

'The truth. I was making enquiries about the same woman; the woman photographed with Gault. It was the only way I could do it,' he added, knowing how lame it sounded.

Disbelief showed plainly in the faces of both superintendents.

'From a prostitute, Mr Hansen?' McGluskie asked disapprovingly. 'Alone with her in an hotel room?'

'Who said she was a prostitute?'

'Isn't she?'

'Near enough,' he admitted. He lowered his eyebrows. 'You're not believing me,' he stated flatly.

'I'm not in the business of believing or disbelieving. I'm putting allegations to you.'

'Where did you get the information? A man's entitled to know his accusers.'

McGluskie's eyes chilled. 'Does it matter, Chief Inspector? What matters is that you were alone with a woman—your secretary, you told Dobkin—for half an hour in a hotel bedroom, using a false name and address.'

Hansen remained silent. He wasn't going to be believed and it fed his inner anger. 'Is that all, sir?'

'No, it isn't,' McGluskie snapped, his chins dropping as he glared at Hansen over his spectacles. 'Were you in the Trattoria Napoli at lunchtime today?'

'I was. Has someone complained I was using the wrong knife and fork?' But he knew what was coming.

McGluskie took a deep breath. 'Don't be insolent, Chief Inspector. Did you have a conversation with anyone?'

'Toffler. As you very well know.' And what McGluskie didn't know of his movements wasn't going to amount to very much. He felt he had been walking around followed by a train of busy, note-scribbling observers.

McGluskie ignored the small jibe. 'This is the man who, through his counsel, accused you of perjury and of planting evidence?' He was underlining the paradoxes of it.

Hansen didn't answer the obvious.

'He sat at your table with you?'

'He did. Uninvited.'

'Do you wish to tell me what was discussed?'

Sloan wasn't saying anything, but Hansen could feel his gaze steady on him, attentive to every tic in his face, every change in his expression. He, and not McGluskie, would eventually compile the report on him and Gault; possibly recommending the action to be taken or not to be taken, giving his assessment of the truthfulness of anything Hansen or Gault might say. It would count for a lot either way.

'He threatened to sort me out if I didn't lay off my enquiries. Which, in fact,' he pointed out, 'he appears to be doing through you.'

'H'm. He shook hands with you when he left? Called you "Bob"?'

Hansen drew a deep breath. 'Sir, I've a great respect for your judgement ... but don't tell me you are even beginning to accept crap like that. An act put on by Toffler to embarrass me, probably for just this purpose here today.' His features reflected the incredulity he felt should be held by them all. 'Can you imagine my being friendly with him after what he did to Gault, after what he accused me of doing?' His anger showed now, his eyes dark and hard with small lights glinting in them. 'Jesus Christ!' His voice rose. 'What do I have to do to make any bugger believe me? Kiss asses with a bible in my hand?'

There was a moment's silence before McGluskie said evenly,

'Please control your temper, Chief Inspector, and don't use improper language in this office. We are in possession of information and allegations to which Mr Sloan will eventually need answers. He doesn't propose questioning you in detail about them until he has made further investigations into them.' He paused, choosing his words. 'However, there is one other thing. It has been known to me for some time that you've been associating with a young married woman, meeting her regularly in your flat...'

'Have you been having me followed?' Hansen asked harshly. 'Watched like a bloody housebreaker?'

'You were not being watched by us,' McGluskie said angrily. There were blotches of pink on his cheeks. 'Is my information correct?'

'Yes. You should also know there is nothing in the Discipline Code preventing my being friendly with a woman—married or unmarried—unless it amounts to discreditable conduct.' His face was white now and a pulse throbbed in the side of his neck. 'Which it doesn't, otherwise you would have done something about it before today.'

'These later matters may throw a different light on your association with women,' McGluskie said curtly. It was obvious to Hansen that his senior considered him a promiscuous, oversexed lecher; not very fussy about who he had it with. 'Also, while we may be justified in accepting you as an unattached bachelor, I don't believe a similar consideration applies to Mrs Barsett.'

'My private life is my own concern.' Hansen was calm only with difficulty, but his voice shook. 'Mrs Barsett's husband knows of our association. If he doesn't object to it—and he doesn't—I see no reason why you should.' He looked from McGluskie to Sloan. 'You're being fed a lot of misinformation by Toffler...'

McGluskie interrupted him. 'Mr Sloan knows nothing about Mrs Barsett. The information about Wikker comes from his wife and certainly he knows nothing about that. The allegation of your visiting the Caulfield Arms and your meeting with Toffler comes from an anonymous letter delivered to the Chief Constable less than two hours ago.' Anonymous letters. McGluskie loathed them for the venomous malice they spread, but no policeman could ignore them or dispose of them without checking them out. 'The information in it is already

114

being checked by Mr Sloan. You yourself admit the substance of it.'

'I admit the facts, not the implications.'

'Who was the woman in your room at the Caulfield Arms?'

Hansen tightened his lips, recalling her distress at the prospect of her husband's knowing, the terror he had seen in her eyes. He couldn't throw her to McGluskie and Sloan that easily. She was a cow and almost certainly a liar, but he'd given her his promise. 'I'm sorry,' he said, knowing it would be taken as a sign of guilt, 'but I can't tell you. I can only say that nothing sexual took place. She was an unwilling informant and I forced her to talk, promising her secrecy.' He pushed his chin out. 'I admit you instructed me not to make any enquiries, but it's my neck—Sergeant Gault's too—that's going to suffer. I'm doing nothing unlawful, nothing more than trying to clear our names. I'd considered what I had to do, what I've done, and I'm willing to take the disciplinary consequences. I've submitted my resignation and it's been refused. So,' his eyes took in both men, 'I've got to be honest. I'm going on with my enquiries, orders or no orders.'

There was nothing immediate to be said to that. Then McGluskie sighed. 'You leave me no choice, Mr Hansen,' he said, 'even if only on the basis of your having deliberately disobeyed my orders. I am recommending to the Chief Constable that you be suspended from duty.'

He still felt for Hansen. He couldn't believe what Wikker was supposed to have told his sour-faced bitch of a wife before vanishing; he couldn't believe that Hansen would hire an hotel room to consort with a whore. But facts were facts until he could disprove they were not.

He read to himself the part of the letter referring to it, turning down his mouth in disapproval at having to consider it. *Ask your Chief Inspector Hansen why he booked Room 17 at the Caulfield Arms this afternoon and why he said he was W. Jackson, 34 Sutton Coldfield Road, Birmingham. He pays women to have intercourse with him and a detective shouldn't do this.*

That he had been friendly with Toffler would have been bloody laughable had not the Trattoria waiters been so emphatically believable when Sloan saw them, supporting more than the letter's allegations. *Why did he,* the letter continued, *meet Edwd Toffler in the TRATTORIA NAPOLI today?*

*Why is he so friendly with him? They are in something dirty together and cooking trouble up for someone.* It had been typed on an Adler Gabriele machine with a shaded typeface and signed *JUSTICE*.

That all of it required thoroughly investigating, he had no doubts. And while it was being investigated, he and Hansen would be cast as unwilling enemies. Were it discovered that Hansen had done anything wrong, McGluskie wouldn't move his two-hundred-and-fifty pound bulk an inch to help him avoid the consequences. A corrupt copper was an abomination to him and once he could assure himself he was, he would treat him as if he had contracted syphilis. And, whatever the bleeding hearts who made up the Council of Civil Liberties might think about the police executing justice on their own colleagues, the detective would get his due measure of justice and mercy, neither a milligramme less nor more and nothing but contempt from his fellows. But McGluskie wasn't the Investigating Officer. Having established the substance of the complaints, he couldn't interrogate Hansen on them.

'Do you want to come in, Andrew?' he asked Sloan.

Sloan said, 'Thank you, Arthur,' and then spoke to Hansen. 'I'm not going to ask you about any alleged breach of discipline. I want information. What did Wikker tell you?'

'He confirmed that the name of the woman in the photograph was Sheila.'

Sloan nodded as if he'd known that all along, although he hadn't. 'Anything else?' He smiled encouragingly.

'He thought she worked for Charlie Glass.' When he saw noncomprehension on Sloan's face, he added patiently, 'He's a local ponce. He owns the Olympian Massage Clinic. You'll find the details in Records.' He didn't tell him he would get no information from Glass with anything less than thumbscrews and red-hot pincers. That was something he would find out for himself.

'What about the young lady you questioned in the Caulfield Arms?'

'She told me the Sheila woman's name. At least, the only Sheila she knew.'

'Ah!' Sloan leaned forward. 'And what was that?'

Hansen hesitated, but only momentarily. He was a copper still and he couldn't wholly obstruct another. 'Sheila Coughlin.'

116

'And you know where she is?'

'No.'

'I see.' Sloan was benignly paternal. 'But you are going to find out?'

'Yes.'

'And when you do, you'll tell me?'

'When I do, sir, you won't need telling. The investigation will have folded up.'

When Sloan asked no further questions, McGluskie said, his voice formal, 'All the allegations will be fully investigated by Mr Sloan. I have already given you my orders. Should you persist in your disregard of them, your conduct can do you no good.'

Hansen blamed neither of them for what they thought. They judged him as men for whom Police Regulations were holier than Holy Writ and knowing that whosoever offended against the greatest of them was destined to be cast into an outer blackness.

McGluskie dismissed him with an impatient flap of his hand, dropping his eyes to his desk and starting to make notes, not looking up again. Sloan watched Hansen leave, the benign expression still on his face. It didn't fool the detective for a single second.

Hansen knew that if the Wikkers stuck to their story; that if the Toffler and Caulfield Arms incidents were not revealed in their proper light, as a policeman he was a dead duck. While none of it would probably support a disciplinary conviction, its dirt would smear his reputation and stick to him for ever.

He had been through the wringer and he knew it. His legs felt boneless and he needed a couple of undiluted whiskies. But, if anything, his resolve was stronger than ever.

# Chapter 13

Needing his car for later in the evening, Hansen left it on the cement approach to his garage at the rear of the apartments. It was a dark night, the sky unilluminated by either moon or stars. The footpath he walked along, leading to the front of his apartment block, was little better than a black ravine lit in muddy-brown patches by too few street lamps.

He had drunk his two large whiskies, enough perhaps to turn the crystals of a breathalyser bright green, but not enough to cheer him up. The interview with McGluskie and Sloan had left him with an eroding worry for Ann's safety. Toffler was proving an even more dangerous adversary than he had judged him...

A dark figure, hurrying around the corner towards Hansen, knocked him staggering backwards, falling against him and holding on to maintain his own balance. Hansen's immediate impression was that he was being attacked and he grasped the man's shoulders in his fists, twisting him and slamming him gasping against the wall. The stranger's hat had fallen off, dropping to the ground. His features showed his pain and astonishment and Hansen released his grip on him.

'I'm sorry, old chap,' the man gasped, sucking air back into his lungs. 'So sorry. I was running to catch my bus.'

'That's all right,' Hansen growled. He picked up the fallen hat and handed it to him. 'No damage done.' But he thought him a clumsy sod just the same.

The stranger put on his hat. 'Your tie, old chap.' There was a soapiness about his voice the detective didn't like. He reached out and straightened the tie, then brushed briskly down the sides of Hansen's coat. 'I'm sorry. I've made you dusty.'

Hansen stepped back. 'It's all right,' he said sharply. He didn't like being handled by another man, even a man neatly

118

and respectably dressed as he was, looking as if he'd been licking stamps late at his office. The detective noticed he wore no gloves. The incident bore all the hallmarks of an attempted pocket-picking, having the apparently accidental bodily contact to cover it.

While the man adjusted his hat square to his forehead, Hansen felt surreptitiously for his wallet. It was there. He took in the man's face. He would know him again. He had also taken note of the initials CC on the inside sweat-band of his hat. 'If you're in a hurry, you'd better go,' he said. He wasn't very happy about it, but knew he could hardly interrogate someone for merely bumping into him. And he could be wrong.

'Once again, old chap,' the man said, 'I'm terribly sorry.' He was also too polite to be true. He should have been as irritated as Hansen was.

The detective waited, his face thoughtful, until the stranger was out of sight among the shadows, walking fast; hurrying, Hansen thought, as if to get away rather than to catch a bus.

As he entered the outer door to his apartment, so the wispy smell of smoke from an autumn fire of leaves reached his nostrils. Inside, he could see the dim red glow of light leaking from beneath the bedroom door. He frowned. Norah shouldn't be here. Not two nights in a row. And no *Commodore* left under the light outside for McGluskie to have reported to him. Nor had she collected Trudchen. He had, and she was at his heels, waiting to be fed.

While whoever was in there must have heard him come in, he nevertheless decided on a cautious silence. He closed the outer door quietly, lifting Trudchen into a chair, walking noiselessly over the carpet to the bedroom and swinging the door inwards, tensed for violent movement.

The only illumination in the room came from the four bars of his electric fire that beat the fierce heat of three kilowatts in his face. By it, in the centre of his bed, he saw a dark blue air travel bag with LUFTHANSA stencilled in yellow on its sides. There was a depression in the bed cover where a body had lain.

The door of the adjacent bathroom was open. Through it he could see the hunched figure of a girl sitting on the lid of the lavatory pan. She was leaning forward, her elbows on her thighs, her face cupped in her hands. From what he could see of her in the half-light, she looked very young, untidy and

119

distinctly unhappy. If she was over sixteen years, she didn't look it. Her breasts were too small to show beneath the heavy-knit blue sweater she wore.

He moved to the bathroom door and switched on the light. She looked up at him blearily, screwing her heavy-lidded eyes against the brightness.

'You missed your cue,' he said roughly. 'You're supposed to be flat on your back on the bed with your legs wide open.' He wrinkled his nostrils in disgust at the thought and said 'Christ!'

She looked a very sick girl and, if intended as a *femme fatale*, was a million miles from being it. She was thin with long straight hair the colour of damp straw that fell over pale pointed features. The geranium-red lipstick on her mouth was jammy and smeared from being rubbed. She wore washed-out jeans with the sweater, both dirty enough for her to have lived in them day and night for weeks. The pupils of the eyes looking up at him were sloe-blue and dilated. Her mouth was open adenoidally, her breathing light and shallow. She held wedged between grubby fingers, a half-smoked greenish-coloured cigarette. The smoke from it hung dead in the air over her head. There was a small puddle of vomit in the bath, together with screws of torn-off toilet paper and two wet cigarette ends.

'How did you get in here?' he asked curtly. He was angry again, but with Toffler, not at the girl. She was too fragile, too hopelessly high on cannabis, for anger.

'Wha' you say?' The words hardly made it past her stiff tongue but they were pure Cheltenham Ladies' College. 'I've been waiting ... Bob?' she said, squinting at him, trying to get him into focus. 'You are Bob?'

'Get up,' he snapped. He grasped her thin arm in one hand and lifted. 'Stand.'

She was dead weight and limp and she fell sideways against him. 'Can't,' she mumbled. 'M'legs ... n-numb. Got to wait for B-Bob.' She twisted her mouth in what he took to be a smile, but it was grotesque. 'You smell ... whisky...'

He let her slump back on the pan lid, her eyes closing. 'Who sent you?' he snapped at her.

When he received no reply, he moved to the medicine cabinet to get a phial of smelling salts he kept there. The mirror door of the cabinet reflected his face, showing smears of geranium-red on the collar of his shirt. He stiffened. then frowned and touched the collar with his fingertips. The stains were the same colour as the girl's lipstick, but she hadn't been that near to him. Then he swore vividly because he had let the stranger go without forcing an explanation from him. The collision outside *had* been contrived. He returned to the girl and caught hold of her arms, shaking her until her eyes rolled back from behind the opened eyelids and saliva ran down her chin.

'*Tell me*,' he shouted, '*who sent you?*' He wanted to twist her stupidly-pretty little head from her shoulders.

'Bob ...' Her eyelids closed again and she slurred her words badly. 'B-Bob Hans'n made me c-come. N-Number eighty-two Marnhull Street ... Ap-p-partment three ... said wait for me. W-We'll have a b-ball, he said. J-Jus' go in an' wait ...'

The words that would damn him, planted in her drug-sodden brain. And she'd say them; repeating them again and again until somebody started believing what she said.

She fumbled with dirty fingers at her jeans, pulling at the zip at the side and standing on shaking legs, holding herself precariously with one hand on the cistern. She was a zombie, trying to do something that had been planted in her brain. 'A b-ball,' she said, mumbling in her incongruous schoolgirl's voice. 'W-We've g-got to have a b-ball.' She was pathetic in her insistence, as mindless as if she were under hypnosis.

'You silly little bitch,' he said without heat. 'Stop it. You don't know what you're doing.' He pulled at her jeans and refastened the zip, pushing her back on to the lavatory seat.

'M-My legs,' she whimpered, her closed eyelids staring blankly in his direction. 'Th-They've gone numb...'

He didn't know whether to believe her or not, didn't know what cannabis could do to a junkie's imagination. A planted trollop. It was old stuff with whiskers on it. But effective, Hansen knew, because it paralleled what could so easily happen. Blatant though it was, there was still the faint flavour of a subtle brain behind it. Had the woman planted in his flat been someone like Sheila Coughlin, a down-to-earth tart, the way out could have been easier. Her story would be capable of being broken under interrogation. He wasn't so sure about this young junkie, although she had apparently fallen down on her job of enticing him into a situation where he could be regarded as having been caught *in flagrante delicto*. Christ!, he suddenly thought, What the hell am I waiting for? This had to be timed to explode in his face. He would have been checked into the apartment by a hidden watcher, a telephone call already made to the effect that one Robert Hansen was engaged even then in fornicating in his rooms with an under-age girl shot to the eyebrows with cannabis. And McGluskie or Sloan would be hammering on his door within minutes.

At any other time, he told himself, he would have picked up the telephone receiver and dialled the Headquarters number, asking them to come and collect. It would be madness to do so now after that evening's exposé of himself as the playboy lecher of all time. No it wouldn't, he contradicted himself. He was being bloody stupid. The whisky he had drunk was muddling his thinking. That was his way out. Telephoning was the *only* way out. He almost ran to the handset at the side of his bed, lifting the receiver and waiting for the purring noise of the dialling tone. It never came and he tapped the studs, receiving only the dead sound of a line with no current running through it. He checked the flex. It hadn't been cut. That would have been too crude, too obvious. There would be a fuse apparently blown, or a disconnected wire in the junction box, and neither would ring true as an excuse for not calling in.

He considered running out, leaving her to it and denying he had returned to his rooms, but that wasn't the answer either. It was too late to conceal his having been there. There were a dozen indications proving he had, and he had still to take into account the watcher outside.

It was then that unthinking desperation took over. To be found now with this souped-up manic girl in his rooms, with lipstick on his collar and, no doubt, something nasty and in-criminating planted in a drawer or cupboard, was the equiva-lent of begging on his knees for instant trouble. Already under investigation and ankle-deep in mud that was sticking, this would destroy the last of any credibility he had. He made his decision quickly, realizing that whatever action he took it would be loaded with potential disaster anyway.

He returned to the bathroom. She was either asleep or in a stupor, still sagging on the lavatory pan lid, her legs astride it, her head lolling against the cistern. Gargling noises came from her open mouth.

Putting an arm around her waist, he hoisted her into an

upright position on boneless legs, holding one of her arms behind his neck in a fireman's lift.

'M'arm,' she mumbled without opening her eyes. 'You're hurting...'

He dragged her through the bedroom and livingroom, her legs jerking in spasms as they trailed behind. He opened the outer door and looked along the corridor towards the head of the stairs. There was no movement and he could hear nothing. The extension of the corridor past his door ended in a cul-de-sac, leading only to a storage cupboard.

He unlocked the door to it and lowered the girl on to the floor inside, clearing a space for her among the brooms and tins of polish and disinfectant. He propped her gently against the wall, then returned to his rooms for the Lufthansa bag and the cigarette-end she had dropped on the bathroom floor. He placed these at her side. She was still in a stupor, looking vulnerable and childishly innocent despite the ugly smear of lipstick. Small veins in her closed eyelids showed blue beneath the transparent young skin. She saddened him. Not too long ago, he thought, she'd been somebody's clear-eyed schoolgirl. He could visualize her easily in a straw boater and a gymslip. Now she was a wreck of a girl who hadn't made the transition from the sixth form to the dirty world outside. And the filthy Toffler had, no doubt, helped her along the way.

He put his mouth close against her ear. 'If you make a sound,' he hissed into it, making his voice ferocious, 'I'll come back and break your bloody neck.' Only the twitching of her eyelids showed she might have heard him. He closed the door, locked it and took the key back with him to his apartment.

He moved fast now, turning on the bath taps to swill away the vomit, picking up the pieces of paper and wet cigarette-ends and flushing them in the pan. He stuffed tobacco in his pipe and puffed smoke furiously in the bedroom, using also an aerosol of air-freshener to replace the smell of burned cannabis with the scent of pine-needles. He turned out the electric fire and smoothed the bed cover, then scuffed over the parallel marks of the girl's toes where he had dragged her over the carpet.

In the livingroom, he switched on the record player, then put on side two of Mahler's Seventh, dropping the stylus on to the second Trio of the *Nachtmusik*. He estimated that it would represent at least forty minutes of playing time and nobody *compos mentis* could accept Mahler's Seventh as a background to entertaining a woman. He knew it was the sort of thing McGluskie would notice and he left the lid open. He poured a whisky, sipped at it and balanced the glass on the arm of the chair he normally used, placing an opened book with it. Then he lit the gas fire and sat Trudchen before it.

He undressed quickly, stuffing the smeared shirt to the bottom of the linen basket, taking out the shirt he had discarded the day before and putting it with the clothes he had just removed. His black and gold pyjamas that Norah had worn the previous night, he placed folded in front of the fire with Trudchen.

It was nine-forty and, to anyone interested, he was obviously intending to make an early night of it. From outside, above the Mahler, he thought he heard the banging of car doors. He increased the volume of the record player and stepped into the shower. With the door open, he could just hear the flutes and clarinets of the *Nachtmusik* above the splashing of the water.

Opening the door to the persistent ringing of the bell, Hansen feigned the natural irritation of a man disturbed in the process of showering. McGluskie had brought Sloan with him and both men took in his bathrobe, his wet skin and hair and the towel in his hand. Their eyes showed nothing of what they had expected to see. Even then, Hansen could think dourly that he was supposed to have answered the door zipping up his fly.

His expression changed to one of surprise. 'I'm sorry,' he said. 'Have you been ringing long?' then adding the obvious, 'I was taking a shower.'

McGluskie was the first of the two to speak. 'Can we have a minute of your time, Robert?' They followed him into the apartment.

Hansen hadn't missed that. He was back to being 'Robert' again. He switched off the record player, leaving the stylus in its track, telling Trudchen to shut up her barking.

'Do you want to get dressed?' McGluskie asked politely.

'No. I was going to turn in for an early night.' He indicated a couple of chairs and his visitors sat. Hansen wasn't intending to make it easy for them. He sat too and took a sip at his whisky, resuming the towelling of his hair. Discipline forbade him offering either superintendent a drink, but it didn't mean he had to go without himself.

McGluskie said, 'We've had another complaint about you, Robert.' His voice was neutral, perfectly balanced so that he could shift it to friendliness or official chilliness without any obvious *volte-face*. The eyes of the two men were busy taking in the domestic scene, not blindly accepting it at surface value but evaluating it, fitting the bits and pieces into a logical, acceptable framework. Hansen had seen McGluskie note the position of the stylus on the record and read the title of it on the sleeve placed in position for that purpose.

'Who am I supposed to have screwed now?' Hansen asked sardonically. He put the towel aside and picked up his pipe, tilting it to show the burnt tobacco in its bowl before relighting it. His attitude was that of a man who was irritated but resigned to hear the worst calumnies, not being prepared to scream with worry about them.

McGluskie blinked and lit a cigarette, apparently determined to bear with Hansen's prickliness. Sloan refused one.

'At nine-thirty,' McGluskie said, 'a woman—cultured voice, sounding a bit arrogant—rang in, asking for the Chief Constable. She eventually made do with me.' That was a joke but nobody smiled. 'She said she wished to complain about the conduct of a police officer.' His expression was non-communicative. '*You*, Robert. She's apparently a neighbour of yours.'

'All my female neighbours have cultured voices and are damned arrogant,' Hansen said. 'And nosy bitches to boot.'

'She refused her name and address on the grounds that she *is* a neighbour, that she doesn't wish to be involved in any ill-feeling. She is, she says, fed up with the sight of a police officer entertaining women night after night in his flat...'

'I knew it,' Hansen said, equally without expression. 'She told you about the troop of Girl Guides I keep hidden in the larder.'

McGluskie wasn't amused. Or Sloan either. 'Quote,' the fat man continued. 'She expects something different from a senior Crown Servant. Unquote. She told me that you had a young girl here. A hippie-type who appeared to be about fifteen years, who she saw enter your flat.' McGluskie looked around him. 'And we can see, of course, that that's nonsense.' He waited, a Buddha's inscrutability on his features.

'Yes, you can.' Hansen's ears, sensitive to noises from the

corridor, heard a sound he thought came from the broom cupboard. He rapped the bowl of his pipe against the rim of the ashtray, then scraped out the dottle with a reamer he took from the mouth of a china frog on the table at his side, creating distracting counter-noise. Neither superintendent appeared aware of anything outside the apartment but followed Hansen's smoker's activities with a mild interest. 'But for all that,' Hansen went on, 'you'd still like to look around the place?'

'Your word would be enough, Robert.'

'No it wouldn't,' he contradicted him bluntly. 'Not for you. Not for me either. I want you to look. The kitchen's that cupboard thing behind you. The bedroom and bathroom are over there. And that's the lot.'

He stayed where he was, waiting with Sloan while McGluskie, his manner misleadingly cursory, inspected the rooms. What he missed wouldn't be worth having.

Hansen saw him sniffing in the doorway of the bedroom, his fat nose wrinkling at its amalgam of smells. The detective touched the dachshund with the toe of his slipper. 'If you can still smell it, blame her. She can't always hold out until I get back.'

When McGluskie rejoined them, he appeared to be satisfied. It was the time, Hansen thought, for the girl to come out of her stupor and start pounding on the locked cupboard door or yelling blue bloody murder. But she didn't, and he was even grateful to her for her forbearance.

'Sorry, Robert,' McGluskie said. He didn't sit again and Sloan joined him standing. 'But it had to be done.'

'Yes.' He still felt intractable, still not intending to make it easy for them. He remained as stiff and formal as a man can in a bathrobe and pyjamas, not conceding a millimetre of mateyness.

Sloan hadn't said one word and that could make him all the more dangerous. It needed only one item of Hansen's carefully-arranged tableau of bachelor domesticity to jar his sense of order and logic and to set him thinking and working things out to an obvious conclusion.

Hansen said, 'You can add that complaint to the rest of the crap you are being fed by Toffler.'

'You don't have to tell me, Robert,' McGluskie said mildly, 'but you know I have to check everything out.'

'It'll be a rape job tomorrow; or a complaint of incest or

sodomy. Christ!' he said irritably, 'Just don't go around thinking I'm a bloody sex maniac.'

'I won't, Robert,' McGluskie promised, but they were easily-said words and not necessarily reflecting what he thought at all.

When they left, McGluskie covered his fool's errand with a friendly jocularity and cynicism about complaints from the public. Hansen saw them to the head of the stairs, feeling the almost tangible threat of an hysterical eruption from the silent cupboard behind his back. He returned to his apartment, seeing them leave in their car from behind the curtains of one of his windows. He couldn't spot the unknown watcher who had fingered him to the woman claiming to be his neighbour, but he would be there, ready to report on events. Toffler's organization, his operational efficiency, was good.

Hansen poured himself another whisky. He was damp beneath his bathrobe, not all of which was from the shower. That hadn't been a pleasant interview. Not with the manic girl in the cupboard waiting to go off like a ticking bomb.

He dressed quickly and took the key to the cupboard with him. He opened it swiftly and stepped inside, switching on the single bulb hanging from a hook above.

She was still squatting on the floor, her forehead resting on her bent knees, the long dirty hair concealing her face. The utter immobility of her made him touch her shoulder in sudden apprehension, then pull her head up from her knees to reveal the dusky plum-coloured flesh, the staring dull eyes, the trickle of thin vomit from between her mauve lips.

There is only one quality of deadness and she had it. It reached out to Hansen and squeezed his heart with cold fingers, shocking him into an unmoving numbness. Jesus Christ! Jesus Christ!, his brain was saying, his features twisted into uncomprehending dismay. He thought that fate couldn't have dealt him a dirtier blow.

He forced his finger and thumb to enclose the thin wrist, feeling for a pulse he knew wouldn't be there, but ready to grasp at miracles. Then he felt under the sweater, the back of his hand beneath one of the ridiculously small breasts, for any murmur of a still pumping heart. For that moment, when all hope for a merciful miracle had gone, he hated her for dying; for landing him even deeper in the dirt. There was anger and resentment in him for his predicament. He wanted to shout at the ceiling of the cupboard, 'Thank you, God! Thank you for bloody nothing!'

Through the partly-open door, he heard the soft footfalls of somebody mounting the stairs from the floor below. He knew his own face would be ash-grey, his eyes staring his anguish, and that he couldn't confront anyone without immediately provoking their concern or suspicion. He switched off the light and closed the door, holding it tight by the handle.

Whatever it was that left the body after death—a new-born ghost, a phantom extrusion of bewildered release—was with him in the stifling blackness of the cupboard. It and the growing smell of vomit in the closed-in space left him shuddering while he fought his stomach's need to vomit itself as he listened for the approaching footsteps as another might the approach of the hangman.

# Chapter 14

The tubercular-thin high-yellow girl with the Afro hairstyle, the sweating shiny face and purple mouth, sang *Bien ... bien ... bien* into the hand microphone, jerking her body in an accelerating crescendo of simulated orgasms, her eyes rolling back in their sockets. Behind her, a black man swayed on his stool as his fingers picked out the music.

The room was in a shaded half-light and foggy with cigarette smoke. The brass disc in the floor was covered by the shuffling feet of a dozen couples dancing. The small tables in the deeper shadows of the perimeter of the room were each lit by a blue-tinted bulb and occupied.

Two women sat at one with drinks in front of them. One was plump, without discernible charm and unlikely to be mistaken for a photographer's model. The other was strikingly different. Her smooth gold hair was long and dropped down over her shoulders. Her fine-boned beauty had been made tartish by the glistening pink paste on her mouth and a vixenish green colouring around her eyes. Artificial lashes, thick with mascara, hung over them like small black fans. Her fingernails were painted a dark bronze. She wore a bright orange blouse pulled taut behind a wide leather waistbelt to outline and emphasize her pointed breasts and a brief white skirt that exposed her long legs and thighs. A silver-metal ankh symbol hung heavy from her neck and she wore a thin chain around one ankle. Her aphrodisiacal perfume reached out through the cigarette smoke. She was a brilliant bird-of-paradise, plumaged to provoke the lust of any male who imagined himself good enough. Some had already thought that, but were finding she was a difficult woman to convince of it.

The woman with her wasn't enjoying the unflattering contrast of the company that had been imposed upon her, but stayed because nobody else was likely to buy her drinks.

It was late when Toffler pushed his way through the crowd to the bar, followed closely by the albino Ash. A cheroot hung from his mouth and it stayed there as he spoke to people. He acted as if he owned the place.

Ann was loose-lipped, showing all the symptoms of having drunk too many gins. When Toffler passed her table, she laughed. It was as penetrating and vulgar as her perfume and it rang clear above the noise of the negress singing.

Toffler looked around, saw her and halted. He put his spread fingers on Ash's chest to halt him too. The big wheel, exhibiting his eminence.

'I know you,' she said, slurring her words, staring at him insolently through the fringes of her eyelashes. 'You're Ed Toffler.'

He walked across to her, standing over her so that she had to look up at him. He took her in, matching her own insolence, from her glossy hair down over her body to her crossed thighs.

''Ello, doll,' he said. 'You're new aroun' 'ere. You've 'eard of me?'

'My husband told me about you.' She giggled. 'He also told me to stay away from you.' She drank from her glass, emptying it and replacing it on the table.

The tight-stretched skin of his face creased in a grin. 'An' 'oos your 'usband?'

'I'm thirsty,' she said to the plain woman with her, ignoring Toffler. She opened a white patent-leather handbag. 'Are you going to have another?'

Toffler reached his hand across and snapped it shut. ''Ave this on me, doll.' He looked pointedly at the other woman and jerked his head in dismissal. She rose immediately and left them. He picked up Ann's glass and sniffed at it. 'A double gin an' Martini for the lady, Ashy,' he said to the albino, 'an' a big brandy for me.'

'You've got a bloody nerve.' She put a cigarette in her mouth and lit it, screwing her eyes against the smoke. Toffler watched her do it, open admiration on his face.

He took the departed woman's chair, mashed his cheroot in the ashtray and tilted the lampshade so that the blue light illuminated her features. ''Oos your 'usband, doll?'

She pushed her hair back from her face. 'Denny.'

'Denny 'oo, doll?' He had been drinking brandy and she could smell it on his breath.

She curled her lips. 'You don't know him?' She made the words derogatory, belittling his ignorance. 'Denny Garvey.'

'Oh, *'im*. I've 'eard of 'im. 'E's inside.' He regarded her thoughtfully. 'I di'n't know 'e 'ad a wife.'

'Well, you know now.'

'Why did 'e tell you to stay away from me?'

She laughed, blatantly provocative, showing her pink tongue.

He stretched his mouth in a grin, a small spark of annoyance in his eyes. 'You tell me, doll,' he said softly. 'Don' 'ave me drag it out of you.'

She hiccupped and said, 'Pardon me,' then, 'Where's that effing drink?'

He pulled the cigarette from her fingers, looked at the lipstick-smeared butt and put it between his lips. *'Tell me, doll.'* There was menace in his voice.

'That's for tasters,' she said owlishly. 'Your lot.' She giggled again. 'It was a joke, I expect, but Denny said you'd chase anything wearing nylon stockings.'

'It ain't no joke, doll.' He looked pointedly at her legs. 'You'd better watch out...'

The albino approached the table and put down two glasses. Without taking his eyes from Ann, Toffler said, 'Look after yourself at the bar, Ashy, an' wait for that 'phone call.'

While she lit another cigarette, he scrutinized her. 'An' that's why you been warned off me?'

'Don't get into a muck-sweat,' she told him scornfully. 'You're shopping at the wrong stall. I've got enough on my plate with Denny.' She scowled as if the thought of the absent Denny had unpleasant undertones.

He wasn't accepting anything she said about her non-availability. Women, he knew, liked to put it on for the first time of asking, but they all ended up begging for it.

'Denny mus' be a good bloke,' he said virtuously. 'I wouldn' like 'is wife to get into trouble. There's characters in 'ere you can' trust.' He sucked at the cigarette he had taken from her and swallowed the smoke, keeping it in his lungs with the toughness of a man used to the harsher tobacco of cheroots. 'You really married to 'im?' he shot at her.

She sipped at her gin, her expression scornful. 'Would it ever make any difference to you?'

He grinned. 'No, it wouldn'.' He inspected the butt of the cigarette, then licked at the lipstick ring around it. 'You tas'e nice, doll, an' you're a looker. I could eat you.' Women came easily to him. His forceful brute masculinity was a challenge to those who wanted their sex raw and dominating. He was big-framed and powerful, his looks vulterine and predatory, his reputation as a womanizer drawing them to him.

'Wha's your name?' he asked.

'Ann.'

'Ann what?'

'Never you bloody mind.' She looked at him frankly, taking in his narrow-waisted Italian tweed suit, the wide-striped shirt and embroidered tie, the chunky jewellery on his wrists. 'My,' she said mockingly. 'You are with it, aren't you?'

'You ain't so bad yourself, doll.'

She examined his lean, sun-tanned features. 'Are you like that all over? Or is it out of a bottle?'

'Why don' you find out? I'm always willin',' he leered. 'I di'n't get it in prison, that's for sure. What are you doin' while Denny's inside?'

She looked down at her fingernails. 'Being a good girl and keeping out of the way of characters like you.' She lifted her eyes to his, taunting him, but letting him know that characters like him might not always be so avoidable, that she wouldn't need to have her arm twisted to take an interest in him.

When he read into it what he wanted, he put an arm around her waist and momentarily she stiffened. 'Naughty,' she said lightly, and pressed the glowing end of her cigarette on the back of his hand.

He jerked his arm away violently. 'You lousy cow!' he growled. 'I ought to clout you one.'

'Try it,' she said coolly. 'But keep your bloody maulers to yourself.' Then she smiled seductively, bringing him back to the bait again. 'At least until you can prove you're a better man than Denny...'

He looked at her incredulously. 'A better man!'

She shrugged her shoulders. 'I suppose you think the gin and Martini makes you one of the big spenders.' She curled her lips, needling him, digging away at his arrogance, blowing hot and cold with him.

He pulled a thick wallet from an inside pocket and tossed

it to her. ' 'Ere, 'ave a dekko at that, doll,' he said. 'Money talks don' it?'

She opened it out, feeling it warm from his body and concealing her distaste. It was fat with ten- and five-pound notes. 'Yeah,' she replied, pushing it back at him. 'It could. As long as it's not all talk and no do.'

His eyes darkened, the lids hooding them. 'There'd be plenty of do. Christ Almighty, there would be. You could bet on that.' He grinned satyrishly at her and lifted his glass, gulping the brandy. 'Le's me an' you dance, doll.' He reached across and pulled her from her chair.

His dancing was crudely sexual; both his flattened hands pressing against her buttocks, forcing her helpless against his body. She held her own hands in front of her, protecting her breasts from the pressure of his hard-muscled chest. She needed all the control she could dredge from behind the few gins she had drunk not to tear her fingernails down his loathsome face. He was her intimate enemy, the filthy brute who had crucified Bill with his boots. And she must never forget it. She couldn't believe he didn't see the glow of repugnance behind the fringes of her outrageous eyelashes. The animal smell of his sweat and the cloying scent of the deodorant he used to disguise it, sickened her as they shuffled between the other dancers. She twisted her head to avoid the brandy- and cheroot-smelling mouth from attaching itself to hers, but unable to stop it nuzzling moistly at the side of her throat. But, in the body contact between them, she had felt more than his animality; a hard bulge lodged at his waist and concealed beneath his buttoned jacket.

When the music stopped and she made it back to the table before he could prevent her, she knew she was going to need all her feminine ingenuity to keep him from trampling her like a bull, and it chilled her. She was glad of the presence of Hansen outside, watching for her, a warming glow against that chill.

The albino was waiting for Toffler and she heard him say, 'No dice, Ed,' and saw Toffler's scowl. Then he said, 'Talk to me about it later. Get some more drinks.'

She said, 'No. I'm going.' She opened her handbag and took out her lipstick.

'I'll take you 'ome, doll.' He was still sweating, his narrow face shiny with it. 'You ain't safe on your own.'

'Like bloody hell you will.' She was sharp with him, smoothing fresh paste on her mouth with her little finger while he watched her hungrily. 'If Denny found out...'

'Well, Denny won' find out,' he sneered. 'The stupid bastard's inside an' I'm 'ere.'

'He's got friends.' She shook her head, putting away the lipstick in her bag. 'Anyway, not tonight. It wouldn't be any good. Perhaps tomorrow.'

'You're sure, doll?'

'No, I'm not. How can you be sure with a thing like that? You'll have to take your chance. I'm not sure yet that I want anything to do with you.' She was beginning to feel like the hard-faced, mercenary bitch she acted. 'Just remember to bring your wallet along. I don't only go for wop suits and pretty neck ties.'

'You're a doll,' he said admiringly. 'I'll be 'ere, wallet an' all. An' it's jus' as well. I got a little job on my 'ands tonight I'm waitin' to 'ear about.'

Outside, not looking for Hansen but conscious that he was checking her leaving, she waved down a passing taxi. When she was back in her room in Commercial Road, she flung off the wig and clothing that were suddenly hateful to her. Just wearing them, she felt, had impregnated her personality with a touch of the tartishness she had adopted to deceive; as if, as an actress, living the part so intensely that off-stage the character hadn't all been rubbed away with the greasepaint. She scrubbed herself furiously in the bath, ridding her body of the last repellent smell and touch of Toffler's pawing and kissing.

When she was clean, she dressed and replaced the wig, dialling Hansen's home number from the call-box in the hall. She needed to talk to him to remove the imprint of Toffler's grossness from her mind. She dialled several times, receiving only a 'disconnected' signal. Then she went to bed to think about him.

Bill had been in hospital for over two months now and her body ached for a physical release. She realized now it could never come from her husband; that she didn't want it to. Hansen disturbed her, and she knew she wanted him to make love to her, wanting the latent desire she had recognized in him to ride roughshod over the residual doubts that reminded her that she was Bill's wife.

# Chapter 15

The footsteps continued up the stairs to die away in silence, then the remote bang of a closed door in the apartment above. Only the rapid pulsing of his own blood remained in Hansen's eardrums. Taking the Lufthansa flight bag with him, he left the cupboard, relocking the door on the dead girl and walking the short distance to his apartment, his feet dragging as if wading through wet cement.

Inside, he sat sombre and brooding in his chair. Whisky was no longer enough and he needed a clear brain for the things he had to do. Thinking under the pressures of another's death was difficult, his claustrophobic few minutes with the girl's body obtruding in his mind, the damning presence of it tied around his throat like a throttling noose. He remained in his numbed trance for a long time, but feeding Trudchen her biscuits during it and, as mechanically, percolating coffee he forgot to pour and drink.

He rationalized the theme of her death to an acceptable level; one he could accept without a dragging sense of guilt. He hadn't killed her, hadn't even been responsible for her dying. No one man had unless, indirectly, it had been Toffler. She had killed herself with the dried leaves and seeds of a plant; by her own weakness and neglect, by nobody in authority giving an effective damn about who supplied people like her with narcotics, even finding apologists for its legal use. She was as certain a cardiac case as he had ever seen, possibly helped on its way by the inhalation of her own vomit. It could happen so easily. At first, he had thought she might have been asphyxiated by a lack of air in the closed cupboard, but the wide crack beneath the door and at its hinges reassured him that he had not been responsible.

He pulled open the zip of her bag and checked through the

135

contents. Two rolled-up dirty handkerchiefs, a packet of seven Kensitas cigarettes, all coloured green, a small bottle of cough linctus that Hansen knew contained the tincture of cannabis in which the cigarettes had been soaked, and two paperbacks —a Solzhenitsyn and a Jean-Paul Sartre. He raised his eyebrows. He himself rarely dug into literature any deeper than Raymond Chandler or Dashiell Hammett. Sometimes a Jonathan Ross. A paper wallet held a few photographs of people like herself, a leather purse contained ten new pound notes— her Judas money, he guessed—and some loose change. There were no documents concerning her identity. She was a nothing, a nameless homeless wanderer who had had the curse of *Cannabis indica* in her veins.

He had examined the lock on his outer door. The tongue showed no signs of being scratched. That meant either a duplicate or a skeleton key had been used to open it. The how of what had been done seemed unimportant anyway.

All this checking was the automatic reflex of his professionalism, masking the need for him to do something about the dead girl. He was close enough to a fatalistic mood in which it seemed proper to turn her over to McGluskie, to accept submissively whatever consequences came his way. He was close enough, but not quite. It wouldn't help her. It certainly wouldn't help him. It wouldn't help to nail Toffler either. Toffler would have been far too cunning to allow himself to be connected with a homeless, drifting junkie. An untalking dead one could be no more dumb than Toffler would. *You clever bastard, Hansen,* he told himself bitterly. Digging himself deeper into the manure pit with his ineptness, needing little help from anyone to do so. Everything he had so far done had been twisted to his disadvantage and used to vilify him, dirty his reputation. He needed only a plague of boils to be a latter-day Job.

He shook himself out of his black mood and went into the bathroom, splashing cold water over his face, then swallowing five Paracetamol tablets and to hell with his kidneys. Examining himself in the cabinet mirror didn't make him any happier. Strain had scribbled tiny red bacilli in the whites of his eyeballs, the lines from his nostrils to the mouth corners were deeper and his skin had acquired a yellowish tinge as if marinaded in nicotine. He needed a shave. He also needed, he told the haggard reflection, some Divine assistance; for God to be on his side for a change; something which, for him, had been noticeably lacking, although Toffler shouldn't be complaining.

He switched off all the lights and, in the darkness, thumbtacked a double thickness of blanket over each window facing into the street. It might discourage the watcher outside to think him gone to bed. Then, switching the lights back on, he percolated more coffee and drank three cups of it, smoking his pipe and thinking out what he was to do.

When it was midnight and the side-street lighting automatically switched itself off, he changed his shoes for a pair with soft crêpe soles and put on his overcoat, pushing his gloves in the pockets. He needed his hands to be bare.

Outside his apartment, in the corridor, he was certain he could feel the psychic presence of the girl waiting behind the cupboard door. It was a sad, lonely emanation. He took the Lufthansa bag with him, leaving it concealed near the rear door before stepping into the narrow alley and rounding the block into the street. Keeping to the shadows, he walked soundlessly, a patch of darker darkness moving from doorway to doorway, examining each car parked against the kerb the length of the street.

When he saw one with a blacker mass than emptiness behind the windscreen, he pulled open its door. The courtesy-light came on and illuminated two men, both blinking, startled by his sudden appearance.

'Are you looking for me?' Hansen was angry, all the repressions of the day's frustrations coming to the surface, his voice thick with them.

The man in the passenger seat, recovering from his surprise and recognizing the detective, said 'Shag off,' with all the insolence of a Toffler-employed thug. He was thick-set and brutal with a pushed-about nose that made him an ex-pug. He survived mainly on his reputation as a boxer. Unfortunately for him, the detective had never heard of it.

Hansen made a savage rasping noise in his throat. He shot his left arm out like a piston and grabbed a handful of necktie and shirt front, jerking the man out like a cork from a bottle, his shoe catching on the door sill, leaving him suspended helpless in Hansen's grasp. The enraged detective lifted him upright, slashing the muscled edge of his open palm across the man's bent nose, doing it no good at all, flooding blood down into his opened mouth. At the same time he released his hold on the shirt front and the man fell back across the bonnet of the car. A foot kicked at Hansen and he grabbed it, pulling its owner sliding from the bonnet to thump soggily on to the footpath. He allowed him to stagger to his feet, then chopped him hard on the side of the throat. A pink-and-white horse-shoe of plastic teeth flew from his mouth and he made a hoarse whistling noise, collapsing on to his buttocks, spewing liquid down his torn shirt-front and into his lap. His eyes, agonized and fearful, never left those of Hansen.

The second man in the driver's seat had made no move to help his companion; had made no move at all other than to put and keep his hands in plain sight on the steering wheel.

'You don't have to hit me, Mr Hansen,' he said quickly. He was a small man, discovering that spying wasn't only sitting comfortably on his backside in a warm car. 'I'm only the driver. Please...'

Hansen, breathing heavily, his anger not yet appeased, wasn't so sure. He reached into the car as the man flinched and seized a personal radio transmitter from between the two seats. It was switched on, emitting a crackling hum, and he wrenched the aerial from it, throwing both back into the car.

He spoke to the driver. 'Get,' he snapped, 'and take your friend with you. If you come back again tonight, I'll get out of bed and give you the same.'

The man on the footpath was scrabbling in the dust for his false teeth. Hansen moved over to him and stamped his shoe on to his gorilla's hand, pinning it to the ground, leaning his one hundred and eighty pounds to keep it there.

'Just a minute,' he said. 'You didn't say you were sorry.'

The man glared at him, then groaned. 'Sorry? Whaffor?'

'For telling a police officer to shag off.'

He groaned again. 'I'm buggered ... Oh, *Christ!* ... I'm sorry.'

'That's better.' Hansen had changed the man's mind for him by screwing his shoe around on his flattened hand. 'I'll know your face again, friend. When you get back, tell Toffler to send someone a little more polite next time.'

He released the hand and the man, clutching his denture in the other, stumbled into the car. It took off fast before the door had been slammed, its rear bumper catching the bumper of the next vehicle and rocking it, turning the corner with its tyres squealing, leaving rubber on the road.

Hansen collected his car from the hard-standing and drove it quietly, the engine only ticking over, to the rear of the apartments. The building was in darkness and quiet with the heavy breathing of sleep. He wedged the entrance door open and ran noiselessly up the stairs.

Opening the cupboard he lifted the body of the girl, holding one arm beneath her shoulders, her legs flexed at the knees over the other. Her face had none of the contentment of the quiet dead. She was beginning to stiffen with the onset of *rigor mortis* and time was becoming horribly telescoped for him. He shuddered his revulsion at the pressure of the cooling flesh against his, the feel of the bony ribs beneath the woollen sweater. Her head lolled and the unseeing eyes appeared to be looking back yearningly at the cupboard they had just left. He swore, the eyes reminding him of what he had forgotten. He turned back and bent his knees, allowing her buttocks to rest on the floor to take some of her weight as he groped for the cigarette-end.

He back-heeled the door shut and jog-trotted down the four flights of stairs, his heart pounding with the effort of holding the girl in his straining arms. In spite of her growing stiffness, her limbs flopped disturbingly He couldn't begin to imagine what he would do were he to meet anyone. His actions were instinctive now, needing to get the body as far away from his rooms as the rest of the night would allow him. At the end of the hundred miles he felt he had carried her, he laid the girl down inside the door and swung his arms, easing the trembling ache in them. Somewhere above him, he heard a door bang. He could only hope it was a restless sleeper getting aspirins or wanting a pee. When he heard nothing more, he moved.

The night air chilled the sweat on his flesh as he checked the alley, then opening the rear door of his car and tossing in the flight bag. He returned for his burden, lifting her again and carrying her down the steps and on to the rear seat. He placed her sitting in a corner, covering her from the waist downwards with a tartan travelling rug. At a casual glance she might be thought a silent, preoccupied passenger, but Hansen knew it would have to be so carelessly casual as to be unlikely. He couldn't—he thanked God—see her himself in the interior mirror. But, before starting, he reached over the back of his seat and closed the lids of her staring sightless eyes with the ball of his thumb.

There was little traffic about and he was confident he was not being followed. Once, during the drive through the town's streets, he heard fluids moving in the girl's body and he stopped to make sure the miracle hadn't happened. It hadn't, and he knew he had been a fool even to consider it.

He drove blindly with no clear plan in his mind, only hoping he would be able to think of something before time ran out, that fate might relent and give him some sugar as a change from the shit he had been getting. It was just as important for him to get back to his rooms. The evidence of her having been there, of her dying in the cupboard would be written in capital letters for any scenes-of-crime detective detailed to run the rule over the apartment. And that could easily happen if McGluskie was fed any further venom by Toffler.

He took a back road out of the city, his headlights cutting clean holes of brightness in the dark night. He was at his highest risk until out of his own police district. His car was known and would be remembered if seen at that hour of the night. Nor dare he stop while in a rural area where a stationary car was always worth a check by a conscientious village constable or a traffic patrol car crew.

And always, he felt her sad presence behind him. It seemed that he had known her all his life; that there had been no remembered time when he had been living free of her.

He decided against dumping her in a field, leaving her to be found fortuitously the following day. They were still too near the city in which she had died and Toffler would get to hear of her finding; putting the facts together and coming up with implications dangerous for the detective. Nor could Hansen accept the mutilation of her face and fingers that would be caused by the gnawing of small animals and insects. He had considered dropping her body from a bridge into an open rail truck, but couldn't accept that either. She would be disfigured and this would cause distress to her parents were they traced and asked to identify her. He cursed the dead girl for being so intransigent a problem. And himself for being more squeamish about dead flesh and tissue than he had imagined.

He turned the car into a slip road, entering the southbound lane of the motorway, pressing his foot on the accelerator, reaching and keeping the speedometer needle on seventy.

When the white Rover overtook him, the STOP-POLICE sign on its roof flashing red, his heart squeezed itself into momentary panic. He braked fiercely and swerved over to the hard shoulder of the road behind the police car. He waited, fighting the fear that put sickness in his stomach, that sent messages of flight to his brain. The constable approaching him would not know who he was, Hansen now being many miles outside his own district. But he may have received information by radio with instructions to stop him. Anything could have happened since he left. He may have been seen carrying the girl's body to his car. The man who had been watching him, who he had dragged from his car outside, may have reported what he knew about the girl entering his apartment.

'Your nearside rear obligatory light, sir,' the constable said through his opened window. 'It's not working.'

Hansen climbed stiffly from his seat and followed him to the rear of his car. He banged the red glass with the heel of his hand and the light came on. 'It's done that before,' he explained. 'I'm sorry. I'll get it fixed.' He found it difficult to articulate from his wooden lips.

'Right, sir. May I see your documents, please?'

They were standing at the side of the car, Hansen not daring to look, but feeling the dead girl to be plainly visible, her livid face to be peering from the inner gloom, distorted and doom-laden for him. He wanted to vomit.

When the constable had finished examining his documents, he handed them back and said, 'All in order, sir. Please accept an official caution for failing to show two obligatory rear lights . . .'

'Thank you,' Hansen mumbled and forced a smile to his face. It was a dreadful parody of one and the hardest thing he had done that day. *Why didn't he go? What's he waiting for?* 'I'm sorry,' he added.

The constable flashed his torch into the car's interior and Hansen's heart contracted, feeling the blood leaving his face. He heard all sorts of irrelevant sounds as he stood, paralysed of all movement; the approaching rumble of a lorry, the far-away mewing of a hunting owl and the nearer ticking noise the radiator of his car was making. Even the metallic click as the constable's thumb released its pressure on the button of his torch.

'Goodnight, sir.' The constable saluted and left him.

Getting in the car without glancing in the rear seat was the second hardest thing that day but he did it, driving from the hard shoulder into the slow lane; watched, he knew, by the constable and his co-driver. He drove for six fast miles in a cold sweat of fear before he lost the patrol car. Then he checked over his shoulder, not being able to see the girl and not daring to stop. When there were no other vehicles within hundreds of yards, he groped with his hand behind the seat, feeling her still body on the floor where it had slid forward and fallen when he had braked. He let his breath out slowly. That had been something useful she had done, if nothing else. Once again, he felt absurdly grateful to her. But what wasn't so useful was that his name, address and car registration number had gone into the constable's notebook.

He was thirty miles along the motorway before he found the answer. The service centre parking area contained more heavy transports than cars, some standing well away from the brightly-lit cafeteria. He drove towards the transports, parking between two of them, then walking with controlled casualness to the cafeteria where he bought a plastic beaker of coffee and a wrapped slab of fruit cake. While he drank the coffee—his gorge rejecting the cake—he scrutinized the parked transports through a window. Only one of them appeared to be neither sheeted down nor carrying a locked container. This exception was loaded with huge grey cement pipes.

When he had finished his coffee, dropping the beaker and the cake into the disposal bin outside, he returned to his car. From there, he moved to the pipe-carrying transport. On the door nearest to him, he read, *P & J Dean Ltd., Bogmoor Road, Coventry 17.* The lower layer of pipes was within his reach, their ends open.

When there was no movement in the parking area, he lifted the girl from his car and carried her to the back of the transports. He did it quickly, not hesitating and with the confidence of a man doing something entirely normal, sliding her head first into one of the pipes, then pushing at the soles of her shoes until she was hidden from sight in the shadowed interior. The Lufthansa bag and the half-smoked cigarette he threw in after her.

Her face had been dusty from the floor of his car and her jaw had dropped to reveal her dry teeth and tongue. He felt

142

keenly that he was deserting her, leaving her to an unknown fate.

She was unlikely to be discovered until the pipes were unloaded and the unarguable inference would be that she had climbed in there for a lift anywhere between Coventry and where the transport finally finished its journey.

She would be circulated low key in *The Police Gazette* as an unknown female found dead, possibly illustrated with a photograph of her taken at the mortuary which nobody could possibly recognize. With any luck at all, her last sad little ride wouldn't interest the newspapers enough to rate more than the briefest of mentions. Nobody was going to worry about her a fraction of the amount he had.

Pulling out of the parking area, keeping away from the pools of light, the thought that he was abandoning her to a lonely journey remained with him, as if an emanation from her was reaching out and touching his brain with a ghostly finger. Their lives had touched as briefly and as tragically as two drivers involved in a head-on collision. She had been the one to die, to leave a trail of debris behind her that he now had to clear up.

Leaving the motorway, Hansen found an unoccupied layby and parked in it. There, as best he could, he cleaned the rear seats and floor of the car, disposing of the vomit-stained rug by pushing it into a water-filled ditch at the side of the road.

After garaging the car, he did another search of the street fronting on the block of apartments. None of the parked cars was occupied, nor any doorway.

Because he knew what the Home Office laboratory scientists could do with their spectrographs and binocular microscopes, what a fingerprint searcher could identify from only a few ridges left by a sweating fingerprint, he eliminated every trace of the dead girl from his rooms with the precision of a professional in scenes-of-crime searches.

Working quietly, conscious of the sleepers above and below him, he cleaned the broom cupboard of the debris of her occupancy. The sweepings from the floor that would contain hairs from her body and head, the fibres and dusts from her clothing, he took back to his apartment.

He rubbed a cloth hard over the surfaces of all doors, over the bed and every other piece of furniture she might have touched and left fingerprints, putting his own back on. The total absence of prints would point suspicion at him just as surely as finding the girl's would. He did the same to the vitreous china surfaces in the bathroom and to the painted walls. He shook and brushed the bed cover over the bath, removing his clothing and doing the same to that. Adding the floor dust from the cupboard to it, he turned on the taps, swilling away the fibres and dusts, the shed particles and powders of the dead girl's presence.

Then he searched the rooms, finding concealed in a drawer a tiny aluminium tube of brown dust that looked like snuff but wasn't. There was nothing original about the planting, but it remained highly incriminating. He washed the cannabis down the hand basin. His lipstick-smeared shirt he scissored into small fragments and flushed down the lavatory pan. It was a good shirt—one of his striped Louis Philippes—and he did it with reluctance.

Finally, he checked his telephone and its connections. The junction box cover had been unscrewed and removed and a wire pulled from its socket. Nobody could prove it hadn't been done accidentally.

That he hadn't been able to check Ann out of the Double Decker was now the lesser of his worries, but he thought about it nonetheless.

It was four o'clock when he took another shower and sat in his chair smoking; exhausted, but unwilling to believe that he could find it in himself to sleep. But ten minutes later he was, his pipe dropping from his nerveless fingers to the floor, the embers sending up tiny tendrils of smoke from the burning carpet until they too went out.


For Gault, there was a clouded waking to the vapourish grey light giving a slow solidity to the interior of his room, a sharper audibility to the tiny remote sounds from the outer ward.

Already there was an aching need in him to urinate, to surrender his helplessness to the nurse's fitting of the gourd-shaped, rubber-flanged bottle over the thing of which he was now ashamed. There would follow the pain of the renewing

144

of the stale bandages, the stabbing needle in his buttock and the swallowing of the capsules that would send him back to his twilight stagnation.

He prayed often, most times praying to die in his sleep. He was desolate even before the day had properly begun. When he felt the nurse's cool fingers on his wrist, timing his pulse, he closed his eyes and prayed again, asking for, willing a response to her woman's flesh.

It was later, lying drugged and almost defeated, that he heard the voices; sibilant, hateful whispers from behind the bedhead. Voices that stopped abruptly when he twisted his body painfully to look. At first, he couldn't understand the words, but as the hours passed he did. Filthy obscenities, remote but audible, about *her*, and about Ann; about his emasculated sexlessness; sometimes in Toffler's voice, sometimes in Sinter's. He answered them, baffled and angry, until the nurse hurried in to soothe and quieten him in his growing madness.

But the voices came again as soon as she had gone, this time whispering insinuating doubts about the need for the amputation of his testicles. A conviction grew in him that he had been the victim of a dark conspiracy, a suspicion that they were hidden somewhere, pickled in a jar of formaldehyde because he knew that was how they kept the severed trophies of their scalpels. It was the thought that the symbols of his lost manhood were to be exhibits for the sniggering inspection of doctors and nurses that made him rise, weak and trembling, from his bed. He shuffled silently to the window overlooking the long fall to the yard below and scratched feebly at the unmovable catch, then smashing angrily at the glass with a plant pot until the nurses came running to pull him away.

# Chapter 16

That he could put on a public face of normality, despite the traumatic and illegal disposal of the girl's body weighing on his conscience, surprised Hansen. But, for all his outward insouciance, she remained no less a burden to him than when she had rested in the broom cupboard.

He was checking through the teleprinter carbons at his desk, searching for any circulation made about her being found, when the Deputy Chief Constable sent for him.

In the penumbra of his guilt, it would have shaken him more had he not been expecting his suspension; had he not known, anyway, that McGluskie would have questioned him earlier about any suspected connection with a dead girl.

Returning to his office, Hansen read the Notice of Suspension with which he had been served. It was addressed to him and signed by the Deputy Chief Constable. In between, in fine detail, it told him that a report had been received from which it appeared that he had, *prima facie*, committed a disciplinary offence, i.e. disobedience to orders, and that he was hereby suspended from membership of the constabulary and from his office as Constable; that during his suspension he would be paid an allowance of two-thirds of his salary and that he might not resign or retire without the consent of the Chief Constable.

It wasn't the end of the world to be served with it. It wasn't fun-making either. Its object was to limit his activities, to stop him interfering with Sloan's investigations. Only, Hansen decided, it would do neither. He folded it in three and put it into his pocket.

As he reached out a hand to lift the telephone receiver and dial Ann's number, the bell rang and it was her.

Although the words were formal her voice was warm, reaching out to him like the pressure of loving fingers. 'Is it all right to speak on the telephone, Robert? I've some information about T.'

'No,' he said. Damn her, he thought. Why did just the sound of her voice, mechanically reproduced as it was over a cable, do things to his breathing. It held the shadow of his being committed to one person and he didn't want that again. 'Where are you?'

'Here, at home.'

He considered it for a few moments. 'I'll come to you, Ann. Can you give me half an hour?' It was, after all, he told himself, a cold workaday morning and no occasion for a repeat of the temptations of his previous visit.

He finished checking the teleprinter carbons. There was nothing from any other force about the finding of the girl. Nor was there any complaint of an assault occasioning actual bodily harm on a male citizen occurring at ten past twelve that previous night in Marnhull Street. He hadn't expected there would be. Toffler would have no sympathy for his inefficient hireling and a complaint could tie him in with the planting of the girl.

Hansen locked his personal papers away, minuting the current crime files back to McGluskie for re-allocation to other detectives. Henceforth, he would be a man apart, a man infective to good order and discipline. His colleagues would speak to him, but carefully. Good careermen had an inbred fear of being judged guilty by association. He would not be allowed to touch an investigation or make an arrest as an agent of the law. He had been stripped of the buttons and badge, of the little protection his status had afforded him. It was ironical that as a private citizen he would be able to claim as many privileges, possibly more, and be less subject to harassment and criticism.

He did a quick check on the records for any known pickpocket with the initials CC. There was nothing. The man smearing his shirt with lipstick was either that rare bird, an unconvicted pickpocket, or had stolen the hat in which Hansen had seen the initials.

Ann opened the door to his ringing, wearing a high-throated blue dress. Her small nose wrinkled and she showed her beautifully white teeth in a warm smile for him. He stepped inside the hall and she held his hand, pressing it with a natural familiar intimacy. He followed her into the room with the remembered smell of coffee fresh in it and she took his coat.

'You look tired.'

He felt tired too, but he smiled. 'I had a late night.' He couldn't tell her he had failed her in not checking her out from the Double Decker. She had obviously survived the experience without damage.

'I tried to call you. There was something wrong with your telephone. Did you leave the receiver off?'

'I found a wire loose when I got back.'

Each was conscious of the other's regard and their eyes hadn't broken contact, the affinity between them an almost tangible current. Their words, Noel Coward-ish and brittle, were said awkwardly, quickly, to conceal their consciousness of a deeper feeling.

'How about you?' he asked.

She busied herself with the percolator, pouring coffee into the tiny gilt cups while he sat. 'You didn't exaggerate about Toffler,' she said. 'He's a disgusting and dangerous brute.'

She told him of her contrived meeting with him, of their conversation, with the accuracy and dispassion of a police-woman giving evidence in a court.

Hansen winced inside as he listened, the dark green acid of jealousy eating at his stomach. That rubbish like Toffler should touch her with his hands was bad enough: that he should so blatantly seek to defile her with his filthy body was sickening. It was with difficulty that he kept his features impassive.

'I couldn't get on to the subject of the Coughlin woman,' Ann was saying, 'but I shouldn't imagine it would be difficult next time. I think,' she added, 'he was carrying a gun.'

'Oh?' That surprised him. It wasn't the sort of recklessness he would associate with the cunning Toffler. 'What makes you think that?'

'When we were dancing.' A faint shadow of repugnance darkened her face. 'I felt it at his waist. Possibly tucked behind the trousers. And he kept his jacket buttoned.'

Hansen didn't like that either. Any thought of her close contact with Toffler, particularly in such a sexual activity as a dance, added to his hatred of the man. 'But you're not sure?'

'No. It could have been a knife, but I don't think so. It

didn't seem long enough and it was chunky.'

He sipped his black coffee and thought about it. 'Do you know when he'll be at the club again?'

'Tonight,' she said carefully. 'I'm meeting him there.'

He scowled. 'Please don't go,' he urged her. 'Leave him to me. If he's stupid enough to carry it again, I'll sort him out on my own.'

'I'm sorry, Robert. I've got to see this through. In any case,' she pointed out, 'I can let you know definitely whether he has the gun or not.'

'If you have to.' He was liking Ann's part in cultivating Toffler less than he ever had. He made up his mind that there wouldn't be anything after tonight. The blonde tart was going to die as suddenly as she had been born. 'You'll bring him outside where I can do it?' Carrying a gun wasn't the most serious crime in the statute books, but it might prove the straw to help break Toffler.

'I'll do that, Robert. He's supposed to be taking me home.' She laughed incredulously. 'I'm his idea of a woman who's fallen for him hard.'

'Not you,' he said glumly. 'It's Ann Pardoe who gave him that impression.'

'There's no danger inside the club,' she assured him, 'but get him away from me outside.' She was serious. 'He frightens me, Robert.'

'I'll get him away,' he promised. 'One way or another. Don't worry about that end of it.'

'I won't. Not now.' She had implicit faith in his ability to do it.

'If he has the gun on him, carry your bag in your right hand. If you are not sure, in the left.'

She nodded.

'And carry an aerosol of hair lacquer in the bag. It could help if he gets nasty with you in the club.'

'I've something better,' she said. 'A pepper gun.'

'It's illegal,' he told her. He knew the sort of thing she was referring to. It would be a pen-type gun, spraying a pepper-gas from a cartridge and harmless in its effects. But capable of stopping a man short in his tracks. 'A woman was fined here a couple of years ago for having one in her handbag. There never has been any justice for a person wishing to defend himself.'

'You don't think I should have it?'

'Of course I do,' he said fervently. 'It makes me happier. But I hope you won't have to use it.'

'So do I, Robert. Was there a job pulled in the city last night?'

'Not that I know of. Not a big one anyway. Why?'

'Toffler mentioned one to the white-haired man he calls Ashy. He said he was waiting to hear about it.'

He shook his head. 'No, I don't know.' But he did, of course. While he couldn't hope the failure of the girl's planting had given Toffler a sleepless night, it might have angered and mystified him.

When he stood to go, she stood with him. She said nothing but everything was there in the deep green of her eyes, in the outgoing tenderness of her expression.

They came together and although he held her tightly, almost desperately, he only touched his mouth gently to hers, more affectionately than passionately and with none of the bite of his aroused sexual excitement. And that had cost him an effort, for to have her in his arms, her belly and thighs hard against his, burned him into a sudden straining need for her. Not since the early days of his marriage had he felt so intimate with a woman, so wanting to be a part of her.

She pulled her mouth from his, her voice shaky. 'I'm sorry, Robert, but I think I'm in love with you. This time of the morning too.' Her eyes were reading his face, looking for answers, for assertions: looking for what women wanted to see in men's eyes when their bodies are separated from the ultimate intimacy of flesh only by thin fabrics.

He said hoarsely, 'Christ, Ann!' There wasn't much a man could say when a woman had said that to him out of the blue. 'Ann...' He tilted her chin and kissed her again. Her mouth was soft and pliant and he felt the strength going from his legs, the resolution from his mind. She made music for him and it thundered in his head like a Wagnerian crescendo of pounding chords.

'You don't mind my telling you? I ... I realized I did last night.' She was anxious, needing to be assured with his words that she wasn't on her own. She laughed nervously. 'I tried to get you and couldn't. I suppose for a woman that's a good enough reason.'

'Darling Ann,' he said, the endearment coming awkwardly,

'I don't know ... but you do terrible things to my breathing.'

She shivered, closed her eyes and put her mouth blindly over his in a fierce and hungry kiss.

And as he tasted the sweet juices of her mouth, he felt the tip of her tongue exploring between his opened lips. He knew that if the arrangement of hormones had anything to do with the explosive compulsive attraction of two people, each for the other, then he and Ann were the exemplars; that a thousand nights might not be long enough to burn out his physical and emotional needs for her. He felt suffocated by her and the thought of her husband having fed on her flesh brought with it the black bile of jealousy. What he couldn't—wouldn't—admit to himself was that he might love her.

Suddenly he pulled his mouth free from her. 'Ann,' he said from deep down in his chest. 'It's no good. We can't.'

She opened her eyes and searched his face. 'Please, darling. What's wrong?'

'There are too many complications. We're neither of us ...' He jerked his head in frustration.

'You mean Bill?' She moved herself even closer to him as if to overcome his misgivings with the promise of her body. The perfume of her flesh was heady.

'Yes, I mean Bill. He's a consideration.' Yet all his body wanted to do with this desirable woman in his arms was to love her physically to the exclusion of that very consideration. He was already wishing that he had never met her. It was all too fast and too intense for him and he felt he was getting out of his depth.

'Sweetheart, isn't he *my* problem?'

'Unfortunately he's mine too,' he growled. 'Remember? He's a fellow copper. There's a loyalty ...'

'*No.* There isn't and I'm not going to let you say there is.' Her eyes were enormous and close to his. 'Bill ... Bill hasn't been faultless. Don't make me say it, darling, but my own loyalty has to be judged by his ... and where does it end ... ?' There was a small desperation in her voice. 'I love you, Robert. I'm not ashamed to say it. I'm a woman and that cuts across every loyalty I have. What I'm doing for Bill with Toffler is my loyalty as a wife ... not as a woman. I'm not prepared to give up my only chance of happiness ...'

'Ann!' He was forcing the reluctant words out, his body wanting her to dissuade him of their meaning. 'He's so helpless. I shouldn't even be doing this. It's wrong and we know it is. He's a colleague ... a cripple in a wheelchair! He's unable ... he can't even hit me, Ann. Not if he was fit and well. That would be a disciplinary offence. Christ, Ann! We *can't*!' She shook him with her intensity and he didn't want to be involved with an intense woman. His mind was in conflict with his body and he wasn't sure which would succumb.

Her open mouth was searching for his. 'Damn you, Robert,' she said fiercely, 'don't be such a bloody martyr and...'

The sudden peal of the door chimes startled them into immobility. 'No,' she whispered pleadingly in his ear. 'I won't answer it.'

'You'll have to,' he said, not certain whether to be glad for his conscience's sake or to curse the fate robbing him of her at the moment of persuasion. 'My car's in the road. Whoever it is will probably recognize it and know I'm here.'

The chimes sounded again and he said, 'Hurry, Ann. This isn't the last day in our lives.'

She straightened her dress and hair and checked her appearance in the mirror near the door. She looked as if she had been made love to, but she left him without further protest.

He put on his coat and sat in a chair, placing his opened pocket book and a pen on the arm of it. The let-down was physically painful and he felt malevolent towards the unknown caller. Then he heard the bass rumble of Sloan's voice and he swore aloud. He picked up the book and pen and went into the hall.

Sloan's eyes showed he wasn't surprised to see him, having obviously noted his car outside. It was an unfortunately timed call for Hansen.

Ann was asking him to call again later in the day.

'No,' Hansen interrupted her. 'I'm just going, Mrs Gault.'

'Ah, Mr Hansen,' Sloan said. 'I didn't know you and Mrs Gault were friends.' He was holding his hat in his hand, his shrewd eyes going from one to the other.

'We aren't particularly,' Hansen said curtly. 'I'm here interviewing Mrs Gault about her husband.' Either way, his answer was going to do him no good at all. To admit to a friendship was as good as putting himself in bed with her. The choice was between two evils and he chose the one least harmful to her.

Sloan looked from the detective to Ann, digesting Hansen's

admission that he was making enquiries while under suspension, but not letting it mislead him. He said mildly, 'I see. Which is what I've called to do myself. Perhaps you'd be good enough to see me when I've returned to Headquarters, Mr Hansen.' He looked at his watch. 'Say, at midday?'

Hansen moved outside and spoke to Ann. 'I'm sorry if I've embarrassed you, Mrs Gault. I'll explain to you on some other occasion.'

Sloan would have been a fool not to have seen the anguish in Ann's eyes or the wretchedness behind Hansen's stiff features, and nobody had ever accused the superintendent of being that.

# Chapter 17

Loyalties, Hansen thought, were awkwardly restricting loads to carry around. Nor were they anything that could be shed lightly. Their roots had their birth in the formative years of his life and were part of him like his hair, throwing out more and more shoots to encompass the added responsibilities of progress. Roots could be extirpated and their stems allowed to die, but this was never a comfortable thinning-out.

How much loyalty, he put to his conscience in self-interrogation, could he uproot, leave to wither, in his growing physical and emotional need for a brother-policeman's wife? Could it be diminished—justified—by a knowledge of its object's own disloyalty? Or Hansen's strong suspicion of it? He had few doubts now that Gault had things to hide. The loyalty that had sent Hansen unhesitatingly to his support in trouble, pushing aside regulations (which in itself was a disloyalty to his profession), courting suspension and getting it, was distinct and separate and not under assault by his conscience. He was committed to that by a sense of injustice and he had no regrets.

These were the questions Hansen asked himself without coming up with satisfactory answers, with no placebo of justification. Although he could argue that he knew Gault only as a Crime Squad Sergeant detailed for a special assignment, a man not of his department; not as a friend but as an occasional colleague, he knew these were equivocations.

*Thou shalt not commit adultery; but, if thou shalt, never ever with the wife of a subordinate officer.* It wasn't specified in Police Disciplinary Regulations as such and, like other heinously unspeakable crimes, had no need to be. That it undermined discipline and good order was enough: that it could only result in trouble of the first magnitude with dismissals and postings and humiliation trailing in its wake was inevitable.

Ann was no casual urge to carnality for him. Had she been, he could have got it out of his system by concentrating his need on Norah. Although he fought it, he thought he could be falling in love with Ann, believing that without her, life would be grey and bleak. He wanted to be with her; to touch her, smell her, even just look at her. On the small screen of his mind that was his visual perception, he could recreate the memory of the deep-green eyes, the small nose that wrinkled at him, the sweetly curving mouth. He could convince himself he had never visualized Norah thus; that she had given him only a transient need that expended lust cancelled out.

No scientist can put a label to love, define it or assess its destructive potential to those affected by its fall-out. Hansen knew only that Ann was in his bloodstream like a potent narcotic; not an addiction he had sought but which had infected him unawares. Infatuation, affection, sexual need; these separate manifestations of maleness were the pale flickerings of emotion against the arc-light flare of the deeper, intenser passion which was the amalgam of them all. His cerebral side recognized that if this was love, it was too apocalyptic an emotion for peace of mind; that it left him vulnerable to again being savaged by a woman.

Sloan patently suspected a sexual attachment (he would call it an improper association) between him and Ann, although he had confined his almost monologic interview with a stiff, unco-operative Hansen to informing him that his admitted interview with her was to be the subject of a report to the Chief Constable; a further disciplinary misdemeanour to be added to the indictment already prepared against him.

He was uncertain, dithering in his doubts, about the wisdom of returning to Ann and facing the issue she had raised, when the telephone rang. His caller bristled the hairs on the nape of his neck in immediate antagonism.

'Alfred Weizsack here, Mr Hansen. I'm sorry to call your private number but I understand you aren't available at your office.' He made it sound as if he knew why and he probably did.

Hansen said, 'No, I'm not,' and waited.

'I wondered if you would do me the courtesy of calling to see me?' The mellifluous, cleric's voice was warm. He could have been an old friend telephoning. 'At my office, of course.'

Hansen's first reaction was to say 'No', to be bloody-mindedly offensive, but that, he knew, was self-defeating. Keeping his distance, keeping himself incommunicado from his enemies from a sense of outrage at being ill-used, wasn't going to help him at all. At the least, it could prevent his knowing what tactics they might be considering. On the other hand, Weizsack could be laying a bait designed to embarrass him further. His was the choice and he chose engagement.

'What about, Mr Weizsack?' he asked.

'Ah, something that could be to your advantage, dear boy.'

'And yours, of course?'

'Yes, indeed,' the solicitor agreed good-humouredly. 'Otherwise I would hardly be calling. So can I expect you?'

'This afternoon is clear for me. Will four o'clock suit you?'

'Thank you, dear boy. I will be waiting.'

Hansen recradled the receiver thoughtfully. A call from his wife—unimaginably unlikely—could not have been more astonishing.

Weizsack would never be thought altruistic or charitably-minded even by his closest friends. Perhaps by them even less so. Obtaining his *Legum Baccalaureus* with Honours, he used his encyclopedic knowledge of criminal law to the uttermost limits of its inadequacies. His object was necessarily money, for it could never have been justice. At its most pettifogging, his was a need to defeat it. The law, while he yet used it, was an enemy. Ethics were things he charged his opponents with lacking. Applying them to his own uses would have crippled him. Justice, as he saw it, was for the man with the fattest wallet, able to employ the most nimble, plausible lawyer; one possessing the ability to refute and confuse facts with specious oratory, to diminish adversaries by accusation as fools or rogues. In short, one Alfred Weizsack, LL.B(Hons). Because his mind sought some form of self-justification, he measured the police against his own yardstick, and believed he recognized self-serving villainy in them all.

Struck off the Solicitors' Roll for embezzling from Clients' Accounts, he had served the year of his eighteen-months' sentence as an apprenticeship in cultivating profitable contacts in the criminal world. Toffler had been one of them. Supposedly employed now as a managing clerk, he wielded in fact—if not in name—a dominant interest in the firm of Soderman, Soderman and Fewler. His erstwhile partner, Fewler, even more elderly than Weizsack, was content to have him practise in his name while he emptied his daily bottle of malt whisky, uncritically signing documents put in front of him and receiving his share of the fees. Which were considerable.

Operational criminals fed money to Weizsack as law-abiding citizens would to an insurance company. He maintained accounts for them, and when they were unavoidably imprisoned or on the run there were standing orders for their families, for their women and spending money for themselves to ease the rigours of a cell. When necessary, and when the security was good, Weizsack subsidized their activities against future profits, taking over their negotiable loot at a usurious percentage, acting as a legal Fagin.

He made his home telephone number available to them to allow for succour for night arrests. He provided a barrister, his crony Sinter, on permanent standby. They worked together like Rosencrantz and Guildenstern. It was not unusual for him and Sinter to hold rehearsals, mock courts, with their clients in trouble, the barrister acting as a devil's advocate to iron out any inconsistencies in their defences. Weizsack was a criminal lawyer in both meanings of the term. That he was accepted by the courts as being competent to instruct counsel under the paper-thin fiction of acting for Fewler, that he could continue to practise, underlined the fact that he took his stance permanently on the blind side of Justice.

It was difficult for Hansen to understand why he wanted the money that went with it, and what he did with it when he got it. He hadn't a spendthrift wife; he didn't gamble, drink heavily or womanize. He lived in a small converted park lodge and if he had more than two suits—or one that wasn't ash-sprinkled and threadbare—he kept them permanently in his wardrobe. His car was almost as old and as unfashionable as his suits. He smoked his daily fifty Players Weights down to the last centimetre of stub, handing them out as meagrely as if they were *Ramon Allones* Cuban cigars. He drank one half-bottle of Portuguese wine a day with his economy-priced businessman's lunch at the Old Ship Hotel. Because he was in his sixties, he was able to sleep under the same roof as his equally elderly housekeeper without inviting innuendo and rib-nudging from those who knew.

At the time of his trial, his bank balance was proved to be

only just teetering over the edge of being in the black and he had refused utterly to account for the disposal of the large sums he was charged with embezzling. He would undoubtedly have received more than his eighteen months but for the emphasis placed by his counsel—Sinter in this case (and it marked the beginning of their association)—on his undisputed mitral valvular disease and his consummate acting as a broken old man only a couple of cardiac seizures away from death.

With his lion's mane of shaggy white hair, his benign ecclesiastical features, the naïve and unbitten could afford to believe him to be an engaging old reprobate. Hansen hadn't a sufficient depth of credulity or enough sheep's wool to be pulled over his eyes to see him as anything but what he was. That he supplied the thinking processes for Toffler's activities, Hansen had no doubt. That he should want to speak to the detective might be the preliminary rumblings of an approaching storm.


At three-fifty, Hansen locked the door to his apartment. He inserted a hair pulled from his head between the door's edge and frame, resting it on the tongue of the lock visible in the narrow space. He left the building by the front door, entering his car standing at the kerb and driving away without a sideways glance.

After making sure he was not being followed, he returned by a circuitous route through side streets to the rear of the apartments. He walked quickly through the back doors and mounted the stairs silently to the rooms he had just vacated.

The hair remained undisturbed in the lock and he let himself in, locking the door after him and removing the key. He kept well away from the windows overlooking the street.

Then he lifted the telephone receiver and dialled Weizsack's office number. 'I'm sorry, Mr Weizsack,' he said, keeping his voice low, 'but I've had to call in at Headquarters first and I won't be able to get away yet. Would five o'clock suit you?'

'Certainly, dear boy,' Weizsack said. He would probably accept he was telephoning from Headquarters, but it didn't matter now if he didn't. Hansen considered it too late for anyone to alter the timing of the events he guessed had been laid on.

He replaced the receiver and waited. When it rang a minute

later, he let it ring. It might be Weizsack checking. He couldn't be sure and he would only know by answering it. When it stopped, it occurred to him it could have been Ann and he cursed himself for not chancing it. He had the need in him to be with her; a need far from being wholly carnal. To have talked to her would have gone some way to easing his deprivation. Now he had nothing to do but to sit and wait and think about her. He dared not smoke and that was a deprivation too, but he sucked tobacco-tasting air through his empty pipe and for ten minutes watched a rectangle of weak sunshine crawl slowly across the carpet like thin golden lava, listening to the afternoon's traffic noises floating up from the street.

When he heard footfalls in the corridor, he put his pipe down and stood. The quietness of the room was broken by the confident rapping of knuckles on the outer door.

Hansen moved swiftly and soundlessly to stand with his shoulders against the wall behind the open inner door. After a few silent seconds there was more knocking, then the slight chinking and scrape of metal on metal as the lock wards were turned. He heard whispering and footfalls going away towards the head of the stairs. The door handle, needing oiling, squeaked as it was turned, briskly as if whoever it was twisting it was in a hurry to get in, then the sound of the door being closed gently and a fumbling with what Hansen imagined to be a wedge to prevent a surprise entry.

He waited until the intruder was in the room, looking around and getting his bearings. He pushed the open door away from him, shutting it with a heart-stopping bang. The man with his back to him jerked in shock and swung around.

'Looking for me, Ash?' Hansen said. The mere sight of the albino rasped strips away from his composure.

Ash's mouth dropped open, his tongue wagging. He was momentarily stunned, not sure of the evidence of his senses, sudden pink staining the translucent paleness of his face. His eyes glittered behind the dark glasses. He put his hands in the pockets of his belted raincoat, then clamped his colourless lips together.

'Are you looking for me?' the detective repeated harshly.

Ash's head turned, seeking a way of escape, his body held tight and ready to move when his mind willed it.

'The only way out is past me,' Hansen said. He smiled mockingly, then stood in front of the door. 'Why don't you try it?'

The albino's lumpy shoulders twitched and he sucked in his stomach. 'You'd better let me go,' he said. His voice wasn't much above a whisper and he emanated deadliness.

'Who sent you, Ash? Toffler? Weizsack?' He had obviously come to check on the missing girl, but this was something Hansen couldn't ask him.

'I don't know what you're talking about. You invited me here.' Despite everything Ash represented to Hansen, the detective noticed that he spoke well and with none of the uneducated uncouthness of Toffler.

'And you've witnesses to prove it, I suppose.'

'Yes.' The albino had paled back to his normal complexion, his eyes never leaving those of Hansen.

'I asked you to pick the lock as well?'

'I didn't pick it,' Ash whispered. 'I knocked. You let me in.'

'All right. So your accomplice picked it.'

'I haven't an accomplice. I'm on my own.' He was all controlled venom, but he was grinding his back teeth, the jaw muscles bulging. 'You're trying to fix me, Hansen. You'll find it's your word against mine.'

'You worry me.' Hansen was wary now. The albino was like a white-furred animal with a twitching tail, preparing to spring. 'I'll pick him up outside after I've taken you in.'

'You're not taking me in.' The words hissed out and a thin line of bubbled spittle appeared on his lips. 'You're not even a copper now...'

Hansen realized without too much surprise that there was going to be violence, that Ash could even kill him. His hatred of policemen, the humiliation of Hansen's outwitting him, could be the catalyst driving him to a frenzied savagery. Nor did Hansen himself wish to take the albino homosexual in like a led sheep. Not believing, as he did, that Ash had been with Toffler when Gault was mangled and destroyed as a man.

He moved sideways, his eyes fixed on Ash, lifting the telephone handset, its cord trailing as he returned to cover the door. He held the heavy base hooked on his little finger and started dialling the Headquarters number.

Ash withdrew his hands from his pockets. Over the knuckles of one clenched fist was a heavy brass stunner. It was a murderous weapon, capable of exploding the teeth from the detective's jaws or splintering his skull. With his other hand, he removed his sunglasses, tucking them in his breast pocket. He

160

was methodical, not hurrying, but not slow either: a man very confident of his ability to do a professional job and looking as if he was going to enjoy doing it. His uncovered eyes were a luminous glowing pink, vicious and hating.

Hansen spoke over the mouthpiece of the receiver. 'Take that thing off, Ash.' Although he was now angry, his face white and his eyes a dark orange, he was poised and supremely confident, knowing what he had to do. 'You're in trouble enough without adding to it.' Then he ground out his dislike of the homosexual. 'You poove...'

The call signal was sounding in his ear when Ash came at him fast, mouthing incoherent obscenities.

Hansen watched the brass knuckleduster flashing dull yellow in an arc but already moving forward inside it and, as it thudded numbingly on his shoulder muscle, stiff-arming the base of the handset with stunning force into the albino's face. The blow jarred and wrenched his arm, flinging Ash backwards, a bone cracking loudly over the meaty sound of impact and bringing, almost instantaneously, blood welling from the ruin of his nose and mouth.

Ash's arms flailed empty space, his fading brain willing them to hit at the detective, but they swung aimlessly as he fell backwards on his heels, smashing into a table before falling to the floor, unconscious before he hit it.

With the receiver still pressed against his ear, Hansen heard the switchboard operator saying, 'Police Headquarters. Can I help you?'

'Yes,' he said calmly, 'you can. Detective Chief Inspector Hansen here. Put me though to the Operations Room.' He was surprised the instrument still worked. There was a gaping split in the casing of the base and, through it, he could see the silver domes of the bells and the tangled wiring. Some of the plastic fragments were missing and he couldn't see them on the floor. They could be in Ash's face. He was prepared to guarantee that as Toffler's *force de frappe*, the albino hadn't much future.

When the inspector answered him, Hansen asked for an escort to be sent to collect an intruder he had found in his rooms, telling him that if both ends of Marnhull Street were sealed off, Ash's accomplice might be picked up. He added that Ash should be taken to the Hospital Casualty Department for treatment en route.

When he replaced the receiver, he moved Ash from where he was bleeding on the carpet to an area of uncovered floorboards. He clipped handcuffs on his wrists and searched him. He was twitching in the pit of his unconsciousness, his breathing liquid through his smashed mouth. It wouldn't be very many minutes before he opened his eyes.

There was nothing in the wallet Hansen took from his pocket to identify him, nothing to connect him with Toffler. It contained a pad of photographs of nudes; young men with prominently displayed buttocks. Hansen's nose creased in disgust. 'You filthy bastard,' he growled at the unconscious man.

He returned to his chair and filled and lit his pipe, waiting and wondering not very traumatically what McGluskie and Sloan were going to make of it.

# Chapter 18

Weizsack offered his hand when Hansen was shown into his office and the detective took it. Dissembling like a bloody politician, he thought sourly. The hand was warm and friendly, the thumb pressing some sign which Hansen recognized but to which he did not respond.

'Sit down, dear boy,' Weizsack said, beaming. The blue tinge of his disease was discernible on his lips. The wrinkled greenish-black suit he wore could have been profitably thrown out some time before World War II as being out of fashion. Its shoulders and lapels were sprinkled with dandruff and cigarette ash. His shirt looked a prison issue and his bow tie was greasy and limp. One arm of his spectacles had been repaired with white adhesive tape. To Hansen, he was a man patently old enough, or wealthy enough, to afford to be uncaring of his appearance.

His office went with him. It was low-ceilinged and dark. A row of faded green Halsbury's *Laws of England* and an untidy pile of the *Solicitor's Journal* filled a shelf behind him. The walls were a dirty cream, more or less embellished with coloured prints of Victorian judges and barristers-at-law. Stacked in a corner, sombre and neglected with accumulated dust, were several large black deed boxes. His desk was a chaos of pink-taped documents, loose papers, uncleared tea-cups and unemptied ashtrays.

He picked out a packet of cigarettes from the jumble, hesitated and waved it vaguely in Hansen's direction.

The detective shook his head. 'No thanks. I smoke a pipe.' His expression was neutral. 'But I'd prefer you switched off the tape recorder before we start.'

Weizsack looked shocked, the cigarette packet frozen in mid-air. 'Mr Hansen,' he protested, 'I assure you ...'

'I know you do,' Hansen said calmly, 'but switch it off just the same, please.'

Weizsack shrugged and pulled open a drawer in his desk. 'No offence, dear boy. It saves me making notes.' He shook his head. 'You've a very suspicious nature.'

'Yes, I have.' Hansen stood and looked into the drawer, waiting while Weizsack pressed a piano key on the machine, seeing the tiny ruby light darken and the revolving spools halt. 'Thank you, Mr Weizsack,' he said and sat again.

The solicitor lit his cigarette, blowing out the match and putting it carefully aside as if intending to make use of it for another purpose. 'Ah, yes. Well, first of all, dear boy, I can assume, I believe, that we both have the interests of justice very much at heart. And in that respect, it shouldn't surprise you to know that I have the highest admiration for you both as a man and a policeman.' The dishonest flattery came out smoothly and sincerely. 'I have watched your career with the greatest interest...' He waited, beaming goodwill.

'I'm glad,' Hansen said drily. 'I wouldn't have guessed it.'

'Ah, we are poor judges of our own condition, dear boy. You may imagine, therefore, how much it distresses me that we seem to have found ourselves in, so to speak, unhappy opposition.'

Hansen wanted to laugh aloud. Weizsack couldn't be expecting him to believe this oratorical lawyer's slush. He was too clever, too cunning.

'Isn't it in the nature of things?' he said. 'I'm employed to bring criminals to justice; you, apparently, to get them off the hook.'

'True,' Weizsack agreed, as if Hansen had said something profound. 'But need we be enemies in the process?'

Hansen said nothing.

'I'm an old man, dear boy, and a sick one.' He knocked a fist on his chest and coughed. 'I wouldn't want to leave this world having enemies.'

Hansen smiled tightly. 'Now wouldn't appear to be a good time to leave it then, Mr Weizsack. I don't think Sergeant Gault feels very friendly. Nor I, for that matter.'

Weizsack shook his head, looking like a bishop saddened by man's wickedness. 'You misunderstand—I fear deliberately— the principles motivating the role of defending lawyers. A client's interests are sacred to me, as they are to all my legal brethren. You don't blame me for putting them first?'

'I'll reserve any comments about that until I've seen my solicitor,' Hansen said nastily. It didn't please him that Weizsack should treat him as if he were a naïve bumpkin.

Weizsack laughed silently, his shoulders shaking. '*Touché*, dear boy. You're a clever one, if I may say so.' But the watery blue eyes were cold and unamused.

'If you think I am.' He shrugged away his momentary irritation.

'But I do. Only prejudiced, dear boy. And a perfectionist, too.' He shuddered ostentatiously. 'You are probably murder to live with. Somebody,' he said earnestly, 'has to represent a man like Mr Toffler. Would you have him thrown defenceless to the mercy of a jury? With no one to put his version of the facts to the court? When I consider the tremendous weight of the Crown's organized investigational and scientific expertise pitted against that solitary, unfortunate individual in the dock ... such men need a champion, dear boy, and, unworthy as I am, I do my poor best.' He smiled, seemingly at his own phrasemongering. 'Anyway, we are living in an amoral society. And who is going to care about Mr Toffler's guilt or innocence in ten years' time ...'

'I am,' Hansen interrupted him, uncompromising. 'What did you want to see me about?'

'Of course. Forgive me. I love the law and an old man wanders.' He shuffled the papers in front of him. 'I understand you are in trouble as a result of the line of defence adopted by our good friend, Mr Sinter? That you have been suspended from duty?'

Hansen showed his teeth. 'Nothing that isn't going to be remedied.'

Weizsack looked doubtful. 'Ah, dear boy. I wish I possessed your sublime confidence. From where I am sitting, it appears to me that you have been harshly treated by your superiors.' He waited for an answer and when it didn't come, resumed. 'Which brings me to the point. It *is* possible in this imperfect world of ours to, ah, negotiate agreements; to—can I put it?—arrive at a mutually satisfying compromise.'

'You mean you want to do a deal? That you're prepared to advise Toffler to retract?'

'Oh, he couldn't *retract* what he sincerely believes to be true. But he can adopt the position of not pressing the complaint.

I understand it needs a statement in writing from him, even though he has already made it verbally under oath before one of Her Majesty's Judges in open court.'

'I see. This would include not pressing the frame-up against Sergeant Gault?'

Weizsack looked pained. 'A frame-up? My dear boy! A solicitor, a counsel, needs must accept the instructions of his client in good faith. It would hurt me should you believe otherwise...'

'Does it include him?' Hansen interrupted, disregarding the platitudes.

'If you insist. But you do realize that this would depend wholly on the continued anonymity of the, er, witnesses to the circumstances of Sergeant Gault's misfortune. Unhappily, despite our most vigorous enquiries, they have not been traced.' He lit another cigarette from the remnant of the old, but his eyes never left Hansen, seeking some indication of an answer from the detective's features.

'And the terms?' Hansen asked bluntly.

'Ah, there are no terms. Merely an earnest desire that your future should not be unduly prejudiced by this unfortunate circumstance.' He pulled at his lower lip with finger and thumb, thinking out his next words. 'To be frank, dear boy, we have long been in need of an experienced ex-police officer with CID experience whom we can consult for advice in criminal cases we are defending; to conduct what necessary enquiries there may arise, to attend courts as our representative...' He waved a hand to indicate the scope and magnitude of the duties. 'There would, naturally, be a commensurately high salary. In short, I am empowered by Mr Fewler to invite you to join us on the cessation of your duties with the constabulary.'

When Hansen started to speak, he held up his hand. 'A moment, dear boy. The crux, so to speak. This, ah, appointment would necessitate your having a clean sheet as they say, with no previous convictions. Mr Fewler is—to make no bones about it—a stickler for the good name of the firm, insisting on the absolute probity of its employees.'

Hansen stared at him. Weizsack's face didn't reflect the incongruity of what he was saying, his apparently unconscious hypocrisy. Hansen wanted to point out that he himself might not qualify for the job; not having served a term of imprisonment for dipping his fingers in the till. And that he would rather work in the corporation garbage disposal plant than with Weizsack.

He said, innocently, 'You mean he wouldn't like my character tarnished by my finding Sheila Coughlin?'

For a moment the eyes glinted, the features frozen into angry immobility. 'I beg your pardon? Sheila who?' Naming names to a solicitor was an embarrassment, tying him down to facts and things that might be remembered.

'I thought you knew, Mr Weizsack,' he said mildly. 'She's the woman who was paid by Toffler to be photographed with Sergeant Gault. When she surfaces we might have the beginnings of a charge of conspiracy to pervert justice.'

There was a short silence while Weizsack struggled to recover his benignity in the face of this barely-concealed threat to himself. Then he said, 'If you'll forgive my saying so, dear boy, one of the indiscretions of young men is their tactlessness. It would be highly improper for me to comment on the defence of a client.'

'I'm so sorry,' Hansen said sardonically. 'Is that all you have to say to me?' He was impatient to go. The man was just wasting time. Which might have been his intention. And to sound him out on what he was doing about Toffler.

'You'll not consider Mr Fewler's offer?' If Weizsack was disappointed, he dissimulated it well.

'No.' Hansen looked at his watch and stood. 'I've been here long enough. You'll excuse me? I have to return to Headquarters. I arrested a man breaking into my apartment this afternoon and I've to interview him about it.'

There was a shifting of different expressions on Weizsack's face that verged on the comic. He was disorganized for a short moment, not knowing what to say. Then the geniality returned, although the eyes remained sharp and wary. 'Is he anyone I'm likely to know?' he managed to get out.

'He could be,' Hansen said carelessly. 'I've no doubt he'll be wanting you there if he is.' He didn't give the name that Weizsack would probably already suspect. Let the bastard worry until he found out. He added, 'His accomplice got away so we'll be looking for him as well. I'm telling you in case he might be persuaded to surrender himself.'

Weizsack stood. He said the words so softly, so without emphasis, that Hansen might have imagined them. Or they

167

could have reached him telepathically. 'You'll regret this, young man. Believe me, you'll regret it.'

He didn't offer to shake hands when Hansen left and the detective had barely left the building before the solicitor had given instructions to his clerk to get Toffler on the telephone. While he waited, he switched off the second concealed tape recorder. He wasn't happy with it, for what Hansen said hadn't been worth the current expended. But then, he assured himself, you never knew. He lifted out an Adler Gabriele portable typewriter from a drawer of his desk and began typing.

Hansen located Toffler's car in the yard at the rear of the Double Decker club. It was a white Alfa Romeo soft-top and securely locked. He parked his own car next to it, chose a heavily shadowed recess in the angle of wall near the arched entrance and settled himself to wait. A coach lamp under the arch threw barred squares of light across the few cars in the yard. High up in the wall of one side, Hansen could see the illuminated windows of the club and, just reaching his ears, the sound of a woman singing. He checked his watch: it was a few minutes past nine and the sky was clear, the stars bright and cold. He smoked his pipe, the bowl cupped in his gloved fist to conceal the glow of embers when he drew on it.

Before leaving his rooms, he had dialled McGluskie's home number, holding a padded handkerchief in readiness. As soon as there was a connection, without waiting to hear whether it was McGluskie or his wife answering, he pressed the linen pad over the earpiece, blocking out sound. 'Hello? Hello?' he had said into the mouthpiece. 'Double-two, eight nine one? Hello? Are you there?'; a man clearly unable to hear anything on his instrument. He muttered a frustrated caller's irritation and disconnected by depressing the studs. He had then dialled again, the pad still in position, repeating the self-defeating performance. He replaced the receiver, noted the exact time and left his apartment immediately. If he needed the security of the call, he would need it badly.

Earlier, McGluskie had been away from the Division and not obtainable. And that had been just as well. After an hour's patching up in the Casualty Department, Ash had been charged with entering Hansen's rooms as a trespasser with intent to inflict on Hansen grievous bodily harm. This intent, entered on the Charge Sheet, could be challenged if Ash came up with another; which, so far, he had not. The detective was almost certain that he had been sent to check whether the girl was still in his apartment. But the charge preferred against him was sufficient to have Ash remanded to a police cell until he could be brought before a court the following morning. He had, predictably, asked for Weizsack, but Hansen had left before the solicitor arrived. Not because he needed to avoid him, but he did need to avoid McGluskie and Sloan. Ash had, as predictably, refused to answer the charge or to give any explanation for his entry. Even had he wanted to, he would have found it painful. His mouth had lost some of its front teeth and his lacerated tongue had required stitching. What he didn't say with it, he said to Hansen with his malevolent eyes. And the eyes promised bloody retribution. The detective had seen the look before in other men; too often to let it worry him. He had found that badly beaten fighters usually lost as much iron from their stomachs as blood from their veins.

Time seemed to wait motionless with him, every crawling minute one in which he imagined Ann in the company of the filthy Toffler. Cars entered the yard and left while he remained unmoving, a grim dark shadow in a darker mass, only the paler disc of his face breaking the camouflage of his immobility.

It was past eleven when they came and Hansen's heart thumped at the sight of the slim blonde figure at Toffler's side, entering beneath the illuminated archway. Toffler walked as if he had been drinking heavily; treading with exaggerated care, with an obvious conscious regard that he should appear sober enough to drive his car. He hovered over Ann; a famished vulture hurrying to a meal. Hansen believed he could read lust and a winner's insolence in Toffler's expression and he felt a quiet fury chill his face. Toffler was bare-headed, his military raincoat hanging over his shoulders like a cape. Ann walked on his left, holding a white plastic handbag in her right hand while he held her elbow with his fingers, guiding her possessively towards his car. She hadn't seen Hansen and she looked worried.

Hansen waited until Toffler was fumbling at the door lock of the Alfa Romeo with his keys before he removed his gloves and put away his pipe. He walked soundlessly between the parked cars to a position behind his quarry. He reached past Toffler and snatched the keys from his fingers before the astonished man could resist. Ann stood at the other side of the car, staring.

Toffler turned sharply, anger already baring his teeth, slapping a flat hand against Hansen's chest, fending him off. ' 'Ere,' he snarled, 'what the bleedin' 'ell do you think you're doin'?'

The detective smelt the rank odour of brandy and tobacco on his breath. He transferred the keys to his left hand, knocking Toffler's hand from his chest with a sharp blow on the wrist. 'Hands off,' he snapped at him. 'I've information that you are in unlawful possession of a firearm. You're...'

'Oh, no!' Ann put a hand to her mouth and stepped back. 'Leave him alone!' she cried shrilly. It was well done and convincing, but her voice not carrying further than the yard.

'You keep out of this,' Hansen barked at her. To Toffler, he said, 'I'm searching you.' Before Toffler could react, he pushed him backwards off balance against his car, a forearm hard under his chin holding him there, cutting off most of his air. He ran a hand swiftly down the arching body, starting at the armpits, feeling the hard bulge at the waistline of his narrow trousers.

'*No,*' Toffler said thickly, bringing his knee up towards Hansen's groin. Liquor had slowed him, made his actions predictable, and Hansen twisted sideways, taking the kick on his thigh. He grabbed at Toffler's lapels and shook him so that his head snapped backwards and forwards. 'Don't,' he growled, 'or I'll do the same to you as I did to your pansy boy-friend.' He shook him again, his hipbone tight into Toffler's belly, jamming him against the car and preventing his moving, Hansen's elbows blocking the moving of his arms.

The detective was spoiling for violence. It would have suited him as a man, if not as a police officer. And, despite his suspension, he remained one. He ached to hit Toffler, but he wanted to do it in his own time, free of other considerations.

There was no fear of Hansen in Toffler, but not even the brandy he had drunk could blur his realization that there was little chance of escaping from this, only a worsening of it. He needed Weizsack's wily mind with him now. Even so, if Hansen hadn't been between him and the archway, he might have chanced a run for it, disposing of the gun before turning and coming back to deny any possession of it.

'You pox-ridden bastard,' he panted, the cords in his neck standing out with the strain of his resistance. 'I'll get you for this.' Like Hansen, he fought the violence rising hot in him, choking on the lust to smash the face of the detective he hated with all the venom of his resentment to authority; for his hatred of the man himself. As deep, was his humiliation at Hansen's hands in front of the doll; his frustration at the promised screwing being snatched from him by this stupid prick of a policeman.

There was little to choose between them in this as each weighed the options open to him. They strained together silently. It was as much a contest of wills as of physical strength.

Toffler recognized that resistance by violence would add to the charges against him; assaulting the law while in possession of a firearm could, with his record, sink him so deep that even Weizsack wouldn't be able to salvage him. Evading arrest now would only postpone it, not avoid it. He would be a hunted man, crawling from hole to hole, losing his stature, weakening his organization.

Suddenly Toffler relaxed, his body submissive in Hansen's grasp. Both men were breathing heavily.

'That's better, Toffler,' Hansen said. He held him with one fist pinning his lapels, holding him off balance, while he wrenched open his jacket, the buttons parting and the fabric ripping. He groped behind the waistband and pulled out a wash-leather bag held behind it. It was small, containing something solid and heavy. Once it was in his hand he released his hold on Toffler, allowing him to stand upright. On the periphery of his vision he saw Ann walking quickly away and under the arch to the street outside.

'You can stop acting tough,' he told Toffler. 'Your tart for tonight seems to have left you.'

Keeping him within his view, he unbuttoned the bag and removed the pistol. There was sufficient light for him to recognize it as a .22 short-barrelled automatic. He pulled back the slide and a cartridge jerked out, glinting in its small arc to the ground. It had been in the barrel, ready for firing. He pulled the magazine from the butt, checked it was loaded and put pistol and magazine into separate pockets. Then he stooped, picking the cartridge from the ground, his eyes not leaving Toffler's hands, still suspicious of his easy surrender.

He straightened himself. 'Right,' he said. 'You are not obliged to ...'

'Get stuffed. I'm sayin' nothin'.'

Hansen continued as if he hadn't been interrupted. '... say anything, but anything you do may be given in evidence.' He waited, then said, 'Who was the woman?'

'Bollicks.' He was sullen now and careful of what he said. 'I want to see my brief. Mr Weizsack.' Weizsack, he was confident, would find a way out for him.

'When we get to the station.' Hansen used the keys, unlocking the door of the car. 'Inside,' he ordered.

When Toffler was in the driver's seat, he unlocked the passenger door and climbed in. He dissembled his antagonism, forcing himself to show a surface imperturbability.

'You know the way,' he said, handing him back the keys. 'Take it slowly and don't rupture yourself trying to call me Bob.'

# Chapter 19

Station Chief Inspector Rodgers ran his Charge Room like an efficient business, processing the human merchandise passing through it to the cells or to freedom with dispassion and experienced fluency. He sat at his desk on a high stool, his cap foursquare and uncompromising over his forehead, the enormous leatherbound Charge Book open before him. Unofficially, he referred to it as *The Book of the Damned*. His features were a professional mask of impassivity; a mask that surprise would never crease. It was an emotion drained from his system years ago by unpredictable humanity.

He listened judicially to Hansen's account of his arrest of Toffler, examined the pistol and its magazine and tied manilla labels to them. Then he asked a glowering Toffler if he wished to say anything before being charged.

When he repeated his demand for Weizsack, Rodgers pulled the telephone handset nearer and dialled the number already familiar to him. His conversation was as brief as Weizsack's, the solicitor asking him to defer the charging until he arrived.

While they waited, Toffler's personal description and identifying characteristics were entered on the Charge Sheet; separated from his henchman Ash, had he known it, by only the sheets of two drunks, a tearful female housebreaker and a man found carrying an electric typewriter he claimed he had bought from an unknown man in a bar he was unable to relocate. Having been searched to his underwear by an escorting constable, the items found were listed and sealed in an envelope. Toffler had refused to countersign that they were his, being as bloody-minded and intractable as a man could be.

When Weizsack arrived, he included Hansen in the amiable greeting which had much of a pontifical blessing in it; a man able to say *pax vobiscum* without incongruity and one who had invested in universal geniality as a means of profit.

He was allowed the use of an anteroom to speak to Toffler privately. When they emerged twenty minutes later, Weizsack looked perturbed, shaking his head as if he couldn't quite credit the possibility of what he had heard. Toffler's insolent sneer was back on his mouth.

'Are you actually going to accept a charge against Mr Toffler?' Weizsack demanded incredulously of the Chief Inspector. He kept his eyes away from Hansen.

'Yes, sir. Actually,' Rodgers assured him, 'right now.' He was impervious to the Weizsack type of outraged protest. He cleared his throat and nodded to Hansen.

The detective moved to Rodgers's side and read from the sheet. 'The charge against you, Edward Toffler, is that you on the twelfth day of December at eleven-twenty p.m. at Friar's Yard in Shoreditch Street, had in your possession a firearm, to wit, a Yashimoto .22 pistol, without being the holder of a firearms certificate at the time; contrary to Section One of the Firearms Act 1968.' He then told him that he wasn't obliged to say anything unless he wished to do so, but that anything he did say would be written down and might be given in evidence.

There was a short silence until Weizsack spoke. 'My client wishes it to be recorded that he has never seen the pistol before tonight when Detective Chief Inspector Hansen produced it, alleging he had found it on Mr Toffler's person.' His voice shook with indignation and he compressed his lips when he had finished.

Rodgers said patiently, 'Let him say it himself then, Mr Weizsack.'

He started writing while Hansen stood by, unable to conceal completely the derisive contempt he felt.


When McGluskie arrived, Weizsack had left the station and Toffler, his application for bail refused, was in a cell with his issue of a red rubber mattress, three grey blankets and an air-filled pillow. Having spoken to Rodgers, McGluskie took Hansen aside to an interviewing room. He wasn't happy and said so at length.

'I just can't believe you'd do this, Robert,' he said sadly. He sat his huge elephantine buttocks on the edge of a small

174

metal table that sagged under his weight.

'That I planted a pistol on Toffler?' Hansen replied ironically, wilfully misunderstanding him. He knew McGluskie would be with him in thinking that Weizsack was taking the same dirty pitcher to the same dirty well too often to be believed by anyone but a jury.

'Damn it, no! Putting yourself in a position where he can say you did.'

'I had no option, sir. I received the information; I telephoned you. When I couldn't get you, I went. I had to get to the club quickly, not knowing when he was leaving.' Hansen was telescoping events; not actually lying for he chose his words carefully, but bending the truth. It would be just passable only so long as McGluskie wasn't in a probing mood.

'You were suspended, Robert. Your being under investigation already made Toffler the last man you should have handled.'

Hansen shrugged. 'It was an emergency and I'm still a policeman until I get my Discharge Papers. Would you have had me do nothing? Let him get away with it? I don't want to be dramatic, but that bullet up the spout wasn't there for fun.'

'No, it wasn't. And it could have been in your belly.'

'Or somebody else's. And all the more reason for my doing what I did.'

McGluskie wasn't so sure. 'You've put yourself in the wrong, Robert.'

'I don't agree. No court is ever going to accept I planted a gun on him.' When he said it, he knew he was being simpleminded. Given Weizsack's tortuous cunning and Sinter's ability to prove that black was white, it would.

'I'll get that painted on your coffin-lid. Weizsack'll make it sound like malicious persecution, using your previous case to his own advantage. You'll be skinned alive ... crucified.'

'No.' Hansen was definite. 'They're going to find themselves up shit creek. Too bloody clever for their own good.'

'Mind you don't find yourself there,' McGluskie said sharply. 'What about the woman who was with Toffler? Who is she?'

'She skipped off while I was dealing with him. She'll be easy to find,' he promised.

'For Christ's sake!' The fat features showed exasperation. 'She'll be Weizsack's witness, not ours. She'll back Toffler up with anything he wants her to say.'

Hansen kept his face straight. 'I've apparently more faith in the honesty of witnesses than you have, sir.' His words were making him appear naïve to the point of being stupid, but now wasn't the time to volunteer information about Ann.

'You've changed, Robert,' McGluskie said disgustedly. 'I've never known anyone so determined on slitting his own throat...' He stopped, suddenly looking shrewdly at Hansen with his enamel-blue eyes. 'Just a minute! You were told about this pistol business by an informant?'

'Yes.' That was the necessary truth: Ann was an informant. Of sorts.

'And is your informant a woman?' He cocked his head, showing his big square teeth.

*You crafty old bastard*, Hansen thought. Aloud, he said, 'Yes.' McGluskie wouldn't ask who she was, the identity of informants being as secret as membership of the Mafia.

'It could be that your confidence in this witness is because she's the same woman?'

Hansen smiled then. It wasn't much of a smile, but better than nothing. 'It could be,' he admitted.

'Ah!' McGluskie sounded less unhappy. 'I won't ask anything more, Robert. But, naturally, I must report your latest act of indiscipline to the Deputy Chief.'

'Yes. You'll confirm my trying to call you?'

Derision came and went as fast as a camera shutter on McGluskie's features. 'My wife received two cut-off calls, yes. Whoever it was apparently couldn't hear her.'

'At eight-forty, sir. Just so you will know I tried.'

'I'll accept you called, Robert. It'll be mentioned.' He climbed ponderously from the table and took his cigarettes out. 'You forgot to tell me about Ash.' He was apparently engrossed in the lighting of his cigarette.

'You know what happened?'

'I read your preliminary report,' he said blandly. 'I don't know that's all that happened.'

'Well, it was.' Hansen told him of his appointment with Weizsack and the conclusions he had drawn from it, leaving out nothing but his suspicion that Ash had probably been looking for the girl.

'Mm. What do you think Ash wanted, Robert?'

Hansen pulled a face. 'Your guess can't be worse than mine. Just a straight beating up with his brass knuckles apparently; waiting for me to return from Weizsack's office. Whatever it was, it proves Weizsack is up to his neck in Toffler's villainy. Perhaps,' he said pointedly, 'you'll now accept what I've been saying about him.'

'I've never disbelieved you, Robert,' McGluskie said mildly. 'And I don't need telling that Weizsack's a villain. But he didn't commit a crime offering you a job. And he'd deny the business about not pursuing the complaints anyway.' He took a folded sheet of notepaper from his pocket. 'Delivered at the Enquiry Desk this evening by unknown hands,' he said. 'Addressed to the Chief Constable and marked Private and Personal. Typed on the same Adler Gabriele as before, incidentally. Read it.'

Hansen read it, knowing that McGluskie's eyes were watching him.

*Why did Chief Inspector Hansen visit A. Weizsack, Solicitor, this afternoon? Ask him where Arabella Stephenson is. JUSTICE.*

'My friend,' he murmured, but his heart missed a beat at the name Arabella Stephenson. He handed the note back to McGluskie. 'Apart from mentioning my visit to Weizsack, it doesn't mean a thing.'

'I'm glad you told me about that, Robert. Who is the woman?'

'I've never heard the name before,' he said. But he hadn't any real doubts who she was. Or had been. She had to be the dead girl.

McGluskie wasn't wholly satisfied, but he let it go. There were a dozen different ways in which he could do a name check and Hansen was under no illusions he wouldn't. He wasn't anywhere near being off McGluskie's hook.

'Do you want to say anything else, Robert?' he asked.

'Not about Toffler or Ash. But could I ask how Mr Sloan's progressing?'

'No you can't, but I'll tell you anyway.' McGluskie still worked at his loyalty to his Detective Chief Inspector despite his suspicion that some sort of fire must accompany smoke. It shamed Hansen that he, himself, was deceiving him. 'Wikker's still missing and the woman Coughlin hasn't been traced. Nor the photographer, of course, and I'm afraid Weizsack's correspondent who signed himself A Wronged Husband is still anonymous. Charlie Glass has never heard of the Caulfield Arms Hotel. He's never employed a Sheila Coughlin and the women working for him as masseuses are all novitiates waiting to enter a convent.' He didn't sound too happy about Sloan's unspectacular progress either. 'Saddest of all is that Sergeant Gault is unable to be re-interviewed because he's been moved to a psychiatric ward.'

Guilt depressed Hansen because he hadn't been in to see the sergeant; guilt because of his own association with his wife; guilt because not only was Gault a physical wreck, but apparently a mental one too.

'Is it serious?' he asked.

McGluskie turned down his mouth. 'Serious enough. Between you and me, Robert, he's suffering from acute melancholia or something like it. Anyway, they say he tried to jump out of a window. He's that bad, I doubt if there'll be any question of further action against him, whatever the outcome of Mr Sloan's enquiries.'

Hansen felt anger stir in him. 'Which won't help him at all. He needs to be cleared.' His own responsibility for Gault hung on him like a leaden overcoat. 'You can tell Mr Sloan to start with Wikker.' He had intended doing it himself, but doubts of his own capabilities had crept in with the anger. Nothing was going right for him. 'I was in Bernard Street this evening and I checked on the hotel. There's a crate of empty beer bottles in the back yard. Two of the bottles have been emptied *very* recently. And there's a room at the top of the building with someone in it. If you use binoculars on the window, you can just see a crack of light. Wikker and his wife live in the basement and his guest rooms finish at the fourth floor. I'm sure he hasn't gone anywhere but upstairs...'

He was interrupted by a knocking at the door. A sergeant put his head and shoulders inside and spoke to McGluskie. 'Excuse me, sir. A telephone call for Mr Hansen.'

'All right, Robert,' McGluskie said. 'I'll leave you to it. Next time you call me, try and keep your thumb out of the earpiece. It works better that way.'

Hansen took the call in the deserted Parade Room.

'Mr Hansen?' It was a woman's voice with a touch of Irishness in it. A nice voice, he thought, but a frightened one.

'Yes?' he answered.

'You're looking for me...' She trailed off.

'Oh? I am?' He must have been tired. It didn't register with him straight away.

'This is Sheila Coughlin, Mr Hansen. I want to talk to you.'

It had been as simple as that.

'And *I* want to talk to you,' Hansen replied. 'About a dirty photograph.'

'Yes, I know.' She paused for a moment. 'I tried to get you before, but they didn't know where you were.' Her voice faded as if she had turned her head away from the mouthpiece.

'Stay where you are. I'll come straight away.'

'No! Please, no! I think I'm being watched.' Nervousness thinned her voice, made her brogue stronger. 'Not tonight. Tomorrow.'

'You need not worry,' he assured her. 'The man's inside.'

'I know. I've just been told. That frightens me, Mr Hansen. If he's in trouble, I shall be too.'

He could hear her anxious breathing; shallow and uneven.

'All right.' He sensed her to be ready to run at any moment. 'When and where tomorrow?'

'Do you know the Limping Duck caff?'

'Yes.' It wasn't the sort of place that embarrassed its customers with flowers or a menu.

'Will you be there at eight in the evening? Just wait ... don't ask for me. And, Mr Hansen...'

'Yes?'

'Can I trust you?'

'You have to, haven't you?'

'Yes.' She didn't sound wholly convinced. 'You've got to come on your own.'

'Will you know me?'

'I'll know you.' She closed down on him.

He didn't bother trying to trace the call. To do it and set up a search for her would only result in frightening her further. And he had to see her before Sloan. Being on his own was going to be good enough after all. His previous doubts vanished as he breathed in the sweet, invigorating scent of success.


It was two o'clock and the windy dark streets were in sleep when he braked his car to a quiet stop in Commercial Road and switched off the lights. He walked the length of the road, doing what had now become an automatic check on the parked cars and doorways.

The house was in darkness and he cursed his oversight in not asking Ann which room she occupied. He reached inside the window of his car and tapped lightly three times on the horn-button, then standing where he could be seen and known by his shape.

She came out of the door quietly, running when she recognized him, her yellow hair bouncing on her shoulders. She went straight into his arms, her mouth finding his.

'I was waiting, darling,' she whispered. 'I thought you'd never come.'

'Hell fire and eternal damnation wouldn't keep me away,' he said thickly, 'and that's what I expect I'll get.'

She tilted her head back, her eyes gleaming in the darkness. 'Are you coming in?'

He shook his head. 'I can't stay.' He could feel a phantom Gault standing behind him in the shadows; his one eye mad and reproachful, his mangled crotch a blotch of crimson. 'In my car,' he said.

Inside, she clung to him, smoothing her fingertips softly like pale feathers over his face, her mouth warm and moist and loving him. 'I can't explain what you do to me, darling, but it's pretty total.' Her months'-long abstinence had made her body's need a sharp bright pain.

Hansen fought the rising desire in him to love her and it gave him a remoteness, a holding back, she noticed. She stiffened slightly but kept her body pressed against his.

'You can't be more total than I am,' he said and smiled. 'But you're singeing my shirt. Tell me what happened tonight.' Always-on-the-job-Hansen, he thought sourly, and she's going to end up hating my sanctimonious guts.

If she resented the rebuff, it didn't show. 'Robert, I was frightened ... I thought at first you weren't there. He was horrible...' Her body shuddered.

'He's booked, Ann, and inside until tomorrow.'

'Was it a gun?'

He kissed her on the forehead. 'You're a good copper lost to the department.' He told her what had happened after her flight from the yard. 'Did you get anything from him about Sheila Coughlin?'

She shook her head. 'I said I was a friend of hers; that I hadn't seen her about for days, but he just looked mean and said she was a bloody cow he didn't want to know about.

He was full of that albino man being arrested and beaten up by the effing coppers.'

'He's in a cell too. And you've just been kissing the effing copper he was complaining about. Toffler said nothing else that was useful?'

'No. He just had me and the albino on his mind.'

He touched her yellow hair. 'Can you take it off? I don't like Ann Pardoe very much,' he said gently. What he meant was that Ann Pardoe had been with Toffler; that, deliberately schizophrenic, he had to keep the two Anns apart.

She slipped the wig off and it was to him as if she was suddenly naked of clothing, the Ann who was driving him insane with his need to possess her. The controlled desire he had held in check rose in him and he hurt her with the savage constriction of his arms, the fierce pressure of his mouth on hers. The music thundering in his ears was Wagnerian again, as dark and tumultuous as a night-storm at sea. Then, as suddenly, he released her, moving upright in his own seat, his face sombre in the shadowed interior.

'Ann,' he said, his voice shaking, 'it's no good. Not yet. We're murdering each other.'

'*I'm* not,' she said simply, her eyes luminous, trying to see behind his expression. 'I love you, Robert.'

He groaned his despair, keeping his eyes from her. 'It's not enough. There's still Bill ... Christ, darling! Don't make me forget him.'

'*Damn Bill!*' She bit her bottom lip. When she was with Robert, her husband became an amorphous figure, retreating to the dark corners of her consciousness. 'No, I'm sorry. I didn't mean that.' Her words hardly reached him. 'I thought loving you would be enough.'

'It isn't,' he said bleakly. 'I want you, Ann, enough to do anything. Anything but take you away from a sick husband.' Gault was in the rear seat now with Ann's yellow wig. *I'm tired*, Hansen thought. *I've got the poor bastard on my brain.* 'You know he's in a psychiatric ward?'

'Yes.' Her eyes were moist, her fingers twisting. 'You're tearing me to bits, darling.'

'I'm tearing holes in myself,' he said grimly. Everything about her; the sweetly-perfumed flesh and hair, the magic of the body he had never seen, the intimacy of her mouth, even her clothing; all were overwhelming attractions to him. Not to touch her was a torture. 'You weren't surprised?'

'No. He's ... he's always been highly strung ... depressed if things didn't go right for him ... aggressive sometimes. When I saw him this evening, he told me he didn't want me ... didn't want to see me again. Told me to stay away from him.'

'He could have thought that was the best thing for you. But hoping to God you wouldn't.'

'*No.*' She was vehement. 'He meant it. Bill isn't the kind of man to be that noble. You don't know him, Robert.'

He took her hand in his. 'Ann, darling,' he lied earnestly, not wanting to hurt her. 'For the moment it's enough for me to know you love me.' He hesitated, then said, 'And that I love you,' not knowing for certain whether he did or not, but believing not.

Love, he reflected bitterly. What the hell do I know about love anyway. He had used a word without knowing its real meaning. Believing it without proof. It hadn't even a quanti-fiable level in terms of emotion. Going to bed with the woman one loved was supposed to be the ultimate God-given fulfil-ment of its intensity and purpose, somehow sanctified by reli-gion into a sacramental rite. So, what about Norah? Was that a sort of love too? Had it to be a selfless consuming need for one woman, allowing a willingness to forgo, if necessary, the sharing of bodies? As he was doing now? And how unselfish, how bloody self-sacrificing, had it to be before it ceased to be a mere physical indulgence? And all this painful, emotionally charged denial with no promise that what they felt for each other wasn't as ephemeral as their driving lust. He had thought he loved his wife until she proved him wrong. He knew that if he could think only with his loins he would suffer less and be a happier man.

Ann touched her mouth to his cheek. 'I can never believe it is enough, darling, but you don't give me any choice. Only, don't murder me for too long ...'

'Only Ann Pardoe,' he promised. 'After tonight, she's dead. I'm seeing Sheila Coughlin tomorrow evening.'

'Oh?' She lifted her eyebrows. 'You've found her?'

'She found me.' He told her of the telephone call. 'And you,' he said, 'are very likely to be looked for by Toffler to corroborate his statement that I planted the pistol. So I want you to leave first thing in the morning; before he gets bailed.'

'I shall be glad to. He's a foul beast. He ...'

'No,' he interrupted her, not wanting to know. 'Don't make me hate the bastard more than I already do. I want to sleep tonight.'

He retrieved her wig and handed it to her. It hung from his fingers like a silky golden octopus. 'Let Ann Pardoe go to bed and have her last few hours in peace.' He held her chin in his fingers and kissed her mouth gently; with affection, without passion.

'If you really think about it,' he said smiling, 'I must love you. Otherwise I'd have already been in bed with the Pardoe woman.'

Late that night, Gault had again attempted violence on his hateful, useless body.

Earlier, while he had lain unconscious from the stunning effects of the injection he had been given, they had moved him to a different ward. It was a similar room to the one he had vacated, but with no exterior window. Only one that was overlooked from the larger ward outside. He was now under observation.

He had spent the day with his nightmares, struggling to stay awake, fighting the stupefying drugs despite the relief they gave him from the ragged anguish of his crotch.

They had let Ann visit him and he hated her for her physical wholeness. And for other things. She sat by the side of the bed, smelling of a whore's perfume, he thought, and of the outside clean air, her green eyes showing the pity he didn't want, that filled him with a sour anger. Behind the pity, he imagined he could discern her steady contemplation of him as a useless, impotent encumbrance.

When she attempted to wipe the fluid running from beneath his eyepatch, he jerked away, not wanting her to touch him.

'No,' he said. 'I've something to tell you. Something important.'

She must have sensed from his expression he was going to be unpleasant, for her face clouded over and she bit her lip. 'You shouldn't say anything, Bill. Not until you are better.'

'Better?' He found his anger difficult to control. 'How am I ever going to be better? You know they've done it?'

'Yes ... I'm sorry.'

'Like hell you are,' he said nastily. When had she ever really wanted him? Hadn't it been her neglect, her coldness, that had pushed him at *her*? He turned his face away from her so that she could see only the back of his head. 'I don't want to see you again.'

She was silent for a while. 'Why, Bill?'

'I don't want you looking at me as if I'm a bloody freak.'

'I don't think you are,' she said gently.

'No? Well, I am.' His voice was empty, with no emphasis. 'Nor am I going to be about while you're bitching around, getting what you want from somebody else.' He knew she would. Any woman would. He knew she had already. And who with. He had searched her face when she first came in, trying to see in it the signs of sexual satisfaction, any subtle hint of the man's love. He clenched his fist. He wasn't jealous, nor could he be, he told himself. Not of her.

Her face went thin, her fingers twisting together on her lap. When at last she spoke, she was as unemotional as him. 'I was about, Bill,' she said quietly, 'while you were. But do we have to go into that now?'

'Yes, we do.' He turned his head to stare at her with his single eye. 'And what do you mean? While *I* was?'

'I knew you were going out with another woman.'

The sort of sneaky guess he had anticipated she would make. Well, he wasn't going to deny it. Not now. 'That's right,' he said. 'She gave me something I never got from you.'

'It couldn't have been love, Bill.'

'How would you know? Anyway, you don't have to worry about that any more.'

'I'm not worried. I want only what is right for you.'

The lying bitch, he thought, and he mimicked her. *'Only what's right for you.'* He suddenly shouted. 'There isn't anything that can be right! Why don't you go? I don't want you here!'

She winced and looked at the door, compressing her lips. 'Do you have to advertise it, Bill?'

'Why not?' he said harshly. 'Things like that don't matter. Not to me. You don't love me any more.' It was an assertion, not a question.

She hesitated, then said, 'If you say not.'

*'Do you?'*

'No, I don't, Bill.'

There, he had got it out of her. What he had suspected. 'You're a bloody cow,' he said softly. 'Who have you been having it off with?'

'You won't believe me, but with nobody.' She accepted his insult because of where and how he was.

'I don't,' he said. He glanced at her cunningly. 'What about Hansen? Haven't you been entertaining him? Bouncing around with him on my bed, in my bloody house?'

The flicker of her eyelids and the faint staining rising up her throat, confirmed the information he already had. He had received the short note yesterday, before his operation, mailed to him enclosed in a Get Well card. It had been typed and was as anonymous as the card.

*Don't worry about your wife. She is being well looked after by Detective Chief Inspector Hansen. A FRIEND.*

When she didn't reply, he said, 'Well?' His eye was injected with threads of blood.

'Nothing you are suggesting has happened between Mr Hansen and myself.' She had difficulty in getting the equivocation through her stiff lips. Her intention of telling him what she had been doing to prove his innocence, her reason for meeting Hansen, vanished in the consciousness that, but for Hansen's loyalty to her husband, she could not have said even that. But her conscience and honesty demanded she said something. 'It's true, though, that he and I are in love. We couldn't help it...'

He interrupted her, mimicking her again. *'In love. We couldn't help it.'* His expression changed and he was vicious. 'You dirty whore! You've been screwing him behind my back ... while I'm here in hospital.' Saliva bubbled at the corners of his mouth and he raised his voice again. 'With that filthy sneaking bastard Hansen...!' He used obscenities and described what they had been doing with incredible filth while Ann rose from her chair, her face paper-white.

When he had finished and turned his back to her, she whispered, 'I'm truly sorry, Bill. I hadn't intended telling you yet.' Behind the real pity was a soft contempt and a sense of relief that she was at last free. What he had said went far in minimizing the guilt she could not help feeling.

As she opened the door, he said woodenly, 'Don't come back. Don't ever come back.' She had gone through the ward and out into the corridor when the tears brimmed from his engorged eye and he lay for a long time kneading his fingers into the linen of his pillow.

It was later, when the ward outside was quiet with sleep, that he yelled and tore frantically at the bandaging until blood welled and ran on to the sheet beneath him and the raw pain of it took away some of the agony of his mind.

# Chapter 20

Hansen found what he had been looking for in the *Daily Telegraph* pushed into the letter flap of his door before he had risen from his too-short stay in bed. He read it over the coffee and pipe of tobacco that was his breakfast, before leaving for court and the remand appearances of Toffler and Ash.

It was at the bottom of page two; short, and happily inconspicuous.

### GIRL FOUND DEAD IN BASEMENT
*The body of an unknown girl was found by children yesterday in the basement of a derelict building in Jamaica Street, Stepney. A police spokesman said foul play was not suspected, but they were seeking to identify her.*

The brief description that followed made her almost certainly the girl Hansen had put on the transport, the Arabella Stephenson of the anonymous letter. Being found dead in a basement at fifteen years didn't apparently warrant any more space than six lines and Hansen knew she was lucky to get even that as an obituary.

He guessed that the driver of the transport, finding the body, panicked for reasons of his own; probably not wanting to be involved in police investigations, he dumped her in his turn. Hansen promised himself that when he was clear of the mire he was in—if he ever was—he would see that she was properly identified. The thought of her lying in a nameless grave bothered him.

Were the finding to be as minimally reported in the other dailies, he wasn't concerned about the risk of either Weizsack or Toffler seeing it and connecting it with the missing girl. He had seen a copy of *The Times* on Weizsack's desk, and he doubted whether Toffler read anything.

Weizsack had apparently decided that pleading for a man charged with breaking into Hansen's apartment could create tactical difficulties in his defence of Toffler, who had accusations of his own to make against the detective; a defence that could not afford to acknowledge a lieutenant who might be making similar allegations. Even the Chairman of the Magistrates, notoriously partial to Weizsack's pleas, might have found that hard to stomach.

So Ash stood alone in the dock, tight-faced, palely furious and bandaged; a man who obviously suspected he was being thrown overboard. His application for bail was objected to and rejected and, despite being the obvious loser in his encounter with the detective, he was ushered down the steps to spend the next seven days in custody. But not without a final malevolent glare at Hansen.

Weizsack, who insisted that Hansen give in evidence his client's reply to the charge, was successful in obtaining bail for the openly sneering Toffler.

When Hansen left the Law Courts, Ann was waiting for him, her blue mini parked on the far side of the square. She wore a fawn suède-leather coat against the cold wind scarifying the grey streets and, with it, a floppy-brimmed green hat that matched the eyes she had hidden behind dark glasses. Her face was without make-up. It would have been difficult to recognize her as the blonde tart Toffler knew. But when Hansen climbed in the car, he said, 'Move, Ann. Toffler will be out any minute.'

She pulled out obediently into the stream of cars, silent until they turned a corner.

'Good morning, darling,' she said smiling. 'I still love you and I've got news.'

He touched his fingertip to his lips, then pressed it on to her cheek. 'It's been a long time. Keep moving and tell me the news.'

'Why are you looking so stern, Robert?' She was teasing him.

'Because you are driving me up a wall. I didn't get any sleep.'

'I'm glad.' She smiled gently.

'Yes,' he said dourly. 'Love's a wonderful thing. Tell me the news.'

'Weizsack telephoned me this morning.'

'Christ, no!' He was dismayed.

'It's all right, darling. Not at my home. At Mrs Quigg's establishment for young theatrical ladies. I was just leaving.'

'That means Toffler had you followed.'

'No,' she said calmly. 'I gave him the number last night.'

His eyebrows chopped down. 'You did! For God's sake why?' He wanted to say that had been a bloody stupid thing to do but held his annoyance in check. He could, he discovered, be as irritated with someone he loved as he could by anybody else.

'He asked for it.' She reached sideways and squeezed his arm with her fingers. 'Don't be angry, Robert. I couldn't play it by being too unco-operative, and it's done no harm.'

'What did Weizsack want?' He wasn't completely mollified.

'What you said. Toffler needs me as a witness. Weizsack didn't go into details, just asked me if I would call at his office at three this afternoon. I'm his "dear young lady", so he wants something from me.'

She waited silently while he thought about that, negotiating the car deftly through a crowded roundabout, calm and relaxed. She was as competent as she was beautiful.

Weizsack's invitation was something Hansen believed he could turn to his own advantage. In the sober, civilized daylight he could rationalize his fears for Ann's safety as being old-maidish. He thought his growing love for her had developed an over-protectiveness in him, blinding him to the toughness and professional capability she must have possessed as a Woman Detective Inspector.

'Do you mind resurrecting Ann Pardoe?' he asked at last.

She smiled. 'I didn't book out after the call, Robert. I knew you'd want me to go.'

He stared at her. 'Only for this afternoon.'

'Only for this afternoon,' she agreed.

'Drive me to Headquarters, Ann. I've an interesting handbag I'd like you to see.'

He brought the handbag out to where she waited at the far, obscured end of the visitors' car park, telling her to drive him back to the Law Courts where he had left his own car.

'This,' he explained to her, once out on the road, 'appears to be an ordinary leather handbag with a telescopic umbrella strapped to its side. It isn't. It contains a tape recorder that will run for an hour. The microphone is concealed in the handle of the umbrella. You press down this switch that's part of the handle frame and put the bag on a table or chair, pointing the umbrella handle more or less in the direction the talking is coming from. It's highly sensitive, so if you're near it don't talk loudly. It will pick up the conversation in an ordinary-sized room. In Weizsack's office, to be specific.' He added, 'I've borrowed it without permission and it cost the Police Authority over a hundred pounds, so for God's sake don't lose it.'

'It's silent, darling? It won't start buzzing on me?'

'As a grave. The recording part is padded in a false bottom. Put what bits and pieces you have from your own bag in it. And, Ann, I don't need to tell you not to act as an *agent provocateur*. Let Weizsack say his piece without prodding. If he tries to encourage you into perjury, I want it legal and admissible in evidence.' He laughed. 'He'll have his own tape recorder revolving like mad, so be doubly careful of what you say. Incidentally, you didn't actually see me find the gun on Toffler?'

'No. His car was between us anyway. I left when I saw you were coping very adequately, my pepper-gun clutched in my hot sticky hand in case any of his friends arrived.'

'That's something you'd better put away with your old photographs. I don't think you'll need it with Weizsack.' He pulled one of her hands away from the steering wheel, turned back the glove on it and touched his lips to the back of her wrist. 'On second thoughts, I'm not so sure even about that unprincipled old bastard.'


Hansen was let into Ash's cell by the sergeant-gaoler and the door closed after him.

The cell had been designed with an obsessive fear in mind that a trouble-making percentage of its future occupants would either attempt suicide in it or use it to propagate anti-establishment sentiments. The walls were tiled like a public urinal and free of the obscene *graffiti* that a whitewashed surface invited. A sunken push-button on which it was impossible to dangle a noose, flushed the lavatory. The pan was sufficiently constricted to prevent a determined man from immersing his nose and mouth in the water. Each corner of the cell was visible from a glassed hole in the door to an inspecting gaoler. Eating utensils were of soft plastic, the blankets impossible to rip into self-strangulating ligatures. Since one man had patiently torn his foam-rubber pillow into fragments and swallowed most of it before choking to death, pillows had been filled with nothing more lethal than air. But there was nothing to stop a desperate inmate from smashing his skull against the tiles or the heavy iron-bound door except the noise he would make doing it. It was a self-mortification often practised by drunks.

Ash, lying on his back on the wooden box-bed, was dressed only in his trousers and a singlet. He was without shoes or socks because a man could strangle himself in a few minutes with shoe-laces or with two socks knotted together. That he could do it equally well with either trousers or singlet was ignored because nobody had so far attempted it that way.

After lifting his head and seeing Hansen, he closed his eyes and turned his back on him, lying on one side facing the wall. His nose and chin were hidden under strips of white surgical tape.

The cell was unbearably hot, and always would be since a long-forgotten prisoner had complained loudly and bitterly in open court about its former frigidity.

Sweat started on Hansen's forehead and he opened his top coat. From the brief glimpse he had had, he thought the albino had been crying. But it could be his light-sensitive eyes suffering from the removal of his dark glasses.

'It looks as if you've been abandoned, Ash,' Hansen said casually. 'You're in here and Toffler's outside.' He waited, but Ash's back remained motionless. 'Before they take you off to gaol,' he continued, 'I wanted a few words with you.' He chose what he had to say carefully. 'About someone called Arabella...'

The effect was instantaneous. Ash twisted around and was up on his bare feet in one movement, facing Hansen. *'What about her?'* The words came glutinous but intense around his lacerated tongue. He was near enough for Hansen to smell the sweat from the body that, despite its muscular lumpiness, was as pale and smoothly-fleshed as a woman's.

Hansen stared at him. 'Sit down,' he said coldly. 'You're in no condition to start being tough. And I'm sure they didn't give you back your brass knuckles.'

Ash returned Hansen's stare for long seconds—the detective was certain now that he had been crying and he felt contempt for his weakness—then obediently sat.

'I'm not going to start anything,' he said submissively. He was giving Hansen's face a searching regard which discomfited him. Then he lowered his eyes, appearing satisfied with what he had seen. There was none of his previous venom about him.

'Where is she?' he asked, an edge of entreaty to his words.

Hansen looked at him curiously. Her whereabouts seemed important to the albino. 'Certainly not in my apartment,' he said. 'I didn't know you cared for little girls.'

Ash glared at him, a spark of the old abrasive hatred in his eyes, pink flushing his skin. 'You've got a dirty mind.'

'Yes, I have. I've picked it up dealing with people like you. Why do you want to know where she is?'

Ash swallowed his momentary anger, revealing to Hansen that the girl mattered very much to him. He could be heterosexual, Hansen conceded to himself, but it seemed unlikely. Young boys, young girls; they didn't often attract the same appetite.

'I have to know,' he said at last. Sweat ran from his body, darkening his singlet; oozing from the skin of his temples and dampening the incongruously-white hair.

'Tell me why.'

The swollen tongue wagged his hesitation before he said, 'She's my sister ... my step-sister.'

Hansen blinked, dismayed, his breath catching in his throat. There were going to be complications he hadn't foreseen when he decided to interrogate Ash. The girl wasn't going to rest quietly at Stepney after all. She was now back into his immediate considerations, a ticking bomb ready to blow up in his face.

'And you let her be used as a plant by Toffler?' he accused him incredulously. 'You're lying.'

Ash jerked his head as if to clear away an irritating fly. 'No,' he said, 'it's true. Where is she?'

Hansen frowned. 'Isn't it a bit late to start worrying about that now? You knew she was a junkie?' Ash in his persistence was putting him on the defensive and he hadn't an answer to give him without lying. Even to Ash, he couldn't lie about a death.

The pink eyes lifted and held his. 'There wasn't anything I could do about that, Mr Hansen.' The 'Mr' showed the measure of his need for answers. 'I didn't believe anything wrong would happen to her with you.'

The faith he put in a policeman's decency when it mattered made Hansen contemptuous, although he didn't show it. 'What makes you think it has?'

'Has it, Mr Hansen?'

Hansen felt his skin chilling. Ash knew or suspected something serious had happened to his step-sister. It explained his anxiety. And made him dangerous. 'I said, what makes you think it has?' He used his words as carefully as he would tread bare-footed through broken glass.

The albino looked down at his hands clenched over his knees. 'Do you believe in dreams?'

'If you're asking do I believe they mean anything, no.'

'I saw her the night she was taken to your place.'

Hansen stiffened, holding his breath. God help me if he saw me taking her away, he thought. 'You were there?' he asked as if it didn't concern him that much. 'With those other two characters?'

'No.' He shook his head impatiently. 'In a dream. Well, a sort of dream.' He put his tongue out and touched it with his broken teeth, wincing. It was bleeding slightly from the talking. 'I'm not sure. I thought I was awake, but I couldn't have been.' He wiped sweat nervously from his forehead with his handkerchief. 'Some dreams you don't take any notice of. This was different. She was there, Mr Hansen. In my room like ... trying to tell me something.'

Hansen stared at him astounded. He couldn't disbelieve him, couldn't argue against a manifestation which had its truth in what he, alone, knew. He recalled his own experience in the broom cupboard, the frightening sensation of an emanation from her dead body. If he could perceive it—and he had never thought himself psychic—how much more might her stepbrother. The grave wasn't as silent as he had been led to believe, but it was straining the logic of his earthy commonsense.

'What was she trying to tell you?' It was an effort for him to keep his voice steady; to maintain his role as the unemotional interrogator who didn't believe that the dead ever came back to give evidence.

'I don't know,' Ash said helplessly. 'I couldn't hear what she was saying. But I know she's dead, Mr Hansen,' he said flatly.

Despite the heat of the cell, the detective went cold again, but he kept his expression stern. 'And if she is, you think I'm

193

responsible?' Toffler and Weizsack seemed prosaic and common-place problems by comparison.

'No. If I did, I would kill you.' He said it simply, as if Hansen would understand that. 'But she's dead all right. I saw her so plain and I had that feeling ... you know?'

'A premonition?'

He nodded. It was difficult to read his expression behind the mask of tape. 'You don't get that in ordinary dreams, Mr Hansen.' He was reliving the visitation, his voice low and introspective. 'She was moving backwards, getting smaller ... going down a long black tunnel away from me. I felt that her shoulders were being squeezed tight ... as if she was in a coffin. And she was saying things I couldn't make out ... and sad ... so sad.' His fingers twisted restlessly, pulling at the fabric on the thighs of his trousers. 'When I woke, I was crying ... and I don't do that. I felt as if she was still in the room and I lay there in the dark, trying to get her back ... to see her again. *I've got to know*,' he burst out with fierce intensity. '*I've got to.*'

'Is that why you broke into my apartment? Expecting to find her there?'

'Yes. When nothing happened, when you came out and bashed Gandy and he pushed off...' His expression showed he had a poor opinion of Gandy although he hadn't done any better himself. '... I got even more worried. That's when she left, isn't it?'

'Yes. Just afterwards.'

The albino sighed. 'I told Ed I had to know what happened. I couldn't rest. So it was fixed you'd be out. Only,' he said, grimacing behind the taping, 'you weren't.'

'You'll make a statement?' He had to avoid answering Ash's question about where she was. If he could. But he knew now he couldn't callously lie about her. What he couldn't judge was which was the kinder for Ash; knowing, or not knowing. And if he told him, he himself would be sunk. It was too late now for acceptable explanations to McGluskie, even were he able to depend on the albino's goodwill. And he was as unstable as a rabid dog. In a few hours he could be as vindictive as he was now complaisant.

'No,' Ash said. 'I'll plead guilty, but I'm putting nothing on paper.'

'Will you repeat what you've told me to my Chief Superintendent? About the plant, I mean.' He was probing, not wanting him to. Not yet.

'No. I'm only telling you because you're the one who knows. The only one,' he pointed out. 'Otherwise your governors wouldn't have left you like they did.' He brushed these considerations aside. 'Mr Hansen, I know you wouldn't have hurt Arra, but you know where she is. You've got to tell me.'

Hansen came to a decision and pressed his thumb on the bell push at the side of the door, summoning the gaoler. 'I don't understand about your premonition,' he said, 'but it was right. I'm sorry, but she *is* dead.'

Ash blinked and lowered his head. 'I knew it,' he whispered.

Hansen hardened his voice. 'She died of an overdose of drugs, Ash, and that's something you and Toffler will have to take the responsibility for.' He could hear the gaoler unlocking the cell passage door in the silence that followed.

'Where is she?' The albino's voice was defeated. There was nothing left in him now but what passed for his conscience.

'You've got money. Ask the Station Chief Inspector if you can buy today's *Daily Telegraph*. What you want is on page two. Take it from there yourself. I've told you,' he said, 'against my own interests. If you've any decency in you—which I doubt—you'll forget what's passed between you and me this morning.' The gaoler was outside the door.

Ash looked up at him with his suffering eyes. 'I shan't tell anyone,' he said, 'but I'll tell *you* one thing. Ed Toffler's going to do you. *Really* do you.'

# Chapter 21

Weizsack came to the outer office where Ann waited and greeted her. He held her hand in both of his and beamed. She had tied her yellow hair in a ponytail and wore a green trouser suit beneath a fawn woollen coat. Only the heavily made-up face and the heavy aura of her perfume made her tartish.

'My dear young lady,' he said. 'How very kind of you to come.'

Her first reaction to him was that he was a nice old man and likely to be thought cuddly by small children. But the policewoman in her saw that his eyes were assessing her behind the smile and the florid welcome.

Toffler was waiting in the inner office. His swagger and the insolent bravado on his mouth showed he had put behind him his belittling arrest of the previous evening.

' 'Ello, doll.' He came over to her and put his hands on her shoulders. He held a cheroot between his fingers. 'I 'ope you 'aven't been worryin'.' He was flash in an oatmeal jacket, narrow blue trousers and an orange polo-neck sweater; a brightly-feathered vulture against the seedy-plumaged Weizsack.

She twisted her shoulders from his grasp. 'I haven't worried,' she said, her voice cool. 'I thought you'd still be inside. With Denny,' she added.

'What, keep me in?' He smiled nastily. 'They got the wrong bloke for that, doll. 'Ansen'll get 'imself clobbered over this. Mr Weizsack's goin' to tear the bastard to bits.'

Weizsack showed his teeth. 'You talk too much, Edward. Miss Pardoe will get the wrong impression. It is justice we are seeking, not tearing people to bits.'

He pulled a chair forward for Ann and then sat at his

desk. Toffler sat to one side, his legs crossed, the cheroot clenched between his teeth, his eyes never leaving Ann's body. It said much for him that not even a solicitor's office could dampen his satyrism.

Ann opened her handbag and took out a packet of cigarettes, lighting one before Weizsack could offer to and returning the packet to the bag with a decisive click. She placed it between her thigh and the side of the chair, the umbrella handle pointing in Weizsack's direction like a small cannon. She had switched the tape recorder on in the outer office and it was, as Hansen had promised, completely silent, although she could feel the faint vibration of the moving spools against her thigh. But her knowledge of what the bag contained made it seem enormous and incongruously positioned where she had placed it, for normally it would have rested on the floor at her feet.

'Well, my dear,' Weizsack began. 'As you may guess, I have been entrusted with Mr Toffler's defence in this distressing affair of his arrest last evening and his being charged with possessing a firearm. You know about this?'

'I heard the policeman say he thought Mr Toffler had one.'

Weizsack nodded approvingly. 'Mr Toffler is indeed in serious trouble. Despite this, he has told me that he has no wish to involve you. But,' he said smoothly, 'I am afraid I had to insist...'

'I hope he doesn't either,' she interrupted him. 'I don't know anything.'

Weizsack coughed and put his cigarette in the ashtray. 'Unfortunately, my dear, the processes of the law take no heed of our personal wishes. You see, unless we can convince a court of what actually happened, you are in grave danger of joining Mr Toffler in the dock as an accomplice.'

Ann frowned. 'A what?' she asked sharply.

'An accomplice, my dear, to the unlawful possession of a firearm; punishable by three years' imprisonment on indictment.' He wagged his head and pursed his lips. 'A serious charge indeed and one in which it behoves us to reveal to the court the real truth of the matter.'

Ann set her lips obstinately. 'I'm not anybody's accomplice,' she said. 'I don't know why anyone should think I am.'

Weizsack reached for and opened a thick green book. Ann recognized it as Archbold's *Criminal Pleading*. He went

197

through the motions of reading. 'Where two persons are together,' he said, 'each is liable for the acts of the other. So, if Mr Toffler is convicted, you could well be convicted with him.'

The policewoman in Ann winced at this gross mis-stating of the definition of an accomplice. 'If you say so, Mr Weizsack; but ...'

'A moment, please. It is to my knowledge,' he continued, closing the book and patting it, 'that the police are at this very moment looking for you. Whether a warrant has been issued, I am unable to say, but it is a fact that Mr Toffler has been asked to reveal your identity. It was, naturally, refused. Mr Hansen has also called at this office demanding the same information.'

'That's the policeman? Mr Hansen?'

He inclined his head gravely. 'Yes. Mr Toffler is, in short, the victim of a diabolical plot by an unscrupulous police officer who believes he has reason to fear Mr Toffler.'

She lifted her eyebrows. 'He is?'

Toffler scowled and nodded. 'The bastard's out to get me an' we ain't fixin' to let 'im get away with it.'

Weizsack said reprovingly, 'All right, Edward, please leave it to me.'

'That's all very well,' Ann protested, 'but I didn't know Mr Toffler had a gun. I wouldn't have been seen dead with him if I had.'

'That's the crux of the whole matter, my dear. Mr Toffler *didn't* have a gun. But, as you saw for yourself, that didn't stop him from being arrested and charged. Nor need it stop you from being arrested and charged with him.'

Ann drew jerkily on her cigarette. 'What can I do?'

'Ah! Fortunately for Mr Toffler and unfortunately for Mr Hansen, you were there to see what actually happened. Between you both, you will be able to reveal the true facts.'

'But I didn't see anything,' she objected. 'Only *him* being arrested.'

The denigrating 'him' rasped at Toffler and he scowled sourly at this reminder of his humiliation, chewing at his cheroot and wondering why the bitch had to be needling him. He knew only one way he could take the starch out of her, and he had been frustrated twice in doing it.

'My dear,' Weizsack said patiently, 'I have had a great deal of experience with witnesses who believe sincerely that they either know nothing or saw nothing; that they cannot possibly help in the furtherance of justice. A lot of what we see and hear lies buried here.' He tapped a pudgy finger on his temple. 'We can be genuinely unaware that it *is* there until perhaps reminded of it. But there it is, nevertheless; waiting to be brought to the surface.'

'It is?' She hoped she wasn't acting too naïvely, but it was necessary for Weizsack to size her up as possessing a not-too-intelligent malleability.

'You may take my word for it,' he assured her, 'as a solicitor of many, many years standing and with much experience in the frailties of the human memory. Please allow me to go over the sequence of events as I understand them. I am sure that your recollection can be improved.' As he lit a fresh cigarette, his eyes idly scanned the handbag at her side and Ann's own wanted to join them, suddenly fearful that a wire was exposed or that the oddly-shaped umbrella handle, pointing at him, had attracted his attention. Then his regard turned back to her and she relaxed.

'You left the Double Decker Club,' he said, referring to a note-pad in front of him, 'with Mr Toffler at ten past eleven. You walked together into Friar's Yard at the rear in which he had parked his car. The yard is adequately illuminated by a lamp beneath the arch at its entrance. When Mr Toffler was about to unlock the door of his car, Mr Hansen approached him from behind and snatched away his keys. He then told Mr Toffler that he believed him to be in possession of a fire-arm ... you are with me so far?'

'Yes.'

'Mr Toffler naturally denied this, but was immediately assaulted by Mr Hansen and forced brutally against the side of his own car, too shocked by surprise and indignation to offer any resistance. Mr Hansen then went through the motions of searching Mr Toffler, doing considerable damage to his clothing in the process and purporting to produce a gun he alleges Mr Toffler was carrying on his person.' He smiled gently, understandingly. 'You recall this?'

'No,' she said promptly. 'I was on the other side of the car. All I saw were their heads and shoulders as they were struggling with each other.'

Weizsack looked pained. 'It is in Mr Toffler's recollection

that you were standing on *his* side of the car and I am sure if you really think about it, you would agree. Anyway, that is an irrelevancy I don't think we need introduce. It would certainly confuse the court and lead it away from the truth.'

'Court?' she echoed. 'Have I got to go to court?'

'Certainly, my dear.' He looked mildly surprised. 'Either as a witness or as a defendant in the dock. Better, as I am sure you will agree, that you appear as a witness.'

She tapped cigarette ash on to his unpolished parquet flooring as Ann Pardoe would undoubtedly consider natural, and said, 'I haven't got much choice, have I?'

'It appears not, my dear. Now, the gun that Mr Hansen says he found on Mr Toffler was in a small leather bag and this is why, no doubt, you didn't immediately recognize it for what it was. It will suffice for our purpose that you are able to say you saw something in Mr Hansen's hand *before* he started to search Mr Toffler.' When Ann started to speak, he overrode her politely. 'I regret to say that Chief Inspector Hansen is an extremely unscrupulous, unprincipled police officer; already suspended from duty as a result of allegations of his planting incriminating evidence on Mr Toffler. He will stoop to anything to harm him. He will, of course, extend his ill-will to you, my dear young lady, accuse you of lying, of being in concert with Mr Toffler.' He shook his head sadly. 'And you will not even be saying he was holding a gun in his hand. Just a small object about the size of one.'

'I don't remember seeing anything of the sort,' she said uncertainly, 'but if you think I should say I did...'

'And I'm sure you did, my dear. Splendid.' He expressed a small grunt of satisfaction. 'Fix that in your mind; picture it as you saw it. A small object that looked like a bag in his hand before he pushed Mr Toffler against his car.' His pale watery eyes stared at her, willing the words to remain in her memory. 'Did you hear Mr Hansen say something?'

'Yes. He shouted at me, told me to keep out of it.'

'Ah! Obviously not wanting you to see what he was going to do. Remember those words, my dear. And the other thing he said?'

'I don't remember he said anything else I heard,' she said doubtfully.

'I'm surprised. Did you not hear him say, *"That will fix you for Sergeant Gault, you bastard!"*?'

She wondered what he would say were he aware he was talking to Sergeant Gault's wife. 'No. Did he say that?'

He looked indignant. 'That is what he said. And he a police officer sworn to uphold the law.'

'Is that right?' she demanded of Toffler.

He grinned. 'Them exac' words, doll. When 'e planted the shooter on me.'

'You see,' Weizsack said, 'Mr Toffler will testify under solemn and sacred oath to those words. You no doubt recall them now?'

'No, I don't.' Ann Pardoe wasn't being very intelligent under her flowing yellow hair and Weizsack hid his irritation behind an encouraging smile.

'This is the buried recollection I was explaining to you,' he said. 'Think hard about it. Mr Hansen pushing Mr Toffler against the car: *That will fix you for Sergeant Gault, you bastard!* It's logic that if you were there when it was said, you must have heard it. It isn't too difficult to remember, is it?'

'No, it isn't. But won't I be questioned?'

He brushed that aside as a triviality. 'Just remember what we have discussed here and you need not worry. Nobody was ever hurt by telling the truth,' he said unctuously. 'You merely support what Mr Toffler will say; which is manifestly the truth because he is the person to whom it happened and to whom it was said.'

She hesitated, patently worried. 'But if I didn't really ... isn't that perjury? Won't I go to prison?'

'Legal balderdash, my dear. That is certainly what the police might threaten. But it amounts to only that your memory has been refreshed; quite properly on a solicitor's advice.' He made his voice reproachful. 'You wouldn't stand by and see Mr Toffler go to prison because Mr Hansen is prepared to lie, to plant a gun on him, would you?'

She looked at Toffler, her eyes not showing the hatred she nursed for him, but not showing sympathy either. 'I suppose not,' she said stonily.

'Of course you wouldn't. One thing, my dear. I think it advisable to suggest that you hadn't met Mr Toffler before last evening; that he was a total stranger who had casually offered you a lift home.'

'If that's what you consider best.'

'I do. Now,' he said more briskly, 'I know your time must be valuable to you.' He delved under the scattered papers on his desk and produced a thin pad of bank notes. 'I don't think fifteen pounds is too much for your trouble ... for your most helpful co-operation. And, naturally, a final accounting at the conclusion of Mr Toffler's case.'

She took the money and signed the paper he brought to her, acknowledging she had received it for loss of earnings, travelling and subsistence.

'If you will come to this office at the same time tomorrow, my dear,' he said, 'I will have your evidence down on paper for you to see.'

'Is that something I can learn what I have to say from?' she asked innocently, putting the notes in her coat pocket.

'It will refresh your memory. And we may have a small rehearsal later. Just to make sure your recollection of events is correct. I can depend on you?'

'You can, Mr Weizsack,' she answered him, meaning every word. 'I want to see justice done as well. Only one thing worries me. What do I do about the police looking for me?'

'Have nothing to fear now. As long as you are my witness, they will not arrest you. If they question you—and they may —you must say you have already made a statement to me and refuse to discuss anything with them.'

'And that's all?'

'For the moment, my dear.' He did a little bob of a bow, smiling as if giving her a papal benediction.

She stood, lifting her handbag, pushing the operating switch off as she did so. She had a purpose in mind.

Toffler, who had risen also, gave her the opportunity. He put a hand beneath her armpit from behind, pressing his fingers on the side of one of her breasts. 'Come on, doll,' he said. 'Le's you an' me 'ave a drink on it.'

The intimate familiarity raised an angry revulsion in her and she twisted sharply away from him. Her face was coldly contemptuous. 'After seeing you operate last night? Aren't you scared we might meet Hansen again?'

His mouth opened and he flushed, his eyes nasty. 'Now look 'ere, doll ...'

'It took two of them to take Denny in,' she interrupted him. 'I've seen old whores put up more of a fight than you did.'

He goggled at her. 'Where'd you get that bleedin' starch from?' he snarled. 'I'll...'

'*Edward!*' Weizsack's voice cut between them. '*Be quiet! I don't want you to be seen with Miss Pardoe anyway.*' He regarded Ann with a growing puzzlement and suspicion. She couldn't know it, but the elegance and fastidiousness, the poise of Ann Gault was showing from behind the tartish mask.

Ann spoke. 'I've said what you wanted me to say, Mr Weizsack. That doesn't give him a licence to paw me with his filthy hands.' She turned on the furious Toffler. 'Your wallet doesn't even begin to make you a better man than the next,' she said with scorn. 'You're all talk.' She let her loathing for him build up in her. 'Big with women and full of bounce. As soon as a policeman puts a finger on you, you start squealing like a frightened baby. Mr Hansen would make a dozen of you.'

'Get out!' he shouted harshly, his mouth lipless and ugly, the skin of his narrow face taut, 'before I knock you flat on your bloody fanny.'

With Weizsack there, Toffler was frustrated in his fury. Anywhere else, he knew he would have hit this arrogant cow arse over tit, witness or no witness, and then made her scream for mercy before he finished with her.

Weizsack said '*Edward!*' again and Toffler glowered, chewing hard on his mouth, his fists clenching and unclenching. 'I insist there is no more of this.' He stepped between them. Things were coming apart and he wanted Toffler on his own, to have him explain about this unpredictable woman who looked a tart but didn't sound like one. '*Please*, Miss Pardoe,' he said soothingly, 'leave Mr Toffler to me. I'm sure he meant nothing of what he said.'

She was suddenly quiet herself, her loathing not expended but under control. 'I'm sure he did, Mr Weizsack, but it doesn't matter.' She was at the door on her way out and visible to the clerk in the outer office. She held the notes the solicitor had given to her in her hand. She threw them down where they slid across the floor, scattering around Toffler's feet.

'If I give evidence,' she said evenly to the dumbfounded solicitor, 'it won't be for Toffler. And you had better start worrying about what the Law Society might do about *you*.'

# Chapter 22

A copper-coloured sun was dropping fast behind layers of ochre smoke-dirtied air held above the town when Hansen drove through the darkening streets. A frigid ankle-freezing wind pierced the floor of his car, buffeting its flanks and whipping up occasional flurries of stinging dust.

Inside the small hall, Ann pressed herself against the thick wool of his coat, then led him into the livingroom. She looked trim and slender in a grey jersey dress, her dark hair glossy and flicked into curls on either side of her pale cheeks. She wore the faintest shadow of pink on her mouth.

Hansen put the tape-recorder he carried on to a table, removing his coat. She shivered against him, her arms beneath his, her hands flat on his shoulderblades. He couldn't deny even his over-inflated loyalties the magic of her pliable body, the softness of the breasts he felt warm against him or the uplifted face, and he kissed her.

With each meeting, he was conscious they had moved further towards a point where it was becoming less possible for him to control the urgings of his sexual hunger for her. And these produced thunderous emotional storms in him that obscured, he believed, the gentler calmer airs of the affection he needed from her no less than the passion. For him, the pattern of their coming together demanded that the climax of their mutual need should be reached later; the Wagner symphony following the Debussy nocturne. His affection for her was inextricably tangled with his desire to possess her body and the confusion divided him and made him cautious, leaving him unsure that following the depletion of his physical appetite, made furtive by the shadow of her husband, there wouldn't be a revulsion against what he had done. He recognized and disapproved his sexual cowardice—for what man did he know who, in his position, would not?—but feared more that he could be left with regret and disillusion. There had, he made himself believe, to be more between them than two bodies coming together like unthinking animals. And none of that took into consideration the haunting, daunting presence of the sad spectre of the mutilated Gault, the man he was, paradoxically, beginning to resent for his demand on his loyalties. *Good old hung-up Hansen*, he told himself wryly. *The man most likely to develop into a manic-schizophrenic: the man with the two-drawer mind.*

He released himself gently from her. 'I actually came for the coffee,' he said lightly. He could smell its charred brownness in the room.

She cocked her head at him, studying his face. 'I know,' she answered solemnly. 'You're not going to bother with the tape?'

He smiled. 'While I'm here I suppose I'd better. It's good?'

'If you think subornation of perjury, attempted bribery, conspiracy to pervert justice are good, yes. I expect the DPP and his staff could dig out one or two more.'

She gave him the handbag and he removed the cassette from its base, fitting it into the machine he had brought with him. He sat on the settee by her side, drinking his coffee, silent while the tape echoed Weizsack's attempts at corrupting her evidence, Toffler's own voice making him a party to the conspiracy.

He switched it off, satisfaction in his face. 'We can do a ritual burning of your wig,' he said. 'But I felt there was more to come. You cut the recording early?'

'That was the bitch in me, darling. Toffler pawed me and I needed to tell him what I thought about him. It wouldn't do for a judge and jury to hear what I said. I told Weizsack, too, in a way.'

'So they know?'

'No more than that Ann Pardoe isn't going along with their cooked-up defence; that the Law Society might be interested in Weizsack's version of preparing proofs of evidence.'

'They were worried?'

'Toffler was livid. Weizsack, poor dear, was rather lost for words.'

'He's as much a poor old dear as a scorpion, and he won't be lost for them when he wants to sting back. I shall have to tell him about the recording,' he said. 'I'd hate to have him think he'd nothing more to worry about than your unsupported word. And Toffler being there was a bonus for us.'

'It's enough?' She was anxious for his approval.

'More than. After I've seen the Coughlin woman this evening—and she can do no less than clear your husband—I'm going to retire from the conflict with all flags flying; leave the clearing up to McGluskie and Bloodhound Sloan. Weizsack and Toffler have tried to fix me for a Charlie and, so far, failed. This won't stop them trying and I mightn't be so lucky next time.' He waited while she refilled his tiny gilt cup from the percolator. 'I want to put my feet up on a soft cushion and read a book or two without first looking under my bed. And I need to get these hatreds out of my system. You know the beginning of the *Desiderata*?' He quoted it. '*Go placidly amid the noise and haste, and remember what peace there may be in silence.* Well, that's for me. Toffler and Weizsack aren't important enough to have them sour me permanently.'

'You are still going to resign?'

'I don't know.' He frowned. 'It depends on how much unorthodoxy the Chief Constable's prepared to swallow to keep on somebody who can't exactly be his *beau ideal* of a Detective Chief Inspector.' He was thinking of the dead Arabella Stephenson and the very-much-alive-and-loving Norah. Disposing of a corpse as he had done wouldn't, his checking in Harris's *Criminal Law* had assured him, put him in any serious danger of judicial punishment. His suspected adultery with Norah wasn't anything likely to qualify him for a Queen's Police Medal and a commendation in General Orders, but, unproved and discreet as it had been, he would find himself in company with a number of other senior police officers at whom similar suspicion could point an accusing finger. Extramarital sex was a human imperfection that could cut down through the rank structure and not leave too much trauma in its wake.

'I've had enough, Ann,' he said. 'I'm too involved personally to enjoy it. I'm eating Paracetamols by the jarful.'

'And when Bill's cleared?' The words were casual, but her eyes were not.

Hansen felt again the dark cloud of Gault's problems. 'When he's on his feet,' he said, 'I'm going to have to let him know how I feel about his wife. It should be intensely therapeutical for him.' He turned down his mouth. 'The poor bugger won't have much left, will he?' he said savagely. 'A disability pension if he's lucky and no ...'

She stopped him, putting her fingers over his mouth. 'Darling, *don't*. You're being masochistic, martyrish, again. I refuse to spend the rest of my life with a man I don't love; who doesn't love me either. No,' she said when he tried to speak, 'He doesn't. He's proved it a dozen times. Even had I not met you, I would have left him. I ... I don't know how to say this, Robert.' She was wary of his reaction, not looking at him, her voice low. 'I've already told him about us.'

He jerked, startled, his eyebrows chopping down. 'You've what!'

'I told Bill we were in love with each other. Darling,' she cried desperately, 'I had to. I couldn't be less than honest.'

'Christ, Ann!' He felt a tiny stir of anger in him. 'The poor bastard's got enough problems already. It's no wonder he didn't want to see you again.'

'No. I told him after that. He had reasons of his own.' She flicked her hair nervously.

'But before he was put into a psychiatric ward?'

'No, afterwards. Darling, it was the right thing to do at the time.' She was persuasive, her expression anxious. 'I *know* Bill.'

'It couldn't have helped him,' he said implacably.

'Sweetheart, Bill and I haven't been compatible for months. It wouldn't be the end of the world for him. I'm not making excuses or trying to justify what I did.' She chewed at her lip. 'I wouldn't have told you this under any other circumstances, but he has a woman somewhere.'

'You know? Or you're guessing?' It suggested to him a reason why she was anxious to know about the photograph. Why, in fact, she would have doubts. Even a woman who didn't care much that her husband was sleeping around, might still object to being supplanted by a whore and having it publicized in a court. She had once said as much to him.

'A wife doesn't need telling, Robert,' she said simply, her eyes wide and candid, 'when her husband is unfaithful. There's nothing very original about what happened. He was often out until well after midnight, supposedly on enquiries...'

'Which isn't a bit unusual for a CID man, Ann, as you must know.'

'Of course not,' she admitted. 'But a CID man isn't supposed to come to bed with the smell of some vile woman on him,' her nose wrinkled her remembered revulsion, '... with a look on his face that tells you it didn't rub off on him from somebody he'd arrested.' She glanced down at her thighs, pulling the woollen skirt tight over them, hesitating at what she was about to say. 'And, of course, he didn't want me. I had to accept rejection.' Two spots of colour appeared over her cheekbones. 'Do you know what that does to a woman?'

'I know what it does to a man.' He meant himself. There was nothing more chilling and belittling to him than the thought of an indifferent turning away of a woman in bed.

'It did it to me,' she said quietly.

'All right. What did he say when you told him about us?' He held her arm in his fist and squeezed it. 'And no euphemisms.'

'No euphemisms. He called me a dirty little cow. With additions.' She pulled a face. 'He naturally wouldn't believe that you and I weren't ... you know?'

'A natural presumption of guilt, I suppose. You can't blame him. And about me?'

Her mouth twitched and she shook her head. 'Darling, there aren't any euphemisms for that. He just doesn't like you very much.'

'I'll use my imagination,' he said, 'and probably agree with him. And he'll no doubt repeat it when I tell him about us. And when I do, it's going to be important to me to be able to look him in the eye and not feel too much like fourth-rate mice dirt.' He gave her a smile that said Gault was casting a very much shorter shadow. 'Whatever the result, it'll only confirm Sloan's suspicions that you and I have already been having a twice-nightly orgy.' He kissed her lightly on the corner of her mouth. 'Please darling, bear with me. Don't let's start off by hating ourselves...'

She put an arm around him and pulled him to her. 'I love you, sweetheart, when you're so chaste and incorruptible,' she whispered, her hair in his nostrils. 'You'll come back?'

'I'll try,' he said, although he had already made a decision not to. Not that night. Exposing his emotions to the magnetism of her body was undermining his resolution.

# Chapter 23

Hansen waited in the Limping Duck Café with no certainty that he hadn't been manoeuvred into position by either Weizsack or Toffler. It wasn't fretting him but he sat, nevertheless, with his back to a wall. Around him had been left a *cordon sanitaire* of empty chairs as if he were a man suffering the terminal stages of leprosy. He was obviously a policeman and as equally obvious not there just for the pleasure of drinking the cup of thin coffee that steamed on the table in front of him. Most of the men using the café guessed he was there for a purpose, and those with momentarily clear consciences waited to see what was going to happen to someone else.

The wizened proprietor with the scarred forehead not completely covered by his crumpled chef's hat thought so too. He was nervous and irritable behind the counter, quick in his movements as a canary as he fried sausages and shook his basket of chips in a huge pan of boiling fat. Hansen's unexplained presence worried him. He assumed it meant trouble for someone; as a natural spin-off probably for himself as well.

Whenever Hansen caught the wizened man's eye, he would nod amiably over the top of his evening newspaper, unsettling him even more.

At eight-eleven, the telephone at the back of the counter rang, the proprietor taking the cigarette from his mouth long enough to answer it. He replaced the receiver after a brief conversation and walked from behind the counter to where Hansen was sitting.

'You Mr 'Ansen?' he asked accusingly. He had pink-rimmed eyes like a hungover bloodhound.

Hansen admitted that he might be.

'A 'phone message from a lady,' he said. 'She says you're to walk up the street.' He jerked a grimy, nail-bitten thumb vaguely northwards. 'Towards the Cross Keys boozer.'

'That's all?'

'Tha's all, mate.' He collected Hansen's unfinished cup of coffee and returned to the counter, taking with him a clinging odour of cooking fat and sweat, his attitude that of a man acquitting himself of a distasteful task with tact and distinction.

The wind outside had increased to a swirling gustiness that flattened discarded newspapers against walls and hoardings and rattled the shutters of closed shops. Hansen thought he could smell snow on its cold breath.

In the lividity of the mercury-vapour street lamps, doorways and passage entrances were black-shadowed caves. He walked with his gloved hands clenched, ready to drop the first man to step from one and ask for a light for his cigarette.

A taxi, cruising slowly along the kerb, overtook him from behind. Not unobserved, for Hansen had been watching its lights in the glass window of a shop. It braked to a halt at his side, its tyres crunching grit in the gutter. The black glass of the rear door was lowered and the pale oval of a face looked at him and, apparently satisfied, retreated again to the dark interior. The driver let Hansen open the door himself and climb in. The taxi pulled away immediately, jerking the detective back in the seat next to the woman.

His first impression was of her strong sweet perfume that filled the interior of the vehicle. His second, that she was more attractive than he had judged from the photograph; although still looking every scented armful a purchasable commodity in her PVC simulated-leather coat, tightly belted to give her a small waist, and calf-length boots. Her hair was black and long and hung loose.

'Miss Coughlin?' he asked.

She nodded and turned her head, looking backwards through the rear window. 'You're sure you weren't followed?' she whispered.

He recognized her voice immediately although her brogue was less pronounced than it had been over the telephone. She sounded as if she had taken pains to soften it.

'No, I'm not,' he said. 'That café's about as private a place as Trafalgar Square. Everybody in town knows how many times I stirred my coffee by now. You should know too. You were watching me.'

'Sure I was.'

'To see that I didn't bring another detective with me?'

'Something like that.' Her teeth showed white in the semi-darkness. 'If you had, I'd have left you waiting.'

'Where are we going?' He thought her a lot less nervous, a lot more self-assured, than she had acted on the telephone.

She put a finger to her lips, enjoining silence, nodding at the back of the driver's head.

Hansen settled in his corner and relaxed. He was happy about the driver. He had seen him carrying a Salvation Army drum when he wasn't waiting around in the rank. He couldn't be one of Toffler's thugs because carrying and beating a big drum was hard work. He had obviously received his instructions beforehand for he took a circuitous little-used route to leave the centre behind, driving into the labyrinth of dark roads that served a sprawling formless estate at the rough end of the town.

She tapped on the glass screen and the driver halted the taxi near a group of telephone kiosks. She paid him off while Hansen tried to obliterate his features in the shadow from one of the kiosks. Being seen with such an obvious hustler in these circumstances could only suggest he wasn't too many minutes from hopping into bed with her.

With the taxi gone, she said, 'It's only just around the corner.' He walked obediently at her side. It was colder here than in the more sheltered centre, the grass on the black lawns looking as if shaved by the arctic wind. He noticed she still glanced around her, but with caution rather than fear. Being with him probably lessened it.

She opened a sagging garden gate that scraped loudly in the quiet road, leading him to an unlit house that was shabby even in the dark, unlocking the door and preceding him inside. Not until he had shut the door did she switch on a light.

In the hard glare of an unshaded bulb, he could see that his impression of her had been nearly right. She was attractive. But, as he could now discern, used and abused too often and by too many men, her pleasant features beginning to bloat, her body too lush to last much longer without unsightly fat being added to the hips and breasts. Her face was a nice placid one with nothing mean about it; childish rather, as if she had stopped thinking after she left school. The eyes were the warm lustrous brown of an amiable cow, looking as if they could weep easily.

Her overpowering perfume was mercifully killing the sour smell of food debris and damp underclothing in the room. Hansen could feel the scent clinging to the cilia in his nostrils and he knew his clothing would reek of it. He thought it as well he hadn't a wife to whom it would be necessary to explain.

She shivered and, without removing her coat, put a match to a gas fire. She was polite too, asking him to sit.

He squeezed into a square-shaped chair that clamped its chilly sides against his haunches. Old newspapers had been stuffed beneath its shapeless seat cushion. The room was meanly furnished with oilcloth, a brown plastic-covered settee and equally cheap easy chairs. The floor was gritty from not being swept and the unwashed crockery of several meals was still on the table. Beneath it was a phalanx of emptied beer bottles. It was the livingroom of people who probably got their evening's comfort in a local bar and would neither know nor care what the room looked like when they returned to it.

With the fire burning, the woman went to a varnished cupboard and withdrew a sherry bottle and two glasses. She poured the detective a drink and handed it to him. He waited until she had poured one for herself, said, 'Good health,' and put it ritually near his lips, then placing it on the floor near his feet. The sherry smelt as acid as fermenting cider and the rim of the glass was smeared.

She said something in Gaelic to him and sat at the other side of the fire, drinking her sherry in one uninhibited gulp, then lighting a cigarette and relaxing in her chair. She had long graceful legs and didn't mind a policeman looking at them.

'This place isn't yours?' Hansen asked.

She shook her head. 'I'm leaving in the morning.'

'Oh? Where to?'

'Ah, now, Mr Hansen, that's not for the asking. But to Ireland.'

'All right. But in the meantime, you've unconfessed sins on your conscience?' Policemen were often used as surrogate priests and she would be a Catholic, needing some sort of absolution by unburdening whatever it was worrying her. It was in her, needing to come out. It would come easier with the minimum of questions.

'Donkey was going to kill me,' she said calmly, picking a fragment of tobacco from her tongue with a red-nailed little finger.

'Was?'

'I don't think he will now that I've told you.'

'You could be exaggerating his interest in you, Miss Coughlin.' He deliberately put doubt in his voice.

'You don't believe me?'

'I'm willing to be convinced.'

She straightened herself in the chair, laid her cigarette on the metal top of the gas fire and unbuttoned her PVC coat, opening it to her waist. Beneath it she wore a violet shirt-blouse. She undid this to reveal her brassiere to the poker-faced detective, wincing as she did so. The brassiere supported the large breasts in two blue satin hammocks just covering the nipples. All above was lard-pale bulging flesh, horribly criss-crossed with red lacerations, newly scored and puckering the skin. Holding the cuts from gaping were knots of surgical stitching, hanging on the bloody lines like tiny black flies. Her breasts would never again, thought Hansen, hang smooth-skinned over a man.

He grimaced his sympathy. 'He did that?'

'Him and Ashy ... the bastards! They did it with a razor-blade.' She wagged her head, examining the injuries. 'I don't know how I'm going to explain it to Jack.'

'Jack?' She was incredible, he thought; acting no more concerned than if she had been showing him a scratched finger.

'Jack's my fiancé in County Limerick.'

'He must be a very accommodating chap,' he said, 'and I'm sure he'll understand.'

She replied, 'Yes,' quite seriously, not recognizing the irony in his voice, rebuttoning her blouse and coat.

'That was to shut you up?'

'Yes.'

'It was necessary?'

'I was upset, Mr Hansen. I didn't like what the cruel bugger did to your Sergeant Gault. I sneaked in the court to hear how Donkey was getting on. I saw the poor sod—your sergeant,

I mean. Christ! What a mess. Losing his eye, having his bangers mashed up.' She twisted her features into a spasm of sympathy. It was genuine enough. Whoredom hadn't yet dried out the woman in her. 'I was daft enough to say so to Donkey. He didn't trust me afterwards. He never trusts anyone anyway. Then he heard you'd got hold of my name. So it's your fault really,' she said without rancour. 'He knew if you found me, you'd probably make me tell you things. Apart from you having my photograph.' She sucked on her cigarette, swallowing the smoke without blinking.

'So, in fact, telling me is a form of insurance, isn't it? You think that just so long as I know, and that Toffler knows I know, he daren't touch you.' He recognized confirmation in her face. She was too ingenuous for real concealment. 'Why do you say he was going to kill you?'

'He said he would if I spoke to you.'

'And you believed him?'

She touched her breasts. 'Wouldn't you, mister?'

He showed his teeth at her, looking as tough as he could when he wanted, but not meaning a word of what he was about to say. 'Toffler isn't the only bastard you know, Miss Coughlin. Don't forget *me*. If I don't get the truth from you, your Jack is going to be crying in his potheen for a month or two longer while I sort you out.'

'You don't have to be hard with me, Mr Hansen,' she said reprovingly, not disturbed by his threat. 'Sure, and I'm going to tell you everything. Janet said I could trust you,' she added.

'Janet?' He had mislaid the name.

She sniggered. 'Janet Liggett. The girl who got your cufflinks undone. The one who didn't give you your massage. She told me what happened when she got back to Charlie Glass.'

'Don't count on it,' he said. 'I'm not always so nice.' He liked Sheila Coughlin. He pulled his wallet out and withdrew the photograph, displaying it to her. Having met her, he could now recognize her on it. 'Tell me how this came about.'

She inspected it with the sort of expression that led him to believe she was going to ask him for a copy to give to her Jack. It wouldn't have surprised him. 'You'll promise me you won't arrest me if I do?'

'No. I'm more likely to arrest you if you don't,' he said easily.

'I shan't give evidence in a court. Kiss the Holy Book, I won't.'

'If you get to County Limerick—*if*—I don't suppose we'll be able to make you. Tell me.'

'All right.' She lit a fresh cigarette, coughed and poured herself more sherry. She drank most of it in one swallow. 'Donkey put this job to me. First of all, your sergeant had been banging up Donkey's girl. Donkey didn't know that but he suspected, and that was enough for him. This girl—Susan, she called herself—was a right bloody cow, Mr Hansen.' She said it without malice; it was a fact of life she was commenting on. 'I used to be with Donkey myself until he met up with her. And while she was with him, she got this sergeant all screwed up about her. She didn't make any particular secret of it, the bitch. When she'd had a few gins, she'd tell the bloody world. I suppose it tickled her to have a detective sergeant trotting round after her like a performing monkey. He was crazy about her, although she used to laugh about the poor sod when he wasn't there. He wasn't the only one she had, of course. She went right through the bloody card with them all at one time or another. And all for nothing,' she said incredulously. 'Just because she bloody well liked it. All except Ashy.' There was spitting contempt in the way she said it. 'And she used to needle him about his young men. He only didn't fill the bitch in because she belonged to Donkey. But I reckon he told him about her in the end.'

She poured out a lot more sherry, spilling it in her haste to get it inside her. It was loosening her tongue, making her eyes heavy-lidded, and Hansen hadn't to do more than to nod now and then to keep it going. But beneath his grave interest there was a creeping unease, a growing coldness of doubt that he didn't want to take out and examine and recognize for what it might be.

'Donkey,' she continued, licking the sherry from her mouth, 'told me he wanted a dirty picture of your sergeant that he could show to this Susan. That, he reckoned, would fix his duff with her. He also reckoned on sending one to his wife and one to your top brass. He was such a nasty sod about this Susan of his that he was doing the job personal. He fixed the room in Wikker's place and told me how to get the sergeant in there when he gave me the nod. That night, Ashy came in and said the copper was tailing Donkey. Donkey, of course,

215

was leading him to the hotel. I went outside and did my stuff, telling Mr Gault I'd been thumped by a man who wouldn't let me back into my room. The poor sod,' she said sadly, 'followed me in like a lamb. I went straight to the room, but I heard him being bashed down in the entrance. I was stripped off when they carried him in. He was out cold as Donkey said he would be. Christ! At first I thought he was dead. Ashy took the photographs. It wasn't too easy because we had to get his face in the picture but not mine. Once he started to come round and Donkey had to hit him with a cloth-covered cosh that didn't leave any mark.'

She flushed under Hansen's steady regard, although there was no sign of condemnation in it.

'I'm not proud of it, Mr Hansen, but Donkey made me. It's easier to do what he says than not. He's a vicious sod and specially with women. When he started beating him, kicking him while he was on the floor, I tried to stop him. Honest, I did. But he slapped me bloody silly and Ashy pushed me out of the room.'

'How did the photograph come to be used in court?'

'Well,' she said, 'for a start, Donkey obviously didn't expect to get knocked off by you. He didn't reckon on the sergeant knowing who hit him. Once he was charged, the picture wasn't much good except to get him out of trouble. The first I knew he was going to use it was when he took me along to see his brief...'

'Weizsack?'

'Yes. He had a statement he asked me to read and sign. It wasn't in my own name so I didn't mind. I signed it Bridget O'Connor with an address I've forgotten. The brief promised me I'd never be called anyway.' She wrinkled her forehead. 'Peculiar bugger,' she said. 'He spoke all the time as if he really believed I *was* Bridget O'Connor and that the statement was true. I mean, he knew it wasn't but he never let on for one second except at the end.'

'That's because he was having the conversation taped. He could produce it to confirm the statement if he ever got into serious difficulties. And, of course, it wouldn't be his fault that he was given a false name and address. What was the statement about?'

'It said that I'd been Sergeant Gault's lover for some time, that we used to meet and go to the Queensbury Hotel, staying there under different names, but always as husband and wife. My husband was supposed to have caught us at it that night with a private detective and after taking a photograph, beat him up. A load of downright rubbish, Mr Hansen, and I'd have never said it in court. When I'd finished, he gave me ten pounds and told me to stay out of sight for a bit, to forget that I'd ever been there.'

With his hand already in his coat pocket, he switched off the tape recorder that had taken down everything she said through the microphone concealed behind his necktie. 'Tell me more about Sergeant Gault and ... and this woman Susan.' There was a maggot in his brain boring a hole towards a knowing that he didn't want to face. He was, he thought wretchedly, like the man on a lonely road who, having once turned round, walks on and turns no more his head because he knows a frightful fiend doth close behind him tread. But he had to know. He had come this far along the road, unwittingly at first, then shadowed by the growing suspicion.

'I don't know a lot,' she answered him. 'Mostly what she used to say in the Double Decker. Of course, he never got to go in there. They used to meet in the Red Lion Hotel when she could get away from Donkey. She wouldn't leave him alone. Always asking questions about the job. At one time I thought she was doing it for Donkey. You know, screwing him for police information. But she couldn't have been. She'd left Donkey by the time he'd found out about them and that was when he started wanting to get her back. There haven't been many women who've tossed Donkey over and he'd do something about it.'

'Where is she now?'

She shook her head. 'Christ only knows. She left before Donkey appeared in court.'

He asked the question he knew he had to ask and hadn't wanted to ever since she had been mentioned. 'What is her second name, Miss Coughlin?' *Please, God*, he prayed, *let it not be*, but knowing he was wasting his time.

'Didn't I say? Goff. Susan-bloody-Goff.'

Braced as he was to take it, it still hit him like a kick from a horse, the blood draining from his face, leaving him cold with a sick anger. Goff. His wife's maiden name and she had triumphed in her final filthy humiliation of him. From all the loud and coarse-fibred men she preferred for the practice of her promiscuity, she couldn't have chosen one more vile or contemptible, or more hurtful to Hansen, than Toffler with whom to degrade them both.

That Toffler almost certainly didn't know made no difference. He, Hansen, knew. That she meant nothing to him now, that he had not seen or heard from her for months also made none. She was still his wife and carried with her some of his honour and pride. That Gault, the man for whom he had nursed such a priggish and misconceived loyalty, had also been her lover mattered nothing against the enormity of her degradation with Toffler. And Toffler, had he but known it, possessed one of man's most belittling weapons against another. And he would have used it mercilessly. That he didn't know, was the only thing Hansen could find to her credit.

Little of his inner torment, none of the internal bleeding of his pride, showed on his impassive features, but he was pale, his eyes dark.

'Are you all right?' she asked curiously. He had gone suddenly quiet and she was well on the way to being woozy from the sherry, her features blurred with it.

'Yes,' he said, standing and ready to go. 'Bloody wonderful.' He dredged the sick humour from somewhere beneath the humiliation. 'Give my regards to Jack when you see him. Tell him I know exactly how he feels.'


After Ann had let Hansen out of the door, seeing the tail lights of his car vanish around a bend in the road, she sat for a long time thinking about him. Then, to kill the time until he might return, she undressed and took a leisurely bath.

She was seated at her dressing-table making up her face when she heard the chimes of the door-bell. There was no conscious coquetry, no intent to provoke a response in Hansen, in her answering the door in the towelling bathrobe that was all that covered her perfumed nudity.

Her mouth opened in terrified shock when she saw Toffler, an insolent triumphant grin on his mouth, his foot already jammed against the door she tried desperately to close against him.

' 'Ello, doll,' he said. 'We 'ad a date. Remember?'

# Chapter 24

By the time he had found his way back to the kiosks and telephoned for a taxi, waiting for it hunched and morose in the increasing cold, Hansen had reswallowed a lot of the pride that had threatened regurgitation at Sheila Coughlin's disclosure. He tried to recognize that he was being masculinely possessive, that he had neither right nor reason to concern himself with what manner of men his ex-wife chose to use as her partners. While he would have preferred her lovers to be clean-scrubbed and bowler-hatted, he should logically have no reasonable objection to her lovers wearing sweaty undervests, having unshaven jowls. It was Toffler who stuck in his throat. He was the nub of it. He felt he could have suffered, without too much bleeding, the knowledge he had been cuckolded by anybody with a decent accent and good table manners; only being humiliated to the point of outraged fury where she preferred one of the specimens of criminality he was employed to deal with. It was, he admitted, bloody-minded arrogance of a sort.

It was ten o'clock when he was dropped outside the Limping Duck Café and he collected his own car. Driving home, he knew that he needed a succession of large undiluted whiskies and time to rationalize Toffler and Susan to a relative unimportance. They were persisting in occupying his thinking to the exclusion of all else.

He considered telephoning Ann to tell her that her husband was as good as cleared, but the thought was sour in him and he knew he wouldn't. When he had laid the devils that plagued him, he might.

The Opel *Commodore*, glimmering its highly polished orange and black under a street lamp outside his apartment block, was almost a relief to him, although Norah wasn't due for

219

three or four days. The thought of her shone as a golden comfort in his wretchedness. He stood in the darkness of the entrance hall and willed himself to a semblance of normality, clamping down on the tiny marionettes of the two obscene lovers cavorting in his brain.

Norah sat in his chintzy armchair, her legs tucked under her, Trudchen on her lap. A glass of whisky was balanced on one padded arm. She looked pink and wholly uncomplicated in a kingfisher-blue tunic dress, her gold hair curled like the petals of an autumn chrysanthemum. She had kicked her shoes off and they lay in the centre of the carpet. She smiled happily at him, showing whiter teeth than any other woman he had ever known. Everything about her was superabundant and gleaming with magnificent health.

He held her hand for a second and squeezed it on his way to the bathroom for Paracetamols. When he returned, he went to the sideboard and washed four of them down with a massive dose of whisky.

'You needed that,' she remarked affectionately. 'You're looking all saturnine and haunted.' Behind the placid features, she possessed a perceptive intuition of his moods.

'Everybody has his own devils,' he said. 'I've just drowned a couple of mine. Have I mislaid the date?' He managed a smile, thinking it must be his first for several days. Not only was she too soon, but she was dressed. She should have been accoutred in a suit of his pyjamas, smelling of talc and of the perfumed soap he had bought specially for her. But he felt happy that she was there. There were no hidden emotional depths to her that he wouldn't be able to understand and, by just being herself, able to spread a soothing cream over his problems.

'No, you haven't,' she said calmly. 'I came to tell you that I'm heavy with your child.'

He stared, horrified and stunned, his euphoria fled. 'Christ Almighty! You *can't* be!'

'Oh? And why not, Bobbie darling? Haven't we done all that seems to be necessary to ensure it?'

He turned to go back to the sideboard.

She lifted Trudchen from her lap and walked to him, wrapping him strongly in her arms. Without her shoes, the top of her head came to his chin. 'Kiss me, you drunken bum,' she demanded. 'I'm not, but it isn't because you haven't tried. I've always been curious to know just what you'd say.'

He felt weak with relief and managed a shaky grin. 'How many whiskies?'

She rubbed her nose against him, then kissed him moistly. 'You were late coming home, and it's been a long time.' She snapped her teeth at him. 'I could eat you, darling. You'd taste of whisky and after-shave.' She regarded his face thoughtfully. 'It's just as well I came,' she said severely. 'Last time you were a physical wreck. This time you've worms gnawing at you.' She gentled her voice. 'Tell me about it, darling.'

He shook his head. 'I'm just a mixed-up schizophrenic who can't make up his two minds. It'll all come out right in the end.' He spoke more confidently than he felt. He smoothed the flat of his hand down her well-fleshed back to her buttocks, feeling the old familiar happy desire she was so capable of raising.

'No more joking, poppet, and no more trying,' he said. 'Which means no more visits after tonight.'

'Darling Bobbie!' She creased her forehead, her eyes searching his face. 'What on earth do you mean?'

He played it light. 'We are undone,' he said solemnly. 'All is discovered. Parking your car outside my apartment has percolated through official channels to McGluskie. The evil-minded old bugger believes you and I are having it off.'

'Oh, is that all? It's probably only a coincidence, darling,' she said, 'but so does a certain Detective Superintendent Andrew Sloan Esquire.'

He was astonished for the second time that evening. 'Sloan?' he repeated stupidly.

'That's why I'm here tonight, Bobbie.' She laughed. 'Pour me another whisky. Not a titchy one either.' She released him and returned to her chair. 'I've things to tell you.'

'Well tell me, for God's sake,' he said. He busied himself with the whisky bottle. 'Although it can't be anything worse than what I've already had this evening.'

'He called on me this afternoon.' Then she spoke gruffly in imitation of him. ' "Detective Superintendent Sloan, madam. I would like to ask you a few questions about your association with Detective Chief Inspector Hansen." '

Hansen felt a flush rising to his face. 'I'm sorry, poppet,' he said contritely. 'That must have been bloody embarrassing for you. I didn't think he'd go that far.'

'It's all *right*, Bobbie dear. Don't worry. Geoffrey wasn't there. I don't imagine he'd have cared if he had been.' She giggled. 'Then he showed me his warrant card and waited while I read every word on it. I was very, very bridge-playing upper class with him; at my most haughtiest and bitchiest. I said, "Am I to understand you are implying that Mr Hansen and I are having an illicit relationship?" I even straightened up a copy of the parish church magazine on the coffee table to help him on. The poor dear went bright red all the way down to his navy-blue socks. Are they an official issue, pet?'

'Norah,' he growled, 'don't be irrelevant. What did he say?'

'He sort of strangled behind his collar and said, "Not exactly, madam." He kept looking across at a painting of Geoffrey's grandfather who was a suffragan bishop or something in Bechuanaland and that didn't seem to make him any happier either. I said, "Then what *do* you mean, superintendent?"'

Hansen began to feel sorry for Sloan. 'You *were* bitchy, Norah, weren't you?'

She smiled. 'I was protecting my honour, darling. And yours. Poor Mr Sloan. While he was trying to think how to say it, I said, "Would you rather discuss the matter with my husband? I can get him here from his office quite quickly. He's awfully litigation-minded, I'm afraid, and Mr Hansen is one of his very close friends."'

Hansen sipped at his whisky. He suspected his reputation was in capable hands with Norah.

'I said,' she continued, '"If it is any business of the constabulary's, superintendent—which I very much doubt—Mr Hansen and I share a mutual interest in ergonomics." Darling, what *are* ergonomics? I was going to say philately, but it sounded so ordinary and suspicious. Like etchings and things. Anyway, it was the first difficult word that came into my mind.'

'If it isn't in Moriarty's *Police Law* and listed as an arrestable offence,' Hansen said, 'then neither he nor I would have the remotest idea.'

'Well, after some small talk about my car being seen outside here, he said he was sorry to have bothered me, refused a cup of tea and some chocolate oatmeal biscuits and scuttled out as if I'd suggested we should go to bed together.' She showed her dimples. 'Talking of beds, Bobbie darling.' She rose and fell on his lap, fastening her mouth to his, wriggling her big body as if to press him flat into the chair.

He disentangled himself. 'Be serious, poppet. I mustn't see you again. I *am* being investigated and your name has come into it. It's a squalid business and not anything I would...'

'Piffle, darling,' she interrupted him calmly. 'I don't give a bloody damn. Neither would Geoffrey. Nor even his sainted grandfather.' She kissed him gently. 'Bobbie dear, please don't be difficult.'

'I'm not,' he said wryly. 'Just unnaturally noble. And *I* give a damn. And so would Geoffrey if he knew. Sloan won't be discouraged just because you've given him an aristocratic brush-off.' Now was the opportunity to let her know he was in love with Ann—Christ! But was he? He couldn't even be sure about that—that this was where they came to a full stop. Only, he thought grimly, how did you explain to a marvellous woman like Norah that he no longer wanted her. No, he contradicted himself, that wasn't the truth. As he had thought it, so he realized how very necessary she was to him, how dismal his life might be without her light-hearted warmth. He cursed himself for being such a two-faced vacillating bastard. He did want her. Self-evidently he did, as she had already noticed. And that was by no means the only way. There was an affection between them he had always drawn back from analysing too closely. She had to be as much his concern as Ann. What he was doing now was fair to neither of them.

'I'm sorry, poppet,' he said firmly, having made up his mind, 'but I'm not going to let you do it. For your own sake. Perhaps for mine, too.' He tried to get out from under the weight of her Junoesque body and she resisted calmly by becoming flaccid on him.

She cupped his face in her hands and held it immovable. She was strong and determined. 'Darling,' she said, punctuating her words by dabbing her pursed lips on his mouth, 'I am simply not going to be refused. Consider my *amour-propre* or whatever it is; my womanly pride. Geoffrey would be *furious* with you. And while you may not want to, I do.'

She was doing him good with her frank, uncomplicated needs. Even were he to tell her about Ann, he doubted whether she would understand his reluctance. He thought that loving her tonight might exorcise some of the besottedness he had for Ann, take some of the sting from his physical need for her. He kissed Norah back. 'You've talked me into it,' he said. 'But no more after tonight.' He qualified that, not wanting to be brutal with her. 'Anyway, not until I'm no longer under investigation.'

'You're going to be in trouble, Bobbie?' She was serious for a moment.

'I don't think so,' he said off-handedly, making a triviality of a disciplinary enquiry. He would re-assume his troubles when she had gone. 'No more than I can handle.'

She stood, holding his hand and pulling him from the chair. 'Have your shower with me, darling. It's terribly lonely in there and I'm frightened of burglars.'

They stood naked together in the curtained cabinet and he smoothed aromatic bath oil on the polished skin of her shoulders and breasts while she knotted a white towel into a turban on her head. When he had finished and she glistened pinkly, she took the oil flask from him and rubbed his body with her soft hands, her fingers kneading gently.

'Whatever this is,' he said, 'I don't think it can be called ergonomics.' It might have been his imagination, but it seemed to him that her waistline, never wasp-like, had thickened. He put the thought to one side.

She giggled, nuzzling his chest with her lips. 'No, it can't.'

When he turned on the mixer taps they wrestled happily, slippery with oil and water, fighting each other with their mouths in the steaming downpour. The telephone bell rang in the other room.

'No,' she said when he pulled aside the shower curtain. 'Let it ring. It can't be more important than me.' She stepped from the shower and reached for a towel. 'Hurry up with yours before Superintendent Sloan starts beating down the door.'

By the time he stepped from the shower and was towelling himself dry, the bell had ceased ringing.

Before climbing into bed, she removed the receiver from its stand and left it dangling uselessly on its cord. 'It'll only be Geoffrey,' she murmured drowsily as she joined him, 'wanting to know where the door key is.'

While Norah slept deeply, sprawled warm and inelegantly against him, he lay with his mind squirreling away at his re-emerging worries, his devils back with him in his wide-awake thoughts. Although what he had done with Norah had been partly his effort to exorcise his unappeased need for Ann, he felt that he had failed her, much as an unfaithful husband might fail his wife.

Ann, staring terrified at the unexpected appearance of Toffler, screamed. Toffler, his face suddenly vicious, slashed her face brutally with the back of his hand. She fell backwards under the stunning impact, her head hitting the plaster wall, sliding down it to the floor.

Toffler kicked the door shut and leaned over her, grasping her arms and dragging her limp body effortlessly into the inner room, flinging her on to the settee. With her body exposed naked beneath the disarrayed robe, she lay dazed and moaning, a thin tendril of blood coming from the corner of her mouth. She opened her eyes, a glaze of pain showing in them, pulling blindly at the robe to cover herself.

Toffler stood looking down at her, swaying with the brandy he had drunk, evil insolence back on his face. 'So you an' 'Ansen was tryin' to fix my duff was you, Mrs Bloody Gault.' His fists were opening and closing at his side. 'Takin' the bleedin' starch out of me.'

Ann twisted from the settee and stood shakily, then threw herself desperately to reach her handbag left on the chair near the fire.

'No you don',' he snarled. He snatched at her robe and swung her staggering around, hitting her again over her cheekbone. Before she could recover her balance, he was at her, raining blows on her face with his flat hand. 'We 'ad a date, doll,' he hissed between his teeth, 'an' you're goin' to keep it.' When she sagged, he released his hold on her robe and she collapsed to the carpet where she lay motionless.

Toffler, breathing heavily, looked around him, then searched the rooms on the ground floor, checking the location of the rear door, ensuring it was locked. He went to the front door and shot the bolts, returning to pull out the plugs of the two reading lamps, leaving only the fire to illuminate the room. His expression was evil in the soft red light. He looked at the still unconscious Ann and licked his mouth, his narrow features goatish. Then he moved towards her.

\*

She lay limp and spent where he had risen from her. No words passed between them. When he was ready, he stood swaying at the door and stared down at her, insolence back on his features, contempt in his eyes, answering the silent loathing and hatred in hers.

When the outer door closed on his going, she turned her swollen bloody face to the crumpled robe beneath her and began to sob. Her fingernails dug into the flesh Toffler had polluted, wanting to mutilate it in self-disgust and revulsion.

Later, she went into the bathroom. When she had finished what she had to do to her bruised and fouled body, she lifted the telephone receiver and dialled Hansen's number with a trembling finger. She waited, listening to the unanswered impulses, then recradled the instrument. When she dialled again, she heard the disconnect signal.

She went to her bed and lay staring, numb and defeated, at the dark sky of the ceiling.

# Chapter 25

Over their eight o'clock breakfast of bacon and scrambled eggs, Hansen had persuaded Norah that both their interests and reputations would be best served by an indefinite period of no contact between them. Indefinite, that is, until he had been cleared in the disciplinary enquiry.

He decided that he would then tell her about Ann. It had to be an honest, daylight telling; in a place other than his apartment where she could so easily make his resolution come to naught.

He telephoned Ann as soon as the big *Commodore* had made its conspicuous departure from the street.

The voice answering him was dispirited and remote with emptiness.

'What's the matter, Ann?' he asked in sudden apprehension.

'Please come, Robert. Straight away.'

'What *is* it?'

'Just come ... please.' He was left with the sound of disconnection in his ear.

Uneasy with a premonitory fear, he bull-dozed his car recklessly through the morning's build-up of traffic.

She let him into the hall, pale, and silent, her face discoloured and swollen. She had obviously been crying and Hansen's heart sank.

'For God's sake, Ann! What's happened?'

She bit at her lip, hesitated and turned and he followed her. She stood in the centre of the room and faced him. There were cold grey ashes in the fire-basket and the carpet had not been vacuumed to a morning's smoothness. Her face was set, showing no emotion. He could see the yellow and indigo of bruising on the puffy cheeks and a raised lump at the corner of her mouth. Her eyelids were pink and swollen.

'Toffler came here after you left last night.' Her voice was neutral.

The apprehension that had stayed with him, built up suffocatingly in his chest. 'No!' he cried hoarsely.

'He must have followed you, Robert. Then waited until you'd gone.' There was no reproach in the way she said it. It was a passionless conclusion she was expressing.

'He beat you up?' *Dear God*, he prayed, *nothing more. Please, nothing more*, but he knew already that it was too late for whining supplications and his stomach cringed.

She looked at him steadily, almost defiantly and much the calmer of them both. 'He raped me, Robert.'

The floor heaved and slid under him and he shook his head blindly like a mortally-wounded animal. Waves of black sickness drained the blood from his face and he felt his flesh chill. He steadied himself by clutching the table, suddenly wanting to vomit, but fighting it as the sickness changed to a shuddering rage, the black waves gradually receding until Ann and the room stood out with the cold sharp clarity of shock.

Ann stood silent, watching him emerge tortured from his own Garden of Gethsemane. She had made no move to touch him, but her eyes sought for something he wasn't giving her.

He put his shaking hands in his pockets to control them and stared at her. He couldn't—didn't want to—touch her, and he had no ready words for her. His bitter hatred for Toffler monopolized his whole thinking, swelling to such proportions that he felt it would burst his skull. He realized, as if an inner compelling entity was directing him, that he wanted to kill Toffler; not impersonally, not antiseptically at long range; not remotely with a gun; BUT FROM NEAR ENOUGH TO SMELL THE STINK OF HIS FILTHY BODY, NEAR ENOUGH TO TEAR AT HIS FLESH AND TISSUE WITH HIS NAKED HANDS, TO SEE THE HOT BLOOD SPURT, TO SAVOUR THE MUSIC OF HIS SCREAMING IN PAIN AS HE PULPED HIM INTO A NOTHINGNESS.

Hansen was not very far removed from running amok like a crazed elephant. First his wife; now Ann. And some of his aggression directed itself at her for having been raped, for *allowing* herself to be after all his warnings of Toffler's dangerousness. It was the irrational illogic of a man close to the edge of unreason. For Hansen, the thin pallid skin of civilized conformity had split, exposing the raw red of savagery beneath; the berserker who wanted to sink teeth into the throat of the defiler of his women. He was a long way from being the calm, impartial and impersonal enforcer of the law.

He didn't recognize the thick-tongued shaking voice as his own. 'You let him in?'

'I thought it was you.'

'What time?'

'Eleven.'

He forced himself to ask, 'Where?' Vivid mental pictures of a darkened bed and naked writhing bodies made him tremble.

'Here ... in this room.'

His eyes went involuntarily to the settee and he jerked them away, his features twisting in a spasm of anguish as he tried to blank off his imagination. 'Have you reported it?' He knew she hadn't. The room would have been busy with detectives or showing the evidence of their search for finger-prints and traces of Toffler's presence.

She shook her head. 'No, Robert. Nor am I going to.' Her mouth grimaced. 'It's degrading enough ... telling you. And who would believe me?'

He stared at her, his mouth working.

'Even if they did,' she filled in the silence, 'he'd deny it ... say I had been willing.'

'There could be corroboration.'

'Could there be?' she said bitterly. 'I was on my own.' She was blaming him for not returning.

'There's the medical evidence.' He almost groaned aloud when he thought of that and its implications. Clinical proof of penetration, microscopic identification of semen and the stigmata of violence inside her; the sickening impersonal evidence of a forcible intercourse that had already dirtied the love between them.

'You really believe that, Robert? That there is evidence of rape? You believe that would convict him? When I haven't complained until nearly ten hours after it happened? And then only to a man who is personally involved with me? I know exactly what he would say. That he was invited here by a blonde tart he had met in the club. No, Robert,' she said, her expression sad. 'Even you. You're not sure, are you? You're looking at me as if I'm a whore because I didn't die not letting it happen.'

He made a noise in his throat. 'That's a terrible thing to say, Ann.'

She nodded. 'Yes, it is.'

'*Why*, Ann? Why didn't you tell me last night?'

'I tried to. I telephoned you ... there was no answer. Later, when I tried again, I couldn't get your number. There was nobody else I could tell.'

He thought miserably of the shared shower with Norah and the ringing they had ignored, and that didn't help. While they had made their own kind of love, Toffler had been making his with Ann. What Hansen had denied himself from loyalty and love, Toffler had taken.

'You could have come, Ann,' he whispered.

She touched her bruised face. 'Could I, Robert? What do you expect me to have done? He hit me.' Her mouth trembled. 'Then he ...'

'*Shut up!*' he shouted savagely. The thought was a piercing agony, an emotional angina pectoris to him. 'I don't want to know! Leave the bastard to me!' The skin of his face was yellow, his eyes blood-injected, and he breathed raspingly as if he had been running.

'No,' she said still quiet against his violence. 'I don't want you to. I want to forget it.'

'Forget it?' he echoed unbelievingly. 'Let him get away with it? Just like that?'

'Yes. You'll only make it worse for me.' She sounded defeated. 'You mustn't see him. It's over and done with.'

He was angry with her now. 'For you, perhaps; not for me.'

'It's better, Robert.' She thought of what must have been her unconscious body's surrender to Toffler's rampant sexuality, of the shaming guilt she felt. It made a gulf between them that she could never imagine being bridged. The bitterness and humiliation, the exhaustion of her physical need and Hansen's reaction to her tragedy, had combined to muddy the love she had for him. She didn't know what she had expected from him—tenderness and understanding, perhaps; any of the emoliating words a defeated, stricken woman needed—but he had failed her. Lucrece's suicide after her rape by Sextus Tarquinius now made sense to her.

'Robert,' she pleaded with him, seeing the madness in his eyes, 'you are not to.' The thought of what Toffler might say to him was a terrifying one. '*Please ...*'

But there was a black unreasoning suspicion in him that he fought against in vain. His features jerked as he struggled to say terrible words he couldn't get out and he turned and blundered through the door, filled with nothing but a scalding hatred for Toffler that left no room for the love that had led him to it.

The two men, each conscious of the other's enmity, each in his own way both the hunter and the hunted, moved towards their inevitable confrontation; the black thread of their mutual hatred, like love, drawing them irresistibly together.

In the first transport of his destructive rage, Hansen drove to Toffler's flat, parking his car outside, uncaring whether it could be seen or not and hammering his fist on the locked door. When there was no answer, he listened to the unbreathing silence behind it, sweating his angry frustration, wanting to smash it down.

Then he walked the streets, a grim revengeful figure, checking the dozens of bars and clubs in the segment of the city that was Toffler's habitat, visiting basement billiards halls, massage parlours, betting shops, cafés and hotels; anywhere a man like Toffler would spend time away from his address. He spoke to contacts and informants as he had three days earlier in his search for Sheila Coughlin. But, with a difference. Putting the finger on the fearsome Toffler, even contemplating it, was another matter altogether from doing the same to a whore. Merely to be suspected of it was dangerous in its promise of extreme and prolonged physical suffering. The small fish of the criminal world live by tolerance in the omnipresent shadow of a shark such as Toffler. So those who might have known of his whereabouts didn't want to be in the same street as a detective. To be seen talking to one with the faintest expression of tolerance or connivance was to invite immediate suspicion as an informant.

So Hansen received no information that Toffler had been seen or heard of since the previous evening. He could have fled the city for all that Hansen could locate him, but he didn't think so. The detective couldn't see him as the type to scuttle like a scared rabbit. Ash's remark that Toffler was promising violence against him had the smell of truth to it. To accept he had gone, was to do nothing; it was to accept the intolerable affront put on him, to allow the contamination of Ann to go unrevenged.

Snow began to drift softly from a heavy leaden sky while he tried to eat a beef sandwich and drink a tomato juice at a lunch counter before returning to his rooms. His postponed intent needed no alcohol to keep it glowing.

Although he couldn't know, his telephone bell had been ringing at intervals during his absence.

While the nurse cleared his tray of the minced beef and creamed potato he couldn't force past his still-sore jaws, Sergeant Gault feigned a more tranquillized drowsiness in his bed than he actually had. Although the morning's injection had relaxed his body and filled his skull with a cottonwool lassitude, he kept a corner of it sharp and alert with his purpose.

By now, he was familiar with the ward routine. He would be left alone until four o'clock when he was due for a cup of tea (which he suspected wrongly contained a sex-depressant drug) and another injection. He would, until then, be subject to a visual inspection through the window every half an hour. If the nurses remembered. By observing the two in the ward outside, he knew that they occasionally did not. After the trays had been cleared, they would spend time enough in their separate duty room situated away from the window.

When the nurse closed the door behind her, he moved, fighting the lethargy of his limbs and the muffling of his will, pushing back the bed clothing and standing shakily on his bare feet, holding on to the locker to steady himself.

He stood motionless for a few moments before taking his clothing from the locker, feeling his heart knocking in his chest and resisting the desire to return to what seemed now the euphoric torpor of his bed. Dressing with urgency, he pulled on the jacket and trousers of his suit over his pyjamas, concealing its open striped collar with the closed lapels of his top coat.

He waited until both nurses were busy in the duty room, then quietly opened the door, his fingers slippery on the handle. He walked along the central aisle of the ward as if wading through deep water, the bandaging chafing the unhealed flesh of his groin. He looked neither to the left nor to the right, his eyes steady on the white-painted swing doors at the end, walking as purposefully as he could, anticipating the sudden rush of an intercepting nurse from behind. Sweat

232

beaded his forehead with the concentration of his effort. None of his fellow-patients spoke to him; those who watched did so without curiosity.

Out in the steam-heated corridors with the dangerously polished floors, brisk-moving doctors and nurses, porters and kitchen staff with wheeled stretchers and food trolleys, passed him. None gave him more than a casual glance, the patch over his eye-socket explaining his presence as much as anything would.

Instead of leaving by the main entrance, guarded by a porter and a receptionist, he made his way to a flight of stone steps which he descended, his legs wide apart, grunting at the impact each time he put a foot down. He crossed an open yard, leaving dragging marks in the freshly-fallen snow, climbing the sloping ramp that led past the hospital mortuary and out to freedom. The cold air thinned the cottonwool numbness of his mind, sharpening his awareness. He was now in the streets of the city, a third man with the intent to violence in his mind.

He rented a car from an office two streets away from the hospital, producing his warrant card to overcome the girl's initial doubts of his appearance and of the cheque with which he paid the deposit and insurance.

He drove slowly past his home, noting his wife's car in the drive. He waited patiently further along the road until she came out, entering her car and turning towards the city centre. There was cold calculation in his eyes as he watched her.

He let himself into the house, using the key he still possessed. In the bathroom, he scissored off his moustache, shaving the upper lip clean and swilling the hairs down the basin. He dried and cleaned what he had used with a towel, replacing the razor and scissors where he had found them.

He changed his clothing, putting on a thick woollen polo-neck sweater, hiding his old suit and pyjamas at the bottom of the linen basket, leaving no traces to show what he had done. The suit he put on in their place would not be missed unless looked for. He searched for and found a pair of his dark glasses, needing to conceal the identifying eyepatch; then retrieving a soft check hat he had worn once only before discarding it to a wardrobe drawer.

From a cupboard beneath the stairs, he took the over-and-under barrelled shot gun with which he had fired at nothing more animate than bloodless clay pigeons. He broke it at the breech and checked its empty barrels. He found a box of cartridges and took a handful, putting them in a pocket of his coat.

Before leaving, he looked around the livingroom for signs of a visit by Hansen, seeking confirmation that he had been cuckolded. He climbed the stairs for the second time, but slower now and pulling his aching body up by grasping the handrail. He stared blank-faced at the bed he had once shared with his wife, pulling back the blankets and examining the sheets with the meticulousness of a trained detective.

Outside, he ignored the tracks he left in the drive. Snow was falling steadily in a thick white veil and would soon blot out the traces of his visit.

Blood had begun to seep on to his thighs from behind the bandages. His eye socket watered and a persistent pain nagged his jaws where the wires had been pulled out. He felt wretched and exhausted and needing to rest. He stopped the car outside a tobacconist's and bought a packet of twenty cigarettes and a box of matches, then driving to a lane, rarely used in daylight, behind the Central Park. He halted the car beneath a group of pine trees and rested, ignoring the gradual chilling of his body, his imagination projecting vivid pictures of Toffler and Hansen and his wife against the steel shutter of his implacable purpose. He smoked continuously, lighting one cigarette from another, waiting for darkness to fall.

# Chapter 26

Hansen was recording a copy of the conversation taped in Weizsack's office when he heard the slamming of a car door outside and below. Peering down through a window, he saw through the falling snow the foreshortened figure of a sheepskin-coated Ann approaching the steps to the apartment block. He cut short Weizsack's disembodied words and waited, standing, his hands clenching into fists, his teeth gnawing on the inner skin of his mouth.

She had never been to his apartment before, but would see his name and floor number listed in one of the metal-framed tablets at the side of the entrance hall door.

He heard her footfalls approaching his door, the electric buzzer sounding, followed by a waiting silence. The loudest noise in the room was the jerky pulsing of blood amplified in his eardrums and the hissing of his breath. The buzzer sounded again, making him start, and he could visualize her clearly through the two intervening doors. Her face would be pale and sad and certain to unman him. She would run straight into his arms, softening his will to fight. He would be emasculated of purpose as surely as her husband had been of his maleness; persuaded to accept the contamination that had been done to her, swallowing the vomit of his bitter hatred for Toffler. He thought it an impossible price to pay for love.

After a while, he heard the footfalls retreat and die away and there was thin blood in his mouth where he had bitten through the skin. He stood motionless until he heard the car door bang shut and the engine started; until there was silence in the snow-muffled street.

His task was disturbed only once more. The telephone bell rang fifteen minutes after she had left his door and he let it ring unanswered. It had, he thought, a lonely despairing sound to it that went well with his room. After a while, that too stopped and did not ring again.

When he had finished recording the tape, he packaged the copy, together with the tape of his conversation with Sheila Coughlin, and addressed the envelope to McGluskie. Before he sealed it, he printed ARABELLA STEPHENSON: SIMON ASH'S STEP-SISTER on the cutting he had taken from the *Daily Telegraph* and added it to the evidence against Weizsack. McGluskie would need no more to complete the picture. He placed the envelope in a conspicuous place on the table, laying his warrant card by its side. Then he boiled and ate without appetite two eggs and drank instant coffee, needing to fill in the time until the afternoon's light failed. And to do something to take his mind from thinking of Ann.

It was a few minutes before five when he stood in the outer office of Soderman, Soderman and Fewler, having asked for an immediate interview with Weizsack.

When the clerk returned, he was shown into the inner office. Weizsack was seated at his desk and he stood as Hansen entered. Although he did not offer to shake hands, he beamed and bobbed his head courteously enough, indicating a chair to the unsmiling detective. Behind the *bonhomie* was an anxious wariness.

He sat and reached down behind his desk, opening the drawer housing his tape recorder. 'It isn't switched on, dear boy,' he said. 'It will avoid the embarrassment of your asking.' He wheezed as he lit a cigarette and flapped smoke away from himself.

Despite his scepticism of the old man's persistent amiability, Hansen couldn't help responding with a lessening of his antagonism, although it wasn't nearly enough to deflect him from his purpose.

'It was a tape I came to see you about,' the detective said, opening the briefcase he had brought in with him and withdrawing from it a small battery-operated recorder. 'May I?'

'Could I stop you, dear boy?' Weizsack wasn't going to show his surprise at anything, but Hansen, watching him closely, saw there was the slightest suggestion of his bracing himself.

He laid the recorder on the desk and depressed the switch. After a short period of tape hum and the indecipherable noises of movement, Weizsack's voice came clear. *My dear young lady.*

*How kind of you to come.* Then more sounds of movement, and Toffler's easily identifiable *'Ello, doll. I 'ope you 'aven't been worryin'* from further away.

They both listened in silence until Weizsack held up his hand. 'Do we have to? You embarrass me. And it was very naughty and underhand of Mrs Gault.'

Had Hansen expected Weizsack to show cataclysmic signs of alarm or distress over his possession of a tape of the interview, he would have been disappointed. But the blue of his lips did seem more pronounced and the knuckles of his pudgy hands showed white.

He leaned forward and switched the recorder off. 'Don't you wish to hear the bit about my being an unscrupulous, unprincipled police officer?' he asked coldly.

'My dear boy,' Weizsack protested, unabashed. 'How we do tend to get carried away in our moments of forensic zeal.' But his smile wasn't quite so embracing and there was fear behind it. 'I have no doubt you have expressed similar sentiments about myself. For which I forgive you, as I hope you forgive me.'

'And for trying to fix me for another planting job?'

Weizsack shrugged philosophically. 'I am a slave to my client's instructions, dear boy. If Mr. Toffler alleges you planted a gun on him, who am I to sit in judgement and call him a liar?' Seeing the open cynicism on the detective's face, he added, 'Don't underestimate the value of a defence based on the misinterpretation of words. Or of a solicitor's being overenthusiastic in a client's interests. I would plead guilty to a mite of gullibility; being misled by my client, perhaps...' He shook his head sadly.

'You think the Discipline Committee of the Law Society would be misled?'

'Frankly, dear boy, no.' He licked his lips, a glint of unease in his eyes. 'But I need hardly remind you I am already struck off and surely outside their jurisdiction.'

'But not outside the jurisdiction of the criminal courts. Try on subornation of perjury and conspiracy to corrupt justice for size,' he offered. 'Helped along by a young lady called Sheila Coughlin, alias Bridget O'Connor.'

Weizsack flinched and a spasm of distaste crossed his features. 'You are so rudely blunt, dear boy,' he murmured, 'as I believe I have mentioned before. You won't object to my reminding you that you need some corroboration of that tape you have.'

'I have it.'

'I feared you might.' He sighed. 'May I ask what?'

'No.' Hansen came to the point. 'I want Toffler.'

'Ah! The nub, I presume. Why, dear boy?'

'He assaulted Mrs Gault at her home last night.' Although he wasn't conscious of it, his face showed his inner anger.

Weizsack saw it, read into it what he could and looked thoughtful. 'That was—if he did—a most ill-advised action. You wish to arrest him?'

'Yes.'

'You have a warrant?'

'I don't need a warrant to arrest for forcible rape,' Hansen said harshly.

There was a silence in the office and Hansen could hear the ticking of the old Ingersoll watch on Weizsack's wrist. Then the solicitor said, '*Rape?* My dear boy!' He showed shocked concern and it looked genuine. 'You don't mean it?'

'I mean it.'

Weizsack stared at him, searching his eyes. He wagged his head in silent condemnation and there was a sadness there too. 'What an unfortunate young woman. But it has hurt you too?' He missed very little of what was written in the human face.

'Where is he?'

Weizsack pulled at his jowl with a finger and thumb, his watery eyes thoughtful. He sensed a bargaining point and only he knew how much he needed one. 'You think that I—his legal adviser—would help you?'

'Yes.' The detective detached the cassette from the recorder and held it in his fingers for Weizsack to see, saying nothing.

'Ah, yes.' He searched Hansen's expression, then frowned. 'You are asking me to betray a client's confidence?'

'I don't care what you call it, I want to know where Toffler is. Today. Now.'

Weizsack nodded his head at the cassette. 'That is the original?'

Hansen nodded. And it was. He had retained only the copy, anticipating Weizsack's question. He was also saying nothing that could be taped by Weizsack and used against him. He wasn't naïve enough to believe his words weren't being recorded.

Apparently satisfied with his assurance, Weizsack said, 'What if I do not know?'

Hansen pulled a disgusted, angry face and stood, putting the cassette in his pocket and replacing the recorder in the briefcase. He had reached the door and opened it before Weizsack broke.

'A moment, dear boy. Please come back.'

Hansen hesitated and scowled, not making it easy for the solicitor. 'Don't waste my time. Do you know?'

Weizsack bobbed his head. 'You give me no option.'

'No, I don't. Where is he?'

'I will telephone him. You wish to see him straight away?'

'Yes. Not here and not with you around.'

'Oh dear, you *are* asking a lot, dear boy, but point taken. I find it difficult to resist your argument.'

He reached for and lifted the telephone receiver, turning the base so that Hansen could not see the number he was dialling. He spoke into the mouthpiece. 'Edward? ... Ah, yes. I must see you, Edward ... Yes, straight away. No, not in my office. At your apartment.' His eyes held Hansen's. 'There's an important development ... you didn't tell me everything about Mrs Gault ... *No*, not now. Tell me later, Edward.' He looked at the watch on his wrist. 'Say, in half an hour? ... Good. Until then, Edward...' He dropped the receiver back in its cradle, regarding Hansen with questioning interest. 'Dear boy! Are you all right? Your expression ... !'

'I'm all right,' Hansen said shortly. But he wasn't. Just knowing that Toffler had been on the other end of the line, hearing the muffled rasp of his voice escaping from the earpiece, had surfaced the anger he was trying to control and had subdued for his interview with Weizsack.

'There's violence in you,' the solicitor said disapprovingly. 'It makes me unsure that I have done the right thing. And Mr Toffler is an exceedingly dangerous man too. He lacks the constraint of a conscience, I'm afraid. If you arrest him, please do not call me.' He pulled a wry face. 'I will—the Good Lord willing—be taking a much-needed holiday.' He held out his hand. 'The tape, if you please. I have done my little Judas act for you.'

'Not yet. We'll stay together until I know he's there.' There was no need for him to tell Weizsack he didn't trust him.

Weizsack looked worried. 'You'll tell him you forced me,

blackmailed me, into this?' He clutched fingers to his chest and grimaced. 'Please, dear boy, don't push this too hard. I think I am ready to retire. I'm an old man and a tired one ... perhaps with not too long to go...'

'No, probably not,' Hansen said unsympathetically, his face stony. He was immune to Weizsack's trading on his disease, having seen him do it before. 'But try to hang on until I've seen Toffler.'

He sat and filled his pipe, tamping in the tobacco with finicky care, content to wait out the minutes without further talk.

*Detective Sergeant 1002W William Austin Gault! You stand convicted on your own confession. Have you anything to say why the court should not give you judgement according to law?* The words came sibilant and whispered from the dark corners like the hissing of black snakes, mocking him cruelly with their slithery echoes. While he strained his ears to hear what was being said because it was very important that he should, searching the shadows with his out-of-focus eye in the confining yet limitless frightening place in which he lay, soft sniggering laughter started from between his outstretched legs. He heard the scratch of a match and saw the sudden spurt of yellow flame lighting the goatish, leering face of his tormentor; felt the exquisite pain that pierced his scrotum. The flame flared higher until the evil mask blurred and shimmered and ran molten in a greasy wax. He tried feebly to move against the unseen force that was holding him in total rigidity, groaning his impotence. The mask now reformed and smoothed itself to the nearly recognizable features of a woman who thrust the open black gap of her toothless, tongueless mouth at him, pressing the chilled slug-like nakedness of her body against his until his terror-locked jaws opened and he yelled, jerking from the sleep that had crept up and smothered him as he waited.

He looked around him, disorientated in the darkness; not knowing where he was and shaking with the cold, his knee joints and ankles locked stiff against his attempting to move. There was a smell of burning in his nostrils. He fumbled for the handle of the door and opened it, the interior light switching on.

He felt the oddness of his naked upper lip and remembered things through the fog of his confusion. A saucer-sized hole smoked black in the skirt of his coat and he slapped it dead with his hand. In sudden panic he checked his wristwatch, seeing it was a minute or two past six. He closed the door, extinguishing the light that would show him to any passer-by and made a conscious effort of will to relax. His mouth was dry and acrid from the cigarettes he had smoked. When he moved his legs to get the stiffness out of the joints, he could feel that the blood had caked hard on his thighs, sticking the bandaging to his flesh. His mind was still echoing with the nightmarish horrors of his sleep, but clear now of the effects of the tranquillizing drug.

When he had buried his dream, he climbed from the car into the night air and scraped a hole clear of snow on the windscreen; then, back inside and shivering on the chilly plastic covering of the seat, he started the engine to heat the interior. When his hands were warm, he retrieved the shotgun from beneath the rear seat and opened it, pressing brass-capped cartridges into its breech, snapping it closed with the air of fixed purpose and finality a man has only when he has stopped thinking of the issues. As Gault had. He thought only of what he was actually doing, of the sequence and mechanics of his intent.

He laid the gun on the seat next to him and put the car into gear. The tyres crunched and squeaked in the drifted snow of the lane as he headed the car towards his destination and he fought the ripples of nausea he felt from the re-emergence of the pain in his crotch.

# Chapter 27

Snow was still falling, soft white moths swirling in the bars of his headlights, and Hansen turned on the windscreen wipers. Traffic was dense and the journey to Cleveland Road slow.

Weizsack had covered his shaggy hair with a decrepit black Homburg hat and put on a greenish-black overcoat with a blue velvet collar against the cold. During the fifteen minutes they were together in the car, he had covered the coat with cigarette ash and had been uncharacteristically silent. It suited Hansen who had withdrawn his smouldering anger into himself.

When the detective pulled the car into the kerb outside the windswept block of flats—he noticed that there was no white Alfa Romeo in sight—and switched off the engine and pocketed the keys, Weizsack said, 'You won't need me to come any further I hope, dear boy? I would rather not see Edward under these circumstances. Not with you. He might misunderstand.'

'So might I. You're coming with me,' Hansen said curtly. He climbed from the car and opened the door for Weizsack.

Weizsack blinked, but stepped out. He shivered, looking shrunken in his heavy coat. 'Dear boy, no further I beg you.' He held out his hand, palm upwards. 'The tape, please.'

'No. Not until I know he's there.' He looked up at the façade of the building, not seeing any light coming from where he knew Toffler's flat to be.

'He'll be there. I wouldn't lie to you.'

'Yes, you would. You probably have.' He was impatient. 'Don't argue, Mr Weizsack. We're going up.' He grasped the old man's arm and pushed him towards the steps.

Weizsack took the stairs slowly and reluctantly, stopping at intervals to rest while Hansen waited implacably for his panting to subside.

'Dear boy,' he protested, 'you are killing me. I am not allowed to climb stairs.'

The door to Toffler's flat had been painted a glossy dark green with 27 on it in black. A thin sliver of light came from beneath it. Standing before it, Hansen felt the inner tension of anticipated violence grow in him, a determination to execute justice on the man who had escaped it so often. This was the personal Armageddon to which his hatred of Toffler had led him by its own inexorable path. But for all his driving purpose, he knew that the ultimate length to which his need to avenge Ann's rape would go would be governed largely by Toffler's own reaction to his visit. For Hansen, unopposed violence—even against the evil that Toffler represented—was unthinkable.

Weizsack's hand was inside his coat, against his chest, his breathing irregular. In the dim illumination of the landing his lips appeared cyanosed. 'No more,' he whispered. 'Allow me to leave.'

Hansen, grim and unsympathetic, shook his head. He unbuttoned and removed his overcoat, then knocked on the door, standing to one side with his back to the wall.

There were movements inside and Toffler's voice. ''Oo's there?'

Weizsack hesitated and looked at Hansen. When the detective made no reply or motion, he said, 'It is I, Edward.'

A key turned and the door opened, at first to a narrow crack, widening to allow Weizsack to enter when he had been identified. Hansen crowded in behind him, knocking the door from Toffler's grasp, bundling the solicitor to one side.

Toffler moved back quickly, his surprise overlaid by an immediate response of hostility that bunched his muscles and made fists of his hands.

'Wha's this?' he said harshly. He stood wide-legged, prepared to resist whatever was intended.

Hansen withdrew the tape cassette from his pocket and handed it sideways to Weizsack, keeping Toffler within his view. His eyes were a dark yellow now, burning with his hate, the lines of his features deep and sharply etched. Between the two men, Weizsack was an unimportance.

'I'm sorry, Edward,' Weizsack said. He had difficulty in getting the words out and he remained carefully close to the detective. 'I'm afraid Mr Hansen forced me to telephone you by threats. I felt unable to resist him.'

Toffler looked from Hansen to the solicitor. 'You bleedin' twistin' bastard.' He said it without heat, but the words were a deadly threat for all that. 'You shopped me.'

'Yes, Edward,' he said sadly. 'I can no longer be your legal adviser.' He licked his lips. 'Mr Hansen appears to know more than is good for either of us and has persuaded me that you have been less than frank about certain things. In particular, your meeting with Mrs Gault. You may not understand, but I have a strong distaste for sexual violence.' His voice strengthened. 'I want no more, Edward.'

Toffler didn't want him either. 'Piss off,' he growled. 'I'll fix your bloody duff later.'

Then Weizsack was gone with his useless tape and, when his footsteps had faded to silence, Hansen closed the door. He tossed his coat on to a chair and moved stiff-legged until he was within reach of the other man. Toffler gave no ground, but waited. They were together at last, and what was between them was as heavy in the air and as suffocating as marsh gas. It could almost be smelled.

'If you think you're goin' to arrest me, 'Ansen,' Toffler said, ' 'Ave another think.' His strong teeth were bared between the insolent lips.

'I haven't come to arrest you.' Hansen, his leg muscles taut and trembling, was poised on the balls of his feet with all the menace of a bull about to put its head down and charge. He savoured the evil face not a yard from his own, seeing in it the red ruin of his vengeance. 'Don't let my being a policeman stop you doing anything.' He was impatient now, feeling a hard pulse beating beneath his jaw, his anger choking him. 'You raped her, Toffler.'

Toffler stared at him, then jeered. 'You want your soddin' 'ead seen to, mate. The doll loved it. You understan'? She as't me. I couldn' give 'er enough...'

As fury flared in him, Hansen knew that Ann had been right. Even with her evidence, Toffler would never be convicted for what he had done to her. He could see in his mind's eye Sinter smearing her honesty and decency with his debasing innuendoes; using his forensic trickery to label her a promiscuous cow, a tart willingly gratifying Toffler's lust. Her reputation would be legally murdered, her name made dirt, and the lawyers would have struck another blow for Justice. He shivered and swung his arm, the back of his hand cracking high on Toffler's cheek.

Toffler staggered backwards, recovered, then shook his head and smiled. One side of his face was red. 'All right, mate. If tha's the way you want it.' He moved smoothly and swiftly, catching the back of a wooden chair in both hands and sweeping it viciously at Hansen as he came forward.

Hansen slid inside the arc of the swing to get close to him, but having to take the blow on the shoulder already bruised by Ash, the sharp edge of the wood paralysing the muscle, immobilizing his left arm to uselessness. He punched upwards at Toffler's jaw but mistiming the blow, his knuckles tearing an ear at its base. Toffler moved backwards, blood running down his neck and reddening his shirt collar. When he came again, the chair was lifted high over his head and already on its way down.

Hansen threw himself low at him, smashing his shoulder against the hard bones of his shins and as Toffler fell, his legs swept from under him, the chair hit Hansen jarringly on his rib cage and agony sliced into his side. He twisted on his knees and with his hand open and rigid chopped savagely at the other man's throat. Each movement stabbed pain in his side and he knew that a rib had been broken. His world was limited to the small segment of perception that contained Toffler's writhing body and his flailing fists. One caught him stunningly in his mouth and he tasted its sweat, feeling his teeth creak and move, his lips go numb. Toffler was sinewy and tough and a practised brawler and that was how Hansen wanted him. It gave him licence to match it with his own strength and destructiveness. He hammered at the face beneath him with the heel of his usable fist, feeling the back of Toffler's head hitting solidly against the unyielding floor. Blood spread like spilled red paint over the nose and mouth, running on to his blue silk tie.

Toffler's hands came up, his fingers groping for Hansen's face. A thumb jabbed into his bruised mouth, its nail tearing at the inner flesh while the other hand locked itself on the detective's throat, clamping muscular fingers into its soft tissues, searching for the artery, trying to get behind the windpipe. Hansen slashed a forearm across the wrists, knocking away the murderous fingers. Toffler's body jerked convulsively, throwing him sideways and they thrashed over the floor, punishing each other with their fists but too close to inflict crippling damage, until Hansen broke free and scrambled to his feet, waiting for Toffler to come again.

He was breathing in rasping spasms, holding his elbow against the pumping ache in his side. Movement was returning to his left arm, although it was still numb. None of it had diminished his lust to hurt Toffler. He was atavistic now, social niceties and conventions stripped from him by his over-powering anger, no more advanced emotionally than Neander-thal man. He would go on until he or Toffler had been beaten into unconsciousness.

Toffler, ignoring the chair at his feet, crouched, beckoning Hansen towards him with his left hand. In the other he held a small black object. He jabbed with his thumb at it and a blade snapped out, pointing at the detective like a short sword. 'Come on, mate,' he said through his bloody mask, 'we 'aven't finished yet.'

Hansen stiffened. Toffler's face possessed the same deadly intent he had seen in Ash's. He would be beyond the reach of reason or fear of the consequences. Hansen, keeping his face towards Toffler, reached sideways and retrieved his coat, taking his handcuffs from a pocket before twisting it around his left forearm. He put his fingers through the steel circlets of the handcuffs and made a fist of them.

Although Toffler was now between Hansen and the door and could have fled, he made no effort to do so. He was as determined as the detective to fight it out, needing to redeem the humiliation of his earlier arrest and submission. His violence had escalated to murderousness.

Hansen held his protected forearm crooked in front of him like a cloth shield and moved towards his enemy, his metal-knuckled fist hanging low at his side. Any bone it hit squarely would break. Toffler still crouched, but weaved and ducked his body, presenting a bobbing target to Hansen. The arm holding the knife was straight and rigid in front of him. He handled it with the confidence of skill. His narrow features glistened with sweat and blood, his mouth slack with his sneer-ing insolence, the pale butcher's eyes steady on Hansen's, read-ing his intent.

The detective had the momentary impression that he had

done this before; that they were two gladiators fighting to the death in a Roman arena and that it was so stupid, even childish in its deadly lack of reason. He could view the whole man now, clear in every minute detail; the sheep's wool hair that cut his forehead square, the sweat-shiny forehead and the thick brows lowered in bars over the narrowed eyes; the thin ridge of his nose and the dilating nostrils still running blood down to the mouth that was now twisted in an animal snarl. The blood had also smeared the jacket of his tan suit and one of its patch pockets had been torn and hung loose in a flap. He emanated a deadly purposiveness that would neither seek mercy nor give it.

Hansen slid his feet forward, quiet on the muffling carpet, his mouth dry and breathing through his nose as he fixed his concentrated attention on the knife blade that caught and threw reflected light at him.

Toffler attacked first, feinting a lunge to Hansen's belly, drawing his padded arm downwards then driving the blade up at his unprotected throat. As Hansen slipped sideways to avoid it, the second stroke came as fast as a snake's tongue, the point of the blade piercing the fabric of his tie and pricking the flesh of his chest as the steel knuckledusters glanced off Toffler's arm. As Hansen moved forward again, his protected arm pushing into Toffler's face, the blade slid over it and hit him; hard this time as if he had been punched in the chest with a wooden post. Toffler's triumphant grin lasted only until the moment that Hansen's steel fist struck him solidly and tore flesh from the side of his head, open-mouthed dismay replacing the grin, his eyes rolling back as he dropped dark-brained to the floor, taking the knife with him.

Hansen remained standing. There was no pain from the wound although he could see from the blood on the blade that it had penetrated about two inches. He pressed the spot with a finger, resisting the nausea threatening him, the deathly sickness preceding a faint. All his will to violence had fled and he was as emotionally empty as if he had expended his lust on a prostitute. He took a tentative breath, then deepened it when no warning anguish came from his chest. But the broken rib in his side ached like a bad tooth. He saw again in his memory the opened chest cavities of the bodies he had seen operated on in the mortuary, recollecting clearly the tidy, compact arrangement of trachea, veins and arteries and the lobes of the lungs. Judging the position of the wound, he thought the knife could have pierced only the upper part of his lung. He didn't know whether a lung had nerve-ends in it or, if it had, whether they would react to being cut. But he knew the danger of a lung wound causing a fatal embolism, a bubble of air moving through the veins and inflicting sudden death when it reached the capillaries of the brain. He was frightened to move abruptly, or to do anything that might bring on a haemorrhage; anything that might hurt him unbearably. There was little external bleeding at the moment, but that could well mean he was bleeding inside.

Moving cautiously, keeping his body unbending, he unrolled the coat from his forearm and slipped the handcuffs from his fingers. He bent at the knees and stooped over Toffler's inert body. He was snoring and bleeding badly from the torn flesh of his head. A slice of hair and scalp hung over one ear. Unless he was seriously concussed—and Hansen didn't believe he could be—he would be conscious within a few minutes, and Hansen was in no condition to handle even an injured Toffler.

He rolled him carefully on to his side, arranged his arms behind his back and handcuffed the wrists together. Straightening his legs with effort, he stood upright and weaved an unsteady path to the telephone he had seen on a small wall table. His eyes were concentrated on it and, although the periphery of his vision was blurred and colourless, there was a vivid detailed clarity in the telephone as though magnified by a lens. He fought his mind's need to allow his body to rest. There was now a consciousness of hurt from the hole in his chest, radiating outwards in undulations of dull pain to join the sharpness in his side. He thought he could be dying, that he might fall and not reach the telephone. He blanked off the fear, groaning between his teeth and pushing his weakening body to the limit of its strength. He knew Toffler needed medical attention as well and it surprised him that he could care that he did. He was back to an inescapable adjustment to his profession's duties and demands; forced to return to the law he had disregarded in exacting his vengeance. *Detective Chief Inspector Hansen reporting back for duty, sir, having taken temporary leave of absence of his sanity and commonsense.* He wasn't sorry for what he had done, but neither was he glad. Now he was facing the consequences of his going it alone, acting outside the Rule Book. There was no alternative but for him to arrest Toffler for attempted murder. And that was going to bring everything out into the open, making it subject to intensive probing by McGluskie. In his present condition he didn't give a bloody damn.

He lifted the receiver. It hung heavy as iron in his hand as he pressed it to his ear, his finger fumbling uncertainly at the dial.

*'Put it down!'* The words came from behind him, hard and authoritative.

He turned slowly, supporting himself by holding on to the table.

Sergeant Gault stood near the door, tallow-faced and haggard, his legs apart as if balancing on an unsteady floor. His uncovered eye showed the wildness of his mind. Without his moustache, his face looked strange to Hansen. He held a shotgun in the crutch of his elbow, the butt under his armpit, a finger crooked around one of its two triggers. The twin barrel was pointed at the unconscious Toffler.

Cold fingers squeezed Hansen's heart. 'No,' he said. 'We need a doctor.'

Gault shook his head. He had seen the knife at Toffler's side and the blood staining Hansen's jacket and couldn't be in any doubt about what had happened. 'Put it down,' he repeated. He swivelled the gun to point at Hansen. Although it shook in his hands, its movement was positive. 'I mean it.'

There was a tension about the sergeant, a taut desperation that made Hansen stare at him in apprehension. He said, 'No. You put the gun away. I'm calling for help.' He turned back to the telephone, forcing his finger to dial the emergency code nine-nine-nine.

Gault moved with ungainly speed across the intervening space, slashing the barrel of the gun on the hand holding the receiver, knocking it from Hansen's grasp to drop swinging on its cord.

Hansen clutched at his bruised fingers. 'For Christ's sake, are you mad!' The jarring of the blow could have released the triggers.

The sergeant moved back from him. 'Yes,' he said. 'If you want it that way.'

Hansen breathed heavily, but tried to control it. 'I want a doctor. Or doesn't that matter?'

'No,' Gault said flatly. 'It doesn't. You're no worse than I was. You're still on your feet and I'm not going to be put off.' His purpose was clear. He had a motive and a gun and was unbalanced enough to use it. Homicidal mania didn't often wear a clear label, but if it ever did Hansen thought Gault wore it.

'He's my prisoner, sergeant.' He tried to keep his voice steady. 'I've arrested him. I'm ordering you...'

'Ordering!' Anger and incredulity worked in his face. 'Nobody's ordering me to do anything.'

Hansen moved away from the telephone. The dial had been about to click back on the third nine when the receiver had been knocked from his hand. He prayed that it had completed its circuit properly, that there had been a connection and that the call would be traced and followed up.

'Sergeant,' he said. 'Get out. McGluskie's due here any minute. I rang him first.'

Gault's eye was on Toffler who was beginning to twitch and show the symptoms of returning consciousness. 'You're a liar,' he said coldly. 'And I wouldn't care if he was here. It might be just his bad luck.'

Hansen needed desperately to get Gault talking, to divert or arrest his intent until help—if it was coming—came. 'Sergeant, this isn't the way. He isn't worth it. You'll spend the rest of your life in prison regretting it.' He meant in an institution for the criminally insane, but couldn't bring himself to say it.

'You think so?' Hansen wasn't reaching him. 'You think I want to go on living like this? I'm dead, Hansen,' he said fiercely. 'I've got nothing. I am nothing.' His chin trembled and he looked on the verge of crying. 'They've put me in a psychiatric ward already.'

'You're feeling sorry for yourself.' That would make two of them.

'Yes, I am.'

'I'm sitting down,' Hansen said. 'Unless you want me to bleed to death on my feet.' He dragged himself to a chair and let his body go limp in it, but careful not to constrict his chest. There was a full, heavy feeling at the base of his throat and the pain had spread like a slow-burning fire. As he breathed, so he felt the creeping of warm fluid beneath his shirt. He gathered together the remnants of his fading strength, injecting earnestness into his words. 'Sergeant! Let the courts deal with him. I've the evidence you were fixed by him and Weizsack...'

'Evidence!' He spat the word as if it had been filth on his tongue, his single brown eye bulging his anger, moisture running uninterrupted down the channel of his nose. 'You stupid bastard! What good is that going to do me?'

'I've found the woman photographed with you,' Hansen persisted. He had no answer to Gault's agonizing. 'You'll be cleared.'

'Will that give me back my eye? My balls?'

'For Christ's sake. What answer is there to that?'

'He did it.' He was glaring at Toffler. 'Do you know what it is to be like me? I'll be better dead. The bastard should have killed me.' His voice sank to a hoarse whisper, excluding Hansen from what he was saying. 'Like I'm going to kill him. They've taken everything ... given me nothing ... called me a liar ...'

'Self-pity, sergeant.' Talking was draining Hansen's vitality. 'You *are* a liar. Toffler didn't beat you up because you were a policeman doing a job. He did it because you'd been fornicating with one of his tarts.' He waited, watching the effect of what he had said.

'Go on.' His face, turned back to Hansen, was ugly and the detective reminded himself he had a loaded gun in his hands.

'Susan Goff, sergeant. Toffler's leavings.' There was bitter contempt in his voice because she still had the power to hurt him.

'*Shut up.*'

'No. She was Toffler's woman and I'm talking about your getting involved with villains.'

'I didn't know until afterwards.' His voice appeared to be fading and Hansen had to make a conscious effort to hear him.

'But you knew. You knew and you kept on with her. What did you expect Toffler to do? You, a detective sergeant detailed to keep observation on him; wanting a woman he'd put his filthy hands on.' Dear God, he told himself bitterly, I'm talking about my own wife. Susan Hansen née Goff. Every man's dream of a non-stop whore and she had spread her favours around like confetti, the sweetest music in her life the unzipping of a man's trouser fly. She had sucked Gault into the maw of her loins as she had Toffler and dozens of others,

251

encompassing their lusts indiscriminately like a one-woman brothel. And she was his legal wife, the fount of his honour and good name till death or divorce did them part; the demure girl who had stood by his side and said, 'With this body I thee worship.' He laughed and Gault stared at him in surprise. The sergeant didn't know and wouldn't know. Her being his wife was a fact his pride would keep buried. But what hurt him as much was the knowledge that his caustic words about her use by Toffler applied to Ann as well. She had been poisoned and made dirty as if some loathsome slug had covered her body with its slime. He pushed the thought of her from him and continued. 'That's the one thing you don't do, sergeant. You put yourself in his power, on his own filthy level, and that's how he treated you.' He slid his hand cautiously inside his jacket. There was a growing awareness of pain there and when he withdrew it, his fingers were bloody. He took a deep, careful breath, wincing at the tearing feeling it produced. 'You make me want to spit,' he said. 'You've dirtied yourself, you've dirtied the force...'

Toffler groaned and moved his arms and legs, the handcuffs clinking. His eyes remained closed. Gault stared at him and his finger tightened visibly on the trigger.

Hansen could see the telephone from the corner of his eye. The receiver had stopped swinging and hung rotating slowly a few inches above the floor; too far from him to be able to hear sounds from it. There was a quietness from the rest of the building. He felt faint and he struggled against the encroaching darkness that was growing in his mind. Unless he could hold on, even if only with his fingernails, the room was going to start spinning around him and he would be flung from it. Why didn't they come, he thought. They should be racing here with the siren blaring to clear the traffic from the streets and he strained his ears to hear it. All he could hear was a thin hissing noise in his skull like an escape of steam under pressure.

He spoke again to take Gault's attention from Toffler. His mouth was dust-dry and his tongue felt as hard as a leather strap. 'You've dirtied every policeman in the city, sergeant ... we'll have to try and live you down ... jumping into bed with a villain's whore ... they'll lump us all together.' He was conscious of his words slurring and running together from his stiffening mouth. 'All coppers are dirty bastards, they'll say.

One copper screws a whore and we all screw them...'

'Shut up!' His face twitched. 'Who the hell are you to tell me about her? What about you, Hansen? You and Ann. You dirty underhanded bastard! Sneaking after her behind my back while I'm in hospital.' Spittle sprayed with the intensity of his anger, his engorged eye blinking.

Hansen understood now. The crawling suspicion he had had since Gault's arrival was showing its teeth. The reason Gault was indifferent to his injury was its unimportance to his intent and Hansen realized he would be a fool to assume that the gun was for Toffler alone. The muzzle that could spout lead shot into a body to tear holes in the stomach and liver, perforate the gut and slice a heart to shreds, was also for him. For something he hadn't done. The mad bastard was convinced he had been fornicating with Ann.

'Listen to me, sergeant.' He tried to make his voice hard and commanding. 'I give you my word I have not touched Ann in the way you think.'

'She told me.'

Hansen shook his head violently. 'No, she didn't. She told you we were in love. That's not the same thing.'

'No?' Gault thinned his lips, disbelief emanating from him. 'Do you think I'm stupid?'

'Yes, I do. You are if you believe that. It was something neither of us could help, but we did nothing about it. It went no further. It's going no further.' He knew now that it wouldn't. He could never see her but with Gault's tortured shadow in the background, with the knowledge of Toffler's defilement of her body. What he had felt for her hadn't been strong enough, or deep enough, to stand up to that. There had been too much of his body's need in the love he had been suspicious of from its beginning. It had shrivelled at the first stern touch of frost. He wasn't proud that it had.

Toffler opened his eyes, staring at the carpet beneath him. He was dazed and uncomprehending. He tugged at the hand-cuffs on his wrists, then twisted his head to look around him, focussing his gaze on the baleful Gault, his eyes moving down to the gun pointing at him. He read the threat, the implac-ability in Gault's face. Fear twisted his mouth and his jaw dropped. He stiffened and held himself still, his regard of Gault that of a frightened vulture.

'Stand up.' Gault moved his legs further apart and jerked the gun to emphasize his order.

Hansen felt cold, emptied of blood and vitality, his heart pumping frighteningly. He kept his breathing shallow, trying not to expand his chest for the gulps of air he needed.

'Don't, sergeant,' he said. 'He's rubbish and not worth it.'

Toffler, panic-stricken, swivelled his head to Hansen. He made no effort to stand. 'Please, mate,' he gabbled. 'You're the law. Stop the bastard. 'E's bleedin' mad.' The smeared blood on his face and his fear made him a pitiable object.

There was a glare in Gault's eye now and the gun held steady.

'For Christ's sake,' Hansen said weakly. 'Leave him to McGluskie. You're wrong ... we're both wrong.'

'Does 'e know?' Toffler meant his rape of Ann.

'No.'

'Do I know what?' Gault glared from Hansen to Toffler.

'Nothing. He heard me speaking to McGluskie on the phone.'

But he had ceased to exist for Gault and something in the sergeant's expression made him grasp the arms of the chair and lever himself upright. His legs felt flaccid and nerveless and his mouth opened as suffocation took him by the throat. He lurched feebly, unco-ordinated, towards Gault. 'I'm not going to let you do it,' he mumbled.

Gault took a step forward, reversed the gun and struck him sideways on the jaw with its butt. Not viciously, but with enough force to topple him to the floor with pain cutting into his flesh from the broken rib. As he rolled, his head singing, gasping his need for air, he saw Toffler scramble to his feet with desperation in his face, his mouth gaping in a terrible yell of animal fear, running awkwardly for the door, his manacled hands behind him. With his face pressed into the carpet, Hansen watched helplessly as if viewing a slowed-down film; saw the swing of the gun barrel following Toffler's doomed flight, holding it on him as he turned his back to the door in a frantic fumbling for the handle, his face working in the dreadful realization that he was going to die. He stopped his fumbling then and straightened, shouting brave and angry filth at Gault, cut off by the thunderous crack of sound that sent its ball of shot to slam him against the door, punching a hole in the front of his trousers and exposing purple gut and pink tissue until the welling of blood covered and darkened his belly. He stood